OASIS TWO

Douglas W. Garlinger

GTS LLC
Fishers, IN 46038

OASIS TWO

Copyright © 2016 by Douglas W. Garlinger

Cover Photo used under license from Natalia Davidovich / Shutterstock.com
Cover Design by Douglas W. Garlinger

First edition
Printed in the United States of America

ISBN: 978-0-9981653-1-8

ACKNOWLEDGEMENTS

The women in my life:
Angela and Kelly, my daughters,
Emma and Lauren, my granddaughters,
Donna, my mom,
Cheryl, my wife.

(It would be good if you skipped over the sex scenes!)

My friends and professional colleagues:
You told me so often, *"you should write a book.."*
This is not the book you expected, and I would remind you,
this novel is fiction!

I would like to specifically acknowledge the five authors
who have influenced and inspired me the most:
Robert A. Heinlein
Mark Twain
Sir Arthur Conan Doyle
Allen Drury
John Grisham

Warning: Mature Content.
This novel contains explicit adult sexual material and language.
It portrays incidents of human trafficking in the sex slave
industry. It contains graphic descriptions of the heinous
practice of female genital mutilation (FGM) common in some
third-world nations.

DEDICATION

To the untold millions of young girls and women who have
endured the heinous practices touched upon in this book.
To women who live their lives as property and sex slaves.
To women who are stoned to death for the smallest infraction.

Chapter 1

Steve Foulke, the Madison County Prosecutor, stood at the railing of the second floor of the Indiana State House. The sound of children's voices below echoed throughout the chamber. He watched as a group of them were rounded up by their exhausted teachers and herded out the doors. Steve snapped his attention back to the meeting he had been summoned to attend.

The Minority Leader of the Indiana House and the Minority Leader of the Indiana Senate stood with Steve at the head of the stairs as they concluded their meeting on Steve's political future. There were openings in both the State House and State Senate districts where Steve lived. It had been assumed all along that Steve would run for one of them, but he had not decided which one. Now, his face was plastered all over the local news as a result of his prosecution of Mark Campbell for the molestation of his daughters. His name had become a household word in central Indiana.

The chairman of the Party had been conducting focus groups around the state, exploring the possibility of Steve running for statewide office. The offices of Attorney General or Secretary of State were being considered as viable options for Steve.

Steve was interested. He had long had his eye on the governor's office, and the thought of bypassing the legislature altogether in that quest appealed to him. As he said his goodbyes to the group, he headed down the stairs into the crowd below. It was much colder on the lower floor and, as he stepped outside, there was a slight drizzle accompanied by a stiff, winter breeze that chilled him to the bone.

He walked a block and crossed the street to the parking garage and found his car. As he left the garage, he turned north and soon found himself in the Friday, late-afternoon, Indianapolis traffic. His mind began mulling over all the events in his life that had gotten him to this point. This is what he had always wanted, and now it was looking very possible.

Steve had just been counseled to broaden his central Indiana exposure into the other television markets. He already understood this and had taken great care to do interviews with television reporters in the smaller markets of South Bend, Fort Wayne, Terre Haute and Evansville. Northwest Indiana remained a serious problem for him. This part of the state was in the Chicago market, and there was no coverage of the Campbell case. No Chicago television crews bothered to travel the 150 miles to cover the story. It would be difficult for Steve to win a statewide race without votes from the counties in the vicinity of East Chicago and Gary, Indiana.

He was tired of all the political bullshit and the carefully laid plans. A seat in the Indiana House or Senate was his for the taking, but he was only interested in the legislature as a springboard to statewide office and eventually the governor's office. He was highly qualified for the office of Attorney General, but he knew that Secretary of State was the politically smart move. Evan Bayh had traveled that same path to Governor of the State of Indiana and then the U.S. Senate. It was the office of Secretary of State that Steve Foulke was now beginning to set his sights upon.

He turned onto Pendleton Pike from 38th Street to travel the forty miles to Anderson. He decided to go the back way on Pendleton Pike rather than fight the heavy I-465 traffic on an early Friday evening.

He came up to a familiar building on the left and made an impulsive turn into the parking lot. It had not been his intention to stop here, but he just could not help himself. He did not drive an official county vehicle, and there was nothing unusual about his license plate that identified him as a government employee. He looked around carefully as he got out of the car and entered the place of business. His eyes adjusted to the darkness as he paid his five-dollar admission fee. On center stage, a scantily clad redhead danced to the music. He caught her eye and she smiled a big grin at him as if they were old friends. They weren't. He had never seen her before.

He took off his coat and hung it over the back of a chair at her stage and sat down. She strutted over to him and stood towering above him; her ankles were at chest height for him. He looked up at her well-endowed figure and the bikini briefs she had on. She sat down right in front of him, her legs dangling on either side of him. "Hi, Sugar," she said, as she grabbed his head and plunged his face into her crotch. His nose briefly penetrated the hidden folds of her skin beneath her briefs, as his face bounced off her body. She held him within a fraction of an inch of touching her. She clamped her legs around his neck and began rocking him back and forth violently, all the time maintaining the fraction of an inch of separation between Steve's face and her bikini briefs. She suddenly released his neck from the grip of her legs, sat up and thrust her chest in front of his face.

She methodically untied her top as she gazed into Steve's eyes. Steve was grinning from ear to ear when her breasts sprung free. She grabbed one in each hand and placed one on each side of Steve's face, nearly smothering him, as he was enveloped into her cleavage. Her long, red hair dropped down onto Steve's head as she leaned over and breathed heavily into his ear. "Hey, Sugar," she said, "would you like a private dance after this song?"

"Well, you sure know how to get a guy's attention," replied Steve, in a quiet voice muffled by her large breasts. "I just got here and haven't even had a drink yet. In a little bit maybe."

"Okay, Baby," she said. "I'll check back with you later." Steve resisted his impulse to kiss the area between her breasts, mindful of the thought that at least five of the last ten guys had done so. She let go of Steve and placed her index finger under the side of her briefs. That was Steve's cue to slip a dollar bill under the strap. After he had done so, she let the elastic snap back loudly capturing the bill firmly. She turned around placing her rear directly in front of Steve's face for a moment. She wiggled it a bit and gave him another good look at it as she pulled the dollar from her briefs and threw it into the center of the stage. She crawled seductively over to the guy seated a few chairs to the left. Steve heard her say "Hi Sugar," as she sat in front of the man, grabbed his head and plunged his face into her crotch.

The waitress had waited for Steve's mini-adventure to end before asking him for his drink order. Steve watched as the redhead lay on her back with her legs clamped around the guy, shaking him back and forth. It was quite a spectacle. As she wrapped her breasts around the guy's face she breathed into his ear. As she did this, she caught Steve's eyes. She looked at him for a moment, smiled, licked her lips slowly and blew Steve a kiss.

Steve smiled as he heard her whisper into the guy's ear "Hey, Sugar, would you like a private dance after this song?"

The guy nodded in the affirmative, as the sound he attempted to make was completely muffled by the woman's breasts. She pulled the strap of her briefs, as the man stopped licking the area between her breasts and slipped a dollar bill under the strap.

The song ended, and she quickly collected the dollar bills strewn about the center of the stage. She exited down the steps as her replacement was introduced and marched up the steps. The redhead came around and took the hand of the guy seated to Steve's left and led him to the privacy of the couches in the dimly lit back room.

The new girl was a shapely blonde in a cowgirl hat, white panties and a sparkling blue vest. Her shoes had at least three-inch high heels, which occasionally lit up in a display of red, white and blue flashing lights.

He watched her elegant and sultry performance to the tune of "Cowboy." She made her rounds to each of the half-dozen or so men seated around the circular stage. She spent time talking to each customer and was into the third and last song of her set before she finally made her way to Steve. By this time, she had shed her vest, panties and hat. She was topless and had only the smallest G-string imaginable barely covering her most private parts.

"Hard day at the office?" she asked, as she lay down in front of Steve with her head propped up on one arm. She reached out and grabbed Steve's tie and pulled him closer to her. Her face was just inches from Steve's. "My name is Danger," she said, "How ya doin'?"

"Well, better now," said Steve. "Good," she replied and smiled broadly. She kissed the end of her index finger and then placed it on the tip of Steve's nose as she twisted around and sat in front of him. She reached out and began to massage his head and ran her fingers through his hair and down the back of his neck. "You're all tense Baby. You need to relax," she said, as she reached over and picked up his nearly finished drink. She raised it to his lips and tilted it for him to take the last remaining drink from the glass. "Waitress," she said, as she motioned her over to Steve, "this man needs another one of these to relax. One is just not going to do it for him."

The waitress looked down at Steve and he nodded his approval. Danger sat Steve's glass down off to the side and motioned for him to slide back in his seat and spread his legs. She bent over the edge of the stage and placed the back of her head firmly against Steve's aroused member. The top of her head rested on the seat of the chair between Steve's legs as she did a headstand. She held herself perfectly vertical for a moment and then bent her legs at the knee and rested them on each side of Steve's head. Steve looked down at her barely covered privates just inches from his face. The unexpected, faint but pleasant scent of cotton candy filled his nostrils. Danger took her index finger and traced the details of her female form over the small patch of remaining clothing. She then reached out and traced from between his eyes to the tip of his nose. Her hands then gripped the edge of the stage and she brought her legs up vertically and rolled back onto the stage. Her head raised slowly from between his legs as she kept firm pressure on his erect penis with the back of her head. Once her legs were firmly rooted on the stage, she brought her face around to be within a half inch of his penis. She flicked her tongue as if she were about to lick his zipper and then slowly moved her mouth up the length of his body until her lips were nearly touching his. She deliberately exhaled and Steve breathed in the warmth of the sweet-smelling air that had just left her lungs.

"Don't you think you should have a little Danger in your life?" she whispered directly into his face.

Steve was not nearly as confident of his own sweet-smelling breath as he replied "Oh, yeah," while somehow managing not to exhale. He pulled a dollar bill out of his shirt pocket. She turned slightly to the side as he clumsily tried to pluck the fragile thread holding her G-string in place. He slipped the dollar bill under it.

He looked up at a pair of blue eyes and a pearly white smile, perfectly framed by her long blonde hair. She winked at him and then gracefully extended her hand.

"Well, Handsome," she replied, "It was a pleasure making your acquaintance. I'll come around to see you if you are at one of the tables later."

"You do that," said Steve as he smiled.

She pulled the dollar bill from beneath the thin strap and placed it in the neat pile she had created at center stage. She turned her attention to one of the other gentlemen seated across from Steve. Her routine with him was completely different. He had a baseball cap on and he wore glasses. She reached out and turned the cap around with the bill facing to the back. She removed his glasses and placed them carefully to one side on the stage. She then placed her breasts against the side of his face and rubbed the nipple around his cheek, and then did the same on the other side. She raised up and let his face slide down her stomach all the way to her G-string. She removed his cap and placed it on her own head for a moment. She leaned back and picked up his glasses and placed them back on for him to see her. She nodded to him as she grabbed the bill of his cap and removed it from her head and carefully placed the baseball cap back on his head.

The man offered a dollar bill to her but seemed too timid to place it anywhere. She reached out and gently guided the man's hand and helped him slip it under the string. She kissed him softly on the cheek.

"There is something special about that one," thought Steve, as he mentally decided she was maybe twenty-two or twenty-three. He looked over at the door and saw a young, Black girl in a thin jacket talking to the cashier. He watched as the cashier motioned over to the office door and then handed her a sheet of paper.

Steve was immediately intrigued. He picked up his drink and walked slowly past the cashier. She was a petite girl, early to mid-twenties. Her hair was braided in the fashion typical of many young, Black girls. He turned and smiled at her as he walked by. "Hello," said Steve.

"Well, hi thar," she said, with a thick Southern accent. Steve smiled and walked on by. It was an employment application. That meant she needed a job and she needed money. She was from out of state, and Steve figured she needed money right now and desperately.

Steve walked around and watched her as she walked over and found an empty table near the manager's office. She sat down and began filling out the application. Steve went over and sat down at the empty table that would allow him to sit facing the stages and look over the table where she was seated.

At one point she looked up and caught his eyes and smiled a beautiful smile that contrasted her white teeth with her dark skin.

"Are you from Indy?" asked Steve.

"Nah," she said, as she shook her head back and forth.

"You must be cold in that jacket," said Steve.

"Oh, yes," she said, as she made a shivering motion and rubbed her hands against her arms. "It don't usually get this cold in Atlanta, Brrrrrr."

"So, you're a Georgia girl?" asked Steve.

"I guess you could say that," she replied, as she continued to fill out the application.

"What brings you to Indianapolis?" asked Steve.

"Well, I jest got here today on the bus," she said, "and I plan to be back on that bus Monday night, headin' for home. I can't get outa here fast enough."

"Really?" said Steve. "You're only going to be here for the weekend, and you're looking for a job? What's the point?"

"What's the point?" she said mocking him. "The point is that I got a room to pay for and I gotta eat, I need an outfit and I gotta get my har done."

"Your har?" quizzed Steve.

"My har," she said, a little annoyed, as she grabbed a hand full of her braided locks and pulled them in Steve's direction. "My har needs done."

He was a little embarrassed at his trouble with her accent "It looks fine to me."

"Well, it don't look fine to me. I need to make a real good impression on some white folk on Monday, and I want to look my best for 'em," she said, as she tilted her head and batted her eyes.

"Important business?" asked Steve.

"It's family business and it's important. Nothin' would get me back to Indiana 'cept for kin needin' me."

"Important enough that you would take the bus up here on Friday, and then you're heading back to Atlanta on Monday?" asked Steve.

"I got important tests next week, and I gotta be back Tuesday," she said.

She stood up and stuck the tip of her finger on Steve's nose and said, "You got a little bit of nose trouble, don'tcha?" She picked up the application she had finished and said, "I gotta go see the boss man."

"Hey, my name is Steve. Maybe, uh, when you get finished with the interview, you might join me for a drink?"

"Well, I'm Cindi," she said. "If I see you when I get out and you learn to mind your own business and stop aksing so many questions, then I jest might do that," she proclaimed as she walked toward the office door.

Steve sat down and, before he could even pick up his drink, a shapely blonde sat down on his lap and put her arms around his neck. It was Danger. She leaned forward almost touching his lips with hers and whispered, "Would you like to spend a little quality time in the Danger Zone?"

Steve looked over at the closed office door. He figured Cindi would be in there for ten or fifteen minutes at least. "Sure," he said. "I got time for one song."

Danger hopped up and led him by the hand to the rear of the club. She stopped and motioned him up the three steps to the private area. As he went up the steps, she reached out and patted him on the rear and gave it a little tickle with her fingertips. There were three other couples in various stages of close physical encounters. The three girls were earning their twenty dollars per song by rubbing their bodies all over their clients and acting out various fantasies.

Steve sat down on one of the empty couches. Danger sat down next to him and swung her legs over the top of his lap "We'll do the next song," she said, as she grasped his tie and pulled him closer to her. Steve put his arms around her and held her close to him. She rested her head on his shoulders and looked up at him. "You know the rules?" she asked.

"Yeah, I think so," said Steve, "but why don't you tell me? I wouldn't want to break any."

"Well, you can touch anywhere except the nipples and here," she said, as she pointed to the area between her legs covered by a very small piece of clothing. "No kissing on the lips," she continued, "and keep your tongue in your mouth."

Steve kept looking over toward the office door to see if Cindi had come out yet. It seemed like this song would never end. The other guys didn't mind, as they were obviously enjoying the long song.

As the song finally came to an end, Danger stood up, faced Steve, and removed her top. Her breasts sprang free and Steve noticed that each nipple was covered with a small piece of transparent tape.

The DJ was announcing the next group of ladies to take the stage, and Danger stood there smiling seductively, waiting for the next song to start. Suddenly, Steve noticed Cindi standing at the cashier area near the exit door. "Oh, shit," he thought. She seemed to be looking around the room, maybe looking for Steve.

Steve realized that she could turn and walk out that door at any second and he would never see her again. Just as the song began and Danger came closer to him, he said in disgust "Oh shit!" He reached for his phone at the side of his belt and pulled it from the clip. "What is it?" asked Danger.

"It's an emergency text," he said, shaking his head. "I don't believe this! I have to make a call right now."

"It can't wait just five minutes?" she asked coyly as she twisted his tie and brought her face up next to his. "No. I am sorry," he said, as he fumbled in his shirt pocket for the twenty-dollar bill he had tucked there. "Here," he said as he handed it to her and looked furtively over toward the cashier. Cindi was still standing there talking to him.

"I didn't do the dance yet," said Danger. "You don't have to pay me."

"No, that's all right, you spent time with me. Just keep it."

"Okay," she said. "I'll give you a raincheck."

"Right," said Steve, knowing that would never happen. She wouldn't even remember him the next time he came in - that's if he ever came in again. Steve darted toward the door where Cindi was still talking to the cashier. He made a beeline for her and then suddenly lost his nerve. "Maybe she wasn't looking for him," he thought. Maybe she was talking to the cashier about the job. He couldn't stop and talk to her and then leave with her. It was against the rules to leave with a customer or even date a customer. He could cost her the job before she even got it. She didn't even see him as he walked right past her and into the entry way. He stopped and pretended to make a call on his phone.

He waited to catch Cindi's eyes. Finally, she noticed him and smiled. "That was encouraging," he thought. She continued to talk to the cashier for several minutes, and Steve continued to pretend he was talking on the phone. As she came into the entryway, he placed his phone back into his belt clip "Hi," he said. "Did you get the job?"

"I dunno," she replied, as she opened the door leading outside into the cold drizzle. He followed her and she stood shivering under the awning. "They said they really need Black girls but they're not interested in somebody for just three nights. They said maybe they'd call me tomorrow or Sunday if some of the regular girls are no shows."

The upbeat smile was gone from her face. "This is the third club I have been to today and they all say the same thing. I gave 'em the number of my motel, but I don't have enough money to pay for any more nights. I can't go someplace else because they won't know where to call me if thar's work. "Damn, Damn, Damn!" she said.

"You know there's a Black club about a mile from here. Have you tried that?" asked Steve.

"Hell, NO!" she said. "I ain't workin' in that place. I can't make no money workin' in a Black club."

"Really?" he said pondering the reasons for that statement.

"I can make real good money from white guys. I think it's a repressed guilt thing or something' or, maybe they're former Grand Dragons of the KKK trying to make up for their past or somethin'. Who knows?" she said, as she continued to shiver.

Steve worked up his nerve and said it. "You know, I'd like to see you sometime while you're here this weekend."

She looked at him. Her eyes stared straight into his and she smiled. "That'd be nice. You 'spose I might be able to get some help?"

Steve wanted to be careful about what he said next. The whole thing could be a set-up. He still wasn't sure if she was a prostitute or if she just needed some money and was willing to do what it took to get it.

He nodded at her, "It's possible," he said, as he looked directly into her eyes with a tense, nervous expression on his face.

She reached her hand out and took his "Relax," she said, "just chill out."

"Your hand is freezing and you in that thin jacket!" exclaimed Steve. My car is over there. It's probably still pretty warm and I can write down your number."

"Okay," she said, as they both made a mad dash through the cold drizzle to Steve's Ford Explorer. Steve hit the unlock button on his key ring and motioned her to get in. He came around and got in the driver's side. He pulled a pen and paper out of the glove box and handed it to her.

"Give me the name and number of your hotel," he said. She began writing in large cursive letters on the pad. When she was finished she handed it to him. He looked at her name, Cindi, the phone number and room number were written on the paper.

"When can I see you?" he asked.

"When do you want to see me?" she replied

"I want to see you now," said Steve.

"Okay," she said.

"Can we go to your place?" he asked.

"Yep, it's nothin' fancy but it's clean," she said.

"I can follow you," he said.

"Steve, silly boy. I don't have a car, I took a cab to get here," she said.

"Oh," he said, feeling real stupid. He started the car up for the short drive to the motel. He pulled into a convenience store just down the street from the motel. "I need to hit the ATM," he said, as he got out of the car. "I'll leave the car running so you can stay warm."

"What an idiot!" he thought to himself. "I just left my keys in the car with an inner-city Black girl that I just met. What the hell am I doing? If anyone recognized me it would be all over."

He just shook his head as he placed his card in the ATM machine. He didn't know how much he should withdraw. No figure had been mentioned. He finally decided three-hundred dollars, and if that wasn't enough, he would just skip the whole thing. He tucked the cash in the pocket of his suit jacket and strolled down some of the aisles until he found what he was looking for. He picked up a package of condoms and tried to hide them from the view of other customers as he checked out. The young male desk clerk looked at him as he scanned the item and took Steve's ten-dollar bill. The clerk looked out in the parking lot at Cindi sitting in Steve's car. He looked at Steve standing there in his suit and overcoat. The little pimply-faced twerp handed Steve the condoms and change, smiled and said, "Looks like you're going to have yourself a fine evening, Sir."

Steve just glared at him and said nothing, as he turned and walked out the door to his car. Cindi was all smiles when he got back in and drove the short distance to the room.

The room was on the first floor and Steve parked directly in front. As they entered the room Cindi flipped on the overhead light and the desk lamp. "I like a lot of light. What about you, Steve? she asked as she slipped her jacket off.

"Sure," he said, as he nervously looked around the room for a hidden video camera. He took his coat off and laid it across the back of a chair.

There were two beds and Cindi sat down on one next to the nightstand. Steve sat down on the other bed directly facing her. It was an awkward moment for Steve. He didn't know what to say next. He looked at her young face as if he was seeing her for the first time. "How old are you?" he asked.

"Twenty-four," she replied without a moment's hesitation. "I got you by almost twenty-years," said Steve. He was actually relieved at her answer. He had been concerned that she was a lot younger.

He looked at her expecting her to say something, to mention money and negotiate a price, but she didn't. She just sat there smiling, looking back at him with her dark-brown eyes framed by her long, braided hair.

Their knees were nearly touching and Steve put his hand down and brought her foot up into his lap and began rubbing it. "Oh, that feel's good," she said, "I been on my feet all day."

He untied her shoelace and slipped her shoe and sock off. She immediately pulled her foot away and raised the other one. He repeated the procedure. She laughed, "Looks like you're wantin' to get down to bizzness."

She hopped up and said, "I have to tinkle." She walked over to the bathroom and left the door open as she pulled her jeans down and sat down. Steve could not see her directly, but he had a full view of her in the mirror of the door. He felt like a pervert watching her. Yet, his eyes remained fixed on the mirror.

Steve forced his eyes away from the mirror and glanced around the room, until his eyes came around to the nearby nightstand. A half-eaten hamburger, neatly contained in a McDonald's wrapper, was laying on the nightstand. It seemed out of place for her, when everything else he had observed about her was very clean and tidy.

His eyes returned to the mirror. She looked at the door and suddenly realized Steve could see her. She laughed but did not close the door or make any effort to hide what she was doing. She finished and went over to the lavatory, washed her hands and then carefully washed her private parts. When she returned she sat back down in front of Steve and then leaned back on the bed. The belt of her jeans was unfastened.

Steve moved over on the bed next to her and fumbled at unfastening her jeans. "Pesky little button, isn't it?" she said. "I have trouble with it, too."

He unzipped her and began tugging at her tight-fitting jeans to pull them down over her hips. She wiggled a little bit to help him. The jeans were so tight that her panties came off with them.

She lay on her back, nude from the waist down, her legs spread slightly and dangling off the edge of the bed. The nightstand lamp lit the scene, providing a magnificent view for Steve. He slid his hand under her top and began massaging her breasts, first the left and then the right. She crossed her arms, took her top in her hands and pulled it over her head. As she did so, Steve placed his hands under her back. She arched her back and Steve unfastened her bra revealing her breasts and deep brown nipples.

He leaned over her and gently kissed both of her nipples. He then stood up and quickly removed his shoes, tie, and all of his clothes. He threw them on the nearby chair. Cindi looked at him and seemed fascinated by his erect member. She giggled and said, "Ooh, looks like you're already ready for some action."

He picked up her legs from the floor and pivoted her whole body onto the bed. He slid over the top of her and lay next to her. He kissed her neck and made his way up to her lips. She gave him a quick kiss on his lips with tightly closed lips and then turned her head away. "I don't like a lot of kissing on the lips," she said.

His fingers had found the place between her legs and he began lightly massaging her. She groaned a little bit in pleasure. He placed a finger deep inside her, and she wiggled with a bit of discomfort. "I'm very sensitive and I can feel your fingernail," she said. "I don't like fingers inside me."

Steve complied with her wishes as he continued to gently explore the area between her legs with his fingers. He took turns kissing one breast and then the other as she caressed his head in her arms. "They're pretty small," she said.

They were not small. "I think they are a perfect size," he said, as he raised his head above her to take in the entire view. He shook his head and thought to himself, "What the hell am I doing?"

He moved down the bed, spread her legs apart and positioned himself where he had a direct view of her. The light from the lamp on the other side of the room caused her moist skin to glisten. He examined every fold and detail of her female form, touching and massaging her as she wiggled and writhed in delight.

For a while he stopped and just savored the view. "It's kinda purty down thar, ain't it?" she said.

"Oh yeah," he replied.

"Well, are ya gonna to lick it?" she asked.

"I'm thinking about it," he replied. He wanted to, Oh, how he wanted to. He could not help thinking about the danger. He didn't know this girl. He had only met her an hour ago. How could he possibly take the risk of performing oral sex on her?

"I'm about to nut with all your messin' around down thar, so either lick it or fuck it and do it now."

He stood up and stepped over to his suit jacket to get the condom. He turned as he was opening the package. He stood directly over her face with his penis dangling just inches above her. She knew what he wanted.

Her eyes got real big and she shook her head back and forth rapidly and said "I don't give head, Steve. I gotsta know a guy really well 'fore I do that." She reached up and pushed him away from her face and said, "You just slip your little friend thar on him and hurry up."

Steve did as she said and positioned himself on top of her. As soon as he entered her she cried out, "ooh doggies, thar's the first one!" He was glad that she had come so quickly. She brought her legs up and wrapped them around his waist, her hands clasped around his neck. "Thar's another one," she said. He lasted only a few minutes before he came with a barely audible groan.

"You came?" she asked, "uh-huh," he whispered.

"Gross!" she exclaimed, "Get out, get out, get out!"

He was startled by her reaction as he withdrew from her. "I'm very sensitive down thar and it feels so gross and squishy since you came."

He scooted over to the edge of the bed and stood up. Her eyes were fixed on the condom. "Wow!" she said, "You must have been savin' it up for a while." as she giggled and eyed the sagging tip of the filled condom.

He went to the bathroom and she followed. He slipped the condom off and threw it into the toilet. She had run some very hot water into the sink. She wet a wash rag and handed it to him and then prepared a second one for herself. She picked up the bar of soap and washed herself. "I'm a very clean girl," she said, as she handed him the bar of soap.

In a few minutes, they went back to lie on the bed next to each other. "You are a very sweet, young lady," he said.

"You're pretty nice yerself," she giggled. "I nutted three times, the last one was same time as you."

"Well, I am glad to know that," he said. "There's nothing quite like a simulgasm." They held each other for a little while and didn't say anything. She had not said a single thing about money yet, and he didn't know how to bring the subject up.

After a few minutes, she got up and started putting her clothes back on. He did likewise. In a few minutes, they were standing there fully clothed facing each other.

It was awkward, "Thanks for letting me come here," he said.

She laughed at his choice of words and looked straight into his eyes. "Hey, Steve, you can come here anytime you want."

"I don't understand why you were willing to be with me, but I really mean it. Thank you," he said.

"A girl's gotta do what a girl's gotta do," she said with a grin.

He took that as a subtle hint for money. He pulled his wallet out and asked "How much?"

"Whatever you think's fair," she said.

He was now completely off guard. "I don't know, Cindi. You tell me," He said, as he was hoping she didn't quote anything over three-hundred dollars.

"Well, in that case, eighty-four dollars and thirty-seven cents," she replied.

He didn't know what to say, "You're kidding?" he quizzed.

"No," she said. "That's what I need for the room for Saturday and Sunday night. You just go pay the man at the front desk as you leave."

He stood there dumbstruck and put his wallet away. He put on his coat and faced her. He placed his arms around her and they embraced for a long time.

"Why me?" he whispered in her ear.

"You just seemed like a nice guy and I told you already, a girl's gotta do what a girl's gotta do. My room's taken care of now, and if they call me to work tomorrow night, I can make enough money for an outfit, somethin' to eat and I can get my har' done. I'll be fine."

"Will I ever see you again?" he asked.

"That's up to you. I'll be here until Monday morning. Monday night, the good Lord willin' and the creek don't rise, I'll be on the bus back to Atlanta."

"I want to see you again before you leave," he said.

"I know you think that right now, but don't go makin' any promises. You want to see me, just knock on the door. If I answer the door, I'm here.

"I wouldn't want to stop in at a bad time," he said.

"I ain't gonna be in here with nobody else, Steve, so just suit yourself."

He didn't know what else to say. It was true he wanted to see her again right now, but by tomorrow or Sunday he might come to his senses.

They hugged and she kissed him on the lips for only the second time.

He opened the door and stepped out into the cold drizzle. He got into his car and turned on the wipers, as he stared at the room he had just left. The curtains parted a bit and he saw Cindi's smiling face as she waved at him.

He waved to her as he backed out of the parking spot, but he was not sure she saw him. He drove around to the lobby entrance. He went in to see the clerk. He put the $84.37 into the security drawer, and the clerk retrieved it and credited it to Cindi's room.

Steve went back to his car. By this time, it was late in the evening and he took the interstate back to Anderson.

Chapter 2

Steve Foulke woke up and looked at the clock. It was 9:00 a.m. and late for Steve to still be in bed, even on a Saturday. He had tossed and turned much of the night before finally getting to sleep. He got up and as he was taking a shower he pondered the idiocy of the night before. He shook his head as he played the events in his mind.

Then it hit him. The hamburger, the damn, half-eaten hamburger so neatly wrapped on the nightstand. That was all Cindi had to eat. She had eaten half for lunch before she went job hunting and was saving the other half for later.

Like a man on a mission, Steve took a shower, quickly dressed and got in his car.

He headed straight for the Cindi's motel. He did a lot of thinking on the forty-five-minute drive but not enough to make him turn around.

He tried to decide if he was really concerned about her or if he was just looking for a lame excuse to see her one more time. He didn't really know the answer. He didn't want to know the answer. He made a quick stop at the Castleton Mall and then went straight to her motel.

He knocked on the door of her room. There was no answer. He looked at his watch, 10:20. He thought she might still be asleep if she planned to work tonight.

He decided to knock one more time before giving up on the idea. He saw someone pull the curtain to the side and peek out. In a moment, the door opened and Cindi was standing there in her robe with a towel draped over her shoulder.

"Well, hi Steve," she said with a big smile, "I jest stepped out of the shower and thought I heared a knock."

"Denny's?" said Steve.

Cindi looked at him with a puzzled look on her face.

"Denny's?" repeated Steve. "I'm taking you to breakfast and there's a Denny's just down the street."

"Well, that sounds mighty good," she said, as she opened the door to let him in.

"How long will it take you to get ready?" he asked.

"About two seconds," she replied with a crooked little grin.

Steve looked puzzled. "Oh," said Cindi. "You mean how long it would take me to get ready to leave for breakfast?"

"What did you think I meant?" quizzed Steve.

"I thought you meant how long would it take me to get ready to give you what you really came here for."

"What do you mean?" Steve replied defensively.

"You just want to git yourself a little more brown sugar 'fore I leave. Now, ain't that right?"

"I don't know?" Steve stammered nervously and embarrassed.

"Don't go bullshittin' me, Steve. You can lie to me if you want to but don't go lyin' to yourself. You're here for one reason and one reason only and I know it and you know it,"

Cindi said calmly. "After all it is your room, or at least will be, 'cause you paid for Saturday and Sunday."

She walked over to the bed and said "one second, two seconds," as she threw off her robe and jumped backward onto the bed completely nude. She spread her legs in full view of Steve, raised them straight up and said, "Come and git it. It's all yours."

He wanted to protest. He wanted to say that was not why he had come. He wanted to say he was concerned about her and was concerned she was hungry and hadn't eaten for a while. But he didn't.

He just looked at her beautiful, young, black body brightly illuminated by the morning sun sneaking through the blinds. Her legs were high in the air and spread, inviting him over.

He ripped his clothes off as Cindi watched with a knowing grin. He slipped on a condom he had brought in his pocket. He was lost completely in lust at this moment. As he drew closer to her, she looked straight into his eyes and said "This may be your last chance to lick it, Steve. I wouldn't want you tossing and turning in your bed tonight 'cause you'd passed it up again. My granny always taught us girls to be proud of our bodies and that all parts of our bodies were beautiful." She giggled as she continued, "Don't you think it's kinda purty down thar? I am a very clean girl." she said with a smile.

There was no pretense left. Damn right he wanted to. He looked into her eyes and didn't know what to say. So, he didn't say anything. He didn't care what the medical risks were. He just did what he wanted to do to her. He plunged his tongue deep into her private recesses. His tongue explored slowly and gently at first. He had to agree that she was a very clean girl!

"Faster,' she said, "Faster Steve. You ain't gonna break it!"

She came with a long slow moan and shouted, "I'm nuttin' Steve, I'm nuttin'."

After she came, he slid on top of her and penetrated her. She dug her nails into his back just enough to inflict the slightest pain on him. He exploded in just a few minutes.

"Okay, you can get off me now," said Cindi. "Why is it you guys are never heavy until after you come?"

Steve didn't have an answer and moved to the side. Cindi got up and went into the bathroom and turned on the shower. Steve followed her in and threw the condom into the toilet. Cindi slipped a shower cap on her head, tucked her braids up into it, and stepped into the shower.

She stuck her head out of the shower curtain and said, "You can come in here if you want." Steve shook his head, "No, but I might watch if you don't mind."

"Suit yerself," she said, as she grabbed a wash cloth off the wall rack and began to lather it up. Steve peeked around the curtain and watched as her black skin was covered with the white bubbles of the soap and then rinsed by the rush of the water coming from the shower spigot. It was tremendously erotic.

Cindi giggled and pulled the curtain back to reveal his penis springing to life again. She lathered up the washcloth and then reached out and began washing him with the warm soap and water. This was the only time she had touched him with her hands.

The lavatory was an easy reach from the shower, and she turned on one of the spigots. She rinsed the soap from the washcloth and then quickly wrapped the cloth around his penis and squeezed the water onto him.

It was ice cold and Steve gasped.

"That should cool him down a bit," said Cindi, as she pulled the shower curtain shut and left the cold wash cloth hanging on his rapidly shrinking private part.

Steve yanked the cloth off and turned on the hot water of the lavatory. He rinsed himself off with the warm washcloth and walked into the bedroom and got dressed.

Cindi was out of the shower in another minute and dried herself off in full view of Steve. She quickly slipped on her jeans and the rest of her clothes.

"Well, Steve," she said, "you've had your Grand Slam this morning and now I'm ready for one down at Denny's."

They left and drove a few blocks north to the restaurant. Cindi ordered grits with her breakfast. She ate like she hadn't eaten in days. "These grits ain't near as good as my granny's," she said, "but you can't get 'em many places in Indy, 'cept maybe Bob Evans and Cracker Barrel."

Steve enjoyed watching her scarf down her food. "You know you can slow down there if you want. We are not in any hurry."

She laughed "Yeah, I 'spose your right. It's jest I haven't had much to eat the last couple of days."

"I figured that," replied Steve. "After I gave some more thought to that half a hamburger that was on your nightstand last night."

You're still havin' a bit of a problem with your nose, aren't you, Mister?"

"I just wanted to help," said Steve.

"The city is full of girls who haven't had much to eat for a lot longer than just a couple days, why aren't you out buying them breakfast this morning?" She asked.

Steve stammered… "I don't know. I just wanted to help you I guess…"

She cut him off. "You're a nice guy Steve, but you have a problem with the simple truth. You don't really believe that shit you tell yourself, do you?"

"Well," he was defensive. "I…uh, yeah…uh, I didn't want you to be hungry."

"Bullshit," she said. "You fucked me last night and you felt so bad about it that came down here and fucked me again this morning. That's the simple truth, live with it?"

"You don't cut me much slack, do you?" he said.

"Steve, we both got what we wanted. I got me a room until I leave on Monday, and you got yourself some strange, black pussy. Now, you don't owe me anything else, but I do want to thank you for the fine Southern breakfast."

Steve just sat there for a while and finally, he said, "Why me? Why did you go with me?"

"A girl's gotta do what a girl's gotta do," she said.

"What kind of an answer is that?" he asked.

"It's the simple truth," she snapped back, "Look, Steve, you're a nice guy. Somewhere, deep down under that five-hundred dollar suit you were wearing last night, I think thar's a nice guy hiding." She reached across the table and ran her finger along his wedding band. "Now, why don't you just go on home to your wife and if you're suffering some great guilt here, then take her out some place nice for dinner. She's the one that got hurt here, not you or me."

He looked down at his ring. "Yeah, I would like to do that, but I can't," he paused for moment. "That part about me being a nice guy, I think that used to be true, but anymore, I, uh…just don't know what to do sometimes. It gets so complicated I don't know what to do next."

"My daddy always said," began Cindi with a bit of a sparkle in her eye "that when you git yerself in a situation where you just don't know what to do next and it's all closing in on you and you jest don't know how to get out of it, thar's jest one thing to do."

"And what would that be?" asked Steve.

"You just do what's right," she said.

He shook his head "If it were only that simple."

"It is that simple. It's always that simple. It's a simple truth that always works."

"Okay, Miss Philosopher, I'll take you back to your room."

He drove her back to the motel and parked in front of her door.

"Thank you for breakfast," said Cindi.

"And thank you for the simple, if painful, truth," said Steve, as he paused and asked, "will I see you again before you leave?"

"No, I gotta go pick out an outfit today, and tonight I'll be workin' to make enough to buy the outfit on Sunday afternoon, and I gotta go to church in the morning. Monday, I'll be doing my thingy for the white folks and then I'm gonna get my little black ass back to Atlanta. So, this is it, Steve."

Steve reached into his coat pocket and pulled out a small package and handed it to her. "What's this?" she said as she opened it.

"It's gift certificates for the mall," he said.

She looked at them and counted them: six gift certificates for fifty-dollars each.

"That's bunch of money," said Cindi.

"They're good at several malls around town, Washington Square, Castleton, Circle Center downtown."

"How about Sak's Fifth Avenue at Keystone at the Crossing?" she asked.

"That's the Fashion Mall, and they're good there, too."

"Well, that's where I'm headed then," she said.

"Do you have cab fare?" he asked.

"I always keep cab fare saved back. I'll be fine and, besides I ain't taking your cash."

"I figured that, so that's why I stopped and got the certificates. You're funny. You will take the room being paid for and you'll take the certificates, but you won't take the money."

"Well, a girl's gotta do what a girl's gotta do, and they ain't nuthin' illegal about accepting gifts from a gentleman. 'Specially a gentleman that needs to clear his conscience."

He thought about it for a moment and said, "You know, I guess you are right about that."

She leaned over and kissed him softly on the lips - the only time she had done so today. "You take care," she said, as she hopped out of the car. Steve watched as she unlocked her door. She turned and smiled at him and then disappeared into the room.

Chapter 3

First thing Monday morning, in Anderson, there was a preliminary hearing at the Madison County Courthouse regarding Mark Campbell's case.

"So, Ms. Merriman," said John Kosten, "is it correct that your testimony is that in your professional opinion, a child molester that has molested his three step-daughters would have also molested his biological daughter?"

"And other young girls in his extended family that he might have had unsupervised access to," Merriman quickly added.

"And yet," continued Kosten "you can offer this Court no other such female family members who may have been molested by Mr. Campbell."

"Mr. Campbell has an adult daughter who lives outside of Indiana. We have been trying to contact her and obtain her testimony and a physical examination," replied Merriman.

"But it is your testimony that, if Mr. Campbell's daughter could be located, that she too will have been mutilated in a similar fashion as was found in the autopsy of Keisha and Kara and that was also detected in the physical examination of Kima Campbell?"

"My testimony is that she will have been molested in some fashion," answered Merriman.

"How can you be so sure? Couldn't he have only started his molestation recently with his step-daughters and perhaps have been a perfect father with his own daughter?" asked Kosten

"Your Honor," interrupted Steve Foulke "I object to counsel's badgering of the witness. She has answered this question already in a similar form.

"Overruled Mr. Foulke," droned the Judge, "Answer the question, Ms. Merriman."

"It does not fit the pattern. A child molester is not suddenly created one day, but rather his pattern of behavior goes back many years, usually beginning in adolescence. Mr. Campbell likely subjected his daughter to many years of such abuse and then when overseas he married a woman with young daughters who provided a perfect venue for his behavior to continue."

"As an American serviceman with a foreign wife, if she or the unfortunate girls were to come forward, they could lose their status to remain in the United States and could be deported. It gave him great power over all of them."

"So, does it then follow," asked Kosten, "that if Mr. Campbell's biological daughter came forward and testified that she had never been abused, that Mr. Campbell likely did not suddenly turn into a child molester one day and begin molesting his step-daughters?"

"Yes, that is possible, but without the testimony and examination of his other daughter, we are left with the indisputable fact that all of his step-daughters were unspeakably abused and mutilated," snapped Merriman with an air of haughtiness.

"Your Honor," said Kosten, "I would like to reserve the right to call Ms. Merriman for future testimony, if necessary, but would like, at this time to call another witness."

"I object, Your Honor!" exclaimed Foulke. "I have received no notice of any such witness."

"This is a rebuttal witness, Your Honor," replied Kosten, "and I call her to directly rebut the testimony of Ms. Merriman."

"Very well. Proceed Mr. Kosten." The judge motioned toward Merriman, "Ms. Merriman, you may take your seat for now, but you may be asked to return to the stand to give further testimony." Merriman stood up, nodded in the affirmative and stepped down from the stand. She walked over and sat down immediately behind the prosecutor, Steve Foulke.

"Call your rebuttal witness," said the Judge.

"Your Honor, I would like to call to the stand, Cynthia Campbell," said Kosten.

An audible gasp occurred throughout the room. Simultaneously, Foulke and Merriman turned to the rear of the courtroom.

In the back of the courtroom, a petite, young, Black woman in her mid-twenties stood up and began walking forward. She was dressed in a smartly styled, conservative, gray business dress with a vest and jacket. Her Olivia Pope hairstyle projected power. She sported a small black hat with matching purse and shoes. She looked as if she had just stepped out of the pages of a women's fashion magazine. She had poise, beauty and grace. All eyes followed her as she stepped up to the stand.

"Raise your right hand and repeat after me," said the bailiff, as he positioned the Bible toward her left side. She raised her right hand and placed her left hand on the Bible and followed the bailiff, "I, Cynthia Campbell, swear to tell the whole truth and nothing but the truth, so help me God!" She spoke in perfect English with no trace of a Hoosier accent.

She sat down in the witness chair facing John Kosten who stood directly in front of her. "Miss Campbell," began Kosten "please state your name and your relationship to Mark Campbell."

"I am Cynthia Campbell and Mark Campbell is my father."

"It's my understanding that you attend college out of state, is that correct?

"Yes, it is," she replied.

"Have you at any time been contacted by the Madison County authorities in connection with your father's arrest?"

"No, I have not."

"Miss Campbell," inquired Kosten, "during the times you were a young girl, or at any time during your life have you had the occasion to be alone with your father in an unsupervised manner?"

"Yes," replied Cynthia "On many many occasions."

"Miss Campbell, has your father at any time, in any way molested you or touched you in any sexually inappropriate manner?"

"No, Sir. My father would never do that to me or to anyone else and he did not molest Keisha, Kara or Kima."

"I object Your Honor," exclaimed Foulke. "She cannot testify to things she does not know about. She can testify to her own experience with her father, but she cannot testify about her father's actions with her step-sisters during occasions when she may not have been present."

"Sustained," said the Judge.

"Can you answer the question a little more precisely, in light of the prosecutor's objection?" asked Kosten.

"I understand perfectly well, that I may not conjecture about my father's relationship with my step-sisters during occasions when I was not present even though I have known him all my life, but that Ms. Merriman can offer conjecture about that relationship as well as my own relationship with my father, even though she does not know any of us. I repeat, my father never once touched me in any inappropriate manner in my entire life."

"Your Honor," said Foulke.

"Mr. Foulke, she answered the question. There is nothing to object to," interrupted the Judge.

"No further questions, Your Honor," said Kosten.

"Well, I have a few," said Foulke, as he strutted to the witness stand.

"Miss Campbell," he began "did you live with your father the entire time of your childhood and adolescence?"

"No," she replied.

"And why not may I ask?" said Foulke.

"My father was in the Marines. Sometimes he was stationed overseas and we stayed in America. We did spend some time here with him in central Indiana. Sometimes we lived near a Marine base with him when we could, but after Mom died we frequently stayed with our grandmother."

"You say 'We?'" asked Foulke. "Who else are you referring to?

"I have an older brother," she replied.

"How old is he now?"

"Jimmy is twenty-six."

"And how old are you, Miss Campbell?"

"I am twenty-four."

"So, your testimony is that you didn't live with your father that much when you were growing up and that you didn't see him alone a lot?

Cynthia glared at him for a long time. Their eyes locked.

There was something vaguely familiar to Foulke about this girl. He couldn't quite put his finger on it. He did not have to wait long to figure it out.

"The simple truth, Mr. Foulke," she began "is that I was with my father alone on many many occasions while I was growing up, and he never once molested me."

"The simple truth?" repeated Foulke as he slowly realized who he was cross-examining.

"Miss Campbell," Foulke began, his voice trembling. "Where, uh, where does your grandmother live?"

"Atlanta."

"Where do you live?"

"Atlanta."

Foulke was taking deep breaths now. "You go to school?" he asked. "Where have you attended school?"

"Started school in Boston, then I transferred to Connecticut, and now I am going to college in Atlanta."

Foulke was lost now. His questions had become meaningless as he tried to get his concentration back.

"I, uh, I notice that you do not seem to have a Midwestern accent, and it's certainly not a Southern accent. I'm just wondering how it is that you have settled in Georgia but have no trace of a, uh, of a, uh Southern accent."

"Mr. Foulke, I have had the privilege, due to my father's military service, of living in many parts of this great country. My accent is a composite of that experience and, as for Atlanta, that is where my grandmother and brother reside," and then Cynthia Campbell slipped into a deep, Southern accent as she said, "And as my granny always sez, it's kinda purty down thar!"

The courtroom erupted in laughter. Foulke turned pale and walked back to his table for a moment. Merriman glared at him. "What the hell is wrong with you?" she asked.

"She says she wasn't molested!" whispered Foulke, breathing deeply, his heart pounding. "You told me she would corroborate your testimony if we found her."

"She's protecting him," replied Merriman. "She's lying through her teeth. Tell the judge we want a physical examination."

"Your Honor," said Foulke, as he turned back toward Cynthia and the judge. He glanced at her for a split second but was too embarrassed to look straight at her. "It's getting close to noon and I really need some time to prepare some additional questions for this witness. I would ask the Court to break for lunch and allow me to continue with this witness after lunch."

The judge looked over toward John Kosten.

"Your Honor," began Kosten, "Miss Campbell was offered as a rebuttal witness to specific professional testimony offered by Ms. Merriman. Mr. Foulke has expanded his questioning to issues not raised in my direct examination of Miss Campbell. She is my witness and she should not be subjected to further harassment by Mr. Foulke's fishing expedition into areas such as the origin of her accent or lack thereof."

"I will rule on your objection when we return," said the judge.

"Your Honor, "said Foulke, "I need time to prepare some additional questions. It hardly seems prudent to take the time to prepare those questions, if you sustain Mr. Kosten's objection when we return from lunch."

"I can rule on it now if you want, Mr. Foulke, but I guarantee you won't like the ruling if I make it now."

"Fair enough, Your Honor," replied Foulke.

"The Court stands in recess until 2:00 p.m." declared the Judge.

Everyone stood up as the judge exited the room. Foulke watched Cynthia Campbell as she gracefully stepped down from the stand. She walked over to the defense table without looking in his direction.

Her father stood to greet her, but he was not permitted to have contact with her. Foulke looked at Mark Campbell's face as he stood before his daughter. They did not speak to each other, but as the bailiff grabbed Mark to direct him back to his cell, Cynthia stood erect for a moment and acknowledged her father with a perfectly executed Marine salute. His hands were handcuffed and could not return the greeting, but his face beamed with pride and satisfaction toward his daughter.

It was if Foulke was seeing the man for the first time. "What if I am wrong?" he thought. There was only circumstantial evidence to implicate Campbell.

His thoughts were interrupted by the whining voice of Ms. Merriman. "Look at those two over there," she said. "They think her testimony is going to win this thing for them. It is not uncommon for a sexual abuse victim to lie and protect her abuser. If they think they are going to get away with this, they have another think coming." Merriman stormed down the still-crowded aisle and into the hall.

Foulke watched Mark Campbell being led out the side of the courtroom and he waited until Cynthia had made her way out into the hall before he left by a side door. He peeked down the hallway at the commotion of the news reporters and cameras surrounding Cynthia for a statement. John Kosten immediately intervened and helped her through the maze of reporters until he directed her to a door where they both slipped through, leaving the frustrated reporters behind.

Foulke just shook his head and walked back to his office. He was supposed to be working on some questions for Cynthia

Campbell, but he could not concentrate. It was all closing in on him. He didn't know what to do. He sat and stared out the window at the Indiana winter.

The silence was shattered when the phone rang. He answered it to hear an excited Merriman say, "I got her! I got the little wench!"

"What are you talking about?" asked Foulke

"Cynthia Campbell. She has an outstanding arrest warrant for failure to appear in a drug case."

"She was charged with possession?" asked Foulke.

"No, but she was a material witness in the case and didn't show after being served a subpoena."

"And how long ago was this?" asked Foulke.

It was almost seven years ago," replied Merriman.

"She was seventeen-years-old then. She was a minor."

"Maybe," Merriman said with glee, "but the arrest warrant is still outstanding and its drug related. That means we can arrest her and do a full cavity search."

"No!" snapped Foulke.

"What do you mean, No?" asked Merriman.

"I mean I am not going to arrest this girl on a seven-year-old case that I don't know anything about."

"Well, I have the full case file right here in my hand," said Merriman.

"Don't do anything until I get there and look at it."

"Too late," said Merriman, "I just dispatched a deputy into the conference room to place her under arrest."

"Well, you get your ass in there right now and stop him. The last time I checked, I was still the prosecutor here and you have no authority here. This is not a Child Protective Services case."

"I don't understand you today. I thought this would be right up your alley. But as for authority, I don't need any. I'm just a citizen telling the local sheriff where they can find a law-breaker," replied Merriman.

Foulke slammed down the phone and raced out his office for the courthouse conference room. He found Merriman in the room. He could see through the window that a deputy, Cynthia Campbell and John Kosten were also in the room.

He burst into the room. "What is going on here?" demanded Foulke.

"You tell me," Snapped Kosten, in an uncharacteristic show of anger.

Foulke turned to the deputy, "Tell me what happened." He looked at Cynthia Campbell sitting calmly at the conference table. She maintained all the poise of her entry into the courtroom earlier. Foulke looked directly at her as she caught his eyes and pulled her arms from under the table. She glared at him as she placed her handcuffed wrists in full view on the table.

Foulke closed his eyes and looked away from her.

The deputy recounted the story of Merriman's discovery of an outstanding arrest warrant on Miss Campbell. "I came over and found her at the courthouse and placed her under arrest. Mr. Kosten intervened immediately and demanded that we not question her or remove her from the courthouse without the specific approval of the judge. I viewed that as a reasonable request, although Ms. Merriman here is not too pleased with that decision."

"Steve," said Kosten, "this is one of the shabbiest stunts I have ever seen you pull, and I have seen a lot of your stunts. This young woman has come from up from Atlanta at her own personal expense and great inconvenience to testify on behalf of her father. You are trying to rattle her and discredit her with this deplorable stunt."

Foulke looked at Merriman "Let me see the file."

She handed it to him and he skimmed through the pages quickly. Foulke spoke aloud as he reviewed the file, "This is a seven-year-old case that resulted in a conviction of a minor on charges of possession of less than thirty grams of Marijuana. It appears Miss Campbell was present in the car at the time of the arrest and failed to appear as a witness for the State. A warrant was issued for her arrest."

"That's right," said Merriman, "and we are perfectly within the law to take her into custody, in connection with this drug case, and search her."

"Search her for what?" asked Kosten "Drugs that she may have in her possession from seven years ago. I don't think the Indiana Supreme Court would quite buy that interpretation to authorize a body cavity search."

Foulke interrupted, "It says here that the defendant plead guilty pursuant to a plea bargain. The warrant shouldn't have been issued. The warrant should have been canceled, and I will personally see to it that it is canceled."

"Deputy, you take those cuffs off Miss Campbell right now, and you escort Ms. Merriman out that door and away from this area.

"Miss Campbell, I deeply apologize to you on behalf of the Madison County Prosecutor's Office and Sheriff's Department."

"Mr. Foulke, this little indignity pales into insignificance when you consider what this red-neck county has done to my father, my step-sister and the bodies of Keisha and Kara, who still have not had a funeral, because of your office's use of this situation for whatever sinister purpose motivates it. I most decidedly do not accept your apology." She spat the words at him.

Foulke did not know what to say. He turned and followed Merriman and the deputy out of the room. Merriman turned to him in the hall, "This is not over yet, Mr. Foulke."

"Yes Shirley, it is over. Now just leave her alone."

"I will not. She holds the key to Campbell's conviction. If we can examine her, it will prove that Campbell's guilty. If we let her testimony stand it will set him free," said Merriman.

Foulke thought for a moment. "And what if a physical examination of her revealed no mutilation, what would you say then?"

"Believe me, Steve, I know the pattern. After I examine her and interview her, she will admit it. They always do. He is guilty. He molested his step-daughters and he molested his daughter. I would stake my reputation on it," replied Merriman.

"And just what if we force her into an examination only to find she has female genitalia as perfect as any Penthouse magazine?" quizzed Foulke.

"You disgust me!" shrieked Merriman. "Believe me, I am right about this."

"Shirley, I am dead serious. Humor me," said Foulke. "If it turns out that she has not been molested, then does that mean that Campbell did not molest the step-daughters."

"I am not the least bit concerned about that microscopic possibility," replied Merriman.

Foulke stopped in his tracks and let her continue down the hall, where the deputy was waiting for her at the elevator. Merriman and the deputy were engaged in an animated conversation as they stepped into the elevator and the doors closed. He turned back to see Kosten leave the conference room alone and start down the stairs.

Cautiously, he retraced his steps and peeked into the conference room to see that Cynthia was still sitting there alone. She looked up at him and said nothing. He knew he shouldn't be seen talking to her alone, but he couldn't help it.

"Cindi," he began. "My God, I am sorry."

"Really?" she asked. "I don't think so."

"Cindi, if I had any idea that you were Mark Campbell's daughter, I never would have gone with you Friday night."

"And just whose daughter did you think I was?" asked Cindi. "Just whose daughter did you think the rich, white, plantation boy was going to get when he decided to jump the fence for a little fun?"

"My God, this could ruin me if it gets out. Having sex with a principal witness and the daughter of the defendant I was prosecuting!" lamented Foulke.

"Ruin you!" she exclaimed.

"Why is it that your life is more important than mine?" she asked. "Why is it that it's more important what your people say than it is mine? What would I tell my father? What would I tell my grandmother? It ruins me just as completely as it ruins you."

"A point well, taken Miss Campbell," conceded Foulke. "You know when you walked up to the stand and I first saw you, there was something familiar about you but I just couldn't figure it out for the longest time. He changed the subject "Nice outfit, Saks?"

She smiled ever so slightly. "Yes, kind of nice don't you think?" It was on sale for seventy-percent off. It's the kind of an outfit that makes the white folk sit up and say, "Hey, she must be all right."

"Glad I could help you," he said.

"Glad I could help you. It was your conscience money," she shot back.

"I don't do that, believe me, I don't do that. It was just one of those things that happens sometimes."

"Yeah, well I don't do it either, but a girl's got to do what a girl's got to do," she said.

"Your accent is a little different today. So, which one is the real you? I actually liked the braids better," said Foulke.

"Well, which one's the real you, Steve?"

"I don't know anymore. I just don't know," he replied.

"Well, I got you there, Mister, 'cause I know who I am, and I'm not the least bit confused about my life. By the way, did your wife at least get a good meal at a fine restaurant out of the deal?" chided Cindi.

Foulke looked down at the wedding band on his finger. "No, Cindi, that wouldn't have been possible. She was killed in an automobile accident."

Cindi snapped her eyes shut and muttered, "Oh, shit," under her breath. "I'm sorry. I didn't know, but don't you go turning human on me now. I've worked up a good, healthy dislike for you, and I don't want nothing spoiling it."

"Well, if my wife were here, I think she would agree with you, if she could see what I have become," said Foulke.

"My father is innocent, you know," she said.

"Well, he obviously never mutilated you," said Foulke.

"I saw all my step-sisters. I knew what had happened to them, and it happened before my father ever met them. It's what they do to little girls in West Africa. It's what they do."

"Well, I considered that," said Foulke, "but Merriman was so certain, and it all happened so fast. She said they were not from the right part of Africa for that. I relied upon her professional judgment."

"It's easy to verify. The UN has experts in this that could have testified to the hideous custom. You just never tried to find out the truth. You didn't want to know the truth."

"It was not that simple," protested Foulke.

"Oh, I forgot," said Cindi, "you have a problem with the simple truth." She looked at her watch. "I will see you in court at 2:00 p.m.," she said, as she walked out the door.

Chapter 4

Emotions were running high in the streets of Anderson. Parents were upset about the forced examination of their daughters in Campbell's class. The age-old feelings of bigotry lay just below the surface in many of the old-time, white residents of the county. The Black population of the county had remained largely silent on this particular case since it involved a Black man's molestation of his own Black step-daughters.

Steve Foulke was well known in the Black community. He typically received eighty percent of the Black vote. So far, this was not a case about race, and local Black leaders did not want to see it become one.

The poor, white trash, on the other hand, had no such reluctance to demonstrate their disdain for Campbell and what he was accused of. For a few days the normally harsh February weather became milder. Temperatures reached the mid-fifties. The good weather had brought out some of the worst elements of Madison County society. A street demonstration of rowdy elements carrying nasty signs decrying Campbell, appeared. This was followed by a sizeable contingent of the Ku Klux Klan marching down the street in front of the courthouse.

Confederate flags were unfurled and there was much commotion in the streets. Indiana had always been the northernmost Southern state.

There was that dirty little secret from the 1920s when Indiana was home to the strongest contingent of Ku Klux Klan members in the country. In those days, twenty-five percent of adult, white males in Madison County were members of the Klan. Their great-grandchildren were out in force this day to express their latent but ever-present hatred.

As news spread on television and radio of the demonstrations, more troublemakers poured in from all over east-central Indiana. Within a few hours, the streets outside of the Madison County Courthouse turned very ugly.

The Madison County Sheriff Department, Anderson Police and the Indiana State Police struggled to gain control of the situation. The Indianapolis television stations were on hand to beam the civil disturbance live to all of Indiana. This did not help as more people poured into town to see what was going on. It was national news.

By late morning, the authorities had arrested dozens of the worst demonstrators and hauled them off to jail. The Indiana weather finished the job of restoring order by turning colder, spraying the remaining malcontents with a freezing rain.

The Madison County Jail was crowded. The new arrivals from the morning's arrests were booked and taken to a facility with too few guards and a bulging inmate population.

When Cynthia exited the courthouse doors, she saw the drenched remnants of the morning's demonstrations. Cardboard signs and discarded banners with racist slogans littered the street, as she walked to a nearby restaurant. A few die-hard bigots were still milling about and gave her icy stares, more frigid than the freezing temperatures that now gripped the city. She had once lived among these people and she wondered what they would do if they knew she was the proud daughter of Mark Campbell. She was not afraid.

In a few minutes, Cynthia was eating lunch in the warmth of a restaurant a few blocks from the courthouse. She noticed Steve Foulke as he entered accompanied by a Black female. Steve stopped and looked carefully around the restaurant.

The two made a beeline for Cindi's table. "Miss Campbell," began Foulke, "this is Belinda Jackson, a deputy prosecutor from my office."

"Hello, Miss Campbell," said Belinda, with a smile as she reached out her hand to Cynthia. Cynthia just looked at her and barely acknowledged her as she stared at Foulke.

"Miss Campbell, Belinda will be transporting you to the Indianapolis airport. You have a reservation for a one-way ticket to Atlanta on Delta Airlines leaving at 6:00 p.m."

"And what about my 2:00 p.m. court appearance?" quizzed Cynthia.

"I plan to withdraw my objection and you will not be recalled to the stand. I will make a motion for the case to be postponed. You are free to leave town. Belinda will take you to pick up your things, drive you to the airport and pay for your ticket.

"I don't think so Mr. Foulke," replied Cynthia, "I am not running out on my father, he expects to see me at 2:00 p.m. and I will be there for him."

"Miss Campbell," replied Foulke, "you must understand that Shirley Merriman is very powerful in this county. She is absolutely convinced that you hold the key to proving the charges against your father. I have been able to vacate the outstanding warrant Merriman used to detain you, but I can't promise you that she won't come up with some other tactic to get what she wants from you."

"You forget, Mr. Foulke, that I used to live in this town, and I am well aware of Shirley Merriman's reputation. I know lots of stories about girls gettin' their kids taken from them by Merriman's so-called Child Protective Services. She don't scare me none," declared Cynthia, as some of her Southern drawl crept back into her words.

Belinda stood there with a puzzled look on her face, watching the exchange between her boss and this witness. She had not seen this spark in Steve for a very long time. There was something going on here and she didn't know what. She had worked for Steve for several years and had always known him to be a straight shooter.

"Child," interrupted Belinda, "you best listen to the man."

Both Cynthia and Steve were startled by Belinda's comment and they turned toward her. Cynthia and Belinda's eyes locked on each other for the longest time.

Cynthia was certainly not one to back down, but as she stared at Belinda, she could sense that there was true concern in the woman's eyes. She thought about the all-night bus ride to Atlanta and her very-important tests this week that she could not afford to miss. She thought about how much she wanted to get out of this God-forsaken town. If Foulke was telling her the truth, then her dad would understand why she left. She could come back next weekend to see him. Her dad always told her that if she didn't know what else to do, then just do the right thing.

"Okay, Mr. Foulke," began Cynthia, "here's what I will do. I will let your deputy prosecutor take me in the car, but we will not leave town until the hearing is over. I will call my dad's attorney and tell him that I can be in court in fifteen minutes if I am called. When he calls and tells me that I can leave town, then and only then will we begin heading for Indianapolis. Agreed?"

Foulke took a deep breath "Agreed."

"Belinda," began Foulke, "you can stay here with Miss Campbell until she finishes her lunch. I'll get back to the courthouse and let Kosten know we are in agreement and get ready for the 2 o'clock hearing."

After Steve left the restaurant, Belinda looked at Cynthia for the longest time, studying her, staring at her.

"What?" said Cynthia, after she could no longer take the scrutiny.

"I don't know, Child," replied Belinda. "He lost his wife a while back and has been lost ever since. He and his wife were a great team together. I worry about him. Sometimes I think the Devil got a hold on him. Back in the day he was a good man: did good for a lot of people. But he's just not been the same since he lost her. But with you Child, for the first time, I saw the passion for justice in him that he used to have every minute of every day."

"Well, I don't know him," snapped Cynthia, "and to me, he seems to be the typical, white, asshole that I have been dealing with all my life. He's after my daddy now and, as far as I am concerned he is the enemy."

"Is your daddy guilty? Did he touch those little girls?" asked Belinda.

"No, he did not!" shouted Cynthia. "My father is a good man. He is nothing like the man that Merriman and your asshole boss are trying to make him out to be. He is good and decent and honorable."

"Okay Child, Okay, I believe you believe that, and I'm going to give you some advice that you better listen to," said Belinda, "You prove that to Steve Foulke, and your daddy will have the best ally a man can have in this town. 'Cause Steve hates injustice and he has a lifetime record of helpin' the folks that need help if they deserve it."

Chapter 5

The courthouse had been recently remodeled, to create new holding areas for prisoners. If anyone had stopped to actually think about all of the powerful forces at play, they could easily have predicted the next event.

Mark Campbell was sitting by himself, having lunch at a table in one of the small holding areas provided for inmates appearing in court that day. He and others were watching the events on the noon news, as some of the new arrivals from the morning's events appeared in the holding area. Steve Foulke had left specific instructions that Campbell was to be sequestered from the rest of the inmates at all times.

The same deputy that had detained Cindi outside the courtroom at Merriman's request was the same deputy that placed Campbell into the holding area, in violation of Foulke's instructions.

Mark Campbell sat quietly eating his lunch, as a large, white man carrying a food tray passed behind him. Mark felt a sharp pain in the back of his neck as the food tray crashed into him.

The six-foot lunch table was overturned by a second white man. Campbell was quickly wrestled to the floor and the side of the overturned table placed across his neck like a see-saw. Campbell struggled mightily to keep the table from pressing against his neck. The first man pressed on one end as he kicked Campbell in the head. The second man pressed on the other end of the table as he kicked Campbell in the side and stomped on his torso.

An alarm went off as two deputies ran to subdue the assailants. A third deputy stood at the door watching events unfold, while making no effort to intervene. The two inmates continued to kick Campbell even as the two deputies had drawn their weapons and were pointing them at the prisoners. One deputy shouted that he would shoot if they did not stop.

Several more deputies appeared outside the locked door. In what seemed like an eternity, the door was opened by the deputy standing inside, and a small army of deputies rushed in. The violence was quickly ended, as both prisoners were subdued and handcuffed by the deputies.

Campbell's body lay motionless on the floor as one deputy checked his pulse. "He's alive!" exclaimed the deputy, "as Mark Campbell opened his eyes and moaned an indistinguishable sound.

"We need medical here stat!" shouted the deputy.

It was only seconds before emergency medical personnel and equipment appeared.

Mark Campbell was lifted onto a gurney and transported to St John's Hospital. He was conscious and his vital signs were good.

Steve Foulke saw the paramedics place the gurney into the ambulance as he got back to the courthouse. Sensing something was seriously wrong, he ran up to the deputy standing at the door.

"What is going on?" screamed Foulke.

"It's Campbell. He got roughed up pretty bad at lunch in the holding area," said the deputy.

"He wasn't supposed to be in there," exclaimed Foulke. "I left strict instructions that he was to be kept separate and guarded at all times."

"I don't know," said the deputy. "Ask Jenkins, he put him in there."

Foulke ran into the courthouse and saw Deputy Jenkins down the hall. "Jenkins!" he cried out "What in the hell were you thinking? That's twice today you have pulled this crap!"

Foulke saw an empty conference room. "In here, now!" said Foulke.

Both men stepped in the conference room and Steve shut the door.

"What in the hell is going on here?" demanded Foulke.

Deputy Jenkins was as white as a sheet. He sat down in a chair, placed his head in his arms on the table and began sobbing.

Steve Foulke had known Deputy Bill Jenkins for twenty years. He was just a few months away from retirement. There wasn't a finer man in the sheriff's office and here he was sobbing like a little kid.

"Bill, Bill, what is it? Tell me?" said Foulke.

"I can't, Steve, I can't," he said, his voice cracking.

"Bill, I have known you for a long time. I know the kind of man you are. There is something going on and you have got to tell me," Pleaded Steve, as he placed his hand on the deputy's shoulder. "Off the record, Bill, off the record. Anything you tell me, Okay?"

After a few seconds, Bill regained his composure and, when next he spoke his voice was strong and unbroken.

He sighed, "It's my daughter, it's my grandkids. I have three of them, and they're the center of my life."

"I don't understand, Bill. Are they okay? What's wrong?" asked Steve. "What's that got to do with this?"

"It's Merriman," he began. "She's out to get Campbell no matter what it takes. She made me cuff the girl, and she made me put Campbell into the holding cell with the others. She had it all planned, but I didn't know she was going to hurt him like that, I didn't know." Jenkins said solemnly.

"Bill, you're not making any sense," said Steve.

"My daughter got into a big fight a few months back with her boyfriend. He started it and he hit her, and she hit him back. He came after her and was going to hurt her bad. She picked up my grandson's baseball bat and smacked him with it. It was all in front of my grandkids. The neighbors called 9-1-1 and the police showed up. They couldn't sort it out at the scene so they took both of 'em downtown. CPS showed up and took the kids. That's when I got the call from Shirley Merriman." He spat her name out when he said it.

He continued, "She knew my daughter from some of the county employee parties we used to go to. She said she knew this was not something my daughter would ever be involved in. Steve, you probably know this, but I didn't - if you have a physical confrontation in front of a minor child, it's a felony. Well, she said she could help. She said she could make it all go away, and we could get the kids back that night. She said she was taking a huge risk but, she had known me for so long, she was willing to do it. But she had to know right then because once the kids were processed into the system, it could take months or more to get them back. I said I would do anything. Just let my daughter and the kids come home with me, and I would do anything to repay her. "Okay," she said, "but someday I will need your help.' I went and picked my daughter and the kids up that night, and they have been living with me ever since. In a few weeks, I am going to retire and have plenty of time to spend with them. I can't wait. They are at such a good age," his voice cracked a little bit.

"And then what happened today?" asked Steve, but he knew the answer.

"Merriman came to me this afternoon and told me to arrest that girl and I did it. That seemed harmless enough. But when you foiled her plan, she was enraged. That's when she said I had to put Campbell with the others…and I did it. She made a point of reminding me that paperwork sometimes gets lost at CPS, and you never knew when it might get found again. Steve, you gotta believe me. I didn't know she was going to hurt him like that. I'm sorry."

Steve was sitting beside Jenkins now. He reached out his hand and clutched Jenkins' wrist and said, "It's okay. We will figure this out. I need to find out how serious Campbell is. If it's bad, Bill, there won't be anything I can do to help you," said Steve.

"I know that, Steve. I shouldn't have let this happen. In my entire career, I have never done anything like this," said Jenkins.

"I know that, Bill," replied Steve.

"There is more," said Jenkins.

"Oh, crap, what is it?" asked Steve.

"I am not the only one Merriman has power over. There are plenty of others and I don't who know they are. It could be anyone: someone you would never even suspect," said Jenkins. "But I know this - she got the original judge to re-issue the warrant for the girl's arrest. She knows your office bought a ticket for her in Indianapolis on the 6:00 p.m. Delta flight. They will be waiting there to arrest her and bring her back here."

"Unbelievable," said Steve. "Well, I can go to the judge and take care of that."

"Don't be so sure, Steve. Oh, I know you can get it done in a day or two, but can you get it done now, today? If not, then Merriman will have gotten what she wants from the girl and Campbell will be toast, if he is not already," replied Jenkins.

"You are right. Time is on her side." Steve started thinking about Cynthia's tests tomorrow and how important they were. How much it could completely wreak havoc with her life if she wasn't in school tomorrow. What was he going to do? As an Officer of the Court, he had firsthand knowledge that Cynthia was not mutilated in any way… "carnal knowledge" you might say, he thought. He had an obligation to come forward and explain that. In doing so, he would destroy his own career, and her standing with her family, and taint Campbell's case.

"I'm ready to turn myself in, Steve. I know I have done wrong. This will probably cost me my retirement but Merriman's got to be stopped, and I'll do it if I have to," said Jenkins.

"Let's not get ahead of ourselves, Bill. We have time and I need to build a case against her. It could all blow up in our faces if she finds out too soon that you are ready to come forward. Tell you what Bill, I want you to consider this conversation as part of a highly confidential investigation of Madison County corruption. I am going to need your assistance and it could be dangerous. You are to keep your mouth shut about it until I say so," said Steve.

"Okay Steve, I will do anything you need. Thanks," replied Jenkins. "Maybe I can still make retirement before this comes out.

Steve's next stop was the courtroom at 2:00 p.m., but, as he got there, he could see nothing was going on inside. He saw

John Kosten talking on the phone, it sounded like he may have been speaking with Cynthia but he could not be sure.

"John, John, what do you know?" asked Steve.

"Well, your goons downstairs have beaten up my client and he has been transported to St. John's or St. Vincent's, whatever it's called now," replied John.

"I saw the ambulance, How is he, do you know?" asked Steve.

"No, I don't' said John, but I am going over there to see him as soon as they will let me in. You know, Steve, you have really done it this time. I can't believe you have teamed up with that zealot Merriman and are going after Campbell the way you are. It doesn't make sense. You used to be one of the good guys. What has happened to you?"

John's words cut like a knife. He and John had political differences and legal differences but John Kosten was one of the finest men in the state of Indiana, and John's words cut deep.

"I don't know John…I don't know," said Steve.

I will meet you over there and see if I can help get you in," said Steve.

Just then Steve's phone rang. It was Belinda. Steve slipped down the hall for some privacy. "Hello," he said, "Belinda."

"Yes, it's me," she said.

"Have you heard about Campbell?" he asked.

"Yes, Cynthia's attorney just called her. She is frantic. She insists on going to the hospital to see him," said Belinda.

"Take her there and wait until I get there. Her attorney is headed over there now and I will get there as soon as I can," said Steve. As he ended the call, he thought to himself, "Cynthia has a phone? Of course she does." He just shook his head, amazed at how stupid he was.

Steve ran downstairs and got in his car and made the ten-minute drive to the hospital. When he arrived at the front desk, he had no trouble getting the room number and headed for the elevators.

When he stepped off the elevator, he saw John Kosten and Cynthia talking. She was emotional and John was holding her as Belinda patted her on the back.

"What's his condition?" asked Steve.

"We don't know," replied John. "They won't tell us anything and they won't let us see him."

"You bastard!" screamed Cynthia, as she lunged for him and tried to pound him in the chest. John and Belinda were able to restrain her, and she just glared at Steve with tears streaming down her cheeks. "I want to see my daddy!" she cried out.

"I'll make it happen," said Steve, as he stormed into Campbell's room. A deputy tried to block him and Steve said, "Don't you even think about it deputy."

The deputy stepped aside and Steve entered the room. There were two doctors and a nurse tending to Campbell. He looked pretty bad. Steve knew one of the doctors quite well.

There was blood on the side of his face. His abdomen was exposed and there were cuts and scrapes. Campbell's dark skin hid any sign of bruising. They were starting to clean him up.

"How is he?" asked Steve.

"He is one hell of a tough Marine," said one of the doctors. He's skinned up some, bruises and contusions. We will know in a few minutes if he has any cracked ribs, but we don't think so."

"Hold on, ssshhh," said Steve quietly.

Steve went to the door. There was quite a bit of noise in the hall, and the deputy could not have heard what was just said.

"Deputy," said Steve "you don't need to stand outside the door. He's not going anywhere. I want you to step down the hall and give his attorney and his daughter some privacy."

"I am not supposed to let anyone in to see him," replied the deputy.

"Yeah, well, I am countermanding that order," Steve said as he looked over at Cynthia, who was watching him intently with a quizzical look on her face. "Maybe, deputy, you would like to tell me who is giving you orders, and I will be glad to discuss it with that person."

The deputy said nothing and complied with Steve's directive and stepped down the hall. Steve motioned for John and Cynthia to come in.

As Cynthia brushed past him, Steve whispered. "It's not as bad as we feared."

"Daddy!" She was horrified when she saw him and ran to his side, started to put her arms around him but suddenly realized she shouldn't touch him "Where does it hurt?" she asked.

He had opened his eyes for the first time since Steve had been there when he heard Cynthia cry out "Daddy!"

"Honey," Campbell said, in an unbelievably strong voice, "I am fine, just a few cuts and bruises. I will be fine."

With that reassurance, Cynthia put her arms around him and got blood all over her arms and top. The doctors and nurses were horrified.

"You must not do that," cried out one of the doctors, "It's not safe."

"I don't care," said Cynthia, as she continued to caress him and soothe him and gently touch him. She kissed him on the forehead and looked at the doctor with defiance."

Steve changed the subject. "You were saying, Doctor, about his condition?"

The doctor replied "He's skinned up some, bruises and contusions. We will know in a few minutes if he has any cracked ribs, but we don't think so. He will be sore for a while but he will be fine and can be out of here in a few days. He is one hell of a tough Marine."

"Ma'am, Miss, we can't allow you to do that. We will clean him up in a few minutes," protested one of the doctors.

"If you think this Marine is tough, you should try his daughter," said Cynthia as she glared at the doctor and continued to clean his wounds.

"Not so fast, Doctor. I want you to keep his condition confidential. He is in danger back at the courthouse and the jail. I need to figure out how this happened before he goes back. Can you do that?" asked Steve.

"Sure, Steve, whatever you need. We will keep his condition unlisted and let your office do all the talking."

It wasn't long before Cynthia and the nurses had Campbell pretty well cleaned up. Cynthia had gotten her father's blood all over her new outfit, but she clearly did not care.

Neither the doctors nor the nurses were too pleased with Cynthia's assistance, but they said nothing more.

"Can we give them some time alone?" asked Steve.

They wanted to protest, but they didn't and everyone including John Kosten, left the room and stood out in the hall. Steve could see Cynthia smiling and the two of them talking. Unbelievably he even saw Mark Campbell smile and raised his hand to caress the side of his daughter's face. Steve was so touched. Who was this man that he was prosecuting?

Merriman was clearly wrong about the molestation of his own daughter. Why should he believe anything that Merriman thought or said?

Kosten was watching Steve intently and John broke the silence when he said, "Welcome back to the side of the good guys."

Steve looked at him and their eyes locked.

Finally, Steve replied "Thanks, John. Coming from you, that means a lot to me. I have been gone for a while."

After a few minutes, they all went back inside. "Cynthia," said Steve, "you must go now?"

She had cleaned all the blood from her hands and arms and attempted to get it off her clothes. Her outfit was still stained with blood.

"I need to change clothes. I have other things in Belinda's car," said Cynthia.

"No, not here," said Steve. "You can do that downstairs. Belinda will get your things. We need to go John. You can stay with Campbell as long as you need to."

He looked over to see Campbell's smile as Cynthia left his side. She turned and blew him a kiss as she exited the door. Campbell's smile got even bigger until she was out of sight, and then suddenly, his face was gripped with pain as he began to take deep breaths to control the intensity.

Steve shook his head. "My God," he thought, "I sure have been on the wrong side of this one."

He quickly caught up with Cynthia. "Make sure the deputy has a clear view of the blood on your thousand-dollar outfit. I want him to see it, and I want you to look distraught, very distraught."

Cynthia understood immediately and cried out in a sob, "you motherfucker, Foulke. He's gonna die, he's gonna die," and then she broke down completely. A nurse had come out of the room with a blue smock and had to chase Cynthia down the hall. Cynthia continued to cry and sob uncontrollably, as she took the smock and stepped into the elevator.

It was just Steve and Cynthia alone in the elevator. Her sobbing stopped as quickly as it had started and a big smile came over her face. "How did I do, Steve?" she asked.

"Academy Award winning, I would say," said Steve.

"I am not sure what you're up to, but it sounds like it's good for my dad. So, thank you," said Cynthia.

Belinda was at the elevator on the first floor when the doors opened. She had Cynthia's bag. Cynthia took it and went into the bathroom to change.

"What are you up to?" asked Belinda

"You will know soon enough," said Steve.

When Cynthia emerged from the restroom she looked perfect. Not a trace of the drama she had just been through.

"Change of plans," said Steve, "The original judge has re-issued the arrest warrant for you. So, you are coming with me. They found out somehow that you have a 6:00 p.m. flight in Indy and they plan to arrest you there at the ticket counter."

Cynthia's eyes widened but before she could say anything, he said, "Belinda, get one of your friends or nieces that looks a little bit like Cynthia to ride with you down to the airport and walk up to the ticket counter and see what happens."

"Okay, Boss, I hope you know what you are doing," said Belinda.

"I do," said Steve. "Miss Campbell, you come with me."

Steve and Cynthia left the hospital and rode in Steve's car to his house.

Chapter 6

"I am taking you to Cincinnati for a direct flight to Atlanta," explained Steve. "There are several flights and the seats are wide open. We will get the ticket there."

"Cincinnati!" exclaimed Cynthia.

"Yeah, they have direct flights to Atlanta, and you can get home earlier and get some rest for those tests," said Steve, as he pulled into the driveway. Steve took Cynthia in the front door. He said, "Give me a minute," and headed into another room.

Cynthia looked around, the room definitely had a women's touch, but it was a bit cluttered and needed dusting badly. She scanned the mantle, the end tables and hutch. She saw a myriad of family pictures with Steve and his wife. Cynthia stared in disbelief at one particular picture taken at Black Expo that captured her attention. Steve was receiving an award and standing next to him was his proud wife. She was Black!

Cynthia was stunned. She had this guy pegged as an absolute asshole. Now, she sees his wife and then there was the deal at the hospital. The plaques and pictures were everywhere. There were many pictures of the couple at community events, as well as the two of them at vacation spots. She just did not know what to think. Was this guy the enemy or not?

Steve emerged from the other room. "We can go now," he said. He and Cynthia returned to Steve's Ford Explorer and headed for Cincinnati.

"Thanks for taking me to see my dad. You have no idea how much that meant to me," said Cynthia, in the most sincere and respectful tone that she had ever used with him.

"Actually, Cynthia, I think I do," said Foulke. "When I saw you salute your father when you left the courtroom, it forced me to look at your father for the very first time. And then being with him in the hospital, I must say that I was impressed with the man I saw and the daughter he raised."

"My dad is a good man, devoted to his family, his country and his God. Me? Don't be impressed with me, Steve. I am not worth it. I am certainly not the woman he believes I am, but one day I will be."

"What do you mean?" quizzed Steve.

"You could get in a lot of trouble for this; taking me to Cincinnati, I mean," said Cynthia changing the subject.

"Yeah, I suppose I could, but then there are a lot of things in the last year or so that I could get me in a lot of trouble," Steve replied.

"You mean like frequenting strip clubs and taking the dancers to a motel?" she asked with a trace of a smile.

"Well, that and more, much more. At a strip club, you can get conversation and intimacy. Some of the girls are starved for real conversation and they like to cuddle up on your lap and be nice to you and breathe in your ear. I miss that even though it's counterfeit in there. They always want to take you into the back, but I usually don't do that, I just feed them a twenty every fifteen minutes or so and I can have all the conversation and intimacy I want," said Steve.

But then that's not always enough, is it?" replied Cynthia.

"No, it's not," sighed Steve, "and usually the girls will not date a customer. Besides, it's dangerous because a strip club is a public place and I could be recognized, so I don't go often. I have to look elsewhere."

"Elsewhere where?" asked Cynthia.

"There are a couple of escort websites where you can find girls that will do what you want," said Steve. "And it's safer and more discreet, but still dangerous."

Did you ever do this before your wife died?" asked Cynthia.

"No, God no!" exclaimed Steve. "I never once cheated on my wife, never even thought about it. But, when she died, something inside me died and I have been all screwed up ever since. It's crazy. I won't date although I have had plenty of opportunities. I would feel like I was cheating on her. But, if it's not a real relationship, then I can handle that?"

"So, you only see prostitutes?" said Cynthia.

"I don't think of them that way. I pay for their time and companionship and, if something happens when we are together, it's just between adults," said Steve.

"Try telling that to the judge," said Cynthia.

"Yeah, I know."

"You know, Steve, you have to stop lying to yourself. You frequent prostitutes and you need to say it and admit it, because that's what you do and that's what an escort is," replied Cynthia.

"I just don't see it that way," protested Steve.

"Well, that's because you have a problem with the simple truth. I don't. I am honest with myself and I don't sugarcoat the truth," said Cynthia.

"What do you mean?" asked Steve.

Steve turned to look at her. There was a trace of tears glistening in her eyes. Suddenly, the loud horn of an eighteen-wheeler sounded when Steve drifted into the next lane. Steve quickly corrected the steering and got back in his lane.

"Sorry," he said.

"Yeah, that would have looked good in the papers tomorrow." said Cynthia.

They both laughed. Steve wanted to look at her but didn't dare take his eyes off the road. He positioned the visor so he could see Cynthia's face in the visor mirror without turning his head from the road.

"What you just said, I'm not sure I understand." declared Steve.

"I'm just saying a girl's gotta do what a girl's gotta do," she replied. "The good Lord gave me certain attributes and I have to use every advantage I have to get where I'm going. I get financial aid and a U.S. Marine scholarship, but it's not always enough and I have to have a place to live."

He glanced at her for a second but dared not take his eyes off the heavily traveled I-465. He continued to look at her in the visor mirror, and he could definitely make out tears streaming down her cheeks.

"I understand, or at least I think I do," said Steve.

"No, you don't, Steve. You have no idea what it is like to not have options. I do whatever I have to. In three years when I am out of school, I will have a very different life. But you…you are not going to change your life until you get found out or self-destruct…although that's the same difference."

"I've already self-destructed," said Steve.

"No, you haven't, you asshole! You're in mourning. You're still dealing with the loss of your wife and you're just fucked up. Who wouldn't be? I saw the pictures of your wife. She was beautiful and she was Black! That was a big surprise and I have had to rethink everything I ever thought about you. You need help, but you won't admit you need help, so you are going to self-destruct, ruin your whole life and never be Governor," said Cynthia. "You know Belinda said that, back in the day you were a good guy but you are so lost now that you may never find your way back."

"And you're not lost?" quizzed Steve.

"No, I am not. I am in a bad place right now, but I choose to be. I am not lost. I know the way back. I just can't take it yet," she said. "A girl's gotta do what a girl's gotta do."

Steve had a moment to glance over at her as he merged onto I-74 toward Cincinnati. It was dark and the traffic was suddenly very light. An occasional car or truck passed them in the other lane.

They were both quiet now. She was right, Steve thought sooner or later he was going to get caught and that would be that. It would be the end of his life as he knew it and it would dishonor his wife. And yet, he was unable to stop.

Steve's phone received a text alert. Steve looked at it. It was from Belinda.

"you were right. Marion and Madison Sheriff detained us at Delta counter. Merriman was with them. She was livid when she realized my cousin was not Cynthia. ;)"

"Looks like they tried to arrest you at the Delta counter in Indy. Ms. Merriman is not happy," said Foulke.

"That's fine," said Cynthia, "I hope she doesn't get over it!"

Cynthia's phone rang and she answered, "Hi, Granny."

Steve could not hear the other side of the conversation; he could only hear Cynthia. Her voice was soft and tender and understanding as she spoke.

"Oh No! Really?" she said, "Granny, look, she's young, she's just nineteen, she's gonna bump her head a few times. We just gotta love her and get her through it. She will figure it out and she will be okay. I know, I know. Look I sent you $50 at Walmart so you would have gas money. I didn't know I was going to be back tonight. I will text you the confirmation number. Tomorrow after school I will bring by another $100 for Tyra, Okay, Granny, I love you."

Steve didn't know what to think, but he was impressed with her in a way he could not express. "How can you give her money when you don't even have enough for yourself?" he asked.

"I have to help. They don't have anyone else. I have to. It's family." she said with determination.

"Oh, my God, I see it now," Steve said, with a sudden burst of enlightenment. "It's not just school. You have to help your grandmother and your family and who knows who else? You are the grown up that comes to everybody's rescue and saves the day."

"You are too smart sometimes for you own good," replied Cynthia, with a wicked little smile that Steve could see in the mirror.

The smile quickly disappeared and was replaced by a somber expression. There was a prolonged silence as he saw Cynthia in a totally new light. He had a new-found respect for her and her commitment to her family. He wondered how many of the online girls he had been seeing had the same kind of challenges.

Finally, he asked, "So, what was the deal with the Southern accent, the braids and that whole routine."

"Well, that's Cindi. That's who she is. You already answered your own question. She's the dancer, that cuddles up on your lap and talks innocent and you feed twenties to her nonstop. The guys love her precisely because she's Southern and seems so open and honest. And if you do go into the back with her, you get your money's work, but never quite as much action as you want. Cindi doesn't go have sex with customers. Now, I did with you but that was a unique situation, because I didn't work there. I knew I would get all the money out of you that I needed. You were easy pickins'."

"Didn't realize I was that transparent," replied Steve.

"You all are. Men are very simple. Just feed 'em and fuck 'em, that's all a girl's gotta do." declared Cynthia.

"You're pretty cynical," said Steve.

"Well, I know what I am talking about and I have a right to be cynical."

She looked down and saw Steve wiggling a little bit, as he moved his hand to his groin.

"Rearranging the furniture there, Steve?" she said sarcastically.

"What?" said Steve.

"What?" she mocked him as she reached her hand over the console separating them and grabbed his erect penis through his pants. She then placed her other hand under the console latch and raised it up as she unbuckled her seatbelt. She quickly removed all of her clothes and hung her panties on his rearview mirror in the center on the windshield. She unbuckled his pants and slipped his underwear to the side. She stroked him for a few seconds. She then pressed her body very close to his in a very sensual manner. She placed her lips against his right ear and kissed him on the ear and neck as she unbuttoned his shirt. Then she kissed his chest and stopped to give attention to each nipple. She was unbelievably sensual until she broke the mood and said, "If you come in my mouth, I will rip your nuts off." And with that, she placed her head in his lap and took him entirely into her mouth.

Steve did not know how he was going to keep from coming but her words echoed in his mind and he controlled himself. It was amazing. This girl was somehow prolonging the act. She was not going after the head or the sensitive parts. Instead, she just expertly pleased him for mile after mile. A couple of times he drifted to the right and the tires sounded off the rumble strips along the edge of the road. She would stop long enough to say "Keep your eyes on the road and don't kill us." While she worked on him she had slid his underwear and pants farther down his legs leaving everything exposed to her attention.

After a while, she stopped and said, "Now don't kill us. Slide the seat back as far as you can." He reached down for the switch and moved the motorized seat back. With that, she straddled him and pressed her breasts against his chest. She reached down and placed him inside her without a condom.

For mile after mile, she rode him, kissing the side of his neck and once in a while kissed him on the lips. Several times the tires drifted over to the rumble strips and each time she said, "Don't kill us."

Sometimes her shoulder would get in Steve's way and he could hardly see to stay on the road. On a couple of occasions, he looked down at the speedometer to see that he was going 80 miles an hour, He quickly slowed down and as he approached a semi going 55 mph, he decided not to attempt to pass. He just kept it at 55 mph safely behind the truck. This was the most erotically sensual event of his entire life.

Finally, when he could take no more, he said, "Cynthia, I'm pulling over up here."

Steve merged to the right into the lane that led to a rest stop. He stopped the car in a secluded spot. The center console posed a logistical problem. Cynthia slipped between the seats over the console into the 2nd row of seats. She tossed her luggage into the 3rd row seat. Dan followed, as he struggled to remove one leg from his trousers. Cynthia placed a condom on him and then positioned herself on the seat to accommodate him.

They kissed passionately. Cynthia held him tightly with her legs wrapped around his waist. Her head occasionally banged against the armrest but she did not seem to mind. When they were finished, she rose up in the seat and again kissed him passionately on the lips. Then she reached back for her bag. She pulled out some baby-wipes. She carefully removed the condom. She cleaned herself and Steve. She then put on some fresh clothes. She stepped outside and fixed herself in the cold evening air. The bright dome light lit up the Explorer like the noonday sun as Steve scrambled to pull his pants up. He got out of the passenger door and got back into the front seat. Steve got on his phone and surfed the web to the Delta site. He picked a flight for her.

When Cynthia finished dressing, she got back in the front seat. Steve pulled out of the rest stop and on to I-74. He merged onto the I-275 loop, and it wasn't long before they started seeing the signs for the airport. The airport was actually on the other side of the river in Covington, Kentucky.

Steve parked his vehicle in the short-term parking and walked Cynthia to the ticket counter. Steve had already paid for the e-ticket, and she had no problem getting her boarding pass and checking her one bag,

As they walked to the security gate, Steve sort of stammered and said "uh, er…uh…do I owe you anything?"

She could have been offended but she wasn't.

"No, Steve, you don't. What you got back there would never be for sale at any price. It was personal. I wanted to do it. I wanted to thank you for letting me see my dad, for you taking the risk of bringing me here yourself, and in a funny sort of way, I did it because you miss your wife so much. It is an unbelievable and inexplicable turn-on to see a man so much in love with his wife."

"Well, thanks, I think," said Steve, "Will I see you again."

"Not in that way, the very personal way you just got, but maybe, when I come back to see my dad." She turned around and walked toward the security checkpoint. She never looked back.

Steve left the airport terminal and climbed back into his Explorer. That's when he noticed her skimpy-pink panties hanging from the rear-view mirror. He left them there until he got back to Anderson.

Chapter 7

Dan Grainger had been held captive for several days in the African nation of Angola. The days had passed slowly. He had spent more time worrying about Callie than he did himself. He wasn't sure how many days had passed since he and Dave were captured, eight days or maybe it was ten. He had scratched a tally mark on the side of the wood in his surroundings. But some days he had forgotten whether he had done it or maybe he did it twice. He just wasn't sure.

He and Dave had been marched down to the river and then crossed it in a whitewater-raft-type of craft. They were placed in an old, dark-green Land Rover with a canvass top. They drove several hours. Dave estimated about 100 kilometers to the northwest. Dan had no idea himself. The Land Rover smelled heavy of perspiration from the two men in the front seat. They did not talk to them during the trip.

They arrived at a fairly large dirt-strip airport running pretty much east and west. Dan and Dave were locked up in a building off of the airport ramp or apron such as it was. It was just a large patch of dirt. They had been questioned for a while in Portuguese but neither Dan nor Dave could understand. At one point when they were looking at Dan's camera, he understood the word "propaganda" which did not sound good. All the while they could hear the cries of someone being beaten outside the building. Then Dan heard the word "magistrate." That did not sound good, either, but Dan chose to think it might be a good thing. The interrogator riffled through Dan's possession and saw the passport. He opened it, looked at the picture, looked at Dan, and said "American?"

There was no point lying. "Yes," Dan said sharply, "I am an American."

"Good," he replied. "Georgie Bush, Good, you…uh…uh," he motioned with his hands to sleep and finally, he said. "You rest."

Dan didn't know which George Bush the man was talking about and he didn't care. George W. had not been President for years. But whatever this guy was thinking, it was a relief.

And rest they did; for days. You can't really rest in such situations of constant stress. They were not being tortured or mistreated. They received bottled water from the United Arab Emirates. Dan was careful what he ate; rice and bread and not much else. Dave was used to some of the local food and ate it. He often offered some to Dan saying it was okay. Dan always declined but did start eating boiled eggs. He needed the protein. "What can they do to an egg?" he figured.

A couple of times they heard a plane land and take off. It was an old, high-wing, twin-engine of some kind, with the engines very close to the fuselage.

Dan spent a lot of time praying. Sometimes they prayed together, but that just wasn't Dan's style and Dave could sense that. Dave would often say "Keep your faith. The Lord would not have brought you this far to have you fail."

One morning, shortly after dawn, they heard a plane coming in for a landing. Dave's ears perked up as he listened intently and tried to get a glimpse of the aircraft from the window but he couldn't for the longest time. Then he did.

"Praise the Lord!" he shouted, "It's my 410. My Lord, it's my 410!"

In a few minutes, they heard their door unlatch. Standing at the door was Johnny, the Flying Doves pilot.

"Johnny," said Dave. "You are a sight for sore eyes."

"I've heard that before, Dave," said Johnny as he gave Dave a huge bear hug.

Johnny immediately turned back around as a middle-aged, white man entered the room. He was dressed in a white suit. He had dark, black hair "This is Pastor Jorge Valente of the Igreja Evangelica Pão da Vida. He has churches in Portugal, Mozambique, Angola and Guinea-Bissau.

"You are safe now, my boy. You're safe," Pastor Valente said, he put his arms around Dan and began to pray in Portuguese and then in tongues.

"Bless you, my boy. You are on God's mission and I am at your disposal. Timothy Doyle and Pastor Adams called me in Lisboa the day you were captured. Jorge Valente's English was very good but he spoke with a definite Portuguese accent.

Johnny interrupted, "I was in the 206 overhead when they nabbed you. Fortunately, I had nearly full fuel tanks and I stayed with you downwind as long as I could. When I was just about forced to turn back due to fuel restraints, they brought you here. I radioed the Doves the whole time.'

"Your Pastor Timothy called me in Lisboa." said Pastor Valente, "and informed me of your location. I have been on the phone for several days from Lisboa and then Beira to arrange your release. Enough talk for now, Mr. Grainger. Gather your things we must be off."

Dave and Dan gathered what little they had and were out the door in seconds. As they left the building, there was no resistance to their exit.

The man that interrogated them was at the door of the Cessna 410 when they boarded up the steps. He smiled.

"America good, Georgie Bush good, Pastor Jorge Valente good."

Dan just looked at him and of all improbable things to say to his captor, he smiled and said, "Thank you."

And with that undramatic escape, the Cessna 410 rolled down the dirt runway and was airborne.

Johnny turned the plane southeast to head for the Lianshulu airport. After leveling off, the sounds of the engine subsided to permit conversation.

Pastor Valente began, "We are headed to Lianshulu to drop us off. Johnny here will take the Stationair and take me back to Beira, Mozambique. You will refuel and grab some lunch. Pick up Ilsa and fly immediately to Bujumbura, Burundi and spend the night at the Novotel Hotel."

Dan's head was spinning, "What are you talking about?"

"Dan, we do not have a lot of time. We will be setting down in Lianshulu in fifteen minutes and I must get back to my church in Beira. It is all arranged. Someone will meet you at the Bujumbura Airport and you will be transported to the Novotel. You will be met at the airport by Joshua and Lori Rogers of the Afrique Iglesias Evangélicas Church. They will transport you to the hotel. Ilsa will stay with them for a while." Pastor Valente paused for a moment to allow Dan to digest what he was hearing.

"Dan," he continued, "the Flying Doves tracked the containers after you were detained. They went to Livingstone in Zambia, where they were transported by train through

Zambia and then down to the port city of Beira, Mozambique. A ship set sail a week ago from Beira with your daughter and all the girls on board, as far as we know."

"We have some leads, but we need help. Tomorrow you will meet with the U.S. Ambassador to Burundi at the U.S. Embassy in Bujumbura. I have known him for years since he was Ambassador to Guinea-Bissau. He is Garth Krewe, from your state of Oklahoma. It is my hope that, as an American citizen, that you can persuade him to get the U.S. State Department to assist us in locating the port that the ship docked."

Dan just sat there in amazement that this man he had just met seemed to have a total command of all the facts involved.

The plane was on final approach now for Lianshulu. As it touched down, Pastor Valente was already gathering his things. The Cessna 410 pulled up to the fuel pumps. Johnny hopped out and motioned the ground crew to top off the tanks. As the rest of the group exited the plane, Dan could see Pastor Adams and Ilsa. Standing next to them was Pastor Timothy Doyle.

Pastor Valente placed his arms around Ilsa and gave her a big hug. "Soon, my child you shall be in Jerusalem with your family," he said.

"Ilsa," shouted Dan, "you look so much better, you have healed nicely from all the bites." She ran to him and placed her arms around him and hugged him.

"Yes, Mr. Grainger, Pastor Adams and his wife have taken good care of me. I am so sorry you were captured," said Ilsa.

"It's okay. I guess somehow, our misfortune brought this remarkable man to our aid."

"Nonsense, Boy, it was the Lord!" said Pastor Valente sharply. "Let us pray."

With that, the three pastors placed their hands on Dan and Ilsa speaking first of Dan. "Dear Lord, guide your disciple's steps in his search for his daughter and of so many others. We know that no task is too great for you, Lord Jesus. Protect Dan's body from illness and show him the way to the truth." The other two Pastors were also laying hands on Dan, and saying "Hallelujah" and "Praise the Lord," and they began speaking in tongues. Pastor placed his hand on the forehead of Ilsa and "Dear God of Abraham," he continued "keep Ilsa safe from harm as she journeys to the Promised Land of her people, where her family awaits her, Amen. And, Lord Jesus, keep Dan safe in the treacherous days ahead, as his path leads into the camp of the enemy. In the name of Jesus, we pray, Amen."

"I am not even going to question what is going on here, I just accept it," said Dan. For the first time in over ten days, Dan began to feel hope again. With every doubt that had overtaken him, how could he lose faith in the company of such great men of God?"

"Pastor Valente?" asked Dan. "The military guy that interrogated us in the beginning mentioned George Bush. Why, what was he talking about?"

"It is just another blessing of the Lord, Dan. That commander is a former member of UNITA, that is the *União Nacional para a Independência Total de Angola.* UNITA has always had a strong relationship with the Bush family. You were captured in a UNITA stronghold province of Cuando Cubango. The U.S. poured in military and financial aid for UNITA for many years. The province favors Americans. There are many provinces where you would have been shot for sport, if they found out you were an American. Dave, on the other hand, may have survived."

"Your plane is fueled and the Stationair is ready to take Pastor Timothy back to Harare and me to Beira. One more thing Dan," continued Pastor Valente. "You must not speak of Ilsa to the ambassador. You can tell any part of your story that you wish, including the collection of the DNA evidence that you stumbled across, but you must not tell him that Ilsa exists or has survived or she must be handed over to the State Department. The Israelis are aware that you have saved Ilsa. They are secretly flying her parents from the U.S. to Tel Aviv. This must all remain confidential."

"You must try to convince the ambassador without the proof of Ilsa. If you speak of Ilsa, she could be taken by U.S. authorities, and there could be publicity that none of us can afford to have right now if we want to find your daughter. He will be forced to act, in the presence of Ilsa as evidence, and report all details of your meeting to the U.S. State Department. It is best he simply come to trust you and act from his gut. If you find Ambassador Krewe skeptical, or you think he is giving you the runaround, hand him this as you leave. It will change the equation in your favor. Leave before he opens it if you can. He will guess where you got it and who gave it to you when he opens it." Pastor Valente handed Dan a sealed manila envelope.

"Dan," said Pastor Timothy, "here is your daughter's passport for Ilsa."

"Here is all of your flight information, Dave," said Johnny, as he handed him some papers. "Your flight plan has been filed to Bujumbura with a stop for fuel. You are cleared over Zambia and the Congo, and here are your forms for Burundi customs, all filled out with your passenger names and passport numbers. You and Ilsa have a temporary entry visa. You will be meeting with the U.S. Ambassador tomorrow. You both have airline tickets from Bujumbura to Addis Ababa. The tickets were required to obtain your temporary entry visa.

"Ethiopia?" quizzed Dan.

"Yes, Dan," continued Pastor Valente. "That is the easiest way to get Ilsa to Israel. We could fly you to Johannesburg and connect with an El Al flight but that is thousands of miles in the wrong direction. Ethiopian Airlines has good connections out of Addis Ababa to Tel Aviv. One more thing - do not tell Joshua and Lori about the missing girls or your search for them or anything. They only know you are accompanying Ilsa to her family in Israel. They believe they are watching Ilsa for you while you attend to business at the Novotel and meet with the ambassador. They are very trustworthy, but there is nothing to be gained by telling them."

Dan shook hands with all the Pastors as did Dave. Their luggage from Pastor Adam's house had been loaded on the Cessna 410. Dan, Dave and Ilsa headed toward the 410, as Pastor Timothy Doyle, Pastor Jorge Valente and Johnny walked toward the Flying Doves' Cessna 206.

The 206 was started and taxiing for takeoff before Dave finished his pre-flight and got settled in the pilot's seat. "Clear!" shouted Dave out the open window. With that, he started both engines and taxied in behind the 206 waiting to depart. The 206 took off and a few minutes later Dave followed

Soon both planes were in the air, with the Cessna 206 headed east and the Cessna 410 headed north. Dan sat in the back side-by-side with Ilsa, as they began the next leg of the journey to Bujumbura, Burundi.

"How long is the flight?" asked Dan once Dave was up and leveled off at cruising speed.

"About 1,750 kilometers. It will be about five hours in the air. I probably have enough fuel, but we will drop down in Pweta, Congo to top off the tanks just to be cautious."

"A little over a thousand miles," thought Dan. He looked out the window and the magnificent scenery below."

He looked over at Ilsa. She did have a striking resemblance to his daughter Callie, but he imagined that many of the girls did. He did not want to think about that, because he knew the girls were selected intentionally to fulfill some specific and depraved sexual purpose. He refused to allow his mind to go there.

She was reading the Torah. "Ilsa," interrupted Dan, "I know you will look back on this one day with some perspective that your years will give you. You should look out the window and take in the beauty in the creation below."

She looked at him with her deep-blue eyes, and her golden hair was highlighted by the sun shining through the window. He was struck by the precocious innocence of her face. "Callie, Callie, Callie," he thought.

"You're right, Mr. Grainger," she said as she placed a bookmark in the pages and closed her Torah and set it at her side. She leaned forward to look out the window.

Dave pointed out a small refrigerator on the plane and a drawer filled with snacks. All three drank some water and munched on whatever was available.

After about three and a half hours, they began to descend at Pweto. Dan could see a small town to the east as they approached over a good size lake.

"It's Lake Mwero," said Dave. "The lake is the divider between the Congo and Zambia."

Dan looked down just as they passed the lake shore and could see a Zambian flag at the water's edge, but just a few feet away across the road a bit was the blue Democratic Republic of the Congo flag with the diagonal red and yellow bar. It was very different from the green and yellow flag of Zaire that Dan remembered from his visit to Kinshasa many years ago.

After landing, the plane taxied for a while until a fuel truck came out to meet them. Dave cut the engines and stepped out to pay for the fuel. Dan and Ilsa went down the steps also. If

Namibia had been hot, this was hell. The afternoon sun beat down on them, with no breeze and the humidity was unbearable. They were still south of the equator and it was summer as if that mattered much. Dan and Ilsa went around to the side of the fuel truck to escape the direct pounding of the sun and stand in a precious bit of shade.

After a short time, the fuel truck stowed its hose and Dave paid with his credit card. Dave motioned them back into the plane, and they were soon racing down the runway and were airborne.

"An hour and a half, maybe a little longer," said Dave.

It wasn't long before a large and very long body of water was visible out the right side of the plane. It was Lake Tanganyika and was several hundred miles long. Finally, the plane was above the water and began to descend. He could hear Dave talking to the tower and he knew it was Bujumbura International Airport.

They taxied to the terminal and parked on the apron. They got out and removed the luggage. A man showed up with a push cart and immediately began helping. The three were directed to customs. Each of them handed the official their passport and Disembarkation Card. Dave slipped a tip to the man helping with the cart.

Their bags were opened and carefully gone through. The customs official carefully looked at each item. Then he placed the bags next to the passport control counter. The official took the three passports. He studied each picture and kept looking back up at the three of them. It seemed the official was looking very carefully at Ilsa and her picture, but he then seemed to look just as intently at Dan's. In what seemed like an eternity, Dave, Dan and Ilsa were passed through customs with a temporary visa.

As soon as they entered the Arriving Passenger area, they spied a couple with a sign that said, "Welcome Dan and Ilsa." They were a young couple, mid-thirties. She was slender with light-colored hair and he was of solid build and wore an African print shirt and khaki pants.

The couple yelled "Over here," as they approached, Lori put her arms around Ilsa and gave her a big hug. Joshua, Dave and Dan shook hands and introduced themselves. Lori hugged them both.

"This way," said Joshua as he motioned the group out of the terminal into the chaos outside. They followed Joshua to a bright-blue Land Cruiser, with the Christian Flag on the side and the words "Afrique Iglesias Evangélicas." prominently displayed on the vehicle. Lori kept her arms around Ilsa and she did not seem to mind. Dave got in the front with Joshua. Dan and Lori sat in back with Ilsa between them. The same man had their luggage from customs and put it in the back of the Land Cruiser and Dave a slipped him another folded bill.

In about fifteen minutes they pulled into a house surrounded by a wrought iron fence and an eight-foot, block wall. The gate was shut and everyone got out. There were lush, tropical plants all around the inside perimeter of the block wall.

"Ilsa," said Lori, "I will show you to your room."

The rest of the group followed Joshua passing through the sparsely furnished home into the courtyard. In the kitchen there were some African women preparing food, and the aroma was a blessing to Dan's nostrils. He had not had a decent meal in a long time. They made small talk sitting under a fan in the courtyard. Mostly Dave asked Joshua about his and Lori's ministry. Both of them were Americans and had met in school. They married and shortly after that felt called to missions work in Burundi. They had a small church in the slums of northern Bujumbura. They fed the children in the neighborhood of the church twice a day. They had services on Saturday and Sunday and on some evenings.

After about thirty minutes, Lori announced that dinner was served. They all found a place at the long table in the courtyard now covered with food dishes. Ilsa sat next to Lori and Dan sat down next to Ilsa.

Joshua said the blessing and got pretty fired up as he did so. Dan found Ilsa's hand and patted it as if to say "This must be a bit too much for you."

After the blessing Lori pointed out several of the foods to Ilsa and described several of the curry sauces, explaining which ones were vegetable only and which ones contained pork, lamb or beef.

Dan thought that was a bit odd but was so hungry he just dug in. Then he realized that Lori was being sensitive to Ilsa's dietary restrictions.

There was hot tomato soup, crackers pita bread and hummus. After that, he piled his plate with steaming white rice and covered it with bubbling-hot-curry topping scooped from a pan. He had bottled water from France and Coke. It was all so delicious. There was apple cobbler or cherry pie for dessert and Dan had both. Dan joined in occasionally with the discussions but mostly listened to Joshua and Dave. They talked with great affection about Timothy Doyle and the Rejoice and Praise Church and the work he did in so many African nations. They spoke about Pastor Jorge Valente. They called him "George the Brave." Jorge was born in Africa. He then moved to Lisbon for his education and became involved with an evangelical church there. He spun off his own ministry, the Igreja Evangelica Pão da Vida with churches in Lisbon and the former Portuguese colonies of Africa. He had churches in Beira and Maputo, Mozambique, Luanda and Lobito Angola and Bissau, Guinea-Bissau. He was fearless in his revival crusades in all of these nations. He also clung to the interesting belief that Portugal would once again rise like the phoenix from its colonial ashes and re-establish itself as a world power just as it was four-hundred years ago!

After the dessert was finished and the conversation wound down, Joshua said it was time to go. This time, an African drove while Joshua studied his Bible in the front seat. It wasn't long before the Land Cruiser drove into a very-depressed area of metal lean-to dwellings and open sewage flowing in a ditch along the side of the road. Dan then heard the melodic music of African praise filling the neighborhood. They pulled up to the open-walled church that had Afrique Iglesias Evangélicas signs all over the structure. Over to the side in a dirt clearing, children clung to their plates and cups, waiting for them to be filled by the women of the church who had been cooking the food for distribution. The parents came in droves to get their children fed a good meal while they listened to the music of praise and the message of love and hope.

"Thomas, will take you to the hotel," said Joshua, as he got out of the Land Cruiser.

Dan had seen these scenes before in other parts of Africa and the world. He had been part of them himself when he traveled with an evangelist from South Bend, Indiana, who operated a Christian Global Feeding Ministry.

"Can we stay for a while and listen?" asked Dan.

"Sure," said Joshua. "Just tell Thomas when you want to go."

"Is that okay with you?" he asked Dave.

"Of course it is. I would like to see the speaker tonight myself. He is from Harare."

They followed Joshua and Thomas directed them to sit in the front row next to an older, silver-haired, white gentleman in the typical khaki pants with many pockets.

Joshua took the lectern and began speaking immediately in a local African dialect. The crowd came alive as Joshua held up his Bible and ferociously proclaimed whatever he was saying with the musicians on stage playing and the crowd following along in song and praise. Then he introduced the gentleman sitting to Dan's right as Gaylord Nash.

Gaylord took the stage to loud applause. He began preaching in English and then paused every few seconds while Joshua repeated what Gaylord had said in the local dialect.

It was an unusual topic entitled "The Devil has no thumbs and he has no toes." The crowd loved it. Dan could not help but think that Gaylord's accent made him sound very much like the actor James Mason. He had a deep, resonant voice that made him very easy to listen to.

After a little while, Dan had taken in enough of the experience and he was very tired. He motioned to Thomas, and the three of them discreetly exited the church shelter and got into the Land Cruiser with Dan in front. They talked some on the drive to the hotel.

Thomas said "Pastor Joshua and Lori good people. I come whenever I can. I have to walk across the city and sometimes sleep at the church the night before to hear Pastor Joshua. I can take the bus part of the way sometimes if I have the fare, but I just sleep on the floor and wait for Pastor to speak. I help the women with food. My life so much better now I find Jesus. I'm so happy."

It wasn't long before they went around a large roundabout and then just after that turned into the Novotel Hotel.

Thomas helped with the bags and insisted upon staying until the two had checked in. Thomas carried the luggage into the elevator and up to their rooms. When Thomas was about to leave, Dan pulled a twenty-dollar U.S. bill from his wallet. "This is for you. Thomas."

"No, no, I cannot," he said. "Too much."

"Please, take it and take the bus whenever you can and come feed your faith at Pastor Joshua's," said Dan.

Thomas did not protest further and smiled a partially toothless grin as he put the twenty in his pocket.

Thank you, bless you," he said as he left.

Dave had already checked out of his own room and was at Dan's door as Thomas left. "Let's get something to drink downstairs," he said.

Dan and Dave went downstairs to the courtyard and sat underneath an awning with a belt-driven fan turning slowly overhead. Dan looked up at the belt that wound in serpentine fashion from fan to fan overhead. It was quite a contraption.

Dan was a Coke drinker, but tonight he wanted something different, a Fanta Orange. There was pizza for sale, too, but Dan was quite full from the Rogers' house. He sipped on his Fanta while Dave drank a root beer.

After about thirty minutes they both went up to their rooms. The room was air-conditioned after a fashion. It was still muggy but Dan had his first good night of sleep and freedom in quite a while. He fell asleep praying for Callie's safety and the safe return of all the girls. After all the miracles he had already received, he had no doubt there would be more.

Dan awoke with a knock on the door, it was 7:00 a.m. Dave told him that Joshua would be picking them up at 8:15 to go to the American Embassy. Dan showered, packed his bags and went downstairs for a quick breakfast in the Novotel courtyard. It was boiled eggs, cereal, toast and a wide range of fresh fruits.   When Joshua came walking into the courtyard, they were ready to leave. Joshua drove them to the U.S. Embassy.

The Embassy was a beautiful stone building and it sent chills up Dan's spine just seeing the U.S. Flag blowing in the morning breeze and the large U.S. Coat of Arms on the wall near the entrance of the building. "How blessed I am to be an American," he thought.

The three of them were ushered into the embassy building. Joshua remained in the lobby. Dan and Dave were escorted past the front desk. There were several U.S. Marines in full dress stationed along the way. They were immediately taken into the ambassador's office and were seated. The walls of the room were wood. It appeared to be a stained oak of vertical narrow slats. The ambassador entered the office. He was over six feet tall with a well-toned build. He smiled as he introduced himself. "I am Garth Krewe," he said, as he shook the hands of Dan and Dave.

The Ambassador motioned toward the Marine standing at the back of the room. "This is Lt. Col. West," he said.

Instead of sitting down behind his desk, he came around and picked a chair facing Dan directly. "I am so sorry about your daughter, Mr. Grainger."

"Thank you, Ambassador," replied Dan. "I am sure you know that is why we are here."

"How can I help?" asked Ambassador Krewe.

"I need the help of the State Department and the U.S. military in the Indian Ocean to find a container ship that left the Port of Beira, Mozambique ten days ago," began Dan.

Dan recounted the story of the lost Oasis 747. He told of Callie's phone calls and the Quonset huts in southeastern Angola. He had to say he didn't know how the girls got to the remote region of Angola. He told the Ambassador he believed the plane landed in Luanda on the morning after the Super Bowl. He pleaded with the ambassador to have the military examine satellite photos of the Luanda Airport for two white

747s and check that against normal schedules. Then Dan explained they found footprints were and believe the girls were loaded into shipping containers and transported by truck and train to Beira. The Flying Doves tracked the containers all the way. There was no time to involve the Mozambique authorities. The cranes loaded the containers as soon as they arrived, and the ship left port right after that. He gave the Ambassador the exact time and day and the name of the ship, the "Quelimane" of Lebanese registry. Dan asked again for the ambassador to enlist the aid of the military to use satellite mapping to track and locate the ship.

The ambassador listened intently. He was respectful to Dan and seemed to empathize with all that Dan said.

Through it all, Dan did not mention Ilsa or anything associated with her rescue. He simply omitted those details and told the story as if they had never found her.

The Lt. Col. was clearly listening as well, on several occasions, Ambassador Krewe glanced over to the Marine at key points in Dan's story as if to say "Did you get that?" The Lt. Col. never flinched or reacted to any of Dan's words.

Finally, as Dan seemed to run out of steam the Ambassador spoke in a deep voice that commanded great authority. "Mr. Grainger, I thank you for your time and sharing the story of your daughter's tragic circumstances."

"Can you help me, please? I have little hope without knowing the ship's destination," pleaded Dan with his voice cracking a bit.

"I will see what I can do, Mr. Grainger. I will relay your story to Washington and pass it on to Defense, if they allow me to," replied the Ambassador, but for the first time, the sincerity in his voice seemed to falter.

Dan stood up. He knew diplomatic double-speak when he heard it. "Ambassador, I know it is a difficult story to accept and requires a great deal of faith to accept from someone you have never met before. You are the only one who can marshal the resources to help me right now." Dan's tone was firm now, no sign of the emotion of a moment ago.

"I want to thank you for your time and consideration, Ambassador Krewe." Dan put his hand out to shake hands and, after doing so, handed him the sealed, manila envelope. "This may help," said Dan, not knowing or having any idea what was in the envelope. He trusted Jorge Valente completely.

Lt. Col. West opened the door as the two men left, and Dan saw the Ambassador opening the envelope. Another Marine began escorting them down the hall to the reception area. As they were about to exit the building, Lt. Col. West came running down the hall, "Mr. Grainger! Mr. Grainger, the ambassador wishes to see you again." He motioned Dan and Dave to come with him.

When Dan entered the office, the Ambassador Krewe and Lt. Col. both seemed a bit shaken. Gone was the professional detachment of both men.

Ambassador Krewe held in his hand a printout of a newspaper article.

He handed it to Dan "Where did you get this?" asked the ambassador sternly, his eyes locked on Dan's.

Dan looked down somewhat dumbfounded. It was a printout of the Anderson, Indiana Herald-Bulletin. The headline read *"Mark Campbell seriously injured in jailhouse attack."* Dan was stunned himself. He wasn't sure why it was significant. He quickly scanned the document and saw John Kosten's name.

"I was told you would know the answer to that question," replied Dan.

"I do know, but I want to hear you say it," said Ambassador Krewe.

"It was given to me yesterday in Namibia by Pastor Jorge Valente of the Bread of Life Evangelical Church of Lisbon Portugal and Beira, Mozambique. Beira is the port the ship sailed from carrying my daughter and perhaps 280 or so other American girls." Dan was almost defiant in his response.

"Sgt. Mark Campbell of the U.S. Marine Corps saved my life," began Ambassador Krewe, "and the life of Lt. Col. West here and dozens of other Americans, as we evacuated the U.S. Embassy in Guinea-Bissau while it was under attack by Islamic Fundamentalists. As we boarded the last helicopters and we were lifting off from the roof of the embassy, Sgt. Mark Campbell disregarded his own safety and single-handedly provided cover for us as we escaped. He held off dozens of Islamic fighters until we were safely out of firing range. He was left behind and somehow managed to elude his captors within the embassy compound. We got word the next morning that he was safe and sound at the Igreja Evangelica Pão da Vida Church under the protection of Pastor Jorge Valente. A few days later we were able to successfully extract Sgt. Campbell, his wife and her three daughters. We also evacuated a dozen other local embassy workers who would have been killed but they too found sanctuary in Valente's church." The Ambassador paused "Tell me, Mr. Grainger, what did he tell you when he gave you this envelope?"

"Ambassador," began Dan, "He said if I thought you were giving me the runaround that I should give you the envelope and leave before you opened it and that it might change the equation in my favor?"

"Well, it did indeed, Mr. Grainger, it did indeed, but not officially. The U.S, Government will not get involved unless you have a great deal more evidence than you have. Even then, it would be too little too late. But you have my attention. There are other avenues and resources that can be utilized.

Good day, Sir, and I will pray for your daughter." The ambassador reached out and shook Dan's hand.

Dan replied, "Sgt. Mark Campbell is being represented by one of my closest friends. John Kosten is one of the most good and decent men in the state of Indiana and one hell of an attorney." Dan turned and left the office with Dave at his side.

Ambassador Krewe turned to Lt. Col. West and said, "We must not let anything happen to Sgt. Campbell, understand?"

"Yes Sir," replied Lt. Col. West.

Chapter 8

Dan and Dave returned to the reception area and joined Joshua. The three left. Dan looked at his watch and saw it was only 9:30.

"How did Ilsa do last night?" asked Dan.

"She was great. She and Lori have really hit it off. It's great to have an American teenager around. In fact, Ilsa insisted on going to the church for the morning feeding of the children and the nursing mothers."

"Really?" Dan choked up a bit, but no one could tell. He thought for a moment what the daily routine must be like for Joshua and Lori, and yet, they seemed tireless in their devotion to helping the people. "Is there a bank nearby?" asked Dan.

"Yes," said Joshua, and in a few minutes, he parked along the busy street and pointed to a bank. "You will need your passport," said Joshua.

Dan got out and walked to the bank and emerged in just a few minutes. Can we swing past your church on the way back to the hotel?" asked Dan.

"Sure," replied Joshua, and in about ten minutes they were again in the unspeakable slums of Bujumbura. They pulled into the church lot and the area was filled with children, some in line and some devouring the bowls or cups full of the food they were receiving. Dan spied Lori over near some nursing mothers, and next to her was Ilsa holding an infant in her arms and feeding the baby.

Dan went over to Lori "Is it like this every day?" asked Dan. Lori nodded. "Where do you get the supplies?" quizzed Dan.

"We get some support from churches in the U.S. and Joshua's parents pastor a church and they help.

"Do you ever run out?" asked Dan.

"Yes," she said with sadness in her face. "What happens then?" Dan asked, but he knew.

"Children die," Lori said in a very matter-of-fact voice.

Dan looked around. Ilsa was holding a baby with a distended belly. There were dozens of mothers nursing their infants. Other infants were being fed by bottles.

"The mothers are malnourished and their milk is not sufficient for the baby to survive," said Lori, "but it does contain the mother's antibodies and that protects the child from many illnesses. We feed the babies formula, when we have it and the older children condensed milk and Muesli. We never know when or where our next shipment will come from."

"Lori," said Dan. The tone of his voice caused Lori to stop and look straight at him, but she said nothing.

"Here, I hope this can help you and your husband in your ministry," Dan said, as he handed her an envelope with the words *Banque de la République du Burundi* printed on it."

She looked at it, saw American currency, opened it, counted it and stared straight at him.

"This is twelve-hundred dollars!" she blurted out.

"I pray it can help," Dan said.

"Mr. Grainger, it will help. Children will live because of your gift," said Lori.

"Lori, the children will live because of you and Joshua," replied Dan.

Dan knew in his heart that the twelve-hundred dollars that the Lord had saved him on his ticket to Harare was not for him, it was for Joshua and Lori to use in their ministry.

Ilsa and Dave just watched as the scene unfolded and said nothing.

"You will come to our home for lunch," said Lori. It seemed to be more of a command than a request.

"We would be pleased," replied Dan.

Joshua headed toward his vehicle, Dan and Dave followed. The drive back to the house was through compelling scenes of poverty. A concrete open ditch along the road contained raw sewage. Dan just shook his head at the children playing near it. Women lined the streets with heavy bags of various types perched on their heads in perfect balance. Their clothes were brightly patterned reds and greens and yellows. Often, you would see children, men and women with T-shirts clearly from the west, advertising sports teams and department stores and American vacation destinations.

They arrived back at Joshua and Lori's home. Dan, Dave and Joshua sat in the courtyard discussing the challenges of Burundi and the mission work that he and his wife were so dedicated to fulfilling. Dan thought to himself for a moment. Anyone could have a bad day at work, but when Joshua and Lori did, children died and others went hungry. This sad fact was true for churches and NGOs all throughout Africa.

There was noise in the background, coming from the kitchen area where the staff was preparing the meal and setting the table in the courtyard.

Ilsa and Lori returned from the church feeding. In a few minutes, they had freshened up and lunch was served in the courtyard.

After lunch, there was conversation and fellowship in the courtyard. Joshua took Dan and Dave back to the Novotel. Dan just sat in his room. There was nothing to do but worry about Callie and the girls. Where were they? Would Ambassador Krewe help? Could he tell Dan where his daughter had been taken? His thoughts also drifted to Jasmine and what challenges she may be facing in Bukhara.

Finally, he just couldn't take it anymore. He prayed and then went down to the Novotel courtyard to get a Fanta. When he walked into the courtyard, there sat Dave nursing some iced tea. Dan sat down next to him.

A waiter soon appeared and Dan ordered a Fanta Orange. Dave ordered another iced tea. Their drinks came and they heard a deep voice say "Put that on my tab, Waiter."

They looked around to see a tall man in dark khakis.

"May I?" asked the man, as he sat down in a chair next to them. He was drinking tea.

"Mr. Grainger, I am Ilsa's uncle, Benjamin Johansohn."

Both men looked at him, startled. "Relax." the uncle said.

"First, let me thank the two you for rescuing my beloved niece from certain death, if not from the wild beasts of Africa, then the human beasts of Islamic terror and slavery," said Johansohn.

"And what do you know of Ilsa's trials, Mr. Johansohn?" asked Dan.

"I know all that you know and much more. I do not have much time Mr. Grainger. You and Ilsa have a flight at 2:10 p.m. tomorrow to Addis Ababa and her final destination is Tel Aviv. Her parents are secretly flying to Israel today. You must choose your destination in the next few minutes," said Johansohn. "Any place you desire."

"I don't understand," said Dan. Dave remained quiet but totally engrossed in the events unfolding before his eyes.

"Let me congratulate you on your successful embassy visit this morning," said Johansohn. "It has immediately opened the door to very-valuable information that corroborates and adds to information we already suspected. We know where your daughter is and the other girls, and for the time being they are safe. They are in captivity in Bukhara and will be trained as sex slaves over the next few years to serve Alim Hassan."

Dan sat in stunned silence. "Bukhara?" he slowly stammered out.

"Yes," replied Johansohn. Bukhara is small city-state that broke off from Uzbekistan a few years ago, under the encouragement and protection of Iran and certain Sunni governments."

"Yes, I know of Bukhara," said Dan, as his thoughts raced about the genius of the Lord in preparing his way in the search for Callie and the other girls. He suddenly was overcome with a feeling of calm and peace, after just hearing the most frightening words imaginable from the Israeli.

"That is unusual, Mr. Grainger, few Americans would know of Bukhara."

"How do you know she is there and safe?" asked Dan.

"I cannot share everything with you, but when you spoke with Ambassador Krewe this morning, you started a process that opened this door. The U.S. government will not help or at least will not help without convincing proof the girls are there."

Dan and Dave just listened.

Johansohn continued, "Once we knew the name of the ship Quelimane, of Lebanese registry, and the date it left Beira, it was not difficult at all to track the ship's movement. After leaving Beira, the Quelimane traveled 6,000 kilometers north to the port city of Chabahar in Iran. We know they were there. Ambassador Krewe has shared with us through back-channels satellite imagery of the girls at the airport in Chabahar. From there the girls were separated into two groups and flown to the city of Bukhara."

"How do you know this?" demanded Dan.

"The city of Bukhara has a small community of Jews dating back 1,500 years. After the collapse of the Soviet Union, many Jews immigrated to Israel but a small community remains. We have reliable contacts in the community that have confirmed the girls are in the Ark of Bukhara, a Royal Fortress controlled by Nasrullah Hassan, the Foreign Minister of Bukhara."

Dan this is all very troubling and will be hard for you to grasp. Nasrullah and his son, Alim, are butchers committed to Sharia Law. And yet, they run the most sophisticated headquarters for pornography and sadomasochist bondage websites in the world. In a secret, underground facility, they have constructed a huge video-production studio where they shoot all forms of this material. They have kidnapped girls and women from all over the world. They keep them captive in the studios to produce every manner of film you can possibly imagine, and I would wager ones that cannot even be imagined."

Johansohn continued with his graphic description. "This includes 'snuff films.' When a woman has outlived her usefulness as a sex slave and cannot be sold to one of the many clients who regularly visit Bukhara for their pleasure, she may be tortured and murdered as a web feature. Sometimes it is interactive with a remote client in another country that directs the torture. Nasrullah and Alim Hassan rake in billions of dollars from this operation. This comes from various websites catering to a particular niche or ethnic preference. They also run a brothel for mostly Middle-Eastern clients who can afford to pay exorbitant amounts for anything they want. Many women are sold to these men."

"Your daughter and all the girls kidnapped with her are destined for this fate but not for several years. These girls will be kept for the personal use of Alim and his father, Nasrullah, after they have been trained. They will not be turned over to the "studio" until they are perhaps twenty, or at least eighteen, after Alim tires of them." Johansohn stopped to allow all he had said to sink in with Dan and Dave.

"How do I get them out?" said Dan, "because I am getting them out."

"I don't know, Dan," replied Johansohn. "We have very-limited resources inside Bukhara, and we certainly have no contacts within the Ark to identify their exact location. Rescue would be nearly impossible, even if we knew exactly where they were," Johansohn said, with clear resignation and regret.

"Well, Benjamin, I serve a Lord who will give me the guidance and wisdom to get them out. First thing, I must go to Bukhara and find out exactly where they are in the Ark," Dan said confidently.

"That is impossible, Dan," replied Johansohn, "It is highly fortified. Very few have free run of the Royal Fortress. You will never find a contact that will help you, and even if you did, his life would be in great danger."

"Well, I just happen, through the grace of God to know someone who lives in the Ark," said Dan defiantly, as he continued. "Yasi Min Hassan, Princess of Bukhara, the only surviving child of Abdullah Hassan, the Emir of Bukhara and the niece of Nasrullah."

Both men just stared at Dan with incredulity. Their eyes widened in disbelief at what he had just said. The silence was deafening. The normally loud background noise of the hotel courtyard patrons seemed to have disappeared.

"Praise the Lord! Hallelujah!" said Dave. "In the name of Jesus, Praise the Lord!"

"Unbelievable!" exclaimed Johansohn.

"Benjamin, book my ticket from Addis Ababa to Bukhara.

"Dan, Dan, you cannot go there without a visa," said Johansohn.

"Then get me one! You have the Mossad. You can do anything," said Dan.

Johansohn just looked at Dan. He had never seen such confident determination in the face of an untrained individual before, especially just an average American off the street. He chose not to dash Dan's hope, no matter how unrealistic. He stood up. "Let me make a call," he said, as he walked over to a private area at the side of the courtyard.

Dan looked at Dave. "Will you pray for me, Dave?" as he reached out his hands. Dave held on to both of Dan's hands with both of his and Dave began to pray. All the right words just seemed to come to Dave as he asked for the Lord's guidance for Dan, and after a short time, he slipped into praying in tongues. Dan had no idea what he was saying. He just held on and accepted the blessings, and he could feel them deep down in his soul.

After a few minutes, Johansohn returned. He opened a small notebook where he had jotted down some information.

"Dan, this is the best we can do," Johansohn began, "You can fly directly to Bukhara. Once there, you can apply at the airport for a 48-hour Transit Visa. You must have an onward ticket to another destination leaving within 48 hours. You can only get a 15-day Tourist Visa by applying in advance from your home country or certain Bukhara Diplomatic missions located in just a few countries.

You must have a letter of invitation from someone in Bukhara or an official Bukhara tourist agency that arranges your hotel and stay in Bukhara. You must have six months left on your passport before it expires, and you must have at least two or more clean pages in your passport for various Bukhara entry and exit stamps and visas. They will not budge on these requirements."

"Crap, replied Dan as he pulled out his passport. He saw that his passport expired in five months. As he leafed through it, he could see had had only three, maybe four, blank pages. "Mine expires in five months," he said.

"That's not a requirement for the transit visa, but you will only have forty-eight hours," said Johansohn.

"Well, that's just going to have to do," said Dan "I will get there, I will contact the princess and she will find Callie and the girls. I will leave and get the visa applied for and my passport renewed. What countries have the Diplomatic Mission where I can apply?"

Johansohn looked down at his small notebook and said "In Europe, just Paris and London. In the U.S, it is New York, Chicago, New Orleans and San Francisco. In the Middle East, it's Teheran, Baghdad, Islamabad."

"Stop right there," said Dan. I am not going to any of those places. It will have to be Europe or all the way back home. I need time to think. How soon do you have to know?" asked Dan.

"We will go ahead and book you from Addis to Bukhara. I don't know, late this evening or first thing in the morning," said Johansohn.

"Your best course of action is to contact a local Bukhara tour agency, while you are there, and make all the arrangements for your return. It will be very busy in just a few weeks and difficult to find accommodations."

"Why?" asked Dan.

"International Women's Day on March 8th" replied Johansohn. "Nasrullah Hassan is pulling out all the stops to host an extravagant, propaganda event designed to convince the world that Bukhara is a great place to be an Islamic woman. Women from all over the world will be attending in their traditional clothing. Even costumes that are very revealing by Muslim standards will be permitted. For this time period only, women will not be required to wear a burka or hijab in the city center."

"Sharia Law will be suspended for the duration of the festivities and all locals will have to vacate the city center during the parade and other activities. Nasrullah is deploying all his normal Ark security to guard a large perimeter around the city center. He is then using the security from the studio to guard the Ark. These men see all the depravity of things going on in the studio and will not be corrupted further by observing the females that attend the main event. This event will be televised to the entire Muslim world."

"What are you suggesting?" quizzed Dan.

"I don't know how you can pull it off, but if your princess can get you to the girls when they are least guarded, it is your best chance to rescue them. I don't know how you can possibly smuggle hundreds of young girls out of the country, but this is clearly the best opportunity to get them out of the Ark."

"Okay," sighed Dan. "That is very interesting. I need to think it through and pray about it. I think I have to figure out a way to use that event to my advantage. Look, Benjamin, I just don't know how to thank you."

"You already have. You are bringing Ilsa back to her parents," said Johansohn

"Now, if I can just figure out how to do that for myself and a few hundred other families in America," said Dan.

"The Israeli government is indebted to you and will not forget what you have done in saving Ilsa. We can only help you in ways that leave no fingerprints of our involvement," said Johansohn.

"I will be taking you up on that offer," said Dan.

"One more thing, Dan," said Johansohn. "You said that Princess Yasi Min Hassan was the only surviving child of Emir Abdullah."

"Yes," replied Dan.

"That's not true. He has a son, Adil Hassan," said Johansohn.

"I know," said Dan, "but he died in an Israeli prison in the Golan Heights."

"Where did you hear that?" snapped Johansohn.

Dan hesitated for a moment and then decided, what the heck, "From his sister."

Johansohn just looked into Dan's eyes, for a while and then said "No, Dan, he was part of a prisoner exchange several years ago with Hezbollah. He is alive and being held in a dungeon deep beneath the Ark known as the Zindon prison."

"Wow, I didn't see that one coming," said Dan. "Why is his own father keeping him in a dungeon?"

"The old man's health is failing, and he doesn't know half of what's going on in his own Emirate. The brother, Nasrullah, and Alim call all the shots. They are the true power in Bukhara. Abdullah is loved by the people, but he is just a figurehead."

"I have some serious thinking to do," said Dan with a sigh.

"I will let you know when I figure it out. Can you give Dave your number?"

"Certainly. Waiter," he called out, as he motioned for the check. Johansohn gave Dave his phone number and he paid the waiter.

"One more thing," said Johansohn. "Ilsa needs to leave Burundi with your daughter's passport. Once on the plane, I will give her an Israeli passport with her own name for arrival into Addis. She can give you back the passport, once you are safely on board. I will be on board also and will accompany her on to Tel Aviv. I will give you your itinerary and flight information after we take off from Bujumbura."

"Okay, I got it. Thank you, more than words can ever convey," said Dan.

"Shalom Aleikhem good evening," said Johansohn, as he stood up. Dan and Dave both stood to shake his hand, and he walked toward the hotel lobby.

The two men sat back down. It was time for dinner and the only thing Dan could see that he was comfortable with eating was pizza.

As the two men ate their dinner, a group of about a dozen local women entered the courtyard in brightly colored garb. They were all dressed the same in a turquoise-colored dress with a coral sash, a white, beaded necklace and a white headscarf around their necks. Each had green and white bracelets on both wrists. They proceeded to the center of the courtyard and began to dance. It was an incredible site and Dan watched transfixed, as his mind began to process all that had happened.

The women danced with beautiful smiles and were clearly very happy to be performing. Dan turned to Dave.

"What is this group and why are they dancing?" asked Dan.

Dave replied "They are practicing for Carnival. Each year Burundi sends dancers and other performers to Carnival in Kigali, Rwanda just 175 kilometers to the north."

"Carnival?" quizzed Dan.

"Yes, although the Hutu Rwandans hate the French, it was introduced to Kigali by the French and is celebrated about seven weeks before Easter," answered Dave. "I think it is coming up soon."

Dan pondered for a moment. "Of Course," he said. "Carnival in Rio de Janeiro, Carnival in Paris," he stopped for a moment, "Oh, My God, Mardi Gras in New Orleans…New Orleans!" Dan almost shouted it out. "Call Benjamin, immediately and just tell him New Orleans. New Orleans is my destination and I must be there before Fat Tuesday."

Dave seemed perplexed but did as Dan asked. When Benjamin answered, he gave Dan the phone. "New Orleans, my destination is New Orleans from Bukhara as fast as you can get me there after the forty-eight hours."

"Okay," replied Johansohn.

"You may have difficulty with so many people headed there for Mardi Gras, but I must be there before then," explained Dan.

"Okay, Mr. Grainger, we will make it happen."

"Another thing, Benjamin," said Dan. "I have another request but it is too delicate to say over the phone. Will we have any time on the flight tomorrow or in Addis Ababa to speak privately?"

"Yes, I think so, if we are brief and discreet," replied Johansohn.

"Thanks again," said Dan, as he handed the phone back to Dave.

Dave ended the call. "Dan," he said "I will be leaving very early in the morning to fly back to Harare. I sincerely wish you the very best. We will all be praying for you at the church, Pastor Doyle and everyone. Godspeed, Dan."

The two men stood up and shook hands for the last time. "I will get the bill," said Dan. Dave headed back into the hotel lobby.

Dan paid the bill and continued to watch as the Burundi women continued to practice their Carnival routine. Dan was suddenly at peace. He had one hell of an idea; an idea so crazy and outside the box that no one would ever think it conceivable. "International Women's Day," he thought. With that, headed up to his room, packed his things and slept soundly.

Morning came quickly. Dan was up early. He had already had breakfast and showered when the phone rang. Joshua was here to pick him up and take him for lunch at the house. Ilsa and Lori were returning from the morning feeding as lunch was served. They all prayed for Dan and Ilsa. Lori hugged Ilsa and said her goodbyes. She gave Dan a big hug, and they parted company for the last time.

Joshua drove them to the Bujumbura airport and stayed with them until they cleared customs. Ilsa passed through with no problems using Callie's passport. Dan and Ilsa headed for the gate.

Once in the gate area, they saw Johansohn. Ilsa knew not to react to her uncle, although she could hardly contain herself and smiled broadly. She did not run to him as she desperately wanted to do.

An opportunity came, while boarding, for Dan to speak privately with Johansohn. "I need a dozen automatic weapons, U.S. military issue, in Bukhara. Can you get them there for me?" asked Dan.

Johansohn's expression did not reveal his utter shock at the request.

He pondered for a moment and did not answer. Finally, "Yes," he said, "Will M249s do?" "I don't know," said Dan, "Just recent issue that any U.S. Soldier or Marine can handle."

"Okay, but not into the Ark, we cannot do that. We will figure a drop somewhere near the city center. That is all we can do," said Johansohn.

"Okay. Let me know somehow, before I arrive New Orleans," said Dan. "A few tranquilizer guns might come in handy, as well."

"Here," said Johansohn, as he handed Dan a jump drive. "Follow the instructions on this to set up secret, encrypted e-mail accounts. It cannot be cracked. It will encrypt pictures, videos and any other attachments you may include. I have an e-mail address that you will see, and you can communicate with me through that."

Dan stuck the jump drive in his bag.

Ilsa and Dan boarded Ethiopian Flight 806 to Addis Ababa with a stop in Kigali, Rwanda. It was a short flight of forty-five minutes on the Boeing 737. He saw several people disembark that were clearly here for Carnival. It got him to thinking more deeply about his options. The layover was just forty-five minutes and they were in the air again and arrived in Addis Ababa at 7:30 p.m.

Even though Ilsa had a flight at 11:00 p.m. to Tel Aviv and Dan had a flight to Dubai that also left at 11:00 p.m., they had to clear customs and collect their luggage as they were traveling as father and daughter and were not able to check their bags through to their destinations.

They made their way through Ethiopian Customs and met up with Johansohn near the Ethiopian Airlines ticket counter. Here, Ilsa could let go. She put her arms around her uncle and began to cry. He embraced her and they spoke in Hebrew.

Ilsa gave Callie's passport to Dan. Johansohn gave Ilsa her own Israeli passport, and the three got in line to check in and check their luggage. Ilsa and Johansohn were on Flight 404 and would be arriving Tel Aviv at 2:40 a.m., where her parents would be anxiously waiting. Dan was on Flight 612 to Dubai arriving at 3:35 a.m. and connecting with Emirates Airlines, leaving at 5:15 a.m. Dan would arrive in Bukhara at 8:45 a.m. Dan checked his luggage all the way through to Bukhara.

Almost exactly forty-eight hours later he had a British Airways flight direct from Bukhara to London Heathrow. Leaving at 8:20 a.m and arriving Heathrow a 1:00 p.m. British Air BA 237 LHR at 10:40 a.m.to MIA 3:00 p.m. then AA 6:30 p.m. to MSY arriving 7:37 p.m. He would arrive in New Orleans the Saturday night before Mardi Gras.

The three passed through security and stopped briefly to say goodbye. Ilsa hugged Dan and he held her as if she were his own daughter. The two men shook hands and said little. Dan watched for a moment as Johansohn and Ilsa walked toward their gate area and then Dan turned and walked to his.

He boarded the 737 and knew he must sleep. Dan always had difficulty sleeping on a plane, but he had to tonight. He would be arriving Bukhara at 8:45 a.m. and had just two days to somehow find Jasmine and tell her of his plan and that her brother is alive. He did sleep.

He awoke as they were descending into Dubai. He could see the lights of the city skyline, with the lit structures reaching to the sky. He could not make out the buildings themselves, just the lights that dotted the pattern of their structure. He had a fifty-minute wait in the transit lounge.

He boarded the Emirates Airbus 380 at 4:45 a.m. It was full. The plane was huge. Dan had never been on an Airbus 380 before. It could carry over 500 passengers. The Upper-Deck-First-Class section housed a dozen or more private suites with individual sliding doors. Dan was in Business Class in the upper deck. It was a spacious seat that folded into a flat bed.

Surely, he could sleep here. He had a window seat, 15A, just a bit past the wing. Dan had never flown an airplane with such elegance and opulence. Almost all the passengers were men dressed either in western business suits or traditional thobe, an ankle-length, white-cotton garment. Many of the men wore a head scarf of white or white-and-red checkered, held in place by a dark cord of various styles. A few women were on the flight, and they wore similar, ankle-length garments, but they were brightly colored, delicate and embroidered and adorned with gold and silver jewelry. Their heads were covered and they had veils. Dan was terribly underdressed in his khakis and short-sleeve, buttoned shirt. Thankfully, there appeared to be a few Europeans in jeans and less-formal attire.

He wasn't sure of the time difference but hoped to get two to three hours sleep. As the plane took off, there was just enough sunlight in the pre-dawn hours to see the skyline. There were hundreds of high-rise buildings and one towered above them all - the Burj Khalifa at over 2,700 feet. It was nearly unbelievable, He had seen it once before, but still, it was difficult to imagine. In a short while, the plane was at altitude. Dan arranged his seat into a flat bed and went to sleep immediately.

He was awakened by the change in engine sound, signaling a descent. He struggled to open his eyes. He raised the window shade and peered out into the desert terrain below. From his window he could see what he imagined must be Bukhara, standing out as an unlikely oasis in the remote terrain below. Dan was very familiar with the city's history now. It was a desert oasis populated by 500 B.C. and, perhaps, a thousand years before that. It was on the Silk Road of trade between many civilizations - Egypt, Persia, Asia Minor, India, China and Central Asia to the north. Even Marco Polo was believed to have lived in Bukhara for a while, before continuing his travels to Cathay. Bukhara was a center of ancient religions, including Zoroastrianism and an early Buddhist monastery on the oasis.

As he was thinking about what little research he had been able to do on Bukhara, he suddenly realized something obvious that should have occurred to him before. The city of Bukhara was founded on the site of an ancient oasis along the Silk Road. "Oasis," he thought. "That's why the bastards named their retail stores Oasis. It was a subtle but direct link to the true owners of the Oasis Corporation."

He disembarked the plane and collected his luggage. There were hundreds of people in line but he saw a different area for those needing an entry visa. He filled out all the paperwork. He showed them his onward ticket to London and New Orleans. He needed to pay the $150 fee for a 48-hour visa in local currency. He went to the Currency exchange counter and exchanged $500 U.S. into the local currency. He returned to the visa counter and paid his fees. His passport was stamped there and then again as he went through customs with his luggage.

Cabs were lined up when he stepped outside. He conveyed in English the best he could the name of his hotel. In a few minutes, the cab pulled up to the Hotel Bukhara Palace. Fortunately, the desk clerk spoke English. He set his clock to 10:00 a.m. local time. He had about forty-five hours to make contact with Jessie and get out of Dodge.

He took a shower and freshened up in his hotel room. In a few minutes, he began his walk to the Ark a little over a mile way. He wanted to walk to get the feel of the city and the locals. It was warmer than he expected. He saw a display that said 13 degrees Celsius. He knew that was in the mid-fifties, Fahrenheit. It was quite comfortable walking in the sun. There was the constant drone of call to prayer always in the background.

Then he saw it. A literal fortress surrounded by a large tiled area two-hundred feet or more across. He continued walking west along the south side of the sloped fortress walls. On the west side was the typical Islamic Arch main entrance, painted white and on each side a tall minaret. All along the south and west side of the Ark, there was a bazaar filled with people. Women in burkas, men in Islamic garb, children playing. He crossed the street to a wooded area along the west side of the Ark. He found a bench and just sat there staring at the impenetrable fortress that had withstood the attacks of a hundred armies over the years. "What the hell was I thinking? How stupid am I?" he thought to himself. He sank into complete despair. He wanted to cry but he fought back tears, lest he draw unwanted attention to himself. He sat there for a long while until finally, he had to eat something. He walked over to one of the many food vendors and found a Coke and something he thought he could actually eat. "How am I going to find Jasmine?" he thought.

He surveyed the area around the Ark. Men and women were playing both backgammon and chess, but gender segregated into two playing areas. Their tables were covered with long table cloths that blew in the gentle breeze. A teapot sat on each table, and the players sipped tea as they played. Bukhara had a long history of chess dating back nearly 5,000 years

He saw a group entering the Ark and suddenly realized you could purchase a tour. He searched for a tour-guide location and found one that offered English. He purchased a tour. The guide spoke a little English. They went inside the courtyard. Some of the online reviews he had read said the inside was run down and not at all spectacular. This may have been true a few years ago, but today it was clean and very spectacular.

People were taking pictures. Dan had his cell phone with him that was useless as a phone in Bukhara. It did have a camera and Dan took some pictures just to fit in with the tourists. During the tour, the guide spoke of Emir Abdullah and Princess Jasmine. The guide also spoke of Foreign Minister Nasrullah and Alim. They passed a gallery displaying portraits of all four of them. The tour guide gave individual information about them. It was the first time he had seen a picture of Alim.

As they were continuing thru the Ark, they often passed uniformed soldiers. Someone asked who they were. The guide explained they were members of the Elite Guard of the Ark and that there were 300 of them.

Toward the end of the tour, they passed another group of the Elite Guard led by a man in a long, white thobe with a white ghutra headscarf and a black, agal cord. The man caught Dan's full and undivided attention. It was the man that jumped him in Sydney. He was sure of it. Dan asked who the man was. Sure enough, the guide said his name was Al-Qadir Ravshan and he was an advisor to Alim. Dan was able to snap a picture discreetly. He had to be very careful not to be spotted by the man.

The tour lasted about forty-five minutes. Dan tipped the guide and learned he could remain in the courtyard, until late evening when it closed.

He continued to mingle among the vendors and shops. There was a contingent entering the main entrance. He strained to see as the crowd began to gather in excitement at their presence. He heard the word "Emira" being shouted out. He didn't really know what that meant, but he knew in his heart it was her. It had to be. He could see people throwing flowers and trying to hand her flowers, but still, he could not see her well enough to be certain. He was standing next to a flower vendor and suddenly realized what he should do. He quickly bought a few Arabian Jasmine flowers and plunged into the crowd elbowing his way to the approaching entourage.

It was the princess. It was Jessie, just as beautiful as he remembered. She was dressed in pure white with a scarf covering her head, but no veil. He could see her face clearly. As she came near, he shouted "Pikake for the Princess, Pikake for the Princess." The crowd did not even seem to notice what he said amongst the shouts of others. But she did. She had heard the word Pikake. She knew that Pikake was the Hawaiian word for Jasmine. She turned slowly, smiling reaching out and touching the hands of many in the crowd. She looked straight at him and reached out her hand as he thrust the flowers into it. For a moment, their fingers touched. He could feel the electricity of their touch in his soul. "Pikake for the Princess," he said again.

"Thank you, dear Sir, Mahalo," she replied. "May the Peace of Allah be upon you until we meet again," and she nodded her head slightly toward the southwest. He acknowledged and tilted his head toward the southwest and mouthed the word "trees." She nodded ever so slightly that she understood. To be sure, he immediately turned and headed southwest in the courtyard, although he had no destination inside the courtyard. He pointed beyond the wall and nodded.

He had done everything he had hoped for. All he could do now was to leave the Ark and cross the street and sit on a bench and hope she understood, hope she came. If not, he still had tomorrow.

Chapter 9

It was nearly dark and he had been sitting there for several hours wrestling with his doubts that she would come or maybe could not come. He saw a woman approach and walk past him. She was covered head to toe in a burka like a hundred other women he had seen that day.

"Dan," a voice said from under the burka, "follow me at a distance."

And he did. He stayed twenty feet behind her and suddenly she turned into the wooded area and disappeared behind a large stone structure. He didn't see where she went, "Down here," a voice whispered.

He followed the voice and slipped behind a stone panel that closed behind him. It was dimly lit from what appeared to be a candle burning along the wall, but it was an artificial light of some kind.

The woman threw her head covering off and there she was standing before him and she did not look happy.

"What on earth are you doing here? You will get us both killed," Jasmine said.

He put his arms around her and pulled her close. "There is going to be a wall between us until you kiss me. Kiss me," Dan commanded.

And she did. They kissed passionately for several seconds locked in an embrace. Jasmine pulled away "Okay. You made your point. The wall is down. Are you out of your mind?" she said tersely, trying to sound angry.

"Yes, I am," replied Dan. "Callie is here. She is being held in the Ark with all the other girls.'

"Are you crazy? How is that possible?" She demanded

"They were kidnapped by Alim and your Uncle Nasrullah for their harem. That's not all. They will eventually in the years to come be sold to others or sent to an underground studio within the Ark to produce sex tapes sold online all around the world. It is going on right now with hundreds of other girls. They have been kidnapped from all over the world. It is a multi-billion-dollar operation all from underground in the Ark," blurted out Dan.

"I know the Ark. I know every tunnel and secret passage in the entire fortress. It's not possible," said Jasmine.

"Maybe you did five years ago. Maybe they have added others," said Dan.

"Well, I can find them if they are here. I can find them," she said. Jasmine wanted to believe him but she wasn't convinced. How well did she really know this American? He may have descended into a deep grief over the loss of his daughter that had made him irrational.

"There's more, Jessie. There is more," said Dan.

Jasmine sensed a change in Dan's tone. He was already serious, but he was even more serious if that was possible.

"What is it?" she asked, almost fearing the answer.

"Your brother, Adil. He is alive and is being held in the Ark as well, in a deep dungeon called Zindon prison."

"I know that place. It is actually outside the Ark, 200 meters to the northeast. It is just a tourist site now," protested Jasmine in apparent disbelief.

"No, Jessie, he was traded by the Israelis as you told me. The trade happened and Adil did not die. Nasrullah and Alim have kept him prisoner all these years," said Dan.

Jasmine just slumped into Dan's arms for a moment. "Praise be Allah," she said. "Give me the strength and wisdom to find my brother."

Jasmine composed herself almost immediately. "Come with me," she said, as she took Dan's hand and led him down the darkened corridor. Dan's eyes had adjusted to the darkness now and he could see pretty well. Jasmine had a small flashlight. They walked for a long time until Jasmine finally stopped. "This is different," she said. "This tunnel was not here before. It led only to the Zindon Prison outside the Ark." Cautiously, she started down the corridor. They approached an area where, to the right, hundreds of pinpoints of bright light pierced the upper part of the corridor. She tried to peer into one of them but she just couldn't get her eyes positioned correctly. They were sounds, too, a lot of sounds. They passed several other corridors that forked off in different directions. Jasmine turned down one and the light got brighter. There was a door with light seeping all around it. Carefully, she slowly cracked the door. The light was bright. No one seemed to be around. They slipped through the door and found themselves on a catwalk twenty feet above the floor below. It was a huge lighting grid with hundreds of lights shining down on the area below.

"This is your studio, Dan," she whispered.

Indeed, it was. There were dozens and dozens of mini-studio sets open on one side. Nearly all had a bed but some were other scenes. One could have easily been a hay barn in Iowa or a ranch in New Mexico. Another looked to be a Munich beer hall. All the studios had one thing in common…sex. There were nude women and women engaged in every form of sex imaginable and a video crew and cameras taping it all. Over to the left, they could see a bondage scene, with a young girl bound to a stockade being violated on both ends with men lined up to take turns. A man cracked a whip on the girl's back whenever she offered the slightest hesitation or resistance.

Dan tapped Jasmine on her shoulder and motioned her back towards the door. Once back inside Dan asked, "Are you okay?"

"Yes, yes, it is more than I imagined, but yes. We must be careful. Let's find Callie and Adil." They made their way back along the corridors. Dan was confused sometimes about which way they had come. Jasmine never seemed to the least bit lost. When they arrived back at where the new area began, Jasmine headed down a different corridor. "This tunnel should take us to the Bug Pit," Jasmine said.

"Bug Pit?" Dan thought, but he wasn't going to ask. The tunnel was especially damp and dank, obviously quite old. Jasmine slowly slid a rock to the right and peered in for a moment, then slid the rock farther, and they both stepped into what could only be described as a dungeon. The smell was unbearable. The pit was covered with an iron grate. There was a ladder descending into the pit. It had a hinged barrier across it blocking anyone trying to climb up the ladder from below.

Jasmine pulled out her flashlight and shined it down into the pit. There was human figure down there lying on his back. He was clothed in rags. A few rats scurried into small holes in the bottom of the pit. Jasmine gasped.

"Allah, Allah, give me strength, Allah," she said.

"Adil, Adil," she whispered loudly to the man below. "Adil."

He did not stir. Jasmine picked up a small handful of pebbles from the dungeon floor and carefully, one at a time, threw them at the man that was perhaps twenty feet below. He began to move and opened his eyes and looked upward.

"Adil, Adil." she said "Is that you and then she muttered something in Tajik.

The man mumbled unintelligibly and weakly and could not be understood.

"Adil, Adil, it is Yasi Min, Adil."

The man seemed to find a new strength in his voice. "Sister, is that you?" The man said softly in English.

Dan tried to stop her but it was no use. She disengaged the contraption at the top of the ladder and Jasmine began climbing down into a virtual cesspool below. "You stay," she said sternly and handed him the flashlight.

Dan pointed it toward the steps as Jasmine made her way down, There were insects crawling all over the ladder. She practically screamed but swept them away and continued one step at a time.

"Brother, Brother, what has Allah permitted?" said Jasmine.

"Alim and Nasrullah, they put me here. I don't know how long I have been here, forever I think," said Adil. "What are you doing?"

"I am coming to you." she said.

"No, Sister," Adil said sternly. I am covered in lice. I have sores all over me from the insects and rats. I have worms in my legs. You cannot get me out of here without preparations, Please, Sister, listen. Allah has forsaken me long ago, and I have forsaken him," said Adil.

Jasmine stopped. She couldn't bring herself to continue into the abyss after hearing his words. His wisdom was correct. There was no way to rescue him now. "Okay, Brother, not now, but soon, I will come back for you."

"It does not matter, Sister, just seeing you and hearing your voice before I die is more than enough for me," Adil said.

"You are not dying on me or Father. You two are all I have," protested Jasmine.

"I have a son," blurted Adil. "I have a son and a wife in Israel, Adonijah is his name. Sister, you have a nephew."

"Adonijah is a Jewish name!" Jasmine replied, "Is your wife a Jew?"

"No, Sister, she is a Christian Arab. Her name is Farah. She visited me in the Israeli prison. Just find her and help her and my son. I can die in peace if I know you will do this. Promise Sister," pleaded Adil.

"Yes, Adil, I promise, but first we save you," She started back up the ladder in defeat.

Dan helped her off the ladder. They repositioned the ladder device. Dan helped her brush the bugs and filth out of her hair and from her gown. They slipped back through the tunnel and moved the rock back.

"What am I to do?" asked Jasmine. I cannot tell Father yet. He will alert the guard and the whole fortress will be in conflict. I won't be able to find Callie and the girls. I must think," said Jasmine.

Dan just listened with relief. He had been afraid Jasmine would forget about saving the girls when she discovered her brother. He should have known better and was angry with himself for even thinking she would forget the girls.

"We will go to my room to think and plan," said Jasmine.

She led Dan through a maze of secret tunnels until once again she slid a stone back and they were in her quarters. It was a magnificent suite to rival the most luxurious hotel. It had a balcony that looked out upon the Ark courtyard below and another that looked out beyond the walls of the Ark. Her bedroom had a large, four-poster, king-size or larger bed. There were a couple of servant's quarters off of her room. Each with a private bath. "We will bring him here," she said. "We can take things to clean him as best we can and disinfect him before we bring him up. I have servants I can trust with my life. They will help."

"Dan, you must go. I will continue to look for the girls tonight and get Adil moved up here," said Jasmine.

"Okay," said Dan, as he showed his phone to Jasmine. "Do you know this guy?"

"Yes," said Jasmine. "He is one of Alim's advisors, Al-Qadir Ravshan."

"This guy tried to kill me in Sydney," said Dan. "I didn't connect the incident with you until I saw him this afternoon."

"This is not good," said Jasmine, "but I am not sure what it means. If Alim can connect you and me, then both of our lives are in danger."

Jasmine guided him back to the secret entrance across the street in the wooded area. "Get, rest Dan. I will come for you in the morning and we will continue to search," she said.

"Here, Jessie, take this," said Dan.

"What is it?" asked Jasmine.

"It is a jump drive with special encryption software so we can communicate by e-mail. I have created an e-mail address for you and you will see mine when you open it. You do not have to load anything onto your computer. You can launch the program from the jump drive. Send me a test e-mail before morning so I know it is working." said Dan.

Jasmine sighed, "Okay." Without either realizing it, they both leaned into each other for a brief kiss, as if it was the most natural thing in the world.

Dan looked around carefully and slipped out of the tunnel. The rock closed behind him and he walked the thirty minutes back to the hotel.

Jasmine returned to her quarters and summoned her most trusted servant, Kaliq. He was an ethnic Tajik and was loyal to Jasmine and her father. He had been with the Emir for many years and had known Jasmine since she was a child.

Jasmine explained that an American she knew in Hawaii was in Bukhara. He had given her information that led to discovering Adil in the pit. She also told Kaliq that Al-Qadir Ravshan had attacked the American in Sydney and tried to kill him. Kaliq was an extraordinarily wise man.

"Al-Qadir Ravshan is a very cruel man," said Kaliq. "He takes sadistic pleasure in preparing condemned women for stoning. If he knows anything of you and the American, he is a threat to your life, Emira."

"I know," said Jasmine.

Kaliq summoned additional servants that were loyal to the princess. Two men and two women. They were all ethnic Tajik. Dan was not mentioned, but Jasmine shared her discovery with them. They were appalled and immediately sprang into action. In a few minutes, they returned with lice disinfectant, soap, DEET insect repellant, clean clothes, several gallons of water, a Red Crescent stretcher, a rope and a pulley. They all followed Jasmine to the Bug Pit.

Kaliq went down into the pit and rigged the rope to pull Adil up. He then guided Adil from below on the trip up the ladder as the others hoisted him up. Jasmine took pictures. One day soon she would show her father what Nasrullah and Alim had done to Adil.

They removed the rope and pulley and replaced the ladder guard and slid the stone back. They extended the wheels on the Red Crescent stretcher and were able to slowly maneuver Adil through the tunnel. They brought Adil to one of the servant's rooms in Jasmine's quarters, and the women went to work cleaning him up, disinfecting him and treating his wounds.

Kaliq asked permission to speak. "Yes, Kaliq?"

"Emira, Alim will come looking for Adil in the pit or the jailer will make a routine inspection. We must do something to prevent them from knowing he has escaped."

"What can we do?" she asked.

"I would ask that you leave that to my discretion," said Kaliq.

Jasmine instinctively understood that Kaliq wanted to spare her knowing the details. She realized it was best if she didn't know.

Kaliq left immediately and took Adil's clothes with him. He tracked down Al-Qadir Ravshan in the Ark. This man bore a resemblance to Adil. Within the hour, Kaliq had taken Al-Qadir barely alive to the pit, cut out his tongue, covered his hair and beard with lice and put the same tattered clothes on him that Adil had worn. He injected him with a drug that would keep him quiet for days. He was left at the bottom of the pit alive and largely unresponsive. From twenty feet away, his own sister would not have known it was not Adil.

Dan slept well at the Hotel Bukhara Palace. He had a plan to get the girls out of the Ark, but he had no plan to get them out of Bukhara. He prayed for guidance.

In the morning, he checked his encrypted e-mail. There was a message from Jasmine. It was not a test. It said her brother was very sick and had Guinea worms, and it is a wonder they did not kill him when they moved him. She did not know what to do.

"Oh shit!" muttered Dan. A week ago, he would have known nothing of a Guinea worm, but after researching Bukhara he knew now. It was a worm that could be three feet long inside the leg of the victim. If not removed properly the victim could die or suffer serious infection and other complications. Jasmine said she did not know what to do. She could not call for a physician.

Dan e-mailed Johansohn and waited for an answer as he took a shower and got ready to walk to the Ark. The answer came within fifteen minutes. There was an Orthodox Jewish doctor in Bukhara who was willing to help. He gave Dan his address. Dan e-mailed Jasmine that he knew someone in Bukhara that could help and to await further instructions. Dan took a taxi to the man's house in the Jewish section of Bukhara. He was indeed Orthodox, in the traditional black suit and the payot curls on the side of his head. Dan explained the situation in detail. The doctor was already willing to go to the Ark, knowing it was a great risk.

They went back to Dan's room and he e-mailed Jasmine to meet him and the doctor in the wooded area. She e-mailed back almost immediately. They took a cab and were dropped off near the Ark. The two men discreetly slipped into the entrance when the stone slid.

Jasmine was there with her flashlight "A Jew!" she said in total surprise.

"Yes, Princess I am a Jew and I will show you how to save your brother. It is a lost skill that 100 years ago any physician in Bukhara could have performed, but not now," replied the doctor in English.

Jasmine just muttered, "Dear Allah, how much more will you require of me?"

The doctor entered the servant's quarters and found Adil on his back on the bed. "My Lord," he said, "the Bug Pit leaves its mark."

He carefully examined Adil all over. He pulled out a scalpel. "Son, this will hurt but anesthesia is of little value for you. You will be experiencing a fiery pain as the Guinea worm is removed." He made three small incisions in one ankle and two in another. He removed five small round stick-like devices from his bag. With his forceps, he dug into the incisions one at a time and pulled the end of a white worm from Adil's ankles. Five of them, each a little larger around than a piece of cooked spaghetti. He began to wrap each worm around one of the sticks. He massaged the area above the wound and poured hot water on the worm.

"Watch carefully," he said to Jasmine and the two female servants. He began to tug very carefully at one of the worms and it began to come out slowly. Adil writhed in pain for every millimeter the worm was pulled. "Now, try it on the others," he said. Jasmine tried first and removed less than an inch. The two servants tried with about the same result. Jasmine tried again on the fifth worm.

"Careful. Yes, careful, very good," he said to each of them as they worked at the delicate task.

"That's all there is to it," the doctor said as he closed his bag. He left the scalpel and forceps. "Every twelve hours do this just as you did. Do not hurry. If you can get two or three centimeters then be satisfied. You must be patient.

"This is called dracunculiasis, named for a fiery dragon of pain while being extracted. If you pull too hard, you will break the worm and leak high levels of foreign antigen, which can lead to anaphylactic shock and the fast death of your very sick and weak brother," the doctor said calmly.

Jasmine understood. She and the servants had all heard of it. It was thought to have been eradicated long ago from Bukhara. Adil would have gotten them from whatever disgusting and contaminated water he had consumed in the Bug Pit.

"How long will this take," asked Jasmine.

"It depends on the length of the worm, at four to six centimeters a day two weeks, three weeks, maybe more maybe less. No one knows. Just be careful and patient," said the doctor, as he handed her two medicine bottles. "Give him two of these to ease his pain if required. It will make him drowsy. This one should be put on his sores and bites. You can get any antibiotic at an apothecary shop."   One of the servants immediately gave Adil two of the pills and began applying the antibiotic.

The doctor pulled an IV container set from his bag. He set up a makeshift IV pole and inserted the IV into Adil's left arm. "Keep him hydrated, I am sure you can come up with additional IV bags where you get the antibiotics," he said.

The doctor picked up his bag and headed toward the tunnel entrance and said, "Now get me out here, every second I am in this place I am in danger."

Jasmine guided the doctor and Dan back to the entrance. She was a mass of conflicted emotions. Just before the doctor slipped out, Jasmine said, "Thank you, Doctor. My grandmother used to tell me when I was small that the Jews and the Muslims were cousins. Shalom Aleikhem." The doctor smiled and said, "Aleikhem Shalom. Your grandmother is very wise."

Jasmine was truly grateful, and yet, when she smiled it was obviously forced. "Princess," began the doctor as his eyes locked on to hers, "Today if you hear His voice, harden not your heart, Psalm 95. My child, I have seen your father at times in Registan Square. He is a good man at heart, not like your uncle. Princess, your father is being slowly poisoned to keep him weak. Get me a sample of his blood and I will find an antidote, if one exists."

Jasmine just stared at him dumbfounded. A lifetime of hatred in her heart for Jews and yet, this man had already saved her brother's life and now revealed the likely cause of her father's debilitation. Her mind and her heart battled to make sense of what was going on around her.

She muttered once again, "Shalom Aleikhem," and the doctor replied, "Aleikhem Shalom," and exited the tunnel.

Dan and Jasmine returned to her room. Adil was resting comfortably now.

"I looked last night for more passages to no avail," she said, "Let's go again," and they did.

They searched many of the passages with no success. They came across different entrances to the studio lighting grid, and the non-stop video production continued every time they peered at the scenes below. After many hours, they gave up for the day and returned to Jasmine's quarters.

She looked at Adil and a little more of each worm had been wound on the stick by the servants while she was gone.

"I am sorry, Dan, that we did not find Callie. There are many more places to search. I will find them if they are here," said Jasmine.

"They are here," said Dan. "My source is reliable. The studio is here, your brother was here. Callie and the girls are here. I will be back before March 8th with a plan. Let me know when you find them."

"And you trust your source that much?" said Jasmine with a bit of disdain.

"I could tell you more, but your mind is closed," responded Dan.

"I know who your source must be. I do not need to hear it said, and I do not even want to think about it," said Jasmine.

Jasmine guided Dan back to the entrance. She stepped out with him. Are you sure that's not too dangerous?" he asked. "The way I am dressed, no, and she pulled a hijab over her head and walked with him staying a proper distance from his side.

They walked through the bazaar as the vendors hawked their wares. There were posters everywhere about the International Women's Day events. Dan could not read them. They were in Arabic or Farsi or Tajik or Uzbek or who knows what thought Dan.

Dan could only pick out the words International Women's Day and March 8.

"I and my staff book all the entrants into the parade and other events. We have women and girls coming from all over the world wearing the traditional clothing of their countries. Many Middle-Eastern women will be wearing ornate burkas and hijabs, of which they are very proud. We will also have delegations from Asia, Europe, Africa, the Americas and the Pacific Rim," explained Jasmine. There will be a march from the Ark to the Sports stadium."

One poster caught his eye and Dan just stared at it in disbelief.

"What do you know about this group?" asked Dan.

"It is the Japanese Dance Troupe. They travel all over the world doing traditional Japanese dance and dance from other countries. They are quite good. I have seen them in Paris," said Jasmine.

"And I have seen them in Sydney," said Dan triumphantly.

"How will they get here?" asked Dan.

"I think they are doing Tashkent or Almaty next, so it could be rail but probably by air. They have their own Japan Airlines

747. I booked them. I can check the details if it matters that much," said Jasmine.

"Oh, it matters greatly, my love," said Dan. "This is how I will get all the girls out of here. We just have to get them to the airport."

"What did you say?" quizzed Jasmine.

"It matters greatly." said Dan.

"It matters greatly, MY LOVE!" said Jasmine.

"It's just an expression, a harmless term," replied Dan.

"Yes, a term of endearment and here in Bukhara that could get us both executed. I know another American expression, you need to watch it, Bub," said Jasmine.

They had come to the corner, and Dan decided to walk the mile or so back to the hotel. They parted without touching or doing anything that could draw attention.

"See if you can get the tour schedule of the Japanese Dance company," said Dan, as he turned and headed east toward the hotel.

He slept well. He arose early and was at the airport by 6:30 a.m. While waiting at the gate area he picked up the brochures of several Bukhari official tour companies and other local hotels. Next trip he might have to stay farther out toward the airport, to be sure, and be outside the security perimeter. When he boarded the British Airways plane and the flight attendant greeted him in the King's English, he already felt like he was home.

Jasmine awoke early, as always. She had not slept well. She had gotten up and checked on her brother several times. She just sat and watched him for a while. He looked horrible and yet, compared with how he looked the day before, the change was astounding. She pondered why she could not find Callie. What was she missing? Finally, she called for Kaliq to arrange for a helicopter.

She told her father she wanted to visit some of the people outside Bukhara living in the rural areas. The helicopter was ready for her just to the north of the Ark. She told the pilot to leave slowly and circle around the Ark so she could see the people below. He circled twice as Jasmine studied the outline of the Ark. She could see the faint scar of recent excavation. The perimeter of the walls had been extended to the east. She could see now that the entrance to the Zindon Prison was now connected to the Ark Walls. There was a much larger area to the east, inlaid with ornate tiles that was not inside the Ark walls. An entire neighborhood to the north was gone and covered with tile outside the wall, while an even larger neighborhood to the east was now inside the walls. There were divisions in the walls along the far east. There were at least two partitioned courtyards with large pools. She pointed to them and asked the pilot in Uzbek what they were. "It is the harem of Alim and Nasrullah," replied the pilot. "I am not permitted to fly over it."

"I understand," replied Jasmine. "I hadn't noticed it before. It is new?"

"Yes, built in the last few years since your father's return," he replied.

Now, she was confident that she knew why she hadn't found the girls. They were somewhere in the new construction. She had the pilot sit down in a small village a few miles outside Bukhara. Many in the village ran out to see her. The people loved her and told her so. They spoke of hope for a new and better life now that she had returned. She toured the village and accepted the invitation of some to enter their homes. In one home, two small girls were lying on a bed clearly in pain. She went and sat beside the girls.

Their private parts were bandaged just as she had seen so many times in her youth in Sudan. She could hardly contain her anger. She wanted to scream, but instead she said, "You have purified the girls?"

"Yes, just this morning," said the old grandmother with a toothless grin.

Jasmine placed her hands on the girls and hugged and kissed both of them and said a prayer to Allah in their language. Both girls managed a weak smile, as if proud that they had endured the pain and wanted the princess' blessing. Deep inside Jasmine was bursting with anger. She had failed these girls. She had failed herself. She had failed her grandmother who had protected her from this brutal savagery.

How could she ever save all the young girls from this fate when their own mothers and grandmothers proudly perform the butchery themselves? What life-changing event had brought her grandmother to not only challenge the hideous practice but to find a way to minimize the effects of the mutilation on her own granddaughter? Jasmine knew her grandmother took her to Paris and had the procedure performed by a French surgeon. She knew that much to Nasrullah's displeasure, Jasmine met the technical requirements of the custom, even though she was not visibly mutilated in the way all the other girls were. Nasrullah had lost his own daughter to the heinous act and despised Jasmine even more for her survival.

Jasmine went straight back to the helicopter. During the flight back, as they approached the eastern part of the Ark walls, she studied the terrain carefully as they landed. She summoned Kaliq.

"Can you get me the construction drawings of the new wall and harem?" she asked

"Of course, Emira," Kaliq said and he left.

Jasmine entered the tunnels again and went to the new area. She kept her compass bearing as best she could. If there was a secret entrance, it should be along here but it was not apparent to her. She was confident that the architects would remain true to the original construction of the Ark and have created a secret way into the harem. But then, she also knew they may not have known of the existence of all the tunnels that she knew so well.

She returned to her quarters and checked on Adil. His color looked better already. He had been connected to an IV by the servants. She also went to check on her father. He, too, was on his daily IV treatment ordered by the doctors, when suddenly it hit her. Poisoned! Jasmine knew how to draw blood. When no one was in her father's room, she drew two vials and stored them in the refrigerator of her quarters, along with one of her father's IV bags.

She then checked on the information on the Japanese Dance Troup and sent it all to Dan, along with her discovery of the new harem courtyards. She left out the harem part and just mentioned the courtyards to the east. She asked Dan to arrange for a rendezvous with the Jewish doctor, to accept the sample of her father's blood and one of his IV containers.

It was several hours before Kaliq returned with a jump drive. She put it in her computer and began searching the drawings for clues. The studio was easy to find, as it was built adjacent to an existing tunnel. The Architects seemed unaware that the existing tunnel also connected to a network of other tunnels deep inside the Ark. She studied the drawings for a long time and could not find any secret passageway. She got out a calculator and painstakingly began to add up dimensions of walls and hallways and rooms. There were some that did not add up. Then she knew. Certain walls had to be several feet wider than the drawings indicated. She marked up the drawing on her computer carefully examining each wall and highlighting the discrepancies. When she was finished she had defined an elaborate group of tunnels running within the new addition. Now it was time to explore as she did many years ago.

She had printed out some of her marked-up drawings to refer to while she searched for the tunnel. She was convinced of where it had to be. Finally, she stumbled upon the way to open the new tunnel. She stepped inside. It was only about four feet wide. She carefully paced off distances as she walked. She marked her turns with a small chalk mark, barely noticeable, lest she get lost like she used to when she explored the Ark. She came to the area she suspected, and carefully slid open an exit. She was behind a fountain in the pool area.

She watched for a while. It was the harem. A diverse array of women frolicked around the pool entertaining themselves in the absence of their master. They were all races and ethnicity. She saw no sign of young blondes from America. She made her way to what she believed was the other courtyard. Again, the exit was hidden behind a fountain. She watched carefully.

She could see dozens of girls, all white and all blonde. This had to be them. She was so excited she could hardly remain quiet. She studied the attendants to the girls and their dress. She could hear that the attendants spoke English to the girls while serving them. She made her way back to her quarters and waited until evening. She dressed as one of the attendants to the girls. She fixed her hair the same way. She returned and slipped into the courtyard in the darkness. She hid until she spotted the girl she believed to be Callie. She waited until Callie wandered off by herself. This was dangerous. If Callie reacted in the wrong manner, it would be disastrous. She approached Callie carefully

Callie was looking up at the sky to the southwest. Jasmine looked up to see what she was looking at so intently. It was the constellation Orion.

Jasmine broke the silence "My child, we call those stars Al Jabbar."

Callie turned and looked at her startled. "I know it by a different name. How do you know which one I was looking at," said Callie somewhat sarcastically.

"Child, may I tell you a story? But you must remain quiet. You must not react. You must just listen and remain quiet. Can I trust you Child? Our very lives will depend upon it," said Jasmine.

"Sure, suit yourself. You don't need to be so melodramatic," replied Callie.

You are looking at Al Jabbar. In ancient Muslim astronomy, he is known as 'Al Jabbar', the giant. In Greek mythology, you know him as Orion. You must remain very quiet, Child, and guard your emotions. In Indiana, your grandfather and father taught you about the constellations."

Callie turned sharply, her eyes widened, "How do you know what I was taught?"

"Quiet, Child, quiet. Maintain your composure. Can you do that?" Jasmine asked.

Callie nodded her head yes.

"Orion was always your father's favorite, even from when he was a small boy. He used to tell you and your sister that if ever you got lost, just like Orion, he would circle the globe hunting for you for all eternity until he found you again," said Jasmine.

Tears began to form in Callie's eyes, but she maintained her silence as she stared into Jasmine's eyes.

"You have your father's eyes, Callie. He was here yesterday and he will be back as soon as he can to get you and all of the girls. He told me where to look for you. Something only I could do. Now I can tell him I have found you," said Jasmine.

"You cannot tell anyone, not any of the other girls. Do you understand? Not anyone."

"I can keep the secret. Who are you?" asked Callie. "How do I know you are telling me the truth?"

"I am Princess Jasmine of Bukhara. That is where you are."

"Oh, you have got to be kidding me," scoffed Callie. "Jasmine? Jasmine? What is this, a Disney movie? Can't you just summon up Aladdin and a magic carpet and fly us all out of here right now?"

"You have your father's smart mouth," said Jasmine. "My actual name is Yasi Min. Your father sometimes calls me Pikake. You can call me Jessie if that helps."

"No, Jasmine, I want to believe in the whole, new-world fairy tale, complete with a beautiful dark-skinned brunette, a regular Aloha Princess. Way to go, Dad," said Callie.

Jasmine's eyes widened. She blushed but there was no way Callie could see that.

"I must go now. Follow me," said Jasmine.

Callie followed her to the fountain entrance. Jasmine took one of the flowers at the entrance and said, "If you see a flower broken and, on this ledge, then I am here waiting on you. It could be days before I can return. If we miss each other look for a note. Do you have access to anything electronic? asked Jasmine.

"Yeah, it's a regular Apple store here. We have DVD players and iTunes players and DVDs out the wazoo," said Callie.

"Good to know," said Jasmine.

As Jasmine was about to slip into the tunnel, Callie suddenly dropped all pretense of skepticism and put her arms around Jasmine and held on for dear life and said, "It's been so scary. It's been so scary. Thank you, Princess Jasmine. Thank you. I'm sorry I was so smart with you. Tell my dad I love him."

"I will," said Jasmine, as she slipped into the tunnel. Jasmine took a few steps and then began to sob almost uncontrollably. There was a still and quiet voice deep within her. This voice so often came to her when she was in the deepest despair. She could hear it now. She wanted to believe it was her grandmother trying to comfort her. Whatever it was, it worked. "Allah," she said, "how much more will you require of me?"

Callie watched Jasmine go. She composed herself and wiped her tears. Callie looked up at Orion and said, "Thank you, Jesus."

Chapter 10

Dan landed in New Orleans on a Saturday evening before Mardi Gras. He picked up his rental car and drove over the Huey Long Bridge and came into Gretna the back way. There was no way he could have gotten a room in downtown New Orleans this close to Mardi Gras. He stayed at a La Quinta Inn on the west bank about a mile from Algiers, very near the Crescent City connection bridge. He had stayed here many times before. He checked in and freshened up after the long flights from Bukhara, Heathrow and Miami.

He wanted to drop into the bed right then, but he went online and found the number of the New Orleans expedited passport agency. He called the twenty-four-hour line and made an appointment for Monday morning. He looked at his watch, 9:30 p.m. Central. He could be in the French Quarter by 10:00 p.m., still early for a Saturday night during Mardi Gras week. Parking would be a bear, so he had a cab called for him.

The cab took him over the bridge and sailed through the toll tags lane. He had the cab drop off him off at Canal and

Bourbon Streets. He walked into the French Quarter past the Royal Sonesta Hotel and the Desire Oyster Bar. The crowd was thick and drunk. Even if someone passed out, there wasn't room to fall over. He never ceased to be amazed at the Milwaukee-school-teacher types who looked up at the men and couples lining the French Quarter balconies. They tempted the women below with a few strings of beads.

Sure enough, up went the normally timid girl's blouse, showing off her bare breasts to hundreds of people whom she did not know. The flashes of cameras were going off capturing the moment. Then her reward, a few strings of beads thrown to her from up above that she could have bought for a dollar in any store lining Bourbon Street. Then there was the smell, that unique blend of dried urine, vomit and beer. It was the hallmark of a good time on Bourbon Street.

He made his way beyond the Maison Bourbon, his favorite jazz joint in the whole world, better than Preservation Hall in his opinion. The street vendors would shout at him and others, "Betcha I can tell you where you got dem shoes," they would say. Inevitably, some sucker would bite and lose his ten or twenty dollars.

Now, he was approaching what he considered real evil - Marie Laveau's House of Voodoo at 739 Bourbon Street. Just another block or so. The crowd was a bit thinner this far up, but the spectacle was more provocative. A man standing in the middle of the street was sucking the head of his own penis as onlookers hooted in approval.

"Oh my God!" he thought to himself, as he forced himself to go forward and into the bar full of patrons that were definitely not his type. They stared at him. A couple of guys smiled at him and a few got closer to him as if to make a move on him.

He slipped into the back room. It was an orgy. A mass of huge bare breasts, bare asses and penises were everywhere. At least, the ones you could actually see. Most of the penises were sliding in and out of the various orifices of the participants. One thing was missing and that was vaginas, at least naturally created ones. You could see several that some well-meaning surgeon had attempted to craft for its owner. There was a lot of noise and music.

The music was loud and ironically appropriate; the frenetic organist was pounding out a familiar refrain, as the vocalist joined in for the final words.

There is a house in New Orleans
They call the Rising Sun
And it's been the ruin of many a poor boy
And God I know I'm one

Dan went up on stage where the band was playing. As the song came to an end, he motioned them to stop. They complied and he grabbed the mike. "Ricky Gibraltar," Dan said loudly as his words resounded throughout the bar. "Major Ricky Gibraltar is your sorry ass in here somewhere?"

The bar became so silent you could hear a pin drop, except for a few who were so near another orgasm that their moans also penetrated the room as well as other places.

A beautiful feminine face popped up out of the sea of flesh. The mascara around her eyes had been smeared and her lipstick was all over her cheeks, although it might not have been hers.

"Danny Boy," she said in a sultry voice, "What brings your straight, white, Christian ass into a place like this?" She shouted to the band "Band, play Danny Boy!"

The band started playing "Danny Boy" and the crowd cheered.

"Ricky, I need your help, I need your help bad," pleaded Dan.

Ricky stood up. She made her way through all the flesh. Her perky 36D breasts bouncing as she did so, and her penis was at full attention. Ricky motioned for the band to stop playing. Ricky got to the mike, "As you were," she said to the crowd. The band started playing and the orgy continued.

Ricky motioned Dan into another room and closed the door, where at least they could carry on a conversation. Ricky slipped on a robe.

"What is it, friend, what's wrong?" asked Ricky.

"You look good, Ricky. The operations have clearly gone well so far," said Dan. "If you were just a few years younger, you would be a cinch for Miss America, as long as the swimsuit wasn't too tight in the crotch."

"What is wrong, Danny? You told me you would never come to this place again in a million years. What in the hell is wrong?" demanded Ricky in her soft feminine voice.

"It's Callie," began Dan, but he couldn't continue. His voice cracked and a huge and painful lump closed off his throat and his eyes began to tear up.

Ricky put her arms around him and pulled him close to her chest. His cheeks were pressing against Ricky's breasts. "There, there now, Baby," she said.

Dan's voice returned, "I don't think this is helping, you son-of-a-bitch." Dan pulled away and told Ricky the highlights of what had happened in rapid fire succession.

"I see," said Ricky, as she listened intently to every word Dan had uttered. He understood why Dan was here.

"You need a squad of Special Forces T-Girls to take the Ark," said Ricky, "kill some sadistic pornographic slime and get 275 girls safely to the airport, assuming you can get the damned 747 in on the plan, and then return to the festivities and blend in as a bunch of harmless, frolicking broads."

"Yes, that's pretty much it," said Dan. He sort of chuckled when he heard how absurd it was when said out loud. "Does it matter? Navy Seal, Army Ranger, Army, Marine or Air Force Special Forces?" asked Ricky.

"You know it doesn't. Whoever you pick is fine with me. I have no such skill or judgment for such things," said Dan.

"Okay," said Ricky. "I'm staying at the Royal Sonesta. I should be up and around by 2:00 p.m. Meet me at the restaurant R'evolution Bienville Room for breakfast."

"Okay, Ricky, see you then." Dan walked the four blocks over to Decatur Street and got a cab at Jackson Square, went back to the La Quinta, got into bed and fell sound asleep.

He awoke and looked at the clock. It was almost noon. He had slept for a much needed eleven hours. He showered and got ready. He checked his encrypted e-mail and read two messages from Jasmine. The first explained her suspicions about the new addition to the Ark walls and her plan to find a tunnel to the two courtyards. It also contained all the information on the Japanese Dance Troupe. They were touring in Europe. He scanned the cities: Frankfort, Paris, Vienna, Prague, Budapest, Riga and Istanbul. Bukhara was on March 8, then Tashkent and Almaty in Central Asia. Dan would have to study this later to determine the most practical city to connect with Mr. Toguchi.

He opened Jasmine's next e-mail. It was simple. "I have found her and all the girls. I spoke with her. She knows you were here. She said tell my dad I love him. She has your eyes."

"Praise the Lord, Praise the Lord!" exclaimed Dan. "Thank you, thank you. It is all coming together with your guidance."

He took a cab to the Royal Sonesta. The crowd along Bourbon Street was nothing compared to the night before. He entered the restaurant. He looked around and saw a beautiful woman with light brown hair, nicely dressed in a designer gown with plenty of cleavage exposed.

"Ricky, you're looking good," said Dan as he sat down.

They both ordered eggs benedict and orange juice.

"Danny Boy, you are a fine figure of a man." She looked around at some of the other women. "Ooh, they're jealous that I am with you and they're stuck with their sourpuss of a husband. Except that girl over there, her man is a generous sugar daddy."

Dan didn't bother to look.

"Danny, I been thinking about your plan, you have a huge hole in it that isn't going to be viable," said Ricky.

"What part?" asked Dan with great concern.

"You cannot get 275 girls, especially the littler ones to walk 1.2 miles to that stadium and keep them all together. You are going to lose some of them. No matter how hard you train them. You don't have that kind of time. As soon as they hit the open streets of a Muslim city, they are going to be petrified. It will all fall apart and there is no second chance," said Ricky.

Dan sighed. He was always confident Jasmine could get them out of the Ark and that he, with Mr. Toguchi's help could get them from the stadium to the plane in the buses. Those were the two really hard parts he had thought.

"Danny," began Ricky, "it is always the thing that you figured would be the easiest that blows the operation. I don't know how you planned to keep them together as one group for over a mile. I am already recruiting some other former Special Forces T-Girls for this operation. Instead of a dirty dozen, we will be the glamorous dozen. Clean-cut beautiful women with big tits. When these Muslim dudes see us getting off the plane their eyeballs will pop out with lust. Those men have no restraint you know. They are idiots. They see a girl's ankle or her bare shoulder, they cream themselves right on the spot. Repressed sons-a-bitches."

"Ricky, do you really think this can work," asked Dan in a moment of doubt.

"Of course, Danny Boy," replied Ricky. You must never forget the V.I. Warshawski principle."

"What's that?" asked Dan.

"Never underestimate a man's ability to underestimate a woman," replied Ricky with a beautiful smile on her face.

"Oh, I see your point," said Dan.

"I already have enough forces lined up. You would be amazed at how many want to go back and take out these Muslim degenerates, who have taken so many defenseless women in bondage. Part of the deal, Danny, is after we get your girls out, we pick our time and take the studio and free all those sex slaves too. We won't move until all your girls are safe. You can then warn your princess, and she can get her brother and father somewhere safe."

"Danny," continued Ricky, "we know these websites. We have done a lot of checking on them since last night. They all seemed to be working out of Southern California, Hollywood, Glenview or Studio City. They're not. They are all fronts for the Bukhara regime, just as the Oasis stores are. They are devoted to one thing and one thing only, the debasing of women, sex slavery and Internet web porn. We are going to kill the mothers and let Allah sort them out."

"Do you all have passports?" asked Dan ignoring what Ricky had just said.

"This is not our first rodeo, Danny. We not only have current passports, we have them in our names that can also be feminine, you know like Ricky, and we have them showing our gender as female. Those are the only girls I contacted," explained Ricky.

"I should have known. I just didn't expect you to be this far along so quickly. I should have known," said Dan.

"We still need to work out a lot of details. Do we come as our own group, or do we come somehow associated with a fictitious group of 275 girls, or better yet, somehow associated with your Japanese group," said Ricky.

"I don't know?" said Dan, "I haven't thought that part out yet."

"We will be working on it. I think we need some floats, maybe three or four of them to carry the youngest girls, and the older girls can walk along and we can keep them corralled and not lose any of them. Ask your princess if she has any flatbed wagons, and we will build the floats when we get there, if there is a place we can work. Another thought is we can mess with their minds. Across the river, here on the west bank, is Algiers. I am thinking we could come as the Algiers Kreole Krewe and make it look like Mardi Gras or Carnival," said Ricky.

Ricky continued to think out loud. "One group of 275 girls is just too many. No one country will send that many girls except your Japanese Dance group that is performing. We need to change their hair color. They can't go out as blondes. Maybe we could have a Balkan group and vary their costumes, Gypsies, Bulgarian, Hungarian, Serbian and Macedonian. Girls with dark hair and have a Balkan theme to the floats. I just am not sure, Danny."

"Here," said Dan, as he handed Ricky a jump drive. "On this is encryption software. Just follow the instructions. I have created an e-mail address for you, and you will see mine on there."

"I'm very impressed, Danny," he said with a smile.

"Okay, let's toss the details around later," said Dan. "I will go to the passport office tomorrow to get my passport renewed and then to the Bukhara Diplomatic Mission to get my visa. I will also get you money for your charges. Somehow, I have to figure a safe way to pay for your tickets. It's going to be a chunk of change."

"Okay Danny Boy," said Ricky, as she signed the check and put it on her room. She got up and wiggled her rear across the room as many of the men tried to sneak a look at her as she went by.

Dan returned to the west bank. He got in his car and went to a nearby Walgreens that he saw from the cab. He got several sets of passport pictures. He remembered a nearby church he had once visited. He thought they had an evening service. He went in and sat near the back. He took in the power of being among believers as they sang in praise and worship. The pastor delivered a sermon relevant to Dan and probably a hundred others in the congregation. He left the service with a renewed and strengthened spirit. He stopped at the mall next to the La Quinta for an Italian meal at Semolina's and then returned to his room.

In his room, he downloaded all the U.S. Passport forms and a copy of the Bukhara visa form that he already had. He filled out all the information on all the forms and printed them out in the lobby.

He rested in his room for a while, watched some television and went to bed.

The next morning, he went to the passport office on Canal Street as soon as it opened. Even with the appointment, he had to wait over an hour before he was called to speak with a processor. He explained that he needed a multiple entry visa to Bukhara and that he could not get one with less than six months on his existing passport. Normally there was a requirement that the applicant provide a travel itinerary showing travels plans in the next fourteen days before a passport renewal would be expedited. They waived that requirement upon seeing that Dan had just left Bukhara forty-eight hours ago and had a 48-hour visa in this passport. He was told he could pick his passport up at 2:00 p.m.

He walked over to Riverwalk and spent his time walking around the mall. He passed a store selling international cell phones and ended up buying a large-screen, quad-band smartphone that claimed to work everywhere including Japan and South Korea. He got ordered a shrimp po-boy in the food court and sat outside to eat on the terrace along the Mississippi. He watched the river traffic and the traffic crossing the bridge.

At 2:00 p.m. he picked up his new passport. He then walked the five blocks to the Bukhara Diplomatic Mission housed in an office building along St. Charles Avenue. He made arrangements with an official Bukhara tourist agency while he waited. It was three hours before he emerged with a multiple-entry visa and the proper Bukhari papers affixed to his passport.

He went back to the hotel and went online to check his American Express account. He had spent over $8,000, and he was going to have to find a way to get it paid before the end of the month. When he opened up his account transactions they were paid. He couldn't believe it. It was all paid. Who would do that? The Israelis maybe or Ambassador Krewe at the State Department. He looked at the dates and saw two payments. As he studied them, he realized the first was right after he charged the ticket from Honolulu to Sydney to Harare. A second payment was after that. Then, he realized. It was Jasmine. Only she would have known his need that early. She must have gotten his card number while they were in Maui.

"Praise the Lord!" he said. "He was going to have to charge $25,000 or more to get tickets for Ricky's T-Girls. He didn't know how he was going to pay that one, but he didn't care. He was okay for now. He booked tickets for Prague to intercept Mr. Toguchi. After Mardi Gras, everyone would be leaving on Wednesday. He decided he would leave early in the morning, the day of Mardi Gras. His connection was in Miami.

Dan hated early-morning flights. It was Fat Tuesday and Dan's plane took off from New Orleans at 6:00 a.m. The passenger next to him was reading the Times-Picayune. An article caught Dan's attention. "An Oasis survivor found." He was both dumbfounded and scared to death that word had gotten out about Ilsa. When the passenger folded up the paper and tucked it in the seatback, Dan asked and opened it up to the article.

It was a Hawaiian girl, Lani Kealoha. She had been picked up by a yacht off of a small island south of Bimini in the Bahamas. She had been taken to Freeport. Authorities had not interviewed her yet. The NTSB was coming to interview her, and her parents were arriving today from Honolulu. "Oh Shit," Dan thought, "I have got to get there and keep her from blowing the rescue." Not only that, her life was in danger. Nasrullah and Alim would have to silence her before she could reveal she was never on the Oasis plane.

Dan landed in Miami and went to the American Airlines Admiral's Club. He explained that a personal emergency had caused him to delay his trip to Prague. He needed to go to Freeport and postpone Prague a few days. It was not a cheap ticket change but they arranged it all for him and rerouted him and his luggage to the Bahamas.

After he had his changed ticket, he began looking at flights from Honolulu the evening before. It could have been Delta or American the best he could tell. The earliest the parents could get there was 10:45 a.m and as late as 6:00 p.m. Dan's flight arrived at 2:42 p.m.

When Dan arrived Freeport and cleared customs he got a cab to the hospital. He spoke with the hospital desk and learned Lani's parents were not there yet. He told them he was meeting up with Lani's parents. He positioned himself in a waiting area where he could keep an eye on everything. He just waited and grabbed some unsatisfying food from a vending machine.

More than three hours passed and he saw them.

"Kahekili! Kahekili!" shouted Dan.

"Dan, Bruddah what are you doing here? Lani is alive!" exclaimed Kahekili.

"That's why I am here. Have you spoken to her yet?" quizzed Dan.

"On da phone when she called last night and told us she was here," answered Kahekili.

"Has the NTSB or other authorities interviewed her yet?" asked Dan.

"No, no one has. The hospital won't let anyone talk to her until we get there. The NTSB is coming sometime tomorrow," said Kahekili.

"How is she?" asked Dan.

"Well, she sounded pretty good to us," said Kahekili.

"Kahekili, you can't let anyone interview her yet. My daughter is alive also. If Lani talks, Lani's life, my daughter's life and the lives of all the other survivors will be in immediate danger." said Dan.

"What you talkin' about man?" Lani is the only survivor.

"Let's step over here where we can talk in private," said Dan. Dan told Kahekili and his wife the highlights of the whole story. Kahekili shook his head in disbelief.

"One of da things you are telling me is they tried to kill Lani because she was not a haole?" asked Kahekili.

"That's my theory. They only wanted the white, blue-eyed blondes. All the other girls were just cover for their plan," said Dan.

"I get it Bruddah, I get it," said Kahekili. "Let me think. How much time do you need for me to keep her from talking?"

"March 8," replied Dan, "but you have to take her some place no one can find her 'til then."

"Well, dat's not dat far off," said Kahekili. "You know we are outside U.S. jurisdiction, and da NTSB has no official power here. I think Lani needs some time to recover before she speaks with anyone after such a trauma, don't you, Bruddah?" Kahekili said with a twinkle in his eye. "We have friends in Trinidad."

"If she is up to it, I need to hear her story." said Dan.

Kahekili nodded, "You can come with us to the room."

As they turned to go to her room, there were some reporters with cameras wanting to talk to him. Dan motioned him to refuse, but it was too late.

"I want to thank da hospital staff here for caring for Lani," said Kahekili, "and da people on the yacht who rescued her. We are glad dat she is alive. She was pretty much out of it and we haven't been able to speak with her much. She knows dat her muddah and I were coming as fast as we could."

The reporters chimed in, "We thought she was in good shape with no serious injuries."

"You read dat in the papers or hear it on TV?" asked Kahekili.

One reporter said, "The early reports were that she was fine."

"Where did dat come from? I don't know dat. They didn't tell us dat, and we would like to have some peace. Mahalo," said Kahekili.

"Has the NTSB spoken with her?" asked a reporter.

"No one has spoken to her including me or her muddah, and no one is going to until I say so," said Kahekili, and with that he walked off from the reporters.

Kahekili turned to Dan and said, "How did I do?"

"You did great."

Dan followed Kahekili back to the hospital administration desk and listened as Kahekili instructed them that absolutely no information whatsoever should be released about Lani's condition to anyone and that included the NTSB. "This is my kama'aina friend from the Big Island, and he is helping me with Lani," said Kahekili.

Kahekili turned and walked back toward the patient area and motioned Dan to come along. As they got to the door where his wife was waiting, Kahekili turned to her with tears in his eyes and made sure that everyone watching could see them.

Dan walked into Lani's room. She was sitting up smiling and looked good.

Both parents hugged her and tears were in all their eyes. After a while, Kahekili pointed to Dan.

"This is Dan Grainger." He has a daughter on the Oasis flight, and he was in Maui with me when we both first heard about the crash.

"Who is your daughter?" Lani asked.

"Callie, do you know her?" asked Dan.

"Everyone knows Callie, Mr. Grainger. She has a strong personality and we all loved her. I am so sorry," replied Lani.

"You don't have to use the past tense, Lani. She is alive as well as all the girls who were actually on the flight, but you weren't on the flight were you?" said Dan.

"No, Mr. Grainger, I wasn't on that plane and none of the girls who have been found were either," said Lani. "The Oasis plane did not go down the way they said."

"I know that. Have you told anyone else that you were not on the Oasis plane?"

"No. The people that picked me up did not speak English. When I got here and they started talking about me surviving the Oasis plane crash, I knew something was up. I wanted to tell my makuakane first," said Lani.

"Lani, I have explained to your dad you cannot tell anyone anything about what you know or experienced. It has to remain a complete secret until March 8. But I would like to hear what happened, if you don't mind telling it," Said Dan, "and I am so sorry but I need to record it."

Lani looked at her dad, and he nodded okay.

She told Dan and her parents all she knew about being taken to some kind of a warehouse. She described it the best she could remember. "I know we drove mostly east," she said. When she got to the part about the girls being drowned, she broke down uncontrollably as she described how they struggled. She explained "I just held my breath when I was forced under the water. They fished us out of the tank and put us into seats. I played dead the whole time. They put us on a plane. They put life vests on us. Later, when they dumped our seats from the back of the plane I unfastened my seat belt and safety vest and threw it off on the way down. I dived the way I have my whole life. I was afraid I would hit too hard if I had the vest on. I held my breath again as I hit the ocean, and it stung so much. I hit with such force. When I surfaced, it was dark but I could see some of the other girls floating in their seats. I checked on them but they were all dead. She started to cry. "I took the life jackets off three of the girls. I'm sorry."

"I found two seat cushions and I had three life jackets. I was able to get some of the metal pieces from the debris floating around. I used it as a knife when I caught fish. I saw some search planes but they never saw me. I was able to drink a little from the rain. After a couple of days, I could see lights at night to the northeast. I just kept working my way towards them. I was afraid the current was going to take me right past it, but it didn't. I never made it to the lights. I came across a small flat island before I came to them. So, I just stayed there on the land. I figured sooner or later a ship would come along. I was able to catch fish and there was some kind of a grape tree that I ate for fruit and used for shade. I would drink the water off the leaves when it rained. I made a bowl out of twigs and leaves so I could catch some water when it rained. Finally, one day, this yacht passed by and I caught their attention. They picked me up and took me to some town on another island, Port Royal, and they brought me here."

"Have you told anyone else this story?" asked Dan.

"No," she said.

"Lani?" asked Dan. There were two little African-American girls."

"Yes, Keisha and her little sister, Kara. They didn't make it. We were the last three that were alive," Lani said. "Strange thing, though, there were these four Black guys, really dark skin, and they didn't speak English, but Keisha could talk to them in some other language. We all thought for a minute that was a good thing but it wasn't. They took the two of them into another room for a few minutes," Lani hesitated for a moment, looked at her father and then her mother, and continued, "they raped them, even little Kara. I could see through the door, and they were laying on the floor bleeding. One of the men came out with Keisha and carrying Kara. I could see their underwear still laying on the floor. That's when I knew they were going to kill us," and her voice trailed off.

"After I came up from the dive. I checked to see if any of the girls were still alive, I came across one of the Black guys floating in the water. I am sure he was dead but I didn't check," said Lani.

Kahekili and his wife sat and listened to her story in horror. Lani's mother kept a tight comforting embrace around her daughter as she had told the story.

"It is a miracle from the Lord that kept her safe," said Dan totally amazed at her story.

"Da Lord protects all of us who believe, Danno." said Kahekili. "She has my Maui blood, and on her muddah's side from Waikiki, she is a Paoa cousin with the same bloodine of Duke Kahanamoku."

Dan was speechless. He was absolutely amazed that Lani was descended from swimmers and divers that were among the greatest in the entire history of the world.

Kahekeli and his wife remained silent for a moment and then the concerned father said "Let us pray," and the three held each other tightly as Dan watched and listened.

"Heavenly Father," began Kahekili, "we thank thee for this day, and thank thee for the moisture we have received." Dan was suddenly very interested in the prayer as Kahekili asked for blessings to nourish and strengthen our bodies and he spoke of Almighty God as the fountain of all wisdom. Kahekili ended with "Bless that we will travel home in safety. In the name of Jesus Christ, Amen."

Dan was moved and he sure needed a fountain of wisdom to figure out what the Lord expected him to do next.

"You are Mormon?" asked Dan.

"Yes," said Kahekili, "We attend regularly in Lahaina. But we often go to Temple at Laie. I teach a class on Polynesian studies at the University. I also host island LDS Church history tours leaving from Ka'anapoli."

Suddenly, Dan knew how to dress the girls in the International Women's Day Parade. "Not just Hawaiian?" asked Dan "You teach about other Polynesian cultures like Maori, Tahiti, Fiji and Samoa?"

"Yes, and Marquesas and Tonga, but we refer to Maori now as Aotearoa," replied Kahekili.

"We need floats, Kahekili," began Dan, "Polynesian theme floats. One larger, one for all the younger girls, and a couple of smaller ones.

"How about a 2/3 replica of the Hokule'a?" asked Kahekili.

Dan's mind was racing and his spirit was dancing, but first things first he thought. "We have got to get Lani out of here. Is there any place you can hide out in the Caribbean?" asked Dan.

"I have family in Trinidad," said Kahekili.

"That would be perfect," said Dan "Now, how can we get the Polynesian gear?"

"I know people, Danno," replied Kahekili, "No problem. I can get costumes for all da girls - Hawaiian, Fiji, Samoan, Tahitian, you name it. Just tell me where to ship everything."

"Okay, give me some time to think and work something out," Dan said, as he bolted from the room.

He sat in the waiting room online, and after a few minutes, he returned to Lani's room.

"Okay, I have two plans. Tell me which one you are willing to do?" said Dan.

"I can put you on a plane to Nassau," said Dan "and then on Air Canada connecting in Toronto to Vancouver. You can stay in Vancouver outside U.S. jurisdiction until March 8, and after that, it's just a six-hour flight to Honolulu."

"Canada, dat's cold Danno," replied Kahekili.

"It's about 55 degrees this time of year," said Dan.

"Dat's cold, Bruddah, what you got dat's warm?" said Kahekili.

"I thought you would say that," said Dan. "How about a cruise? There is a ship from Fort Lauderdale that is docked in Freeport. We can get you there tonight and you can set sail tomorrow. It goes on to Curacao, Bonaire and then Trinidad. You can get off there and stay until the 7th and fly back to Honolulu from there."

"How 'bout a cruise, Mama?" asked Kahekili. "Both Lani and her mother smiled and nodded in agreement."

"Okay, I will go confirm the booking," said Dan. "You tell the hospital you are leaving this evening with Lani. There should be Wi-Fi on the ship. It's expensive but we need to stay in touch. Send me an e-mail once you are on board to this address." He handed Kahekili a note. Create a phony e-mail address once you are on board with Yahoo, or Google or whomever."

The hospital offered no resistance to Lani leaving. Dan had a driver waiting and he took the family to the harbor and watched as they boarded the cruise liner. The driver recommended a hotel close to the airport where Dan could find a room on short notice. Once in the room, he called the American Airlines Platinum desk and booked himself back to Prague. From the Bahamas, he had an American Airlines flight in the morning at 11:30 to Miami, then British Airways to Heathrow and on to Prague. He would arrive by noon the next day.

Dan called John Kosten in Indiana, told him about Lani, and said he would be sending him an audio file with her story. John was glad to hear from him and said he would check with the Dade County Coroner first thing in the morning to see if they still had the bodies of the four Black men that had been recovered, and to see if they had saved samples of the water from the girls' lungs. Dan and John chatted for a while, then John did what he always did. He counseled Dan to remain strong and asked to pray for him over the phone. John always seemed to have the perfect words to say. Dan hung up the phone feeling blessed. He e-mailed the recording of Lani to John Kosten. He had an e-mail already from Kahekili.

He flipped on the TV to an old episode of "The Amazing Race." Dan chuckled as the couples were at some foreign airport trying to book a flight ASAP to some other obscure destination.

"I don't need that," he thought, as he clicked off the TV set.

Chapter 11

The Madison County Coroner was at his office waiting for two visitors. The first to arrive was Madison County Prosecutor Steve Foulke.

"Steve," asked Larry, "do you have any idea what this is about?"

"Obviously, it's related to the Campbell case," said Foulke, "but Kosten wouldn't tell me any more than that. He just said he had to see the two of us…alone."

There was a knock at the door and in walked John Kosten.

"Good morning, Gentleman," said John, as he opened up his laptop and waited for it to bootup. He handed them both a picture of a young girl "This in Lani Kealoha from Maui in Hawaii. You need to know that Lani's father is one of the world's best cliff divers and has taught his daughter well. Lani is one of the girls purported to have been on the Oasis plane when it supposedly crashed."

"Purported, supposedly," said Foulke. "What are you up to?"

"I need the assurance from both of you that what I am about to tell you will remain confidential until a certain event that we are praying for happens soon," said John.

Both men had known John Kosten for years and had never seen him this serious or somber about anything, except when he was actually in court. Both men nodded.

"The case against Sgt. Mark Campbell has two basic elements," said John. "The first is that the condition of the girls was caused by Sgt. Mark Campbell. We will show that assertion to be false at another time. The second element is that Mark Campbell had sexual contact with Keisha and Kara the day the plane left Orlando for Miami."

"Yeah, we know that, John. Do you have a point here?" said Foulke

"Take a seat, gentlemen," said Kosten, "and prepare yourself for an unbelievably tragic account of what actually happened to 24 of the girls believed to be on the Oasis 747. You are going to hear the voice of Lani Kealoha, one of those 24 girls, a witness who was present for 23 murders, two sexual assaults and her own attempted murder."

Crawford turned to Foulke with eyes widened and then back to Kosten and said "My God, John, what the hell are you saying?"

Kosten said nothing. He just clicked his computer."

The two men sat transfixed by the words they were hearing. Steve Foulke's eyes were full of tears. After a few moments, he didn't even try to hide it. Even the Coroner was shaken by what he was hearing. When the tape ended, there was silence for the longest time.

Finally, Foulke spoke, "What do you..." his voice cracked with emotion and stopped. "What do you need from us, John?"

"I need your strictest confidence for now," said John. "I need you to contact the Dade County Coroner and get DNA samples from the four Africans and compare it with the semen from Keisha and Kara. I need you to find an expert on seawater and have an analysis done on the seawater recovered from their lungs compared with seawater that would have been present in the area of the Atlantic near the Fowey Rocks Lighthouse. I need you to see if there is any Dade County Coroner reference to underwear being present or absent on Keisha and Kara when their bodies were recovered."

"Hold it," said the Coroner.

"What is it?" said Foulke.

"I gave Merriman a copy of everything sent by the Dade County Coroner, and I told her myself that there was no underclothing or shoes on the bodies when recovered."

"Merriman knew that!" said Fouke.

"Yes, the shoes I could understand," said the Coroner, "but the other seemed a bit odd, especially since they were strapped in seats when found. It would have been reasonable to believe they weren't wearing any that day."

"And Merriman knew this?" said Foulke again.

"Yes, we discussed it and she knew it," said the Coroner

"Well, she didn't tell me," Said Foulke. "Is there more you need John?"

"Yes." began John. "I need the legal statement of the ship's captain who said the four men fell overboard during salvage operations. When the semen samples come back as a match for one or more of the men, I need you to ponder how that's even possible. How can four men that fell overboard from the ship be a match to girls still strapped in their seats that fell from a 747 and drowned in the Atlantic? This strongly implies the captain of the ship is involved in this deception. And finally, Steve, I need you to open a criminal inquiry into the Oasis corporate office in Carmel, asking for a complete disclosure of the selection procedure used to select the 300 girls. I have tried to get the information myself in a Motion for Discovery for a client I am representing, Annie Grainger, who had a sister aboard the Oasis plane. I have also taken on the Campbells as clients, three more families from Westfield in Hamilton County, and now one from Hawaii. Oasis has stonewalled me. I don't believe they can stonewall a criminal request from you so easily."

"I don't know. I will need to consider it," said Foulke.

"Look, Steve," said Kosten, "I know that Oasis collected DNA samples from every girl they selected and hundreds more that they were considering. I need those DNA samples."

Steve was just trying to absorb it all. He had so many questions but one surfaced first.

"John, it is one thing to request information on the selection process for Keisha and Kara, but the entire 300. How do I sell that one?" asked Foulke

"You say you are trying to determine if there were any specific racial or religious criteria for the selections and to evaluate that possibility you need all the information for all 300 girls selected and all the girls that applied," said John.

"Religious? You know more you are not telling me," Said Foulke.

"There is only so much I can tell you. If you poke around too much too soon, you will endanger the lives of," he paused "let's say up to 276 girls whose bodies have not been recovered."

"You're trying to tell me those girls may still be alive and you expect me to remain quiet!" said Foulke. "That's a lot to ask."

"There is a lot at stake," said Kosten. "I need your help on timing. We are gathering a lot of evidence to prove my client is innocent. If the 276 girls were to suddenly be found that will prove he is innocent. On the other hand, if those girls remain where they are, then the evidence in Campbell's case will go public in a big way. This will provide a second opportunity to save the girls if the first plan fails."

"So, you're holding back evidence that could exonerate Campbell?" said Foulke, "in an effort to safeguard those girls?"

"Mark Campbell insists upon it," said Kosten.

"He is risking his own life knowing he could be free?" asked Foulke.

"That's who Mark Campbell is," said Kosten.

"Yeah, I've begun to figure that out," said Foulke.

"At some point, not yet," said Kosten, "I will ask you to make an official call to Orlando law enforcement."

"Okay, but we can't sit on this too long," said Foulke. "We are talking about a murder scene in Florida for 23 girls."

"We don't know where the murder scene is." said Kosten. "If we reveal what we know without knowing exactly where the actual murders took place, it is possible all evidence would be destroyed."

"I see your point," said Foulke. "You don't really have enough proof."

"Two of my clients with relatives on the Oasis plane have insisted on using what they know to discreetly find the location of the murder scene. I have advised them not to, but there is no legal justification to prevent them from trying. They have promised to inform me if they find anything helpful. I will inform you if they find the murder scene so that you can call Orlando."

"Anything else?" asked Foulke.

"Yes, Merriman," said John.

"What about her?" asked the Coroner, Larry Crawford.

"I believe she was behind the attempt on Campbell's life," said John. "I have absolutely no proof whatsoever, except my gut, or in fact, it is my spirit that tells me that is the case. She is so irrationally convinced Campbell is guilty that she won't listen to reason."

"She is a nut job," said Crawford. "She cannot stand to be wrong about anything. Sometimes, I think she has something on some of the judges because it is like she can do no wrong in this county even when she is wrong."

"What do you mean?" asked Foulke.

"She can always get in to see most of the judges whenever she wants. I've never understood it," said Crawford.

"Steve, it sounds like someone else knows more than they're willing to say," said Kosten.

"Look, Larry," said Foulke, "you told me once you would like to see her taken down a notch. Do you still mean that?"

"Yes," said Crawford.

"Then tell me what you think you know," said Foulke.

"I have no proof, but I hear things," said Crawford. "She has power over some of the judges and some other key people, through her dealings with their children or grandchildren. She uses her power at CPS to bring trumped-up reports, or in some cases real reports of CPS issues. The problems magically disappear from official records or are resolved, if the judge or whoever plays ball. When she needs a favor, she gets it. If she doesn't get the favor, then the issue magically reappears, and the judges' grandkid is put in foster care, and the daughter or son is charged with child abuse, or at least an investigation has to be completed before the child is returned. When the judge or whoever plays ball, voila' the kid's back in the home."

"Now, I suddenly get it. I was aware of one single such story but did not realize there were so many others,' said Foulke. "Okay, all this is confidential, just between the three of us?

"Yes," said Kosten.

"Yes," said Crawford.

"I have a highly secret investigation underway into corruption in the Madison County Court system and Merriman is at the center of that investigation. John, you are right. Merriman did try to have Campbell killed, but I do not have enough proof yet to charge her."

"You can count on me for whatever you need, Steve," said Crawford. "This will be a labor of love."

The meeting ended and all three left with a lot to think about. Foulke returned to his office and drafted a request for the selection criteria and had it hand delivered to the Oasis office by the Hamilton County Sheriff Department. In it, he stated if the information was not forthcoming in forty-eight hours, he would file the request through the Court of Madison County or Hamilton or both, and that would make the information public.

Kosten went to see his client, Mark Campbell in the Madison County Jail.

"How you holding up?" asked Kosten.

"I am fine," said Campbell.

"I have to ask you again. Say the word and I go to the Court with everything I know, and I am certain they will have to let you out and drop the charges," said Kosten.

"We have talked about this before," said Campbell. "Until we know the fate of the other girls, I will stay here."

"There are a lot of new things we know now and we have some proof," said Kosten.

John briefly recounted how Keisha and Kara were murdered and the events surrounding their deaths.

"All that proves, John, is that I didn't touch my daughters and I already knew that. That would change nothing for me, except you would be one step closer to finding who is behind all this, and you're not telling me that."

"I had to ask," said John. "There is more that directly affects you. Merriman is the one that tried to kill you and I believe she will again. You are not safe here."

"I always knew that," said Campbell. "Still doesn't change anything. If she happens to succeed then all you have to do is break the stooge that got me and you will get her. Merriman has overplayed her hand. She has to get a conviction in my case to validate her entire career. She will get careless. If I am released before we bring her down, she will take Kima into CPS custody."

Kosten just shook his head in awe at this man's determination and willingness to sacrifice.

Campbell continued "There are a lot of crazies in here, especially after the couple of warm days a while back when all the protesters showed up at the courthouse and the jail to call me every name in the book. They arrested a bunch of them and now they're in here with me. I get called everything but a white man every day. There are a half-dozen skinheads in here that are as tough as nails. They never actually say anything. They just sneer and grin and everybody makes sure they don't cross them."

Kosten got up and went to the door. "I need to ask you the question again for someone else to hear," He opened the door and in came Steve Foulke.

The two men stared at each other. Steve could hardly look him in the eye when his thoughts turned to Cynthia.

"You can talk freely, Mark," said Kosten.

Steve Foulke did his best to look Mark in the eyes and said "If we can't get you out, we can get you moved to another county. There are things we can do to protect you from Merriman."

"She will just get me another way if I'm out," said Campbell. "Merriman is bad news. You should already know that. If you don't, just ask some poor, Black family or any poor, white family about her reign of terror at CPS. Or better yet, ask some rich, powerful family."

"Just what do you know?" asked Foulke.

"Just what's on the streets," said Campbell, "and that's plenty.

"I'm the bait," said Campbell, "Both of you need to understand. I am the bait and she is the big overconfident shark that just has to have me for dinner. She keeps circling and getting hungrier and hungrier. She can't help it. But all she is going to get is a bad case of indigestion. She's going to get careless. That's the only way I can get her. I am staying right here, Mr. Foulke, right here."

They both understood. Kosten left and Deputy Jenkins came in to escort Campbell back to his cell.

Foulke said, "I want to come with you."

Jenkins looked at him. "Okay," he said.

As Campbell entered the cell block the jeers began. The comments about Campbell messing with his daughters, the racial slurs became more pronounced as Jenkins walked Campbell back to his cell. Foulke followed a few feet behind. Then the spitting started. Most missed but some landed on Campbell's chest and sides. Through it all, Campbell kept his head up and never missed a step until he was back in this cell.

Foulke could sense the tension and hatred. It was palpable. There was no one lower on the inside than a child molester. Foulke looked around at the motley crew of men in the cell block with Campbell. In adjacent cells, there were several particularly nasty-looking skinheads. They weren't saying anything and hadn't done any of the spitting. They just grinned at the events.

Jenkins locked Campbell safely in his cell and Foulke and Jenkins left. Once out in the hall Jenkins motioned to someone and said, "You need to get a mop in there."

As Foulke left the newly remodeled jail he was more concerned than ever for Campbell's safety.

Mark Campbell had also assessed every new threat as he walked the path back to his cell. He had most of the inmates figured out, but the skinheads remained an enigma. They seemed to wholeheartedly support the widespread sentiment against him. Yet, they actually never said anything or joined in. They just watched. Mark was very concerned about them because he couldn't get a bead on them.

Mark became aware that Deputy Jenkins was standing near his cell just looking at him. Campbell caught the deputy's eyes and the two men just stared at one another for several seconds. The deputy seemed lost in thought.

"It's all such a shame," said Jenkins as he turned and left the area. When he returned to his office, he was surprised to see Shirley Merriman waiting for him.

"Bill, I am so sorry, the situation with your daughter has unexpectedly resurfaced. I had no choice but to send someone over to take her children into our protection."

"You said you would leave us alone after I did what you said last time," said Jenkins.

"I have to do my duty to protect the children of Madison County," said Merriman.

"What else do you want?" said Jenkins.

"You should be pleased that I have been able to keep the children together pending our completion of the Parental Assessment Process. They are with one of our finest foster couples. I have allowed your daughter visitation. I didn't have to do that," said Merriman.

"What more do you want?" said Jenkins.

"Have you made arrangements to transfer the list of inmates I gave you?" asked Merriman.

"Yes, I have put them close to Campbell's cell. They will be transferred to the holding area the same morning as his hearing," said Jenkins.

"And you understand what is expected of you the day of the hearing?" asked Merriman.

"Yes," said Jenkins, as he looked away from her.

"Well, I am confident that when we complete your daughter's Parental Assessment, we will arrive at the best outcome for all parties," said Merriman. "And then Bill, you can retire knowing that your grandchildren will be in a place that is in their best interest."

Merriman abruptly ended the conversation and left Jenkin's office.

Foulke had gone home and spent the evening going over court records with several judges and cases involving Merriman. The next day Foulke began making the rounds of judges. He just dropped in on them for a friendly discussion. He talked about the Campbell case a little. He would turn the topic to Merriman and watch their reaction. He would suggest wondering about some of her tactics and if they were ethical. By the end of the day, he had a gut feeling about judges she owned, judges that were scared of her, and judges that weren't. Judge Hardy was one he felt he could trust.

He approached Judge Hardy and asked for a court order allowing him to obtain Shirley Merriman's financial information, bank accounts and other documents related to her net worth. He gave Belinda the assignment of collecting the information.

The rest of the day, he focused on CPS cases. He became very familiar with all the players and procedures. He found numerous cases where a mother was under review by CPS but had her kids back. She was suddenly given a surprise inspection. Often, the children were again removed from the home because the apartment didn't have enough bedrooms and beds in the right ratio for the gender, ages and number of children. Foulke was not very familiar with these requirements. Skimming the guidelines, there seemed to be a fifty-square-foot-per-child requirement. A child that was not an infant could not share a bedroom with an adult. Each infant had to have an approved crib. Each child had to have their own bed. All of the guidelines had good intentions but their interpretation could easily be arbitrary.

He couldn't help but think of his own father. He was the youngest of nine children. They slept two and three to a bed or on the floor or the couch or wherever. According to the guidelines enforced by Merriman, they were abused and could be taken from the home.

How was a young, single mother with two girls and a boy supposed to afford a three-bedroom apartment, and in some cases if the age spread was just right, four bedrooms? They could get by on two if the mother or one of the kids could sleep on the couch, but that was not permitted.

Merriman's enforcement was clearly arbitrary. Sometimes the children were simply returned with no change in circumstances.

He then went to speak with Deputy Jenkins again. He told Jenkins that the preliminary investigation was uncovering a lot of suspicious anomalies. He told Jenkins to stay close with Merriman and keep her trust and not give her any reason to doubt it.

Jenkins reassured Foulke that he had already done that and that he would do what was right.

Foulke then went to see the doctor who had performed the examinations of the girls that attended Campbell's classes. Dan remembered the doctor's well-manicured beard.

"On the day of the examinations," asked Foulke, "did Merriman inform the girls that they had a right to refuse the exam and be examined by a physician of their choosing?"

"I never heard her say that," said the doctor. "I assumed all those details had been taken care of. Merriman said she had a court order for the examinations and she showed it to me."

"Did you read it closely?" said Foulke.

"No, I just took her word for it," said the doctor. "I will say that the school administration was vehemently opposed to the exams. I know they tried to contact the school attorney but couldn't reach him."

"How were you able to conduct so many examinations by yourself without some medical assistance?" asked Foulke.

"Merriman's a nurse," said the doctor. "She always assists whenever I do these exams. However, I have never in all my years done this many exams at one time."

"Merriman's a nurse!" exclaimed Foulke. "I never knew that. I've been in her office dozens of times. She's got diplomas and awards and shit all over the place. I never saw anything about nursing."

"Yeah," replied the doctor, "I saw her BSN diploma laying on her desk years ago. I don't know why she never hung it up."

"Did she actually say she was a nurse?" asked Foulke.

"No, but the diploma was right there in front of my face while we spoke about medical issues and physical examinations for abuse. She displayed a great deal of medical knowledge. She always has. It never crossed my mind that she was not a nurse," said the doctor.

"Really?" said Foulke "And so she is the one that actually touched the girls' genitals during the exam?

"It's uncomfortable enough for the girls with me being male. I avoid," said the doctor.

"Aren't the exams supposed to be private?" asked Foulke.

"We positioned the girls so that the others could not see any of the other girls' privates," said the doctor.

"Okay, thanks," said Foulke, and he left. He went back to his office and did an online Indiana Professional License search for nursing for Merriman. He got back zero results. He called HR and asked for Merriman's resume' and application from years ago to be sent to him.

Belinda entered his office and said, "You need to take a look at this."

Foulke began looking at Merriman's bank accounts "Holy mackerel!" he said, "She's worth over a million dollars!"

"It's all legal, Steve," said Belinda. "I have gone over all of her deposits and her Indiana tax returns for the last ten years."

"Where did she get all this money?" asked Steve.

"Speaking fees mostly and professional consulting fees," said Belinda. "She has reported every penny. I can't find anything that is not supported in her tax returns. When her mother died, she inherited a house free and clear. She sold it and bought the house she now lives in. Everything's legit."

"This is not what I'd expected. I thought there might be some kind of illegal or unethical activity," said Steve.

"She also gives about ten percent of her income to various charities, United Way, Planned Parenthood, Social Workers Across Nations, the Anderson F.O.P and others," said Belinda.

"A solid citizen all the way around," said Steve.

"Well, the people that work for her don't think so," said Belinda.

"Why do you say that?" asked Steve.

"I know several of the caseworkers in her office and I spoke with a few of them off the record. They do not like her at all.

They say she is just interested in the cases that make her look good. She takes cases away from the other caseworkers, if it's a high-profile case or if it involves some VIP or law enforcement family." said Belinda.

"Go on," said Steve.

"They wouldn't give me a lot of details but one thing is clear. No one who works with her likes her or respects her. This includes the Indiana Region 11 DCS Regional Manager. Merriman is plugged in somehow, and even he cannot control her," said Belinda.

"Very interesting," said Steve.

"One other thing." said Belinda.

"What's that?"

"Merriman has been selected this year to receive a Lifetime Achievement Award, and she will be inducted into a Social Work Hall of Distinction. I'm not sure if it's a state or regional association. It has not been officially announced yet. It is a huge honor in her field." explained Belinda.

"Is that like a hall of fame? asked Foulke.

"Exactly," said Belinda, "She has been notified, but it will not be official until the press release goes out. The ceremony occurs in May. One of her co-workers told me she has been more insufferable than usual lately because of it"

"Now that is really interesting. Thanks, Belinda."

After Belinda left his office, Steve looked up the criteria for the Hall of Distinction on the Internet. *"The Lifetime Achievement Award honors social workers who have made outstanding contributions to social welfare and the social work profession. Inductees to the Hall of Distinction have distinguished themselves by promoting a vision of how things could be better in their communities and followed their vision with consistent and concerted action for change."*

Foulke had a lot to think about. As he drove home that night, the old familiar curse came over him. He opened the glove compartment and pulled out his throwaway phone. He scrolled through the contact list trying to make up his mind who to call. He picked a number and sent a two-word text "Available now?"

In a few minutes, there was a reply, "Yes Bae."

Ten minutes later he was knocking at her apartment door. She was a well-endowed, natural blonde and, when she opened the door, she had nothing on but a smile. "Hey, Baby," she said. Steve quickly removed his clothes and laid some cash down on the table.

Thirty-five minutes later. Steve was back in his car on the way home. He just shook his head. "What the hell did I do that for?" he thought. He didn't even like her that much, but she was always available on short notice.

He was relaxed now and put the whole episode out of his mind and re-focused on his work.

Then it suddenly dawned on him. Merriman could not afford to be wrong, just as Campbell had pointed out. She made all her money being a well-known and well-respected child advocate. The Campbell case fit her narrative perfectly. This case was extremely high profile. If it came out that she was dead wrong and had accused an innocent man, her reputation would be tarnished. Her speaking fees and consulting fees would dry up. Her Lifetime Achievement Award and her induction into the Hall of Distinction would never happen.

Now, he understood why Merriman could not afford to lose.

Chapter 12

The Foreign Minister of Bukhara was Nasrullah Hassan. In the last five years, he and his son had developed a multi-billion-dollar enterprise within the Ark. Alim Hassan entered the special harem to observe the new American girls. He watched as they played around the pool and enjoyed the sun.

He would soon be slowly training the 275 American girls for his harem. He would be pleasured for a decade or more with them. When he chose to sell them he would net well over 27 million Euros. That was over 33 million U.S. dollars. He could add $200 million for the insurance claim on the crashed 747. It was a great business.

Alim Hassan entered the subterranean studio to make one of his regular visits and inspections. He walked past scene after scene of hard-core sex. Every imaginable ethnicity and race were represented in his productions. Innocent looking, young Latvian and Ukrainian girls were among Alim's favorites.

Alim had constructed an entire series of shabby-looking, mock restrooms that were used as gloryholes. These were among the easiest films to shoot. The customers viewing on the web selected the type of girl they wanted, Black, White, Hindu, Latina, East European, Filipino, Polynesian, Chinese, Japanese, Thai and so on. Then, the customer could select from the same choices for men to be serviced through the gloryhole trimmed in duct tape. You could pick participants of average build, petite build, large build and any combination in between. The choices were endless for one monthly fee.

Beyond the gloryhole sets were the bedrooms and living room sets. Again, any choice of ethnicities that could be imagined was available. One on one, one girl with many men or one man with many women, all were available for viewing online by subscription.

There were the sadomasochist bondage sets. Chains and leather devices hung from the ceiling and walls. Men and women dressed in leather attire acting out both in domination and submission. In many cases, it was not acting. Members with premium subscriptions had access to actual torture. It was always men torturing women or women torturing and inflicting pain on other women. The sex was brutal and the pain was real. Premium Deluxe members could direct the torture and the sexual action by clicking their mouse or entering a request by instant message.

Alim ran an exorbitantly priced brothel. Leaders and rich businessmen from all over the Islamic world were regular patrons. The occasional wealthy and powerful westerner also visited from time to time. Alim had assembled a high-quality assortment of women for his customers. He would often have western women kidnapped from their country of origin. Their fate was never known, they were just missing. On occasion, he even snatched the women of Europe's royal families.

All the women were carefully trained. Many of them were kidnapped when they were young and trained over a year or more to serve their masters. Some had to be quickly trained and were subjected to unbelievably brutal expedited training. The women were beaten on the soles of their feet so that no permanent marks were left on their skin. The women were completely broken. They were taught to never show one millisecond of hesitation in anything their master asked them to do. In fact, they were taught to anticipate every desire of their master and perform it expertly. If they did not learn these lessons and execute them flawlessly, they either died in training or in the snuff films.

The snuff films were among Alim's favorite exercises. His trusted assistant Al-Qadir Ravshan relished the opportunity of torturing and slowly killing the women in the snuff films. The exact method of death was usually directed by the subscriber on the other end of the Internet connection. Al-Qadir was the man who directed the selection and abduction of women around the world to be brought to the brothel. Al-Qadir had been missing lately and that usually meant he was on the prowl for a new addition to Alim's harem. Alim was never disappointed in the women Al-Qadir delivered to him.

As Alim walked through his studio, he came to the expedited training area. He sold these women for a quick and handsome profit. He stepped into one of the rooms. A prim and proper English woman was being subjected to the cane. She was crying in horror with each strike of the cane on the soles of her feet. She was begging the dominatrix to stop. She was pleading for an opportunity to please the master if only the pain would stop.

The dominatrix stopped and spoke to the woman in a calm and soothing voice. "You will be asked to do many things to please your master. He will ask you to please other men of his choosing. You must never hesitate, do you understand?"

"Yes, I will do whatever Master desires," cried out the woman.

"I know you will, my dear. I know you will," said the dominatrix. "But we must never allow you to forget the cane. If you remember the cane now, you will never have to endure this again. Just one more stroke, my child, one more stroke. The master desires that you ask for the last stroke."

"Will the master be pleased?" asked the woman with her British accent very evident.

"Yes, the master will be pleased," said the dominatrix.

"I wish to the please the master. I will do anything the Master desires. Please strike me with the cane one more time," pleaded the women.

Alim heard the whistling of the cane, and the woman cried out in agony for the last time.

Alim was pleased. He was also aroused. He left the room and found the old woman that was one of his most efficient trainers.

"The American red-head? Is her training complete?" asked Alim

The woman answered, "Yes."

"Bring her to my quarters," commanded Alim.

Alim returned to his quarters. In a few minutes, there was a knock at the door. "Bring her in," he said.

The door opened and two men escorted Rebecca Calloway into his quarters. She was brimming with excitement. "Master!" she said.

The men immediately left leaving Rebecca alone with Alim.

"How may I serve you, Master?" asked Rebecca.

Alim slipped off his robe and stood before her. She immediately removed her gown and dropped to her knees and eagerly began servicing him. She was ecstatic to have the opportunity to please him. She couldn't get enough of him as she caressed him and kissed every inch of his body. When he came, she eagerly consumed every drop not wanting to waste any.

"You have pleased me, Rebecca' said Alim.

"Oh, thank you Master," said Rebecca, almost unable to contain her excitement.

Alim did not penetrate her. He never did with those that had been through the accelerated program. It was one thing to be with a western woman who may have had a limited number of men in her life. He could overlook that in his twisted desire to dominate her while she was defiant. A woman who had been through the accelerated program had been ravaged by hundreds of men in a very short time. Alim would not risk that. His desires were satisfied by her total willing submission. There was no challenge or satisfaction in penetrating her now.

He much preferred training the girls slowly over the course of years, starting when they were young. They would be pampered and spoiled and he obtained great pleasure from the anticipation of watching them blossom. When he grew tired of them, they would be sold or sent to the studio.

Rebecca was older and had to be brought along very fast for a quick sale. He loved taking a prim and proper American or European woman, with their initial defiance, and then totally breaking them.

Alim told Rebecca to put on her gown. He got dressed and he told her to follow. He opened the door and she followed him down the hall. They entered another room. There several Islamic men in the room ranging in age from thirty to seventy.

"This is Rebecca," said Alim. "Remove your gown and display your exquisite beauty to my friends."

She did so immediately and began to slowly walk by each man and give them a very good view. She stopped in front of each man, she bent over, she spread her lips apart just as she had been taught.

"This one is a very-rare American redhead," said Alim. "She is a college graduate. You can see that she is truly a redhead. We have groomed her nicely and left her unshaven. We will shave her if you prefer before you take delivery."

All of Rebecca's years of training in the art of dance had been reduced to erotically performing for the pleasure and arousal of these men. Each man looked her over carefully but did not touch. That was forbidden. After several minutes Alim said, "We will start at 50 thousand Euros."

One man after another nodded as the price rapidly increased. After a few minutes, Alim announced "Congratulations, Your Highness, she is yours for only 115,000 Euros."

The other men quickly left the room, leaving only Alim, Rebecca and the man that had purchased her. "This man is now your master. He will be taking you to his country. It will please me, that you please him," said Alim.

Alim quickly left the room. The royal winner of the auction struggled to raise his thobe above his waist. Rebecca went to her knees immediately, smiled at the man and said, "Thank you Master."

Chapter 13

Dan's British Airways flight through Heathrow to Prague went well. He cleared customs, took a cab and checked into the Hotel Majestic Plaza near the city center and went to find Mr. Toguchi.

The Japanese Dance Troupe was performing three nights in Prague at the Rudolfinum, along the banks of the Vitava River. Dan walked in the main entrance and asked about rehearsal. He showed his ID and was directed to a Japanese group associated with the dance troupe. He asked for Mr. Toguchi and everyone suddenly became very alert. Dan gave his name.

In about five minutes Mr. Toguchi appeared in the hallway.

"Mr. Grainger," said Mr. Toguchi. "How wonderful to see you."

"Mr. Toguchi, I need your help," said Dan.

"I owe you great debt," said Mr. Toguchi. He looked directly into Dan's eyes. "The blessing of Buddha very powerful, has brought you great fortune." He reached into the jacket pocket next to his heart and pulled out the same small

Buddha he had tried to give Dan in Sydney. I have kept next to my heart. The Blessing of Buddha has traveled with you in search for daughter and will remain with you until daughter is safe with father."

"Thank you, Mr. Toguchi," said Dan, as he bowed slightly in his direction.

"Let's go to my office and you tell me how Mr. Toguchi can help."

They went to an office down the hall and sat and talked. Dan told him everything. Dan explained his embryonic plan.

"Your friend in New Orleans is right," said Mr. Toguchi, "Hundreds of young girls very difficult to take care of and move them. They have so many needs and require great care and planning. Mr. Toguchi understand now why use plane to go such short distance from Orlando when bus is more efficient."

"In Bukhara, we will arrive on a Japan Airlines 747 but will take train short distance to Tashkent. May I please offer you my 747? It would be great honor if you accept," said Mr. Toguchi.

Dan started to speak and then his voice froze and his eyes began to tear up. He struggled to say, "I don't know what to say or how to thank you, Mr. Toguchi,"

"There is no satisfaction greater than to save innocent life," said Mr. Toguchi.

"Now, I have idea. We have many costumes for young girls that reflect cultures from all over the world. You decide what you need and we will bring to Bukhara. We arrive three days before event on March 5. We also have materials to decorate all kinds of floats. Tell your New Orleans Krewe that they will have to adapt to what we bring. You understand?" said Mr. Toguchi.

Dan nodded in understanding and said, "We will be doing Hawaiian, Fiji, Samoan, Tahitian and Maori.

Mr. Togucci responded, "We have many music tracks of all cultures. Your daughter's friends all are great performers. I will select graceful, yet simple Pacific Islander routines for them to learn. Princess Hassan can get tracks and videos to them, correct?" asked Mr. Toguchi.

"Yes," said Dan. "She can FTP the large file and burn DVDs for them."

"Ah, yes," Mr. Toguchi smiled as he said "I learn so much about FTP and jump drives and CDs and DVDs after you saved performance in Sydney. Never make that mistake again. Mr. Toguchi rely only upon himself," he said.

"Now you go to hotel and rest. You need rest. You come tonight as Mr. Toguchi's guest. You rest mind during our performance." said Toguchi. Once again, it was not so much a suggestion as a command.

It suddenly sounded to Dan like a great idea. For the first time in as long as he could remember, he did not have a next step he could do now. He went back to the hotel and went to sleep.

He woke up at 6:00 p.m. The performance was at 7:30 in Dvorak Hall. He showered and took a cab to the Rudolfinum. An aide to Mr. Toguchi saw Dan enter the building and immediately went to him and guided him to the box seat with a great view of the stage. Shortly before the show started, Mr. Toguchi appeared and sat next to him.

The two-and-a-half hours were amazing. The girls did many traditional Czech, Slovak and Moravian dances. They did other European dances as well, such as the German Polka, waltz, ballet and even the Irish Jig, And, of course, a brilliantly choreographed Japanese dance. Dan found that he actually did relax a bit, at least for a little while.

Mr. Toguchi asked Dan to come back the following afternoon to pick up the audio-visual materials he was preparing. Dan waited in line to get a cab back to the hotel. He went online to check his American Express charges. They were huge. Almost $17,000 with his ticket changes to go to Freeport and the cruise. He couldn't worry about that now but secretly could not help but hope that the princess would keep footing the bills.

Dan's plan for rescue was still embryonic but his mind constantly turned over every possible permutation. The resources available from Mr. Toguchi, Kahekili and Ricky were invaluable, and their wise counsel was even more so.

It was still just late afternoon in New Orleans when he called Ricky. They briefly discussed the basic plan. He told Ricky of the Polynesian theme. Ricky told him not to worry about any passport and visa expenses, each of the T-Girls was handling that themselves.

Then Ricky asked a strange question. "Dan, did you have any problems with the Bukhara visa with your last name being Grainger?

"No," said Dan. "Why do you ask?"

"It took us a long time to figure it out," said Ricky, "but two of my girls were denied visas. After a lot of analyzing, we figured out that their last names were the same as two of the kidnapped girls' last names."

"You're kidding," said Dan, "Those bastards."

"We just submitted new visa applications with different passport names and altered the hair color of the girls. They were approved," said Ricky, "Then, just for the hell of it, we picked another girl's last name at random and tried an application. It was denied."

"No shit," said Dan. "Praise the Lord!"

"That's an odd reaction," said Ricky.

"Callie is listed on the Oasis records as Callie Brooks, not Grainger," said Dan, "That really annoyed me until just now. I guess the man upstairs knew what he was doing."

"Amen, Brother," said Ricky. "One more thing."

"Yes," said Dan.

"I want to be King Kamehameha. I look fabulous in red and yellow."

"Sure," said Dan.

"Mahalo," replied Ricky.

Ricky gave Dan the itinerary information on the airlines and Bukhara hotel. Dan pulled up the reservations online. It was $31,000 and change. Dan sighed. He called the international number for American Express and explained he was about to make a large purchase for a group event. It was no problem. The agent stayed on the phone as Dan completed the charge successfully. American Airlines and American Express, he loved them both.

He went to bed and slept well. The next morning, he checked out of the hotel and had them hold his luggage. He decided to walk through the Old City to the Rudolfinum. He walked first to Old Town Square to view the Astronomical Clock, and then on to the Charles Bridge and the statue of King Charles IV. A little farther north was the Rudolfinum.

He went to see Mr. Toguchi, who once again emphasized that he had costumes and props and a number of things at his disposal that he could bring on the 747. He gave Dan a special shipping address in Riga, Latvia for anyone needing to send additional items. Mr. Toguchi again offered Dan the Buddha. He saw the look on Dan's face and said, "I know you not take. I keep next to my heart until daughter safe." He placed the Buddha in his left breast pocket. He handed Dan two DVDs and two jump drives. "This is music, many kinds of music; you can create any program you may want. It is indexed by Pacific

Island and cultural customs." He smiled, "You keep backup copies safe and do not leave in boat. You promise?"

"I promise, Mr. Toguchi, I promise."

Dan took a cab to the Vaclav Havel Airport. While there he e-mailed Kahekili to ship the Hokule'a and other Polynesian props to Riga, Latvia by 2nd day air and gave him his DHL account number. He told him to e-mail back the drawings and specifications on the props. He boarded his Turkish Airlines flight to Istanbul.

Dan arrived Istanbul, cleared customs and purchased a $30 visa for arriving Americans. He took a cab for the thirty-minute ride to the Citadel Hotel on the banks of the Bosporus Strait and the Marmara Sea. Dan had no Turkish Lira only Euros and U.S. currency. The driver eagerly accepted a twenty-dollar bill.

Here he would spend the next few days before flying directly to Bukhara. Time to think, time to plan and time to pray.

Chapter 14

Annie Grainger was back in Orlando. Walking through the airport brought back painful memories. It was the last place she had seen her sister. She was on a mission that she alone had insisted upon. John Kosten confirmed that Mark Campbell's trial date was coming up on March 8.

Annie had learned that Mark steadfastly insisted upon remaining in jail until Callie and the girls were free. Someone had already tried to kill him once. His life was in danger every day he stayed in jail. Annie owed him. Mark's silence was preventing the world from knowing that the girls were still alive. That fact needed to remain secret until the girls were free. She decided to come back to Orlando to look for evidence to support Lani's story that someone else had molested Keisha and Kara. If she was successful, that part of the story could come out without revealing the girls were in Bukhara. Annie knew her dad had a plan to get them out, but they might not be out before Mark's hearing. Her dad had said, if she could find the drivers of the truck and the bus, they could prove that things were not as they seemed.

Mark's trial was at 9:00 a.m. on March 8 in Anderson. The girls would not be back in the U.S.A. yet. The best she could hope for was to know they were in the air clear of Bukhara airspace. Her dad had sent the audio file of Lani recounting the events surrounding the murders in the warehouse. Annie had listened to it several times and knew every heartbreaking detail. If her dad's plan didn't work, the publicity from Mark's trial was Plan B to make the world aware the girls had been abducted.

Annie had traveled to Orlando in the hopes of finding the warehouse and finding evidence that would prove some of the girls were never on the plane. The number of recovered bodies had risen to 23. Annie knew Lani was the 24th. The other 276 girls were on the 747. She needed to find something that would be helpful to Mark without letting the world know the girls were still alive somewhere.

She collected her luggage and headed outside. A few hours ago, she had been in the cold temperatures of Indiana. The warmth of the Florida sun was a welcome relief. There was just one small problem in her plan. She was under 21 and could not find a rental car. She needed someone to drive her around, someone as committed to her mission as she was.

Then she saw her ride. Jimmy Campbell was standing next to an old Ford F-150 extended cab with a camper shell. He took her luggage and stuffed it into the area behind the passenger's seat. She looked around inside the vehicle. It was familiar to her. Her dad used to have a Ford F-150 SuperCrew.

"Do you live in this thing?" asked Annie.

"Sometimes," said Jimmy. "I can't trust my car to make it the 500 miles from Atlanta and I can't afford a motel. My granny has owned it forever, from when we used to go camping when Dad was home on leave. It runs good and drinks gas. I left Atlanta last night and pulled over to sleep at a rest area."

"Well, we have rooms tonight at a La Quinta near the airport, you can get a better night's sleep," said Annie, as she handed him the driving instructions to the La Quinta.

In less than fifteen minutes they were at the hotel. Annie went in and paid for the rooms with her dad's American Express Gold Card that she had in her name.

When she came back to the truck, she said, "Did you bring a suit?"

"Yeah," said Jimmy.

"Put it on and meet me in twenty minutes," she said, "Here is your room key."

Jimmy pulled the truck around close to the rooms and helped Annie get her luggage. Annie headed to her room. Jimmy got into the back of the camper, retrieved his suit, and grabbed a few things to take to his room.

In a few minutes, they met back at the truck. "Where to?" asked Jimmy.

She handed him another sheet of driving instructions. "The bus company," said Annie. "You clean up pretty good."

"I'll try not to let it happen again. It's the only suit I have," replied Jimmy.

It took about thirty minutes to get there. Jimmy and Annie didn't say much to each other. Jimmy tried to pry out of Annie exactly what they were looking for, but she didn't give him much. Finally, he said, "Look, I need to know exactly what's going on here."

"I can't tell you everything yet, but this will help your dad if we are successful. Isn't that enough to know right now?" said Annie.

"I don't know. I don't see how anything down here in Orlando is going to help my dad in that hellhole Anderson," said Jimmy.

"Then why did you come?" snapped Annie.

"Cynthia said I had to," replied Jimmy.

"What does she know about it?" asked Annie.

"I told her you called me and wanted me to come down and drive you around Orlando and that you said it could help prove that dad's innocent," Jimmy replied. "She said she didn't know you, but she knows of you and she trusted you and to just do it."

"Then listen to your sister. I will tell you more if it becomes necessary. There is a lot at stake here if we are successful," said Annie.

"I still don't get it," protested Jimmy.

"Well, ponder this," said Annie, "if we can prove that your dad was not the last Black man to have access to your sisters, then the case against him falls apart."

They pulled up to the bus headquarters before Jimmy could ask another question.

"You stay here," she said, as she hopped out of the truck.

Annie went into the lobby and let the receptionist know she was here for her appointment with Mr. Lopez. She sat in the lobby for several minutes until a woman showed up and said, "Annie Grainger."

She followed the women through the halls and into Lopez's office.

The man was seated at a desk and stood up as she entered.

"Miss Grainger," the man said, "I'm Felipe Lopez."

Annie wasn't sure she should extend her hand but she did.

Lopez shook her hand across the desk and asked her to have a seat.

"Mr. Lopez," began Annie, "I am a journalism student at Ball State in Muncie, Indiana. I have a favor to ask you, and I cannot explain why it is important but it is a matter of great importance."

"You have my interest," said Lopez.

Annie pulled out some photographs of all the buses that had transported her sister and the other girls last month. She had captured strategic shots from the video she had taken. She handed them to him.

"You are investigating something that involves my buses?" asked Lopez defensively.

"Yes, Mr. Lopez," said Annie, "Your buses provided the transportation for the Oasis girls from the Hilton to the airport on the day the Oasis plane crashed. This was for Super Bowl weekend. I need the odometer readings from all of these buses, when they left your garage that morning and picked the girls up and took them to the Citrus Bowl, then back to the hotel and then to the airport and back to your garage."

Lopez looked at her for a moment, sighed and said "Miss Grainger, this is not information that we can share with you. It is not that it is confidential, it is just that your request is bizarre and I simply can't do it."

"Mr. Lopez," said Annie, "in less than seventy-two hours there will be a huge national story blow up in your face. I can't tell you about it but I can tell you enough that you can prepare for it. There will be a thousand reporters asking you questions and they will not take "no" for an answer."

Lopez was caught off guard by her steely determination and impressed with her resolve.

"I am sorry," said Lopez, "I cannot help you."

Annie stood up and threw a paper down on his desk. It was the handout that showed the faces of the 17 girls pulled from the Atlantic. "Have you seen this before?" asked Annie.

"Of course," said Lopez. Everyone in Orlando, everyone in the country has seen this."

She threw a few more photos on his desk and said, "Look carefully at this and tell me how it happened that all the girls in this handout were nearly all minorities. Tell me how all of them were on the same bus. Tell me why the girls on that single, red and white bus are the only girls that were recovered from the ocean. What are the odds of that? How is it that no white blondes got on the red-and-white bus that afternoon?"

Lopez studied the pictures. There were several shots of the girls getting on that bus, as well as seeing them seated through the windows. Annie was right. There were no white blondes.

"Let me call someone. I need to check into this," said Lopez.

Annie pulled out her cell phone and called Jimmy "I need you to come in here and meet someone. I will come to the lobby to meet you."

Annie went into the lobby and sat down. Jimmy came in and sat down beside her. The receptionist said, "Mr. Lopez will be with you in just a few minutes."

It was about fifteen minutes and the same woman reappeared and escorted Annie and Jimmy back to Mr. Lopez's office.

"Mr. Lopez, take a look at those 17 girls again." Annie pointed to two of the pictures and said, "This is Keisha and Kara Campbell of Anderson, Indiana and this is Jimmy Campbell, their brother."

Lopez looked at Jimmy. His previously hardened expression turned to compassion, as he extended his right hand to Jimmy and they shook hands.

"I don't know what to say," said Lopez. "I am sorry for your loss."

"Thank you, Mr. Lopez," said Jimmy, "but I think you also need to know that Annie's sister, Callie, was aboard the Oasis plane and has never been recovered."

"I see," said Lopez. "Uh Annie, I had thought that this was some kind of an assignment from your journalism class, but I see now it is something far more."

He looked at the file on his desk. "I have gathered the information you asked for," said Lopez. "I wasn't going to give it to you. I can't give this to you without talking to our attorneys."

"Look, Mr. Lopez," began Annie, "you're getting something out of this, too. I am giving you the PR gift of being able to get out front on this story. When the questions come you won't be caught flat-footed. That has value."

Lopez stared at both Annie and Jimmy for several seconds. He was clearly wrestling with himself.

He picked up the folder, got up and walked around to Annie sitting across the desk from him. He sat the folder down right in front of her and said, "Let me go check on something. I will be back in five minutes." He left leaving Annie and Jimmy alone in his office.

As soon as the door closed, Annie grabbed the folder. Sure enough, there was a list of the buses, bus number, license plates and the mileage logged in and out of the garage that day. She took a picture of the sheet with her phone, put the paper back in the folder and sat it back on the desk.

In a few minutes, Lopez returned. He didn't sit down.

"One more thing." said Lopez. "I don't know what this means but maybe you do. The driver of that bus dropped it off along the curb that night, instead of pulling it into the lot. Nobody saw him drop it off and he's never been back. He had been with us for years. He was a good man. HR has never been able to contact him."

"I don't know what that means either," said Annie, "and I don't want to guess, but it is not good."

"Should we call the police?" asked Lopez.

"I can't tell you what to do. I don't know that any crime was committed by the driver. I have nothing I can go to the police with yet, but I will and soon."

"I am sorry I cannot give you the file," said Lopez, as he picked the file back up from his desk. "I trust that I have been of some help," and then he grinned slightly.

"Thank you, Mr. Lopez," said Annie. "You have no idea how important this is to us, and thank you for doing all that you could."

"I'd like to say I understand, but I don't," said Lopez, "We are going to report the incident to the police and tell them the driver disappeared. I am going to tell them some journalism student from Indiana brought it to our attention and we don't know what to make of it."

"Sounds like a plan," said Annie, "and thank you so much."

"Thank you, Mr. Lopez," said Jimmy, as he shook Lopez's hand. Annie and Jimmy turned and left.

As they were leaving they heard Lopez on the phone saying "Get me Legal."

Jimmy and Annie got back in the truck. "He left that file out on purpose for you to see, didn't he?" said Jimmy.

"Ya think?" said Annie.

"Where to now?" asked Jimmy.

"Food," said Annie, "I'm hungry, then back to the hotel."

"Fast food or sit down," said Jimmy.

"Just pick a drive–thru, I don't care.

"It can be fast food if you want but not a drive-thru. It's just too tricky navigating this camper through a drive-thru," said Jimmy

"Okay. We'll eat in," said Annie.

They stopped at a Denny's. Annie couldn't help herself. While waiting for the food and even after it came, she had spread a central Florida map out on the table. She had the bus garage, the Citrus Bowl, the Hilton and the airport all marked on the map. She was plotting distances. She looked at the picture on her phone of the bus company mileage sheet.

"Okay," Annie said, "the six buses went anywhere from 83 to 86 miles that day. I am going to error on the side of 83. The red-and-white bus went 137 miles. That's 54 miles extra. At some point, it either left from the airport or turned off before the airport. So, the warehouse can be no farther than 27 miles from the airport. And the least it should be is 71% of that distance or let's say 19 miles."

"How do you figure that?" asked Jimmy clearly stumped by her logic. He looked at the map where she had drawn a donut with the airport in the center.

"If it was a straight line, it would be 27 miles. If it was all east–west roads the shortest it could be at 45 degrees due southeast it would be .7071 of 27 or about 19 miles," explained Annie.

"I thought you were studying journalism, not Algebra," said Jimmy.

"You don't know my dad, he made me study this," said Annie, with a smile. "It's triggernometry. Dad always said I was the worst shot in the family."

Jimmy just looked at her, "Either I don't get it, or it ain't funny."

I am sorry to be so obtuse," she said. "C'mon, we got places to go."

They got in the truck and headed to the south. "The southeast quadrant is the most likely search area," said Annie. "We will start at the south 17 miles out to 27 miles and then work our way to the east. I just think it is more likely they were closer to the Atlantic and in the less sparsely populated area of Osceola or Orange County."

It was a great idea on paper. After about two-and-one-half hours of driving through the backroads and wetlands of northern Osceola County, the results were discouraging.

Jimmy finally said "Without a GPS, I don't see how you would find anything out here, even if you knew where you were going, and we don't."

"Oh my gosh…you're right!" exclaimed Annie. "The truck driver and the bus driver would have needed a GPS if he wasn't from here."

She pulled out her phone and played the video she had shot with her camera. She had converted it to play on her phone. She got to the video of the truck she had taken when they were loading luggage. She could clearly see a GPS glowing on top of the dashboard.

"Look, Jimmy, the truck driver had a GPS," said Annie.

They still had a large section of the southeast quadrant to search when Annie said "Plan B."

"What's Plan B?" asked Jimmy

"The Sunblessed Truck Rental Company. Here is the address she said as she handed him a map with directions from the La Quinta. We need a blessing, maybe we can rent one from them today. We have to get that GPS."

They were so far southeast that it took them a good forty-five minutes to get to the truck rental location. It was actually a gas station and had about a half-dozen orange trucks ranging in size sitting on the lot.

"Pull into this strip mall," said Annie "and pull around where we can check out the place."

Jimmy parked so they could look over and see the gas station pretty well.

She searched on her phone and said "This is the only one I could find. Their webpage says it's for local rental only."

Annie thought for a minute and said. "Jimmy, I want you to walk over there and check out the whole process of renting a truck. It was one of their bigger trucks, but not as big as that one."

"That's a 24-footer," said Jimmy. "What about that third one from the left?"

I can't tell from this angle, but I think that one is shorter," replied Annie.

"That's 16-footer so it must be a 20-footer that you saw," said Jimmy.

Annie watched as Jimmy walked over to the gas station. Just before he got to the door a girl in her mid-twenties came storming out of the door. She was crying

"What's wrong, you okay?" asked Jimmy.

"No, I need this job but the pervert won't keep his hands off me," she said. "He keeps brushing up against me and touching my shoulders and rubbing my neck whenever we're alone. It's creepy!"

Jimmy hadn't gone in yet but couldn't help talking to the girl for a moment. She was about 25, a dirty blonde with stringy hair. A few freckles dotted her cheeks. "I'm sorry," said Jimmy, "Is there anything I can do?"

"No," she said, as she sighed "He just gives me the creeps. He's kind of a nice guy in a lot of ways, but I just can't take the touching anymore." She had only stopped for a few seconds and continued toward her car. Jimmy watched as she got in her car and peeled out of the parking lot.

Jimmy stepped into the station to find a guy in blue jeans and a plaid shirt, maybe in his mid-fifties. The man looked up.

"Yes, Sir," he said, "What can I help you with?"

"I want to find out about renting a 20-foot truck to help a friend move next weekend," said Jimmy

"You over 25?" asked the man.

"Yes," said Jimmy.

The man gave Jimmy a big smile and reached out his hand "I'm Gus," he said, "but you can call me Gus."

"Uh, Okay, uh, Gus, I'm Jimmy," said Jimmy, as he reached out to shake hands. Gus had a strong grip.

He handed Jimmy a brochure. "This explains it all son," he said, "It's $35.95 a day, 70 cents a mile, $49 for exclusion-free insurance, $14 for a two-wheeler dolly, furniture pads for $20 per dozen, GPS for $11.95. You got any big appliances?"

"Refrigerator," said Jimmy.

"Twenty bucks for a refrigerator dolly," replied the man, as he pointed toward the window "Need boxes? Got plenty of them, different sizes, peanuts and tape. Whatever you need."

"Can I see one of the trucks?" asked Jimmy.

"Sure, Son," said Gus, "Follow me." He took Jimmy outside and opened up the back of one of the 20-foot trucks. It was clean inside.

"Big enough for ya?" asked Gus.

"Yeah, I think so," said Jimmy.

"Size matters, Son. Make sure you are sure," said Gus.

Jimmy followed him around and opened the driver's door. Gus tossed Jimmy the key. "Hop up there and see what you think. I got to go back inside. There's a customer," he said. "Bring the keys back in when you're done kickin' the tires."

Jimmy looked over the vehicle. It wasn't like he was really interested in it, but yet it was interesting to him. He looked around for a GPS and there was not one there. He did see a ball mount on the dash and a power cord for the place where a GPS could be added.

He went back in and the guy was tied up with customers for a while. Finally, he handed the keys back to Gus. "I locked it up and closed the cargo door."

"Thanks," said Gus. "Wanna reserve it?"

"I will get back to you soon, I didn't see a GPS," said Jimmy.

"I got to keep those locked up back in the cage with the dollies and blankets and stuff," said Gus. "They walk off. I keep the key on me so my employees have to ask me for it."

"Okay, I will let you know soon. Thanks," said Jimmy, as he turned and left.

Annie watched as Jimmy walked back to the truck. As he got in, he said, "He keeps all the GPSs locked up in back." He handed her the brochure.

She looked at it." I know this series of GPS. It keeps an archive file," she said.

"What do you mean?" asked Jimmy.

"If you select a destination, it keeps track of the time and location of your travels. We have got to get access to the GPS that was in the truck that night," said Annie.

"That girl I was talking to," said Jimmy.

"Yes, I saw you had to stop and spend a little time with her," said Annie with a grin.

"Well, she just quit, she didn't like the owner much and he needs help fast," said Jimmy.

"Really," said Annie, "I used to work at a Speedway in Westfield. If I am not back in thirty minutes, go back to the hotel without me. I will call when it's time to pick me up. Annie jumped out of the truck and headed to the gas station.

Chapter 15

Annie entered the gas station to find about a dozen people in line to pay at the cash register. Once in a while, someone would leave the line and storm out in disgust. Annie watched in amusement as Gus tried to keep up, but he was slow. Annie had grabbed a water and a candy bar and was waiting in line. The girl in front of her asked for Newport cigarettes. Gus turned around tried to find them.

Annie spoke up, "Just to your left, third row up, the green box, probably the longs." Gus found them and turned around, "These?" he said to the girl.

She nodded yes and paid.

"You need help?" said Annie as she sat down her water and candy bar. There was still a long line behind her.

"Yeah," muttered Gus, "Someone just quit on me."

"Open that other register," said Annie.

Gus looked at her. He smiled, "Okay, I will call your bluff." He stepped over to the other register and opened it. Annie came around, looked at the line and said "I can help the next customer," and she did. She was taking care of the customers two to one compared to Gus.

In just a few minutes the line was cleared.

"Okay, Young Lady," he said. "That was interesting, you proved your point." He pulled a ten out of his pocket and handed it to her.

"Seriously, I could use the job," said Annie. "I'm only here a few days but every little bit helps."

"It's only 'til I find somebody," said Gus.

"I'm Annie, by the way and I'm from Indiana."

"I'm Gus," he said, "but you can call me Gus."

"Do I need to fill out an application?" asked Annie.

"It's on the computer there," said Gus "but if you're only going to be here a few days, I will pay you cash and keep it off the books."

'Works for me," said Annie.

"Ten bucks an hour. I'll show you around," said Gus.

As they walked by the front door, he put a "Help Wanted" sign in the door.

"Anybody comes in that wants a job, send them to the computer to fill out the application."

He showed Annie around. They went in back and he showed her the stockroom and the cage. Over there is the employee's bathroom. He took a set of keys out of his pocket and opened the cage. Inside she saw the dollies, blankets, and a lot of small valuable stuff prone to being stolen. She tried to be cool about it as Gus was showing her where things were. Once in a while she would pick something up and look at it.

"You rent trucks here, too?" she asked.

"Yep, carpet cleaners too," replied Gus.

"One of the places I worked before did U-Haul," she lied, "so I had to enter all the computer information on the renter."

She looked up on of the shelves and struck pay dirt. She saw six GPS boxes. They were all the same model, and it was the model she knew. She picked one up and shook it.

"It's in there. I got six of 'em. Only rent local and I never understood why people needed a GPS. But about half the rentals take one," he said.

They heard the door buzzer and went back into the main room to take care of the customer. Annie worked for six hours until another employee came in to work the overnight.

"Can you do 2p to 10p tomorrow?" asked Gus.

"Sure," she said, as Gus handed her sixty dollars cash.

"You already gave me ten," she said.

"Signing bonus," said Gus, "See you tomorrow young lady."

It was dark but there was enough light to walk across the lot to a drug store in the strip mall. She called Jimmy and after several minutes he was there to pick her up.

Annie told him everything that happened. She explained that tomorrow she would bring her laptop and somehow she would have to get access to the cage long enough to download the files from all six.

"I don't know how I am going to get the keys and distract him. It will take thirty minutes to download all six, and that doesn't count getting them in and out of the cage and powered up and re-packed," said Annie.

"Even with two people, it would take thirty minutes," said Annie, "How am I going to pull this off?"

"It may take three people," said Jimmy.

"Well, we don't have three people." said Annie. "I don't even know how you can help. I'll figure something out. I always do."

Jimmy sighed "I never did get how you were going to pull it off. I have my own Plan B, when you finally realize you need it, and I guarantee it will work."

"Hey, there's a Target! Stop! I want to get one of those GPSs to practice on and make sure my laptop is all set to go." said Annie.

Jimmy waited as Annie ran into the Target. In a few minutes, she came out with the GPS and a sandwich and Coke from the Target Café. A few minutes after that, they were back at the hotel.

Jimmy went to his room. Annie went to hers and spent some time setting her laptop up with the right software to download the archive files from the GPS.

She knocked on Jimmy's door.

Jimmy opened the door with a big grin "Settle down, Jimmy, I need you to take me and the GPS for a ride, so I can test the archive download. She entered the address for the Hilton and had Jimmy drive there.

"This is where they all got on the bus, Jimmy," said Annie wistfully.

"Okay, back to the hotel," said Annie.

They went to their rooms. It took only a couple of minutes for Annie to connect the USB cable to the GPS and download the file. She took a look at the file and went to bed.

Jimmy called her at 8:00 a.m. "Annie, I need to pick someone up at the airport at 9:20. Do you want to come?"

"Who?" asked Annie.

"Cynthia, my sister," said Jimmy.

"Why?" asked Annie.

"Look, there are things you can't tell me, and there are things I can't tell you," Said Jimmy.

"Fair enough. Yes, I will go," said Annie. She got ready and slipped into the lobby for a quick breakfast. Jimmy came to meet her at 8:45 a.m. and they left for the airport. He parked at about the same place he had the day before. Jimmy stood beside the truck until he saw Cynthia and motioned her over.

Annie and Cynthia certainly knew of each other and Annie had seen her on the news stories about her dad. Her hair did not look anything like the Cynthia she had seen in Indiana. She had long braids. It looked good on her.

Annie said, "Hi, I'm Annie."

"I know," said Cynthia. "I pray for your sister, Callie, every day."

Annie was caught off guard. "And I pray for your dad," said Annie.

"You sure got him a good attorney, and for that I am very grateful."

Cynthia took one look the seating arrangements and said, "I am not sitting back there."

Annie immediately volunteered to sit in the back.

"No," she snatched the keys from Jimmy's hand and said to him, "You squish back there. I'll drive."

"Where we going?" asked Cynthia.

"The La Quinta," said Annie, as she pulled another set of driving instructions out of her purse.

Cynthia took one look at it and said, "Oh, yeah, I know that one and handed Annie back the paper. She drove straight to it.

"You can stay with me in my room," said Annie.

"Well, that would be good, he is such a slob," said Cynthia.

The three of them walked to a nearby restaurant for lunch.

At 1:30, Jimmy was ready to take Annie to the station. He dropped her off at the strip mall just before 2:00 p.m. He watched as Annie, with her laptop, walked across the lot and into the gas station. Gus was there and spent most of his time in the back. Customers were constantly coming and going. Annie spent a few minutes in back devising a plan. She studied the hinges of the cage and decided she could take them apart with the tools Gus had.

Annie just never got the opportunity to spend much time in the back. The only thing she accomplished was to get on the truck rental computer and download the rental agreement on the two 20' trucks for the day of the Oasis plane. Both renters also rented a GPS. Annie took a short break around 6:30, as it was getting dark. She called Jimmy.

"Okay, you were right, Jimmy," Annie said, "What's your Plan B?"

"Just sit tight and do not react to what is about to happen," he said and hung up.

Jimmy told Cynthia they needed to go. Cynthia went outside and opened up the back of the camper. She spent a few minutes cleaning it up and making the bed.

At about 7:30 things had slowed down at the gas station. Annie saw Jimmy's truck pull up and park between two of the large rental trucks. She saw Cynthia get out but she was not expecting what happened next.

Cynthia came in the station. Gus was over by the window arranging some boxes.

"I gotsta go," Cynthia said. "Whar's your ladies' room?"

Gus looked up from what he was doing and saw her. "It's for customers only, Miss," said Gus.

"I got me a thirsty F-150 out thar, an I need a whole big tank of gas to get back to Atlanta. Hi, Handsome, I'm Cindi," she said, as she walked straight over to him and stopped within inches of him. She had on a thin halter top and short shorts. He was down on one knee, and her breasts were practically in his face.

He stared at them but Cindi didn't even seem to notice. She started wiggling her legs and said, "I gotta tinkle. Can't we talk about you feelin' my tank after I'm done. Whar is it?"

"It's in back. I'll show you," said Gus, as he struggled a little bit to stand up.

Cindi put her arms around him and said "Ain't you the gentleman. Let me help you up," said Cindi. She pressed her breasts against his side as she helped him up.

"You're so sweet," she said and kissed him on the cheek.

He led her down the hall to the Ladies' Room. She no sooner shut the door than a few moments later she opened it back up. "I got a problem in here," she said, "this toilet is runnin' and I don't think it's gonna flush. It wouldn't be very lady-like to leave a mess for you to clean up," she said.

Gus took a quick look and she was right. The chain was broken and had gotten caught under the flapper. There was no water in the reservoir tank.

"You gotta 'nother little girl's room?" asked Cindi as she kept wiggling like she had to go.

"We got the Men's room or the employee's washroom in the back," said Gus.

"Well, take me to the back, Handsome." She took his hand and led him out of the ladies' room. He directed her into the backroom and the employee's washroom.

"Now you stay right thar. I might get lost findin' my way back," said Cindi.

Gus was enjoying himself too much to even think of leaving."

In a few minutes, she reappeared at the door. "Oh, Lordy," she said, "I feel like a whole new girl."

"Well, you still look like the beautiful young lady that went in there," said Gus.

"Ain't you the charmer," she said, as she pressed real close to him again. "What's your name?" she asked.

"Gus," he said.

"Well, Gus, let's talk about how I can get my tank feeled up." She put her finger lightly on a button in the center of his chest when she said it.

Gus was getting a little nervous and stammered a bit "Well, Honey, what do you need."

"Oh, Gus, my tank has been runnin' on empty for so long. I really need a good feel up."

"Fill up?" Gus said, "You mean fill up?"

"Yeah, a feel up, I need a real good feel up. You think you can handle that for me Gussie-pooh?"

"I'm sorry," I thought you said 'feel up.'"

"Gus, you naughty boy." She grabbed his right hand and placed it right between her legs. "This is a feel up. I need my truck feeled up with gas, Gus."

She kept her hand on top and continued to his press his hand between her legs. "Haven't you ever needed a feel up, Gus," she asked.

"Uh yeah," he stammered.

"Oh, lookee at that. We got somebody's attention," she squealed. She cupped her other hand between his legs. "Man, that thing is hard," said Cindi. And at the same time, she maneuvered his hand underneath the leg of her shorts. She had no underwear on, and his fingers were right on the promised land.

"Ooh, Gus," she said, "you have such a soft touch." She let him explore her.

"I need a full tank of gas, Gus. Maybe a hundred dollars' worth. I only got ten bucks. Can't you think of somethin' I could do for you to earn that tank of gas?"

"Oh, God, the girl up front could walk back here anytime. I don't know," said Gus.

"Well, that's not a problem," said Cindi. All the time his fingers were touching her and she had her hand cupped over him moving her hand just a little bit. "I gotta camper and we can git in thar and you can feel me up, that's f-e-e-l me up as long you want, long as I can have a full tank of gas."

Gus just took a big breath and sighed. Cindi pulled away from him and his fingers were left floating in the air. As she uncapped her hand, her finger traced a line straight along his member all the way up to his belly button.

"You sell condoms here, Gussie-pooh?" she asked.

"Yes," he said.

"Well bring a nice, thin, orange-flavored three-pack if you got 'em. We are going to need at least two, maybe all three." And with that, Cindi headed out of the back room and left the store. As she passed Annie, Cindi winked at her. Cindi went out to the truck camper and opened up the back.

A few moments later Annie saw Gus come from the back room and stop at one of the display counters. He grabbed a pack of condoms and went out the door. When he got to the back of the camper, Cindi was already lying on the bed. The camper was clean and very well kept.

He stepped inside and closed the door. She reached over and pulled him next to her. She unbuttoned his shirt and then undid his belt. She took his shoes and socks off and pulled off his pants. She folded them up very neatly as he took his shirt off. She folded that too. She took his folded clothes, opened a little pantry door and placed them inside. She took his shoes and socks and placed them neatly on the floor. She removed his wristwatch and said, "I don't want you scratchin' me with this. She put it in his shoe. She then pulled down his underwear. "Ooh, doggies!" she squealed. "That's a mighty fine expression of manhood you got thar, Gus." She touched it and looked it over. "Nice and clean, too," she said, as she let all of the braids of her hair come tumbling down around it. Then she looked up at Gus and kissed it on the side.

"Whar's the condoms?" she asked. He had them in his hand and gave her the package.

"Orange, just like I asked for. You're going to be real glad you got me orange. I can suck on orange all day."

Cindi stood up and opened the small refrigerator. "Beer?" she said. He nodded and she opened it and handed it to him.

"Now you unwrap me," she said as she held her hands up as far as she could in the camper. He pulled her top off and her breasts sprang out. He pulled off her shorts.

Outside the camper, the moment the door shut, Jimmy put a clip through the latch so it could not open. He waited at the side of the camper for a few minutes, and then opened the exterior pantry door. There were Gus' clothes. He unclipped the keys from Gus' belt and headed into the station.

There were no customers in the store at that moment. Annie and Jimmy headed into the back room. He slid a Coke cup over the two cameras. Then Annie took the keys and fumbled until she found the one that opened the cage. They both began taking the GPSs out of the boxes. They then folded the boxes back up and returned them to the shelf.

They carried the GPSs into the main room in a black bag that sat at Annie's feet. Jimmy sat at the truck rental computer as if he was filling out the application for a truck rental.

Annie had her laptop set up below the register so she could wait on customers. One at a time she plugged in each GPS and downloaded the file.

"How much time do we have?" said Annie.

Jimmy chuckled, but with a note of chagrin "All the time in the world. My sister can keep him distracted for hours."

"I can't believe your sister," said Annie.

"There is no stopping her, Annie," said Jimmy, "Granny says she's just like our mama when she was young. She does whatever she wants and no one controls her but her. And, when it comes to family, she will do whatever it takes to protect us."

Annie chose not to say anything. She went back to her task. It took about thirty-five minutes to download all the files for all six units. She had only had five customers to take care of during that time. "Here, Jimmy, you go pack them back up neatly. It will just look like you're going to the restroom again on the security camera. Don't forget the Coke cups."

While Jimmy did that, Annie used the GPS program on her computer to combine all of the files into one file. She then downloaded that file to her new GPS.

Jimmy came out sat down at the computer again and acted like he had finished the application. Annie looked over his shoulder and nodded like he had done it right. Jimmy got up and walked out the door.

Jimmy walked around to the camper exterior pantry door and returned Gus' keys to his belt loop. He then removed the clip from the rear door and walked over to the strip mall. He sent a text to Cynthia.

Inside the camper, the text went off. Cindi heard it and glanced at the screen. Gus was oblivious being totally occupied with other things. A few minutes later Cindi shouted, "oh, I'm about to nut again! That's the third time, Gussie-pooh." She gently nudged him off of her.

Gus had a huge smile on his face as he complied with her wishes. "Thank you!" he said.

Inside the station, Annie realized the GPS couldn't get a good signal, so, she was unable to check if the combined file was working. About that time, she saw the F-150 camper pull up to a pump. She watched as Gus pumped gas for Cynthia. When the pump clicked off, Gus came back in and did something at the register to close out the sale.

Gus went back out and handed her the receipt. "Just over a hundred dollars like you said. Paid in full."

"Thanks, Gus. It was my pleasure. If I ever find myself in Orlando again, you 'spose I could earn a tank a gas some other time?" she asked.

"That would be my pleasure, Young Lady, anytime," he said. "One more thing, you said you only have ten bucks and you're going to go all the way back to Atlanta and leaving tonight?" he asked.

Gus pulled four twenties out of his pocket and handed it to her. "Here you stop someplace and get yourself something good to eat. There is enough there for a room. That would be safer than sleeping at a rest area."

She took it and said "What a fine Southern Gentleman you are that knows how to treat a lady right. Thank you."

Cindi got in the truck and left. She kept an eye on Gus until he got back inside. She then pulled into the far end of the strip mall. Jimmy was there and hopped in. Jimmy said nothing about what had just happened. He did not approve of what his sister had done. He had learned a long time ago that Cynthia Campbell did whatever Cynthia Campbell felt she had to do. He had no room to judge. She had saved his ass too many times.

Chapter 16

Just after 10:00 p.m., Annie came over to the truck carrying her laptop. The GPS had located the satellites now and knew where it was. Jimmy got in back, and Annie got in the passenger seat. She went to the recently found destinations and to the favorites. She found several sites to the southeast, and that is what she focused on. She was looking for a destination name that might match the right distance. She found several possible matches. She then pulled up the file on her laptop and began checking dates, times and destinations. It took several minutes as she kept going between the GPS and the laptop.

"Bingo," she said "This is it. It is to the south and east within the target donut, and I have the time frame near the time when the Oasis plane took off." She reached over and hugged Cynthia and Cynthia hugged her back.

Annie had not yet shared with Jimmy and Cynthia all that she knew. She had heard the recording her dad had made of Lani telling what happened. She thought it best to wait and find the warehouse before telling them the graphic details. All they knew was that they were looking for evidence that would prove their father's innocence.

Annie sighed and lowered her head. "Dear Lord," she started, and when she did that Cynthia reached over and held her hand. Annie started again "Dear Lord, thank you for blessing us today in our work." She paused for a moment realizing that she had just prayed for a blessing on Cynthia's work. She continued "Lord guide us to the warehouse so that we may be able to find evidence to clear the father of Jimmy and Cynthia. In the name of Jesus, Amen."

Annie hopped out of the truck "I will be back in a few. I need to go quit my job."

Annie walked into the station and said "Gus, something's come up and I have to leave. You don't have to pay me for today, but I have to go now. I'm sorry."

Gus looked at her disappointed "Annie, I'm sorry too. You were great. You didn't need any training. You've been a big help."

"Well thanks, Gus, I appreciate that," said Annie.

He handed Annie eighty dollars. "Here is what I owe you. I am not stupid. I know why you're quitting so soon," said Gus. He suddenly had Annie's full attention.

"You do?" said Annie. Her eyes widened. She wondered what he was going to say next. She wondered if she was caught.

"It's about that Black girl, isn't it?" asked Gus.

Annie just stood there petrified.

"I know you know what happened," said Gus. "I am just an old fool. I know it was wrong. But a man like me can't pass up something like that. She was a precious young lady, and we helped each other out. Someday, you will understand."

He paused for a minute, "Actually Annie, I hope you never understand."

Annie then said "Believe me, Gus, it is actually something else. The 150 dollars I have earned here has really helped."

Annie turned and left. As she walked across the lot to the truck, she wondered how much she really did understand about life. This last month was off the charts for things she had never had to think about before.

As she got in the truck with Jimmy and Cynthia, Annie said, "You know, he was so nice to me." She held up the four twenties, "And he paid me the full eighty dollars. I like him, Cynthia, even if he did take advantage of you."

"Annie, bless you," said Cynthia. "Gus did not take advantage of me. I took advantage of him; He never had a chance. He's a nice man. I always try to find something to like about everyone I'm with. His wife died five years ago. He has a son in L.A. and a daughter in Dallas. They never come to see him unless they need money. Gus is just lonely and doesn't have anyone." She paused and held up her four twenties, "And he gave me eighty dollars for something to eat and a place to stay if I needed it."

Then Cynthia said, "And Jimmy back here gets a hundred dollars' worth of gas to get back to Atlanta, and he hardly did a damn thing. He's the one taking advantage."

They all laughed, Annie hit "Go" on the GPS and placed it on the dash. It indicated they could be at the site in about a half hour.

"We need to wait 'til daylight," said Annie, "Let's go back to the hotel and get a good night's sleep. Cynthia put the truck in drive and away they went.

As they got out of the truck, Cynthia headed toward the lobby.

"Where are you going?" asked Annie.

"To get a room," she said, as she held up the four twenties.

Annie said, "No, you can stay with me. I have a double."

"Annie," said Cynthia, "you made that offer before you knew what I might have to do. I won't hold you to it now."

Cynthia was right. Annie hadn't really processed what had just happened. Annie would not have made the offer knowing what she now knew. Then, she had realized she had lied to Gus to get the job. She had actually broken into the cage, and she stole data off his GPS. Who was she to judge?

"No, Cynthia," said Annie, "please stay in my room."

"Okay," said Cynthia.

The first thing Cynthia did when she got in the room was to take a shower.

The next morning Annie, Jimmy and Cynthia checked out of the hotel. Annie set the GPS to guide them to the warehouse. Cynthia drove. Before long they were in a sparsely populated area in northern Osceola County. The GPS guided them directly to an unpaved lane. After some twists and turns, they came to a large metal building. Annie would not have used the term warehouse to describe it. It was a good-sized-corrugated metal building with sliding doors. There was rust showing through in several places, and much of the metal was peeling paint or something.

The three got out and walked around a little bit. It was a beautiful, bright sunny day in central Florida, and yet, the place was foreboding.

"This place gives me the creeps," said Jimmy.

Annie sighed, "Me too and it should," she said.

"I don't want to go in yet. It does belong to somebody, and I suppose we are trespassing," said Annie

"You're all about following the rules, aren't you?" said Cynthia.

Annie didn't respond.

"Let's look around. We need to see if there is a place a C-130 could take off and land," said Annie.

"What?" said Jimmy.

"We need to see if a large transport plane could have landed here," said Annie.

They walked around to the other side of the building. There was vegetation and the ground was very solid. They followed deep tire tracks in the sand, until suddenly, the tracks disappeared.

"Well, I guess that answers your question," said Jimmy. "A heavy plane clearly took off from here." They went to the other end of the tracks and found that the tracks suddenly started. In fact in some places there appeared to be two sets of tracks. They studied the terrain and the tracks in the sand. It became evident that the plane had been parked near the building next to another sliding door. It had then taxied back to the area near the beginning of the tracks. It had been several weeks since the tracks had been made and it had rained. The path of the tires was still clearly discernable. Jimmy began taking pictures with his phone.

They went back to where they had parked. It took all three of them to slide the door open. They parted it just enough to slip inside. There was enough sand on the floor to clearly make out tire tracks of several vehicles. In the center of the room was a water tank and steps up to it.

"This is where your sisters were murdered," said Annie.

Cynthia and Jimmy stopped in their tracks and looked at Annie.

"Say what?" said Cynthia.

"This is a murder scene. We have to be careful not to disturb anything," said Annie.

"You are going to have to explain what the fuck you just said," said Jimmy.

"Jimmy," said Annie, "your sister and I have to be on a plane to Indianapolis in a little bit. We are going to have to report this to the Police. You go up the steps very carefully and see if there is salt water in that tank."

Jimmy went up the steps." Well, there's water," he said, as he leaned down and put his finger in the water and brought it to his lips. "It stinks," he said, "It's saltwater." He kept taking pictures.

Strewn around the floor were several elastic straps and rubber tubes.

"Guys, each of the little girls was bound by these straps and the tubes were put around their legs and inflated with air. Then they were thrown into the water to drown. The air in the tube around their ankles made it impossible for them to keep their heads above water and get air. The elastic straps left no marks or bruises on their bodies. Eventually, they drowned. Any marks or bruises they had from hitting themselves on the tank could not be separated from the trauma of falling out of the sky from a 747. Then they were strapped in seats from a 747 and thrown out of the back of the C-130 into the ocean." Her voice cracked, and tears rolled down her cheeks as she recounted what happened.

Cynthia and Jimmy were mesmerized by the story and without being aware of what was happening the three came together and put their arms around each other. Tears streamed down Cynthia's face, and Jimmy's eyes moistened.

"How do you know this?" asked Cynthia.

"One of the girls survived. Lani Kealoha. She's Hawaiian, and her dad is a famous cliff diver in Maui. She was able to hold her breath. She was able to contort her body and grab a breath of air once in a while. When she was tossed into the sea from the C-130, she dived the way her dad had taught her to her entire life."

Annie paused "My dad found her and has her story recorded. I have heard it a half a dozen times."

"It gets worse. Maybe not worse but worse," said Annie.

Annie walked over to a door entered another room. Jimmy and Cynthia followed. "The girls were held in here," said Annie, and then three at a time they were taken into the main room to be drowned."

Then Annie walked over to another door that led into a small room. Cautiously, Jimmy and Cynthia followed.

"And in here," Annie began sobbing when she saw the blood stains on the floor. "In here, your sisters were raped by a Black African who could speak their language."

"Crioulo?" asked Cynthia.

"I guess. All I know is they spoke to the man in a foreign language."

Cynthia and Jimmy looked around, and suddenly, Cynthia said, "Oh, no."

She walked over to two pieces of clothing laying on the floor. "These are Princess Tiana underwear. Keisha and Kara loved Princess Tiana."

Cynthia started to reach down to pick them up.

"No," said Annie, "don't touch them. We can't disturb the evidence. We have already walked around too much."

Jimmy took pictures, and continued to take pictures as they passed back through the other room.

"We need to go," said Annie.

"What about your sister?" asked Cynthia.

"She was never here," said Annie. "Look, that's enough for now. Except for one thing, all the girls that were white and blonde were not murdered. They murdered minorities and white girls that were not blonde."

They slid the door back shut and got in the truck to leave.

"I have to think," said Annie. "We have to report this to the police, but we have to make our flight to Indianapolis. The police might make us stay if we call them now."

"You worry too much," said Cynthia. "The airport is maybe thirty minutes away. I'm taking us there now."

"Jimmy, don't call 9-1-1. Look up the number for the Orlando police," said Cynthia.

"The warehouse is in Osceola County, not Orange," said Annie.

"Jimmy, can you find your way back here without the GPS?" asked Cynthia.

"If I had been driving, maybe, but no," said Jimmy.

"That's a problem," said Cynthia. "Annie, can you get the coordinates for the warehouse from the GPS?"

"Yes," said Annie, as she fiddled with the GPS. "I got 'em."

"Write them down for Jimmy," said Cynthia. "We have to take the GPS with us just in case the cops take it from Jimmy."

"Okay," said Annie. "I see your point."

"Jimmy, transfer all the pictures in your phone to the memory card and delete all pictures from your phone," said Cynthia. "Give me the memory card and delete your entire call history."

As they drove back to Orlando, Jimmy did as his sister said. He knew better than to cross her when she was in one of these moods. Along the way, they came to another Target and Cynthia pulled in.

"Annie, go in there and buy another GPS identical to this one, and buy a memory card just like this one. Do you have money?" asked Cynthia.

"Yes, I will put it on my dad's card. It's ok," said Annie.

"No," said Cynthia, "Do cash." Cynthia reached into her purse and pulled out two crisp one-hundred-dollar bills and handed them to Annie.

"Make it two separate purchases," said Cynthia.

"Why?" asked Annie.

"Just do it," snapped Cynthia.

Annie caught Jimmy's eyes and she could see he was thinking "don't cross her, just do it."

In a few minutes, Annie came out with the GPS and the memory card.

Cynthia took Jimmy's phone and removed the memory card and put in the new card. She had Annie open up the new GPS and enter the coordinates of the warehouse.

"Now pay close attention, Jimmy." Cynthia followed the GPS instructions all the way back to the site.

"Why did we come back?" asked Annie.

"Give Jimmy the receipt for the GPS," said Cynthia, "Now Jimmy, if it comes up, you tell the cops that we stopped at that Target to buy a GPS so that you could find your way back. Tell them we drove back here, and it took you a while to find the site and mark the location. Got it?"

"Yeah, I got it, Sis," said Jimmy.

Cynthia turned the truck around and headed for the airport.

"Now, call the police department and put us all on speaker phone," said Cynthia.

The dispatcher answered.

"Hello, my name is Cynthia Campbell. This is not an emergency, but we think it could be important for you to take a look at. I am here with my brother, Jimmy Campbell. We are from Atlanta and another girl; Annie Grainger from Indiana is with us. My brother and I lost two of our sisters on the Oasis plane crash last month, and Annie lost her sister, too."

"Go on," said the police dispatcher.

"We don't think our sisters were ever on that plane," said Cynthia. "We think they were kidnapped by somebody else and were killed out in the country not far from Orlando, and then their bodies were thrown in the ocean."

"I see," said the dispatcher, obviously skeptical.

"Anyway," said Cynthia, "we thought we should report it to the police, but Annie and I have to be in Indianapolis in the morning. We have a subpoena to appear in court, so we are flying to Indianapolis in just a few minutes."

"My brother, Jimmy will come down to the station later and take you to the site." said Cynthia, "Is that okay?"

The police dispatcher really didn't know what to say. Finally, the dispatcher said, "Sure, Miss Campbell, you have your brother come down and make a full report, and when he does, we will investigate the matter."

"Okay, bye-bye," said Cynthia. "Well, we reported it."

"The way you said it, even I didn't believe you, and I know it's true," said Annie.

"I can't help that, Annie," said Cynthia "We reported it, and we're not from here, so how do we know what county to call?"

Annie just looked back at Jimmy. She tilted her head and raised her eyebrows. "I see your point," said Annie.

"Annie, we are supposed to call John Kosten if we find the site, right." asked Cynthia.

"Yeah," said Annie.

"You have John Kosten's number?" said Cynthia.

"Yes," said Annie.

"Give the number to Jimmy," said Cynthia.

Annie held her cell phone up to Jimmy so he could read the number.

"Jimmy," said Cynthia, "wait until we are in the air and call the Orlando police station and tell them you found the site again, and it is actually in Osceola County and ask them what to do. Ask them to please not dispatch a unit over the radio. We don't want the press to catch wind of this until tomorrow. Give them the coordinates and meet them there if possible. They will probably give you a number to call. Whatever they tell you to do it, just do it. Call John Kosten right after that and fill him in. He needs to call them and add weight to what you are telling them. They may not take you seriously."

"Okay," said Jimmy.

"John Kosten said he would let the prosecutor know and they would make the call," said Annie.

"Steve Foulke?" said Cynthia.

"Really? He knows about this?" asked Cynthia.

"I think he just found out from John Kosten," said Annie.

"That's fine," said Cynthia as she chuckled. "Annie, Let me see your ticket."

Annie fished for it in her purse and held it up for her to see while she was driving.

"I have a flight back to Atlanta," said Cynthia, "and then I have a flight to Indianapolis later today. I didn't know I was coming here when I booked it. I have to get these braids out and get my hair conditioned and done before court. My flat iron is going to be busy tonight. I am going to see if I can get a flight with you back to Indianapolis, and that will give me more time for my hair."

Cynthia pulled the truck up to the departure terminal. Annie and Cynthia got out and got their bags from the back, and Annie saw Cynthia take something out of a drawer. They went to the ticket counter. Cynthia explained she wanted to get the same flight one way to Indianapolis.

"$267," said the ticket agent. Cynthia handed her three crisp one-hundred-dollar bills. Annie saw her and couldn't help but wonder where she got that money. She chose not to dwell on it.

They boarded the flight to Indianapolis and had seats next to each other.

Chapter 17

Dan's time in Istanbul had been productive. Jasmine had downloaded all the music files from his FTP site. He explained the plan to Jasmine and told her just to give Callie the files in the directory marked "Polynesian," and as a backup plan, the files in the "Baltic" directory. He instructed Jasmine just to tell Callie to think Polynesian Cultural Center, and that would be all she would need to know to choreograph a program. Callie had visited the Polynesian Cultural Center at least a half-dozen times when in Hawaii with her dad.

Ricky informed Dan that he and the T-girls were on their way to Bukhara. Ricky preferred the term T-Girl rather than Trans, Transgender, Transsexual or Trans Woman. Benjamin Johansohn confirmed that all the Special Forces weapons and communications gear would be in place near the Ark. Ambassador Krewe confirmed "unofficially" that passports and government clearances would be forthcoming as needed. John Kosten had confirmed the cooperation of Sgt. Mark Campbell and the Madison County prosecutor. Jasmine confirmed that all was ready on her end and that Callie had the music.

Kahekili confirmed that the Hokule'a and Polynesian props had been shipped. He also told Dan that the elders had picked up the full cost of the shipping and stood ready to assist in any way that they could. Mr. Toguchi confirmed that the Hawaii cargo shipment was in Riga and being held for the arrival of the JAL 747.

It was all in place. Dan sat in the café along the sidewalk having breakfast at the Citadel Hotel. He could look across the Sea of Marmara and the Bosporus straights to the Asia side just two miles away. He contemplated all that he had been through and all that Callie, and the girls had been through. It was incomprehensible that this was happening. He decided to take a morning stroll to the Hagia Sophia and Blue Mosque a short distance away. He was there in fifteen minutes. The minarets of the mosques reached toward the sky.

He looked around at the bustling Islamic society that surrounded him. Yes, there were women in burkas and some with long dresses and scarfs covering their head but showing their faces. But there were also many local girls in western outfits, with shorter skirts, and their arms and shoulders and lower legs fully exposed, many with beautiful young faces and happy smiles. Here was a Muslim society that coexisted with European customs and at least tolerated Christians within their midst without persecution. It was a stark contrast to Bukhara.

He gazed at the magnificent structure of the Blue Mosque, and opposite it was the site of the Hagia Sophia Byzantine church. First built in 360 A.D. by the son of Emperor Constantine, and then rebuilt in 567 by Emperor Justinian. It was the site of the "Mother Church" of Eastern Orthodox Christendom. For nearly a thousand years, it was a church, until Constantinople fell to the Ottoman Turks in 1453. It was turned into a Mosque until 1935, when the secular government of Turkey turned it into a museum. It was a remarkable site to behold in the interior, where mosaics of Jesus, the Virgin Mary and St. John could be seen intermixed with large Islamic roundels proclaiming Allah and Muhammed in Arabic.

Dan left the church/mosque/museum to walk along the fountains between the Blue Mosque and Hagia Sophia. He encountered an unlikely site. A vendor was roasting corn on the cob. One of Dan's most cherished memories with his daughters was his annual trip to the Indiana State Fair, where they would always stop at the Wilson Roasted Corn booth. Dan was feeling very melancholy and at the same time hopeful. He purchased one from the Turkish vendor. It was good and brought back some nostalgic memories, but it still was not a genuine Hoosier "roast'n'ear" slathered with butter.

He stopped one last time at the entrance to the church, dwarfed now by the Mosque and the minarets. He closed his eyes and prayed for a long time, asking for a blessing on his plans and specifically thanking all those whom he could remember that had helped.

There was the Buddhist from Japan, a Jewish doctor from Bukhara, the Seventh Day Adventist pastor from Namibia, Benjamin Johansohn and the Israeli Mossad, Pastor Doyle of the Rejoice and Praise Church in Harare, the Catholic church in Zimbabwe and all the attendees at the Kariba conference, Pastor Jorge Valente of the Igreja Evangelica Pão da Vida, Pastor Joshua and Lori Rogers of the Afrique Iglesias Evangélicas Church in Bujumbura, the Flying Doves, and Ambassador Krewe. Then there was John Kosten, Mark Campbell, Steve Foulke and Mike in Indy and Keith in Hawaii and the Mormon Church, Ricky and the Special Forces of the T-Girls, the American Airlines agents at the Honolulu Admirals' Club and on the phone, the agent at American Express, the understanding passport examiner in New Orleans and most of all, a devout Muslim princess and her aid Kaliq.

He prayed blessings for all of them and all of those he could not remember. Although they were not all Christian, he took liberty with Matthew 18:20 and ended his prayer with "For where two or more are gathered in my name, I am there among them."

He turned around and walked back to the hotel, checked out and took a cab to the Istanbul Ataturk airport for the four-and-a-half-hour flight to Bukhara.

Dan landed Bukhara in the late afternoon. The airport was teeming with arrivals. The airport was bustling with planes from airlines all over the world. He scanned the tarmac and spotted a JAL 747 that belonged to the Japanese Dance Troupe. It took about an hour to clear customs and find a vantage point where he could see the arriving aircraft.

Right on schedule, he saw a British Airways Boeing 767 land and taxi to the gate area. A mobile jet bridge drove out to meet the plane and was positioned to allow the passengers to disembark. In a little while he saw them. A dozen beautiful women appeared as a group. They were dressed provocatively for any venue, but for a Muslim country, it was a sight never seen before. They strutted their stuff while stepping down the stairway and onto the terminal bus. The men stared. The eyes of the Muslim tarmac workers remained fixed on the glamorous dozen.

Dan was on a stairway overlooking customs where he could watch the group make their way through passport control. They made a fuss getting their luggage loaded onto the luggage carts. A half dozen men quickly came to their assistance and helped them all the way through customs.

Dan positioned himself down at the arrival doors where various tour companies were holding up signs for the arriving passengers. Soon, Ricky and her friends appeared. They strolled out of the baggage claim as if they had just finished a shopping spree on Rodeo Drive and were looking for a cab. Dan smiled and nodded his head when he caught Ricky's attention. Ricky grinned and blew him a kiss.

"Nice discreet entrance," whispered Dan, as Ricky and the T-Girls passed by. "We aim to please," whispered Ricky to Dan. A tour guide had spotted them and held up the sign identifying him as their shuttle bus. The luggage, a lot of luggage was loaded into the back of the bus and the dozen girls piled in. They were being watched by every male within viewing distance.

Dan got in line for a cab and was soon on his way to his hotel. He checked in and went to his room long enough to drop off his luggage. He then walked the short distance to the hotel where Mr. Toguchi and the Japanese Dance Troupe were staying. He called up to his room, and in a few minutes, Mr. Toguchi appeared in the lobby. They spoke very briefly, and Mr. Toguchi confirmed the shipment from Hawaii had been off-loaded at the Bukhara airport and was sitting in a nearby warehouse. He gave Dan the address on a slip of paper along with the warehouse number.

Dan suddenly realized he was famished. He walked back to his hotel and found something he could eat at the hotel restaurant. He studied a Bukhara map and figured out the route to the warehouse. It was only a fifteen-minute walk. As he got closer to the warehouse, he could see workers at many of the warehouse doors constructing all manner of floats. Dan entered the warehouse listed on the paper and saw that Ricky and her group were already here working on the construction. There were three 40-foot trailers in the warehouse.

Ricky had studied the construction specifications sent by Kahekili. They had already opened the crate containing the Polynesian *pièce de résistance*. It was a replica of the

Hokule'a, a double-hulled voyaging canoe with dual masts. This float alone, when finished would carry all of the youngest girls without them having to walk. The Hokule'a symbolized the great pride the Hawaiians and all Polynesian peoples felt toward their ancient wayfinding techniques of celestial navigation. The theme that Dan had picked for this group in the parade was "One Pacific, One People."

Dan spent a few minutes meeting the twelve T-Girls. They were all so decent and spiritual about this mission. One by one they expressed their outrage at the kidnappings and the exploitation of all the women in the studio. As Dan was leaving one of them said, "We will get your daughter and her friends out and then we will get the bastards for what they have done to all those other women."

Dan nodded his head. He didn't want to think that far ahead as he had not shared that part of the mission with Jasmine. It was the price he had to pay to secure the commitment of Ricky and the T-Girls. He didn't know how this was going to play out after Callie was safe, but he had to trust the Lord that it would be good for everyone, including Jasmine.

He hailed a cab and was taken to the Ark. He walked to the secret tunnel entrance and waited until the appointed time. Suddenly, a female appeared in the shadows. It was Jasmine. She motioned Dan to come closer.

Neither of them had planned, intended or expected to do what happened next, but they kissed and did so passionately. "Inside," she said, and they continued their passion for the next few precious seconds standing in the tunnel. They held each other silently for a while and finally Jasmine uttered, "What just happened? That was not part of the plan."

"I know," replied Dan, "I'm sorry, not very sorry, but sorry a little," Jasmine could see his grin in the dim light of the tunnel.

"You have not convinced me of your sincerity. Thankfully my burka served its intended purpose and prevented things from going too far," she smiled

"Damned Muslim garb," replied Dan.

Jasmine suddenly got very serious. "Callie has the dance routine all worked out, all the girls know what they are to do. I have secretly watched them rehearse from the tunnel close to where they are being held. They are all well fed and have a pool. There is music, electronic games and movies to keep them occupied."

"Thank you," he said.

"Your Jewish doctor was correct," began Jasmine. "My father has been poisoned with a small amount of cyanide in his IV. His symptoms of weakness, confusion and dizziness have all been from the cyanide. He has suffered some kidney, and liver damage. We have prevented any further doses of the contaminated IVs and have administered the antidote to cyanide poisoning and have kept him hydrated with a clean IV."

"This is very encouraging," said Dan.

"Dan, what am I to think? My father and brother have been saved by a Jewish doctor; my brother has a Christian wife and son. The Jews cared for Adil in prison better than his own uncle and cousin. Allah has been no help at all in blessing those that I love, or me. Sharia Law put my grandmother to death by stoning." She shook her head and came into Dan's arms.

Dan knew when to remain quiet, and this was one of those times. Any comment he might make now in agreement would cause Jasmine to throw up resistance and defend Islam.

"You must go," she said suddenly, and she was right. Dan needed to get back to the hotel. There was much to do at the warehouse tomorrow.

Dan slipped out of the tunnel and into the park. As he walked closer to the Ark, it suddenly hit him. It was as if this was an entirely different city than when he was here last. There were westerners everywhere. Many of the women wore western clothes. There were a few women in traditional burkas. Others were in beautifully colored dresses fully covering them from neck to toe and their faces uncovered. Many of these women were black and appeared to be from African nations. There were women with shorter skirts, with their arms, shoulders and lower legs fully exposed.

It reminded Dan more of Istanbul than the Bukhara he first visited. Clearly, all the usually strict requirements of Bukhara society had been suspended for the International Women's Day. One group was conspicuously absent. There were no local Muslim men except for the Elite Guard of the Ark.

Dan was up early the next morning and off to the warehouse. When he arrived, he could hardly believe his eyes. Before him, on one of the flatbed trailers was an impressive 2/3 replica of the Hokule'a. The masts were shorter proportionally than they should have been to allow the float to exit the warehouse and pass under various overhead obstructions along the parade route.

Nevertheless, the two masts with their crab-claw golden-brown sails replicated the appearance of the craft. The mast closest to the bow had a Hawaiian flag with its eight red, white and blue stripes, and British Union Jack visible even in the still air of the warehouse.

Dan stepped up onto the trailer. The stern and bow of the double hulls extended beyond the trailer a bit at each end. The trailer bed itself had been covered with a dark, smooth, hard material that would permit the girls to easily dance on its surface. Along the hull and edge of the trailer surface were bamboo handrails that would protect the younger girls from falling off the trailer. Ricky's T-Girls were clearly expert Krewe of New Orleans float builders.

The T-girls were already putting the basic touches on the other two trailers. A Fiji and Tahiti theme were being created on one of the trailers and a Samoan and Maori theme on the other. Bamboo mats and bamboo thatch were strewn around the warehouse floor as Ricky directed all the construction. The sides of the two trailers were draped with large green leaves reaching almost to the floor. Dan helped as best he could but the dozen Special Forces worked together so well, anticipating each other's next move. Finally, Dan decided he was hindering the operation rather than helping it. He just watched as the flavor of five Polynesian cultures was created before his eyes.

"This is amazing," someone said, as Dan turned. It was Jasmine in her princess attire. She was touring the preparation of the floats at the warehouse locations. Her entourage remained outside as she took a closer look.

"Hey," said Dan, caught entirely off guard.

At that moment, Ricky came over. Dan introduced Jasmine to him. Ricky bowed slightly and caught her eyes. "I am so pleased to meet you, your Royal Highness," she said.

Ricky locked on to her eyes which was a cultural taboo and then looked over to Dan and watched his reaction, then back to Jasmine. The three were standing well out of earshot of anyone else in the warehouse.

Ricky slipped into his feminine T-Girl persona, "Oh my God!" he said, "Oh, my God!" He looked back at Dan and then to Jasmine "You're in love with each other!" she blurted out "Oh, my God, Danny Boy, you're in love with her!" Dan blushed, but Jasmine's face betrayed no reaction.

"You have quite the imagination, Ricky," said Jasmine, "I trust that you will keep your whimsical observations to yourself."

"Princess," she said, "the secret is safe with me."

Jasmine smiled and held up her little finger. "Pinky swear?" she asked.

Ricky held up hers, they locked fingers. "Pinky swear," said Ricky.

Dan changed the tone and became very serious. "Princess," he began, "there is something I need to tell you that I was hoping would not be necessary, but Ricky won't let go of it."

Jasmine could sense his tone was very grave. "What is it?" she asked.

"Ricky and her compatriots have every intention of launching a second mission shortly after the first mission is successfully completed and the girls are safely out of Bukhara," said Dan.

Jasmine paused and looked at Ricky and then back to Dan "They intend to free all the women captive in the studio and eliminate your uncle and cousin, Alim," announced Dan.

Jasmine stood still for an eternity as she looked at Dan and then Ricky. She was deep in thought. A thousand times she had thought it needed to be done, even if it meant the loss of her father's kingdom. Once Nasrullah and Alim discovered the American girls were gone, they would come after her. The practices she had seen in the last few weeks had convinced her that Bukhara had become synonymous with evil itself. Finally, she said, "You must guarantee the safety of my father and brother," she paused, "How can I help?"

"We will let you know if that becomes necessary," replied Ricky.

Jasmine extended her right hand to her, "As-Salaam-Alaikum," she said. Ricky recognized the great import of a royal Islamic princess extending her hand. Ricky extended her right hand to Jasmine and said, "Wa-Alaikum-Salaam."

The princess turned and exited the warehouse, joined up with her awaiting entourage, and continued her tour of the warehouse area.

Ricky and Dan just stood there and watched her leave. Ricky broke the silence "Well that went rather well, didn't it?" she said.

"Ricky, what the hell were you thinking with all that love crap?" exploded Dan.

"You clearly left out some critical details back in New Orleans when you gave me the highlights," retorted Ricky.

"I told you all that you needed to know," said Dan.

"No, you didn't," insisted Ricky. "You never told me you had slept with the princess, and you certainly never told me you were in love with her. Little details like that can get people killed when you are going on a mission. Love clouds judgment and makes people predictable, but in a very different way," replied Ricky "Now tell me the rest, Dan."

So, Dan told Ricky about meeting Jasmine in Honolulu and hooking up with her at the Maui Sheraton. He told Ricky about the discussion on female genital mutilation. He explained that Jasmine's grandmother had taken her to Paris for the operation. He told Ricky the whole story about traveling to Sydney and the guy that jumped him in the bathroom turned out to be one of Alim's men."

"Hold it right there, Danny Boy," said Ricky. "A guy tries to kill you, and you leave out that little nugget of information? What else have you forgotten to tell me?"

"Oh my God! I forgot about all about it. The film! He had two rolls of 35mm film. There was no camera with him. I tucked the film in my carry-on. I never gave it any more thought," said Dan. "Until now."

"Go get them and bring them to me," commanded Ricky.

"This is important now?" protested Dan.

"It may be. Every piece of information matters," said Ricky, "I won't know 'til I see the pictures. Bring them to my room. Text me the film type."

Dan walked back to his room and began searching through all the zippered pockets of his carry-on bag. He found both rolls. How many X-ray machines had he been through since Sydney? He wondered if the film had been damaged. He texted Ricky, "Tri-X 400."

Ricky scurried out and found a photoshop, She purchased a developing kit and an old, vintage USSR Soviet developing tank for 35mm film. She bought every accessory she could think she might need, as well as a 35mm film-to-digital scanner. When he got back to his room, he texted Dan to come.

Dan took the film to Ricky's hotel room. Dan saw an assortment of items spread around on the bathroom counter. There were a couple of jugs of distilled water, hanging clips for the film, scissors, measuring cups, thermometer and a timer. Dan watched as Ricky trimmed a brand-new roll of film and practiced rolling it into the vintage Soviet developing tank. Ricky heated the chemicals to 20 degrees Celsius and was ready to go. "Good," said Ricky, "It's Tri-X 400. We have a decent chance that it has not been ruined. This is going to take about an hour. You might as well go back to your room. I'll text you."

Dan returned to his room as Ricky went into the bathroom. She shut off all the lights and tucked towels at the bottom of the door to prevent any light from getting in. He processed one roll and then the other. She thoroughly rinsed them off with the distilled water. She did not trust the water from the tap for the final rinse. She flipped on the lights to reveal the two strips hanging to dry. She waited.

After a while, when they were dry, she placed them in the scanner and voila', the perfectly developed film was on her computer in highly detailed, black and white, with no signs of fogging or reticulation. She texted Dan. He was quickly at the door.

"Danny Boy, Danny Boy you have been a naughty boy," Ricky said, as she stepped through the 72 pictures. "You need to look at this."

She turned the computer display toward Dan. Dan paged through the pictures. They were mostly of Dan and Jasmine in Maui. There were some pictures of Jasmine in San Francisco and at that airport. There were pictures of them meeting in the walkway of the Honolulu airport. There were pictures of them walking in Lahaina, sitting by the banyan tree, having a shave ice, eating at the Ohana Blue Lagoon. There were no pictures of them at Haleakala. If only that had been all. There were a couple dozen explicit pictures of Dan and the princess having sex. The photographer had managed to position himself to get a direct shot through the Lanai doors to Jasmine's bed.

"Oh, shit!" said Dan.

"It's more than an 'Oh, shit,' Dan. You told me you did not find a camera on the guy, right?" asked Ricky.

"You think there are more pictures?" asked Dan.

"It could go either way. There may have still been film in the camera you didn't find. There could be other rolls. On the other hand, why would you leave critical film in a camera and fly thousands of miles to Sydney? We just don't know. Why shoot film and not digital? That one I know."

"The guy saw what he shot," continued Ricky, "but whoever he is answering to did not trust him with the pictures he took. Of course, he could have always shot a roll he didn't turn over. There is no way to know. We have to assume more pictures exist and that they are here in Bukhara," reasoned Ricky.

"I am not sure I am following," said Dan.

"Your princess was being tailed before you even met her. Once the two of you hooked up, the pictures were taken. It's a death sentence, Dan. Even if they didn't have the two of you in bed, the walk in Lahaina, holding hands, cuddling on the beach, it's plenty more than her uncle needs under Sharia Law to have her stoned. And you, too, if you're caught here in Bukhara.

"Oh, shit," said Dan.

"Now you get it. Both of your lives are in danger," said Ricky, "We have to get her out of Bukhara, as well."

"One more thing, Dan, just for the record," said Ricky.

"What's that?" Dan asked.

"Did she have an orgasm?" asked Ricky.

Dan remained silent. "Danny, answer the question. I have no prurient interest to satisfy here. Answer the question," demanded Ricky.

"Yes," Dan whispered, knowing full well he was betraying Jasmine.

"Powerful, with after-tremors?" asked Ricky.

Dan clenched his teeth. He hated this, but his friend knew things about people and behavior that was far beyond Dan's understanding. He nodded his head.

Ricky suddenly changed the mood and grinned and said light-heartedly, "You can't ring a chime if the button doesn't work."

"What do you mean?" Dan was totally lost.

"You said she was operated on by a surgeon in Paris. I am telling you, Dan, the surgeon did not remove what Jasmine thinks was removed. He just camouflaged it. I have heard of it being done before. Her grandmother knew what she was doing and died before your girl could be told when she got older."

Dan was still lost.

"Danny Boy, do I have to draw you a picture? You rang her chime, and you are trying to tell me the button isn't there. You may be good, Danno, but nobody is that good. A little minor surgery and she will be totally restored," said Ricky.

Dan was embarrassed, Ricky was not.

"Now, I have to get back to the warehouse. We are nearly finished and almost ready to roll in the morning," said Ricky, as he ushered Dan out the door.

Evening fell, and Dan had a planned rendezvous with Jasmine. A large tent had been constructed right next to the tunnel entrance in the park. It was not the only one. Other tents from other nations dotted the landscape.

He stepped inside the tent and waited. Soon the tent flap opened, and Jasmine appeared. A stack of boxes had been delivered to the tent. Jasmine and Dan began transporting the boxes to Jasmine's room. Kaliq was summoned to help. It took a couple of hours for the three to transport all the boxes.

When they had finished and were in Jasmine's quarters, they could hear Adil calling for Jasmine. Kaliq and Jasmine went to check on him.

"Sister, where is your American friend? I want to meet him," said Adil.

"Adil, I don't know what you are saying," replied Jasmine.

Adil sprang out of bed. Not slowly, like a man who had been ill, but forcefully, as a healthy young man. "You, Sister, are not the only one who can keep secrets," Adil said, as he stepped toward her and embraced her.

"Mr. Grainger," Adil said loudly. "I wish to meet the man who saved my life, now that I am alert enough to thank you properly."

Dan came into the room. Adil extended his right hand and they shook hands. "I owe you a great debt, my friend," said Adil.

"How long have you been up and around, Brother?" asked Jasmine.

"For three days. I thought it best that I not burden you further, as you have a very big project that you are planning," replied Adil.

"What do you know of my plans?" asked Jasmine as she looked over at Kaliq.

"Far more than you realize," said Adil. "And I know my friend, Mr. Grainger, has a daughter and hundreds of her friends are held captive in the Ark."

"So, tell me all that I should know to be able to help," demanded Adil.

And they did. They shared the entire plan.

Chapter 18

The next morning came quickly. It was March 8, International Women's Day.

Dan and Ricky's entire group of T-Girls slipped into the secret tunnel in the park and Jasmine led them to her quarters. The T-Girls set up operations in Jasmine's suite. Her sink was prepared with brunette hair dye. An assortment of brown contact lenses was spread out on the counter.

Jasmine led six of the armed T-Girls to the location where the girls were being held. Adil insisted that he come along. The regular, male guards outside the special harem were not posted. They had been transferred out to the streets, as part of the Elite Guard of the Ark to control the population. Jasmine appeared at the fountain where Callie was waiting. Callie had been practicing all week with all the girls on their routines. All the girls were positioned for Callie's signal. The T-Girls, dressed exactly like the female attendants, came around to the far side of the girls.

Jasmine gave the signal to Callie and Jasmine slipped back in the tunnel with Dan to return to her quarters. Callie gave the signal and all the girls rushed in formation to the entrance of the tunnel. The real, female attendants began to scream and head for the main entrance to sound an alarm. The T-Girls shot the real female attendants with tranquilizer darts. Ricky's group barricaded the main entry doors and quickly turned and followed the girls into the tunnel. The tunnel had been well lit for the girls' escape. The other T-Girls were positioned along the tunnel to guide the girls and keep them calm. Callie was the last girl to enter making sure all the others had already gone before her. Soon the 275 girls began pouring into Princess Jasmine's quarters.

Dan was there with open arms as Callie entered Jasmine's room. "Dad!" she squealed and began to cry tears of joy. "I always knew you would find me! I never gave up." They embraced, and he held her in his arms. The other girls looked on wistfully and hoped that soon they would be in the arms of their loved ones.

The oldest girls went first. Their hair was quickly dyed brunette and they were fitted with brown contact lenses to hide their blue eyes. The twelve T-Girls acted as an amazing group of beauticians and hair stylists. They related to each girl professionally, putting them at ease and discussing typical "girl things." The girls laughed and giggled. Had the situation not been so critical, it could have easily been the beauty shop in an American mall. Then, each girl sat in front of the camera, and a passport photo was snapped.

Outfits were handed out. The girls quickly donned whatever Fiji, Samoan, Maori, Tahitian or Hawaiian outfit they had been assigned. When the process got around to the younger girls, they were all given Hawaiian attire. The older girls helped the younger girls get dressed. Jasmine helped many of the girls.

Dan and Callie spent as much time together as they could. Callie was busy helping the other girls. Dan often stood by helplessly keeping watch at the tunnels with Ricky. Ricky made one last check of the passport pictures on Jasmine's computer and e-mailed them

For all the girls, there were various types of Polynesian sandals and all manner of wrist and ankle leis. There were leis for the neck and Haku lei head pieces to be worn as a crown. It took several hours to prepare all the girls. The parade was in the early afternoon, so they had adequate time. There was bottled water and nutrition bars for the girls to snack on. It could be a long time before they would eat again. Jasmine periodically left her room and made appearances at the festivities in Registan Square.

As far as the girls knew, the T-Girls were, indeed, naturally women. The T-Girls slipped into Adil's room to dress in private, away from the innocent eyes of the girls. The room had been completely cleaned by the servants that morning after Adil had arisen. There was no sign Adil had been recovering there.

When everyone was ready, Jasmine and six of the T-Girls dressed as Polynesian women led the girls down the tunnel to the park exit. Dan followed the girls. A large tent had been constructed right over the tunnel exit. The girls poured into the tent and lined up as they had practiced so many times with Callie.

Soon, only Ricky, Kaliq and Adil remained in Jasmine's quarters as Ricky got dressed. Adil spoke, "You have a weakness in your plan."

Ricky looked at the man "and what would that be?" asked Ricky, but Ricky knew full well what it was.

"You have no one to watch over the attendants if they wake up and no one guarding that entrance," said Adil.

"I know, but the regular guards have been redeployed outside the Ark. I can't spare any of us from the parade, and none of us can pass for a guard anyway," replied Ricky

"But I can," said Adil. "Kaliq has provided Elite Guard uniforms and weapons. If you give me the tranquilizer gun, I can stand guard at the entrance to the harem. I can ward off any visitor except Alim and Nasrullah."

"You're right. The tranquilizer gun is over there," said Ricky.

"One more thing," said Adil.

"What is that?" asked Ricky

"Can you take a passport picture of me and supply a Tajikistan passport as fast as you can a U.S. passport for the others?" asked Adil.

Ricky thought for a moment. "Yes, I probably can. What do you have in your head, or do I want to know?"

"Just trust me," said Adil.

"First rule of life. Never trust anyone who says just trust me," replied Ricky.

"A point well taken. Just trust me," said Adil.

"Okay, I think I will," said Ricky. Adil sat down in front of the camera. Ricky took his picture. She prepared an e-mail and added weight, height, hair color."

"What name are you using, and where were you born?" asked Ricky as she slid the computer to Adil.

Adil typed his birthdate, used his full name and typed Dushanbe, Tajikistan as the place of birth.

Ricky took a look at it and hit send. "No guarantees," he said, "I didn't tell them this one was coming."

"I understand, but I am sure the Mossad can handle the request if they choose," said Adil. Ricky made no comment and his face displayed no reaction.

"You're a tough guy, Adil. Are you a typical asshole Muslim brother when it comes to your sister's honor?" Ricky almost spat the question as she asked it.

"You speak of my sister and the American?" asked Adil.

"Very observant. Yeah," said Ricky.

"The answer to your question is that six or seven years ago, yes. But after I have seen the value of Allah's favor on me, I have nothing but love for my sister no matter what has happened between her and the American."

"Then be prepared to save her," said Ricky. "There may be pictures, explicit pictures, of your sister with the American in Maui. Pictures that will guarantee her execution. Nasrullah or Alim may have them. Will you protect her against those charges?" asked Ricky.

"I will, with my life," replied Adil.

Adil paused for a moment as if lost in deep thought and then said, "I have one more document that I need from your friends on the other end of your e-mails." Ricky sat down at the computer and started the e-mail and then turned it to Adil. "You type whatever you want. It's your request, surprise me," said Ricky.

Adil typed several lines with a very-specific request for a very-specific document. Ricky looked at it before hitting send. "Well, son-of-a-bitch," Ricky uttered. "Even I would have never thought of that." She hit send.

As Ricky finished dressing, Kaliq and Adil donned the uniforms of the Elite Guard of the Ark. Ricky entered the tunnel toward the park and Adil and Kaliq headed through the tunnels to guard the harem.

Jasmine was about to leave the tent in the park and the re-enter the tunnel to her quarters when Ricky appeared. He was dressed as King Kamehameha in a colorful red and yellow feathered cape and distinctive headpiece. His torso was completely covered in matching bright red and yellow fabric. Jasmine was impressed but had little time to enjoy the spectacle. She had to get dressed for the parade reviewing stand.

All the various floats were lined up to the north of the Ark. Here was the moment of truth. One the T-Girls opened the entrance to the tent as King Kamehameha stepped out into the park. It was a beautiful warm, and sunny day at 23 degrees Celsius. There were numerous tents dotting the landscape. There were women and young girls everywhere with colorful burkas and Islamic dress. There were Asian women in the traditional costumes of their nations. Swiss, German, Dutch and Irish costumes could be seen. The assortment of various ethnic outfits was too numerous to count. The girls followed Ricky double file past several floats. The T-Girls kept a close watch on all of the girls, as they were shepherded to the awaiting floats. The older girls helped all the young girls up the stairs to the Hokule'a platform to get into position. They then began to climb on board the appropriate Polynesian cultural trailer where their costume belonged.

Five T-Girls in Hawaiian garb joined the little ones on the Hokule'a platform. The other six T-Girls, in various Polynesian outfits, took their position alongside the other two trailers. Ricky, as King Kamehameha, took up her position at the leading edge of the Hokule'a on the bow, midway between the two hulls. It was early afternoon as they waited for the parade to start.

Chapter 19

Jasmine returned to her quarters. Adil was there dressed in an Elite Guard uniform.

"I want you to summon Father," said Adil.

"No, I cannot," protested Jasmine. His heart is weak. He hasn't recovered from the poisoning. He doesn't even know Nasrullah poisoned him, and he doesn't know you are alive. The shock could kill him. The parade starts in less than an hour, No!"

"You underestimate him. Your life is in danger, his life is in danger, the lives of 275 American girls and who knows how many women here in the Ark are at stake. Father will grasp the severity and rise to the occasion," said Adil.

"You are not giving me a choice. Are you Brother?" said Jasmine "Very well. Where is Kaliq?"

"He is just inside the tunnel waiting for us to decide," replied Adil.

Jasmine went to the tunnel entrance "Kaliq," she said.

In a moment, he appeared. "Go get Father. Tell him I must see him privately before we assemble for the parade," she commanded. Adil slipped into the other room.

In about fifteen minutes Kaliq reappeared pushing Abdullah in a wheelchair.

"What is it, my child?" asked Abdullah with great concern. He looked around at the boxes and general mess of the room. "What has happened here?" he asked.

She knelt down close to him and embraced him lovingly. "Father," she began, "I have kept things from you; very important things. I have little time to explain before the parade begins. Many lives are at stake - yours, mine and your very kingdom."

The Emir listened intently. He had never seen his daughter like this.

"Father, I am about to give you a great shock. You must be prepared," she said.

The Emir nodded.

"Adil is alive. He has been here in the Ark for the last five years, held captive by Uncle Nasrullah and Alim. Father, he was in the Bug Pit for five years until rescued a few weeks ago by me and an American," Jasmine said.

"Alive!" repeated Abdullah "My son is alive! Where is he? Take me to him."

"I am here, Father," said Adil, as he stepped into the room.

The man's face lit up. My son! Praise Allah! My son lives!" said Abdullah as he reached his hand out for him. Adil knelt down next to him with Jasmine. The man embraced his son and Adil embraced his father."

"Show him the pictures on your phone," Adil said to Jasmine. She got her phone from the table and selected the pictures of Adil when he was rescued from the Bug Pit.

"This is what your brother and nephew have done to Adil," said Jasmine. The pictures were graphic, and showed Adil's deplorable condition when he was rescued and brought to Jasmine's quarters.

The old man suddenly held his chest and breathed deeply. He fumbled in his pocket.

"What is it, Father?' asked Adil.

"The Nitro," he replied, "I need my pills." Jasmine had already realized what was happening and pulled the pills from her father's robe and placed a tablet under his tongue. In a few minutes, the pain subsided and Abdullah was breathing normally.

As quickly as possible Jasmine explained about the kidnapped girls, the parade, the American, and the escape plan that had been set in motion.

"Jasmine, I need some time alone with Father," said Adil, "Some things must only be heard from me, not his daughter."

Jasmine obeyed Adil's admonition. She took her clothes and stepped into Adil's small room to continue dressing.

"Father, there is so much to tell. We must protect Jasmine. She has lived in the west. She is involved with the American that saved me, and is saving the American girls. You understand what I mean when I say involved?" asked Adil.

The old man pursed his lips and nodded that he understood.

"She loves him. I don't think she even knows it, but she does. It's obvious when you see them together," explained Adil. "Can you accept that and protect her when the time comes, as it surely will?"

"I will," said Abdullah. "I will not lose her like I lost you. Like I lost your grandmother. I will not lose someone again to Nasrullah's treachery."

"You have been poisoned by Nasrullah," began Adil. "Cyanide in your IV. That is why you have been weak, confused and dizzy. They had to send you to Dubai for medical treatment because they overdid it. When you returned, they lowered the dose. It was the American that uncovered this, Father. It was the American that arranged for a Jewish doctor to save you. The doctor got Jasmine an antidote for the cyanide and made sure your IVs were clean."

"A Jew doctor?" said Abdullah.

"Yes, Father," said Adil, "He saved me from the Guinea worm and you from cyanide poisoning."

"Get me a pen and paper at once," commanded Abdullah. Adil went to the desk and brought a pen and pad to his father.

Abdullah penned two brief letters and signed them. Adil read them. He was astonished at his father's decisiveness and audacity. He placed the royal seal upon them. They were each placed in a royal envelope addressed by Abdullah and the envelopes sealed with the royal seal.

"You must have these delivered as quickly as you can," said Abdullah.

"I will, Father," replied Adil.

Jasmine suddenly reappeared. "We must go to the parade," she announced. She pushed her father in the wheelchair. Kaliq and Adil headed back to the harem to guard it for the duration of the parade.

Dan was seated near the parade review stand in one of the many grandstands that had been set up along the parade route. The scene in front of the Ark was bustling with excitement. The parade review stand had been set up at the entrance to the Ark ramp. He could see Jasmine's father, Emir Abdullah, seated in a royal wheelchair in the elevated center of the stand. It looked like a throne. He was flanked by Nasrullah and Alim on each side. Behind Abdullah, stood Jasmine. An Islamic cleric offered a prayer. The Bukhara national anthem was played and long, medieval looking trumpets sounded, signaling the start of the parade.

There were cameras perched along the parade route and the event was being broadcast internationally. Jasmine's hard work in planning every detail of this event was furthering Nasrullah's evil deception of portraying Bukhara as a beacon of hope and education to Islamic women. Bukhara would appear to the world as an example of women's progress in an Islamic society.

The parade started with women of all ethnicities and dress walking side by side carrying an International Women's Day banner. Many wore purple ribbons. Signs were present decrying violence against women, domestic abuse, child marriage, gender equality, climate change, female genital mutilation and many other causes. Signs abounded promoting solidarity and gender equality expressed in clever slogans.

There were no men and no military marching. Bukhara only had a military numbering just 3,000 and another 300 were the Elite Guard of the Ark. All of them were busy patrolling the parade route and manning roadblocks around the city that prevented the local Bukharans from coming anywhere near the festivities. Their forces were spread incredibly thin which is what Dan and Ricky were counting upon.

Then the floats began to arrive in the area in front of the Ark. It was an unbelievable culturally diverse display from dozens of nations featuring beautiful clothing of every imaginable style and color. There were stylish multi-colored burkas that covered a woman from head to toe and the basic black ones. There was all manner of Islamic clothing from across Africa, to Indonesia to Central Asia. Some revealed a great deal of flesh and some very little.

Dan saw the Japanese Dance Troup float approaching the parade review stand. The float stopped in front of the Emir as many had. Some of the girls stepped down from the float and began performing traditional Japanese dances to music coming from the float. It was a magnificent tease to the stadium presentation later in the day. More floats passed and then Dan saw the Hokule'a and a proud King Kamehameha standing at the center of the bow, the Hawaiian flag blowing proudly in the wind. Hawaiian music filled the area of the Ark as the float approached. A large banner read "One Pacific, One People."

One of the T-Girls blew into a traditional Hawaiian Pu shell horn. The piercing low note of the conch shell resonated throughout Registan Square in front of the Ark. On the deck of the Hokule'a the little girls were dressed in long, flowing Hawaiian, floral-print dresses. They were holding their arms up delicately in the air with Hula motions to the music. Some of the older girls came gracefully down the stairs and joined the girls who had been walking beside the float.

The music changed to another song, "Aloha 'Oe" began to play as Callie came down the stairs of the Hokule'a. She walked gracefully up to the parade review stand and looked directly at Emir Abdullah and Jasmine. The other girls in perfect motion with the music took up positions next to her and behind her. Callie led the group in the very delicate and tasteful flowing motion of the Hula. Callie's brunette hair blowing gently in the wind, her tanned skin did not betray her. There were no grass skirts today that might offend the Islamic government.

All the dresses covered the girls from the shoulders to just above the ankle. The pure white dresses were of a Victorian Holoku style, with long sleeves and green wrist leis that accentuated the Hula motions. Each girl had ankle leis and a white Haku Lei upon her crown and was adorned with a beautiful flower lei around her neck. The crowd was transfixed at the majestic display. Even Nasrullah and Alim seemed taken with the performance. The television cameras caught the performance in HD and broadcast it all over the world.

The Hula is traditionally performed with bare feet, but the uncertain texture of Registan Square and the long walk to the stadium required that each girl wear sandals. Callie had been taught many years ago in Hawaii to keep her eyes on her hands as they majestically formed a narrative of deeply felt emotion. A cultural and spiritual display of harmony and discipline created a sacred continuum that bonded God with his creation of nature and humanity.

Callie broke with that tradition on just a few occasions when she allowed her eyes to look into the face of Princess Jasmine. The two spoke volumes to one another during those few brief seconds when their eyes locked. They both knew this was the last time they would ever see each other. They both knew that a terrible fate awaited them and so many others if the carefully laid plans of Dan Grainger went awry.

As the girls finished their remarkable performance, they gracefully turned and went up the stairs of the Hokule'a just as the music was ending. The older girls took up positions on the float carefully interspersed among the younger girls. At the end of the Hawaiian "Farewell to Thee" classic melody, all the girls shouted out in unison "ALOHA!" The float continued its travel down the parade route. Callie sighed in great relief. The dance had gone just as she planned it.

Immediately, the next two floats came slowly by. The Tahiti and Fiji theme float followed by the Maori and Samoan float. The girls on the floats were waving and performing the cultural dances of that island. A half-dozen of the Maori girls were performing a short-string poi-ball routine in their black and white lined outfits, and the Tahitian girls were doing their dance in bright-yellow outfits. The floats slowed as they passed the review stand and stopped briefly. The parade route was another 1-1/4 to 1-1/2 miles to the stadium and the buses that could carry them to freedom.

Dan left the grandstand and looked up at the parade stand. He could see Jasmine, but there was no way she could pick him out of the crowd. Jasmine looked toward the departing Polynesian floats and scanned the crowd hoping to catch a glimpse of Dan one last time. Alim watched Jasmine as she seemed unusually preoccupied with the departing dancers. He watched her intently as she seemed to scan the crowd as if she were looking for something. Whatever it was, she did not seem to find it. She returned her attention to the parade. Alim suddenly had a very unsettling feeling about his cousin.

Dan began his walk to the stadium by back streets rather than the parade route. When he arrived at the stadium, it was chaos. The Polynesian floats were not there yet, but buses and costumed parade participants were everywhere. He located the six buses chartered for their ride to the airport.

He saw the Japanese Dance Troupe entering the stadium to prepare for their performance. Then he saw the Polynesian floats entering the stadium grounds. He went over to assist. One trailer at a time, the girls were escorted to the correct bus. A courier handed a package to Ricky, still dressed as King Kamehameha. In it were U.S. passports for all the girls and a Tajik passport for Adil. The girls' names were carefully checked off a list as they entered the buses. When all the girls had exited the floats, a final count was made of each bus. Passports were separated into six groups for each bus.

Callie sat at the front of her bus. Dan was next to her. There was some relief, but the tension was still palpable. Two of the T-Girls were on each bus. Ricky was with Dan and Callie. It is impossible to know if any of the girls had figured out that the T-Girls were not naturally female. They had only seen them initially at the harem location, then Jasmine's room, and finally dressed as Polynesians. Ricky had removed the cloak and headdress and her long brown hair dangled to her shoulders. She slipped out of the King Kamehameha costume and was wearing a beautifully colored, Hawaiian print-dress.

The buses began to move. It seemed like an eternity as the convoy of buses slowly made their way to the airport. Suddenly, the convoy was stopped. Dan looked out the window and saw dozens of military men surrounding the buses. There was a pounding on the door of the bus.

The door opened, and without warning, a large German Shepherd appeared. It ran down the aisle to the back of the bus. Several of the girls shrieked loudly in surprise.

Two military men boarded the bus. One of the men stood at the door. The other officer started down the aisle to the back of the bus where the dog was methodically sniffing his way forward from seat to seat and person to person. The German Shepherd was actually very sociable and not at all threatening. Some of the girls even tried to pet him as he checked them out. Most of the girls cowered back in their seats with some fear.

The officer in front looked at Dan. "Passport, please," the man said in English. Dan handed him his passport. He opened it and studied Dan for a while and carefully studied Dan's passport. He handed it back to Dan. Ricky held up his passport, and the man opened it. He looked at the passport, looked at Ricky, and he looked back at the passport again. He studied Ricky's features carefully.

The German Shepherd had made his way to the front of the bus and scurried out the door. Dan was able to look out the window and see the other buses lined up behind him. The dog waited at the door of the second bus. Military men were walking alongside the buses and looking up to the windows at the girls.

"So close," thought Dan. "We are so close to making it out of here. Dan's heart was pounding as he looked at Ricky. Ricky's face betrayed no emotion or concern. Dan was reassured by Ricky's calmness.

Dan knew this was their only shot. Resistance would be futile if they were discovered. The safety of the girls could not be risked in a physical confrontation. There was simply no place to run and hide.

Dan's thoughts drifted to his daughter, Annie, in Anderson. He had instructed her to proceed regardless of whether she knew that Callie and the girls were safe. Annie was the backup plan. If they failed to escape right now, the world would learn from Indiana that the girls were alive this morning in Bukhara. There was an internationally broadcast video of the parade to prove it. Mothers all across America would recognize their own daughters, even with dark hair and brown eyes.

It was up to Annie and attorney John Kosten to succeed. He trusted both of them with his life, and he trusted the Lord. Dan began to pray.

Chapter 20

Annie had to testify in just a few minutes. She stood in the hallway outside the Madison County Court. She was concerned. If Callie and her dad were still in Bukhara, her testimony would endanger them and all the girls. Mark Campbell had already remained in jail long enough, knowing he was in danger from the other inmates. He had nearly been killed once. Yet, Campbell steadfastly refused to permit John Kosten to submit evidence that would show his daughters were never on the flight. He was risking his life until the girls were safe.

Annie was conflicted. Should she testify now, or just try to put it off for a few hours until she knew for certain everyone was safe. Kosten had to fight to get this hearing postponed as long as he had. There was intense, almost irrational opposition from Merriman. She wanted Campbell put away.

Foulke never fought the continuances very hard. He knew Koston had his reasons. Foulke's judgment was no doubt clouded by his relationship with Cynthia. He didn't believe Campbell was guilty of the molestation. He had seen too much of Campbell's character. Foulke believed he had deferred too much to Merriman's office. Foulke also knew that as long as Campbell was in jail, Cynthia would keep coming back to Indiana. Foulke liked that idea a lot.

John Kosten was just a few steps away from Annie speaking with Steve Foulke about the possibility of postponing until the afternoon. Foulke said he didn't think he could get that past the judge. He told Kosten that Merriman had vigorously opposed every delay. He said Merriman was powerful and would find a way to go around him if there was another request to delay.

"I have good reasons," said Kosten.

"I have been patient. You are going to have tell me what those reasons are if we go in there and you expect me to agree to another delay," said Foulke.

Kosten looked over at Annie. "Any news?" he asked. She solemnly shook her head no.

"Okay, Steve, off the record, and I mean way off the record," said Kosten.

"You sound really serious," said Foulke.

"The lives of 275 children are at stake."

"You implied that before. What has changed?" demanded Foulke.

"Off the record, Steve, your solemn word," said Kosten.

Foulke looked into Kosten's eyes. He pursed his lips and thought for a moment. He looked over at Cynthia standing alone several feet away. His gut told him to listen to the man. "You have my word, John," said Foulke with a sigh.

Kosten whispered, "The part I did not tell you is that the 275 girls are alive and we are waiting for word they are safe."

Foulke stared in disbelief "You're shittin' me," Foulke said.

"If the word does not come before Annie testifies, then we have specific instructions from Annie's father to go to Plan B. We tell the world through Annie and Cynthia's testimony how the Oasis Plane was hijacked. We have Lani Kealoha standing by in Honolulu to testify by video. You have heard her story. It will exonerate Campbell. I am asking you to allow me to go with the complete witness list I gave you.

Tears began to stream down Annie's cheeks. John walked over to Annie, "Annie," he said, "what is it?"

Steve Foulke also approached to within earshot. "I have not heard from my dad. He should have let me know by now if Callie and the girls are free. It's probably 6:00 or 7:00 p.m. in Bukhara by now. The parade has been over for a while. They should be out of the country. My dad said his rescue plan might fail. If that is the case, he said to blow the lid off the story on the morning of March 8, Indiana time. They are either safe now, or this is the only way to save them. I have to testify.

Kosten looked over toward Foulke and said, "No word on the girls, but it's a go."

Cynthia had been listening and was just a few steps away. When she heard the "It's a go" comment, she came over to the group. Belinda was with Foulke. He had known John Kosten for a long time. He knew in his heart that Kosten would never fabricate such a yarn.

"Let us pray," said Kosten, as he held his hands out to Annie and Alice. Annie motioned to Cynthia to join in. Cynthia hesitated "Go, Child," she heard a voice say. She turned and it was Belinda standing next to Foulke. "You too, Mr. Foulke, Lord knows you two need prayer."

All six joined hands and created a circle in the hall outside the courtroom. Annie and Alice were on either side of Kosten. Cynthia held Annie's hand with her right hand and her left hand was holding Steve Foulke's right hand, then Belinda connected with Alice. Kosten quietly led the prayer. He asked the Lord for His guidance and prayed that Dan and the girls be delivered from their captors. He blessed Sgt. Mark Campbell for his courage and to keep him safe. He asked for the Lord's guidance for each of them in the pursuit of justice.

It was an unlikely sight. When the prayer ended, Foulke looked at Cynthia but said nothing. His eyes had teared up a bit. Cynthia winked at him and smiled a slight grin and nodded her head slightly. She turned to John. "Thank you, Mr. Kosten," she said. The six then parted and returned to their preparations. An observer at the end of the hall had watched the spectacle. Shirley Merriman was not pleased. She turned to the deputy and said, "Jenkins, something smells real rotten here."

The deputy remained silent. "You better be ready when I call," said Merriman.

People were filing into the courtroom. Foulke had specifically invited Judge Hardy to sit directly behind him in the front row. Television news crews were showing up outside in the hall. Reporters were gathering inside the courtroom.

As Annie and Alice entered the courtroom, Alice spied the same TV reporter she had spoken to at the Hamilton County Courthouse. Alice stopped and said, "I told you Oasis knows something. Oasis is hiding something. Now you are going to see that I am not the distraught rambling mother that you painted me to be. I told you a mother knows these things."

The TV reporter just looked a bit stunned and said nothing. There were no cameras rolling inside the courtroom to catch what Alice had said. The courtroom was filled to capacity.

Mark Campbell was led into the room in an orange jumpsuit accompanied by a deputy. He was led to the defense table. Cynthia was in the front row and their eyes met. They both smiled at each other. Cynthia stretched out her arm and touched her father's shoulder as he sat down next to Kosten. Campbell's wife sat next to Cynthia. The judge entered, and all rose until he was seated. From the rear of the courtroom, Shirley Merriman looked on.

John Kosten said "We need just a moment for one of our witnesses to step outside. Cynthia stood up and walked to the rear door of the courtroom. Her eyes locked on Merriman's. The two women glared at each other every step of the way until Cynthia reached the door. Cynthia mouthed the unmistakable words "Fuck You!" with her lips as she exited the courtroom.

Merriman was incensed.

John Kosten stood up and said, "We now call Annie Grainger to the stand."

Annie was sworn in and sat down in the witness chair.

"Annie," began Kosten. "Your sister, Callie Grainger, was on that fateful Oasis flight, is that correct?

"Where were you when the flight took off?" asked Kosten

"My mother and I were at the Orlando Airport and watched the plane taxi from the gate," replied Annie.

"Did you happen to take any pictures?" asked Kosten.

"I took video of the plane taxiing from the gate as my mom and I watched through a window."

A TV screen had been set up in the courtroom. Kosten motioned, and a video started showing a plane on the ground.

"Do you recognize this video?" asked Koston

"Yes, it is my video of the Oasis 747 with Callie on board," replied Annie.

For a while, the camera was on the tail wing with the Oasis logo, and then it widened out to reveal the entire plane. In just a few seconds, the video showed a light in one of the windows being switched off and on. The camera zoomed in quite a bit and revealed a young girl waving with her face pressed against the window, making a face at the camera. The courtroom erupted in a muted laugh, the crowd realizing they were looking at one of the girls who had died in the crash.

"Is that your sister, Callie Grainger?" asked Kosten.

"Yes, sir," replied Annie.

As the video concluded, the camera widened back out to reveal a wide shot of the plane with the vertical tail wing clearly showing the word Oasis. The video stopped on a still frame of the entire plane. Then switched to a still frame of the just the tail wing.

"What is this picture?" asked Kosten.

"It is the vertical tail wing of the Oasis 747 plane that my sister was on," said Annie.

"Now, just so there is no confusion, please switch back to the full plane and then back to the tail wing," asked Kosten. The video switched back to the picture of the whole plane. "I want you to note the placement of the Oasis logo. Now switch back to the tighter shot," said Kosten. "Annie, you are confident this is the tight shot of the same tail wing?"

"Yes, I created it myself from the video I shot," said Annie.

Kosten handed Annie a newspaper. "Do you recognize this?" he asked.

"Yes, it is a copy of the Miami Herald showing the Oasis tail wing being pulled from the water off the coast of Miami." It was a large, color picture on the front page above the fold.

Kosten pointed to the screen again and said, "can you identify this picture?"

Annie began, "It is the same picture that is in the newspaper that I downloaded from the Miami Herald website."

"It is the same picture. Is that correct?" asked Kosten.

"Yes, it is the same Miami Herald picture of a tail wing being hoisted from the ocean, clearly showing the Oasis logo

"Now, what is this picture?" asked Kosten as he motioned for the next slide.

"This is a picture I created of the two photos of the vertical tail wing side by side at nearly the same camera angle," said Annie.

"And do you have an observation about this comparison?" asked Kosten, as he turned to face the spectators in the courtroom.

"Yes, they are not pictures of the same tail wing," said Annie, as she paused for a moment. "The tail wing hoisted from the debris off the coast of Miami is not from the Oasis 747 that was carrying my sister. The plane never crashed, and my sister and all of the girls on the plane were abducted," said Annie confidently, as she paused for effect and let her words sink in.

Suddenly, the spectators gasped and made sounds. A couple of reporters bolted for the door. The judge pounded his gavel and asked for order in the court.

"How can you say that?" said Kosten.

"Look at the placement of the letters of the Oasis logo," replied Annie. "It's not the same. The Oasis logo on the video I took is closer to the front of the wing and higher up than it is in the Miami Herald picture. It is not the same tail wing."

Everyone could see it. The courtroom was in pandemonium. More reporters ran for the hallway outside to make phone calls. Most of the TV stations had live news at noon. They had to get LIVE ENG/SNG trucks or cellular backpacks to Anderson to broadcast live at noon.

Merriman scurried down the aisle to Foulke. "Stop this. You need to stop this now," said Merriman.

"Why?" asked Foulke. "It's all true."

"It's not relevant," said Merriman. "What happened to the plane has no bearing on the charges against Campbell," said Merriman.

"I have no problem with this line of questioning," said Foulke, "I am not going to object."

"Well, I object to you, and I am going to have you thrown off this case," said Merriman.

The judge was pounding his gavel for order. As the noise subsided, Merriman could be heard saying, "Your Honor, this dramatic grandstand play has no relevance to the hideous molestation of Keisha and Kara at the hands of Mark Campbell."

"Mr. Foulke," said the judge, "Do I hear an objection?"

"No, Your Honor," replied Steve Foulke. "My office is committed to finding out all the truth surrounding the events associated with Keisha, Kara and all of the girls affected by this tragedy in Orlando. Miss Grainger's testimony is assisting this Court in its search for the truth. I have no objection."

"Duly noted," said the judge, "Ms. Merriman, you need to take your seat." Instead, Merriman stormed down the aisle to the back of the courtroom.

"Annie," asked Kosten, "do you have anything else to share?"

"I do." said Annie.

"Do you recognize the girls in this exhibit?" asked Kosten.

The screen now displayed a picture of 17 girls.

"Yes, it is the information sheet handed out at the press conference in Orlando identifying the 17 girls that had been recovered off the coast of Miami." said Annie

"Did you know some of these girls?" asked Kosten.

"Roll the video," said Kosten and the monitor began showing a video of Callie Grainger in a stadium of some kind demonstrating dance steps to some girls.

"This is my sister in the Orlando Citrus Bowl Stadium helping Keisha Campbell with some dance steps, and as I widen out and pan around, you can see a lot of girls. One thing is quite noticeable when you realize it. Almost all the girls are white, and they are blonde. I can tell you from my personal observation that they had blue eyes," said Annie.

"Why is that significant?" asked Kosten.

"Now, look at the handout with the 17 pictures of the girls," said Annie, as the screen switched back to that picture. "Nearly all of these girls are minorities. None of them are blondes. What are the odds of that, that none of the girls recovered were blue-eyed blondes when 90% of the girls on the plane were blue-eyed blondes."

"Anything else?" asked Kosten.

"Oh yes," replied Annie, "I was in Orlando last night with Kara and Keisha's step-brother, Jimmy Campbell, and step-sister, Cynthia Campbell.

"Why was that?" asked Kosten.

"We were looking for evidence that would exonerate Mr. Campbell of the molestation charge, by proving he was not the last Black male to have access to his daughters," said Annie.

"Did you find such proof?" asked Kosten.

"What we found was an abandoned metal building southeast of Orlando. It had sort of a grass strip that a plane could use. It had a water tank filled with sea water. I saw what I believe to be bloodstains and other items on the floor," said Annie.

"Did you report this to the police?" asked Kosten.

"We called the police and explained some of our suspicions," said Annie. "Cynthia and I had to get back to the airport to be here for this hearing. Jimmy stayed behind to meet with the police."

"Thank you, Annie," said Kosten.

Steve Foulke stood up. "I have no questions of this witness, Your Honor."

"We would now call Miss Cynthia Campbell." Said Kosten.

Annie left the stand and walked to the rear of the courtroom where her mother was waiting. When Annie and Alice stepped into the hall, Cynthia was standing there. Annie and Cynthia hugged for a moment. "Thank you," said Annie.

"Thank you," said Cynthia, and then she disappeared into the courtroom.

The reporters then realized it was Annie Grainger in the hallway and surrounded her, peppering her with questions. Annie and Alice had a plane to catch. Her dad said they should go ahead with the flight even if she had not heard from him. Annie did not respond as their questions got louder and more insistent, as she and her mother reached the elevator. Annie made the decision to trust the Lord and believe in her dad. Callie was going to be alright, she had to be. As the doors closed, one reporter shouted, "Give us something."

Annie smiled, "Stay tuned, you ain't seen nuthin' yet," and the doors closed.

Annie looked at her phone, it was 9:35 a.m. Their plane left at 11:51 a.m. from Indianapolis. It was tight, but they should make it. Kosten had arranged for a private limousine. Outside, they found a black Jaguar XJ and driver waiting for them. Their luggage was already in the trunk.

Chapter 21

After studying Ricky's passport for the longest time, he handed it back to Ricky. The Bukhara military officer began walking down the aisle of the bus. Ricky jumped up with a handful of passports and began speaking with him. He spoke English quite well. Ricky was openly flirtatious with the officer, and he smiled. He took several of the passports in his hand and continued down the aisle.

Occasionally, he would open a passport and call out a name. The girl would raise her hand and Ricky would point her out. He would study the picture and then look carefully at the girl. Ricky remained by his side at all times, sometimes bumping into him and holding his shoulder for support as if she were about to fall. When he reached the back of the bus and turned around, Ricky just stood there in her Hawaiian print dress. The officer had to slide by her in very close quarters. He smiled again as he brushed against her. Ricky allowed her breasts to press against the man's chest. Dan was watching the events unfold, and even he could not believe how brazen Ricky was behaving.

The officer returned to the front of the bus and motioned the other man off the bus. He handed the passports back to Ricky, smiled and exited the bus. The two Military men stopped each bus as it passed. The officer boarded each bus and asked the T-Girl to show the collection of passports. He did not look at them. He just looked down the aisle and then left the bus. This was repeated for the next four buses.

It seemed as if it took forever for the buses to arrive at the airport. As each girl left the bus, her passport was checked by a security guard and matched as the correct photo. There was no luggage for any of the girls.

The girls were then shepherded to passport control. At this point, the passport officials had little interest in checking each passport, as they had been handling dozens of such groups. Had they checked closely they would have found an official Bukhari entry stamp for each girl. They opened the passports and stamped their departure stamps as fast as they could.

The T-Girls escorted the girls to the terminal bus and rode with them to the plane. When all the girls were aboard the plane, a final count was made. All the girls were on board and accounted for.

Callie was at a window seat sitting by her dad, on the aisle, as much of this was unfolding. Then quietly she said, "You are coming with us?" but she sensed the answer.

"No, I want to but I cannot. Princess Jasmine risked her life to save you and all the girls. Her life is in great danger right now, even more than she knows. We have to try and save her.

"No, Daddy. I won't accept that answer. Isn't it you that always says to finish a job right before starting the next one?" Callie asked.

"Yes, but," began Dan.

"No, Daddy, please. I am asking nicely. Your mission was to bring me and all the other girls back to their families in the United States of America. I told them you would come for us. We are not there yet. What if something happens to stop us and you are not there to fix it? How will you feel then? You must stay with us until we reach America," Callie said emphatically.

Dan just paused for the longest time. This was actually what Ricky was referring to when he said love can cloud judgment and cause unpredictability. He sighed.

"You are right, Callie. "I will stay with you until we reach America."

She put her arms around his neck and hugged him tightly.

Ricky was about to motion to close the aircraft door when Adil appeared at the stairway ramp. He was still in Elite Guard attire.

"Did you get it?" asked Adil.

"Yes, I did. Didn't know you would need it so quickly," replied Ricky as he handed the new passport to Adil.

"The other document I requested. Were they able to produce it as well?" asked Adil.

"Not yet. That was a tall order," replied Ricky. "I expect to have it delivered in a couple of hours."

"Too late for me," said Adil, "When it comes you must get it to the princess. She will understand its importance."

"You do know that the JAL request for topping off the tanks was denied, due to the great demand this week for fuel at the Bukhara airport?" asked Adil.

"Yes, we need full tanks to reach the final destination. We have enough fuel for a short hop to get them out the country and stop to refuel," said Ricky.

"Let's say 400 kilometers to Dushanbe?" asked Adil, with a bit of a grin.

"Yeah, Dushanbe, Mr. Smart-ass," replied Ricky, "but you knew that already. You don't waste any time getting up to speed or thinking things through."

"When you've contemplated your existence for five years in the Bug Pit, it doesn't take any time to realize the importance of full speed. I have already thought everything through a thousand times," said Adil.

Ricky nodded with full understanding.

"Give me your secure e-mail address in case I need it," said Adil.

Ricky rattled it off. Then he said, "Did you get that?"

"I got it," said Adil, as he scurried up to the door and Ricky motioned it to be closed. Adil walked through the cabin. The magnitude of this operation suddenly hit him for the first time when he saw the faces of hundreds of little girls. He found Dan and placed his bag in the overhead compartment. Adil sat down across the aisle from Dan.

"We need to become better acquainted," said Adil.

The flight to Dushanbe, Tajikistan was only two hundred fifty miles, and shortly after the plane was in the air they had cleared Bukhara airspace.

Callie stood up and shouted the announcement. "We are free! We have to stop soon for fuel and then will be on our way home to America." The plane erupted in cheers from the girls.

Adil had traveled much of the eastern hemisphere in his life, but never to the U.S. He was quite taken by the unbridled spirit of the American girls. They had all been through a tremendous ordeal and yet, their American spirit had not been broken. There were no signs of oppression, no signs of defeat.

Adil got up from his seat, retrieved his bag and entered the restroom. In a few minutes, he reappeared in a long, white thobe with a white, ghutra headscarf with a black, agal cord.

He looked like Arab royalty with his well-manicured, stubble beard and moustache. He sat down just as the descent into Dushanbe was beginning.

Adil got up immediately when the doors opened. Two Tajik military officers entered the plane and greeted Adil warmly. Dan leaned across Callie and peered out the window to watch as the three men disembarked and then began talking on the tarmac. After a few minutes, the three men walked toward the terminal.

A truck pulled up to the stairs, and men began unloading containers and bringing them up to the plane. Some of it, they stowed in the galley. Shortly, they began distributing sacks of food to the girls. There was pizza, and there were hamburgers and cheeseburgers from Burger King. There was water and soft drinks. The distribution had no order to it, but before long, every girl was chowing down on pizza or a sandwich.

Dan stopped one of the JAL flight attendants and asked, "Who did this?"

She smiled, "Mr. Toguchi say American girls need American food."

Dan just shook his head and scarfed down a cheeseburger. When finished he fired up his laptop and connected to a Wi-Fi signal from somewhere on the airport property or maybe the plane while it was on the ground.

Chapter 22

At the stadium in Bukhara, Jasmine tried to enjoy the performance of the Japanese Dance Troupe. She was nervously awaiting word on the 747. The Japanese Dance Troupe completed its performance to a standing ovation. They boarded the buses for the train station. She was getting very concerned.

There was a presentation of awards and recognition to the various participants in International Women's Day. This ceremony dragged on for another forty-five minutes. Alim was becoming noticeably agitated but did not dare leave. It would have been publicly disrespectful to the Emir and those dignitaries in attendance.

Jasmine watched Alim fidget. She had control of the entire day's agenda, and this boring interlude was necessary to give the Japanese girls time to board the train and leave the country. On one occasion, Alim and Jasmine locked eyes, He glared at her and she smiled, which further inflamed him. The text she was waiting for finally arrived.

"OASIS TWO has cleared Bukhara airspace, Dan and 275 girls are safely on board."

Jasmine was relieved. Finally, the event was over. The Emir Abdullah, Nasrullah, Jasmine and Alim exited the stadium. An aide pushed Abdullah's wheelchair. Too frequently, Jasmine would stop and become engaged in conversation with an important dignitary from another nation. Abdullah would converse with them as well, clearly understanding the need to delay their exit. Alim continued to fume. Another text message to Jasmine confirmed the train carrying the Japanese Dance Troup had crossed into Uzbekistan. She smiled and Alim noticed as he observed her looking at her phone.

At a snail's pace, they finally made it to the awaiting Mercedes. Once all were aboard, Alim instructed the driver to hurry back to the Ark. They were escorted by an Elite Guard motorcade.

Once at the Ark, they entered the main entrance and Alim scurried quickly into the Ark without saying a word. He seemed to be on a mission.

Jasmine and her father were escorted to the Emir's quarters.

"Come, Jasmine, we must talk," said Abdullah, as he motioned his daughter to come into his quarters.

"Has your plan succeeded?" asked Abdullah.

"Yes, Father."

"Very well done, my child, I am proud of you," said Abdullah.

"And what about the American? Where is he?" asked Abdullah.

Jasmine was surprised by the question but did not hesitate to answer truthfully "He has left after rescuing his daughter, and I shall not see him again."

The Emir looked at his daughter, "You are so much like your grandmother. My father loved her above all of his wives," replied Abdullah.

"Then why, Father, why did he allow her to be stoned?" asked Jasmine. She had never dared broach the subject with him before."

"He had no choice. She committed adultery and it is the law," he said wistfully.

"You are the law in Bukhara," began Jasmine. "If I were accused of adultery, would you require that same fate for your daughter?"

Without hesitation, the Emir said, "I thought I had lost my son. You are my only daughter. I love you unconditionally. Damn the law! I would never permit it."

Jasmine broke down immediately in tears and her father motioned to her, and she dropped to her knees and sobbed uncontrollably as her father held her in his arms for the longest time.

"Now, Child, you need a good night's rest. You, Adil and I have a nation to rule."

Jasmine stood up, bowed to him and retired to her quarters.

Alim had sensed that something in Jasmine's manner was more defiant than usual. He did not need a secret tunnel to reach the special harem. He walked the main hallways and reached the main entrance to the tunnel. Kaliq saw him coming from his vantage point inside the harem.

He had tied up all the attendants and had tranquilized them again when they started to awaken. Occasionally, an Elite Guard had come by. Kaliq had told them from the other side of the door that he was guarding the harem and they were to leave. No one became suspicious.

Alim would never accept such a story. Kaliq raced across the harem to the fountain and disappeared into the tunnel. Alim tried to enter the main entrance. He pounded on the door and no one came. He called for the Elite Guard and no one came. He had released nearly all of the Elite Guards of the Ark to guard positions in the city.

He ran down the hall until he finally found an Elite Guard at his post. He ordered him to find some guards and come to the harem. Alim scurried back to the harem door and waited. In a few minutes, a half dozen Elite Guards appeared. "Open the door," commanded Alim.

One of the guards fumbled for his key, quickly found it and unlocked the door. It only opened a few inches. It was blocked. "Break it down!" Alim commanded. The guards turned over a large lamp post in the hall and used it as a battering ram. The barricade gave way and the door opened wide enough to enter. Two guards rushed in and Alim followed. The attendants were lying tied up and motionless on the floor. One of the guards began to check them. "They are alive," he said.

"Better for them if they were not," said Alim.

Alim quickly searched the harem. All the girls were gone. All of their belongings appeared to be left behind.

"Jasmine what have you done!" screamed Alim "You will pay this time for your treachery!"

"Guards," shouted Alim. "Search the Ark, search the city. Find the American girls and bring them to me."

Alim stormed out of the harem and down the hall. International Women's Day had been a huge success for the image of Bukhara. As far as he was concerned, Jasmine had outlived her usefulness. It was time to take full control of the Emirate.

Kaliq had made his way through the tunnel and circled around in the main hall. He needed to warn the princess and headed to her quarters. Before he was able to get there he saw Alim and a group of Elite Guards at her door. Alim pounded on her door until she finally answered. He pushed past her into her room.

"How dare you!" she exclaimed.

Alim looked around. It was a mess. All the remnants of the "beauty salon" were obvious. The outfits the girls had been wearing in the harem were strewn about her room. Alim checked all around her quarters. He looked into the room where Adil had been recovering. There was nothing to see there, now, out of the ordinary.

"Jasmine, you have gone too far this time," said Alim, "You will pay for your treachery with your life."

Jasmine was defiant as Alim motioned the guards to take her into custody.

Kaliq watched from the down the hall as Jasmine exited her quarters with her hands bound behind her back, surrounded by the Elite Guard. Jasmine continued her defiance. "Father will never permit this. I have done what is right and just," she proclaimed. "What is the charge?"

Alim motioned for the guards to stop and came around in front of her to face her directly. He looked into her eyes and she did not avert her eyes and stared back at him with obvious contempt.

"Adultery!" Alim declared. "You have been with that American. You will be tried and stoned until you breathe no more."

"Father will not permit this," she said.

"Your father will be unable to prevent it. You are an adulteress, and no mercy can be shown. You have no defense against the proof I have. I have pictures of you with the American in Hawaii," said Alim.

"Take her to the Zindon Prison," Alim smiled as he said it.

Jasmine's iron composure broke for moment, much to Alim's delight. Her eyes closed as she fought back tears. Was he going to put her in the Bug Pit? Would he dare, she wondered? Of course, he would. He put Adil there for nearly five years, but her father did not know Adil was alive.

The Elite Guard marched Jasmine through the halls of the Ark and then outside to Zindon. Alim followed all the way. They entered the prison and she was literally thrown into a cell. Alim personally shut the door with an evil grin.

In a moment, she was all alone in a dimly lit, dank cell. When her captors were out of earshot she broke down, threw herself on the single bed with the dirty, thin mattress and cried out "Allah, Allah, how much more must I endure? Please help me." But no comfort came from her God. She just remained all alone and in total despair.

Alim could not have simply left Zindon. He had to savor his victory by going to the Bug Pit where he believed Adil was still wallowing at the bottom of the pit. He spit into the pit and then relieved himself on the man below. He shouted down at the pathetic figure that he presumed was Adil. He shouted, "Soon, Cousin, I will come back and finish you after I take care of your sister and your father." He walked away in satisfaction that finally Bukhara would be all his and his father's.

Kaliq had watched as all of the events unfolded. He dared not go to Abdullah at this late hour. Adil and Dan were on the plane in Tajikistan. Kaliq had to find this Ricky person. He had no choice. He had such distaste for this group, but his loyalty to Princess Jasmine and Adil overcame his disdain. He quickly went to the hotel.

Kaliq saw the group of "women" as soon as he entered the lobby. Ricky saw him at once and the look on his face. She discreetly went over to him. She pretended not to notice Kaliq and sat down near him. "What is it, Mate?" Ricky asked.

"It is the princess. Alim has arrested her, charged her with adultery and has taken her to the Zindon Prison." He whispered softly but his eyes cried out in pain.

Ricky had to digest the new situation. She sighed deeply and then sighed a second time. She had planned to wait a couple of days before the next mission, in the belief that most of the visitors to Bukhara would be gone. "I see fate has intervened," said Ricky. "We will save her and with no help from your precious Allah."

Ricky stood up and motioned to the T-Girls. They all followed him to his room. Ricky sent an e-mail to Dan who should still be on the ground in Dushanbe.

Ricky told the T-Girls what happened and said, "We need a plan by morning and I don't have one." Ricky dropped to his knees, held out his hands; the other T-Girls joined him on their knees. They held hands and created a crowded circle in the middle of the room. Rick led them in prayer as they all joined in and said, "Praise Jesus. Yes, Jesus. Guide us, Jesus," It was an unlikely sight.

Dan was seated on the plane next to Callie when Ricky's e-mail came through. "This can't be good," he said while opening it. Callie perked to attention and she could see his computer screen, as Dan read that Jasmine was under arrest and in the Zindon prison. She thought she heard her dad mutter something.

Tears welled up in her eyes. She knew what she had to say. Her voice cracked. Her dad was going to try and save Jasmine no matter what she said. She could make it harder for him or easier for him. "You have to go, Dad," said Callie, "You have to go save her."

Dan looked at her, this young girl who had been through so much now telling him he should go. Dan wasted no time, he replied to the e-mail "I will be there as soon as I can." Dan retrieved Callie's cell phone from his bag.

"Here," he said, as he handed it to her. "You left this in a Jeep."

"Oh my gosh, you found it! I didn't know what to do. I finally decided it was no good for anything if it wasn't on. So, I left it," said Callie.

"That Jeep was 6-volts not 12-volts. It was another blessing that you didn't burn up your phone," said Dan.

"I just kept messing with the wires until the phone started charging," said Callie "It was a miracle."

I've had a thousand miracles since I began looking for you," said Dan. He finished buttoning up his computer, grabbed his carry-on, kissed Callie on the forehead as she clung to him, and then headed for the stairs.

Callie could see him out the window talking to a military guard. The man motioned to another military guard who escorted Dan to the terminal. Callie placed her hand on the window and prayed. "We need another miracle, Lord," she said quietly, "Keep my dad safe and help him save Jasmine."

Dan was taken to the ticket counters and he searched for a flight to Bukhara. Tajik Air had a late-night shuttle with seats available. Dan booked it and within the hour he was aboard the Boeing 737 on his way back to Bukhara.

It was a short flight and he was back at his Bukhara hotel by 1:00 a.m. and was able to get a room. He e-mailed his room number to Ricky and tried to get some sleep. He had no doubt they would all get together in the morning with a plan to rescue Jasmine.

Chapter 23

At the back of the courtroom in Anderson, the petite young Black woman in her mid-twenties walked forward. She was dressed in a finely tailored, gray, fitted jacket with a slim, matching dress cut just above her knees. Her hair was styled once again in an Olivia Pope power look. She looked fabulous and fearless. All eyes followed her. This time, Steve Fouke fully appreciated her as Cynthia took the stand.

"Where were you yesterday?" asked Kosten.

"I was in Orlando, Florida," replied Cynthia.

"Was anyone with you?" asked Kosten.

"Yes, my brother, Jimmy, and Annie Grainger," said Cynthia.

"Can you tell us what you found?" asked Kosten.

"We found an old warehouse. We went inside. We discovered a large water tank filled with salt water. There was a trail of bloodstains leading to another room. We went in. We found more bloodstains and two pair of little girl's underwear on the floor." said Cynthia as her voice cracked.

"Did you recognize the underwear?" asked Kosten.

"Well, all I can say is that it was the Disney Princess Tiana underwear. Keisha loved Princess Tiana, and Kara always wanted to wear whatever Keisha was wearing. One was smaller than the other and could have been their sizes," said Cynthia.

"Did you touch anything?" asked Kosten

"No," replied Cynthia, "We left and the three of us called the Orlando police dept."

"What did you tell them?" asked Kosten.

"We told him that the two of us had to fly to Indiana but that Jimmy would be coming by to talk to them," replied Cynthia.

"What happened then?" asked Kosten.

"Jimmy took us to the Orlando airport and he stayed in Orlando," replied Cynthia.

"Have you heard anything from Jimmy since then?" asked Kosten.

"Yes, Jimmy called me yesterday after I arrived in Indianapolis. He said he was at the warehouse. The Osceola County Sheriff was there conducting an investigation," replied Cynthia.

"No further questions, thank you, Cynthia," said Kosten.

Steve Foulke got up and stood directly in front of Cynthia. Their eyes met. He nodded ever so slightly at her with just a trace of a smile. He knew what he needed to do. He was totally on board with Kosten now. He would do as John had asked him. Together, they would be a tag team in the search for the truth and justice.

"Miss Campbell, has your father ever molested you or touched you inappropriately?" Foulke asked.

"No," Cynthia responded firmly.

"Do you have any reason to believe your father has ever molested your step-sisters?" asked Foulke, as he turned around to face the courtroom and stared at Merriman in the back of the room.

"Absolutely not!" said Cynthia.

"You are the sister of Keisha, Kara and Kima, is that correct?" asked Foulke.

"Step-sister, yes," said Cynthia.

"When they first came to the U.S. did you have occasion to see the girls in, uh, a state of undress?" asked Foulke.

"Yes," replied Cynthia.

"Did you notice anything unusual?" asked Foulke.

"Yes, their private parts had been mutilated in an unspeakable fashion that is the custom in many African Muslim cultures. It is called FGM, Female Genital Mutilation and it is widely practiced."

"How is it that you know so much of this practice?" asked Foulke.

"When you have actually seen it once, you can never get it out of your mind," said Cynthia. "I have thoroughly researched it after having seen it three times up close and personal. These precious little girls, my sisters, had their clitoris scraped out of their bodies. The villager or relative that did it used a dirty razor blade. There was no anesthesia. All three told me about it. In Guinea-Bissau where they are from, as many as fifty percent of the girls have been subjected to this hideous procedure. In neighboring Guinea it is as many as eighty percent."

Her words hung in the air, and everyone who heard them was stunned into absolute silence. The courtroom was eerily silent.

"No further questions, Your Honor," said Foulke.

Kosten stood up and said, "I would like to call my next witness, Cheryl Graham

A professional woman in her late thirties took the stand and after the oath was administered Kosten said, "Ms. Graham, what is your occupation?"

"I am an Indiana Licensed Social Worker," said Graham.

"How long have you been a social worker?" asked Kosten.

"Ten years."

"Have you ever met Ms. Shirley Merriman of the Madison County Child Protection Services?" asked Kosten.

"Yes," replied Graham. "I am an adoption specialist at a Christian adoption agency. I work with birth mothers. Sometimes I have a client in Madison County who gives birth to a baby addicted to drugs and Ms. Merriman's office is notified."

"Of birth mothers you have served in Madison County under these circumstances, have any of them been from Africa?" asked Kosten

"For reasons of confidentially, I cannot identify any of the clients by name, but I can tell you some have been from Sudan, Nigeria, Senegal, Guinea and Mali," replied Graham.

"Did any of these girls suffer Female Genital Mutilation in their native countries?" asked Koston.

"Some did."

"How do you know that?" asked Koston.

"My clients would tell me and discuss what happened to them when they were little girls. The doctors also had to be aware of their condition before delivery, as it can make for a difficult natural birth," said Graham.

"Would Shirley Merriman have known about this?" asked Kosten.

"Yes," said Graham. "In cases where drugs were involved she would have been notified and would have had access to records. In addition, in the case of two clients, she and I discussed the birth mother's FGM."

"Have you ever heard Ms. Merriman speak of FGM at any other time?" asked Kosten.

"Yes. When I was in school fifteen years ago studying for my Bachelor's in Social Work. Ms. Merriman was a guest speaker that addressed our class," said Graham.

Kosten handed Graham a thin spiral notebook. "Can you identify this?"

"Yes. It is a handout given to our class outlining topics that Ms. Merriman spoke to us about," said Graham.

"Can you turn to page 12 and look at the map of West Africa?" Asked Kosten

Graham opened the booklet to page 12.

"What do you see?" asked Kosten.

"It is a color-coded map showing the nations in West Africa where the practice of FGM is most common," said Graham.

"Can you identify the nation of Guinea-Bissau on the map and tell me how it is color coded?" asked Kosten.

"It is one of the nations where FGM is very common."

"Thank you, Ms. Graham."

"Can you turn to page 17 and read the heading at the top of the page?" asked Kosten.

Graham flipped a few pages and began reading, "The heading is *Guidelines to Identifying the Perpetrator of Sexual Molestation.*"

"What else does it say?" asked Kosten.

Graham began reading, "The perpetrator of sexual molestation is often the father, step-father, uncle, older brother or an older male cousin. You should always suspect the step-father first. This is even more likely in families when the step-father is or was in the military or law enforcement. Male military members stationed overseas often select their child victims by marrying the mother and bringing the family back to

America. The mother and the victims fear reporting the abuse, due to possible deportation from the United States."

"Did Ms. Merriman cover this topic with your class, as well?" asked Kosten.

"Yes."

"What do you think of those comments?" asked Foulke.

"It is not my area of social work," said Graham, "but to the extent I have experience, I have not seen any truth to the statement that members of the military and law enforcement are more prone to committing sexual abuse than the general population. But more importantly, after Ms. Merriman left, our instructor specifically told us to disregard that statement as untrue. Our professor told us that many studies had shown that statement to be blatantly untrue."

"How did you feel about that?" said Kosten.

"It troubled me that a person as highly-regarded in central Indiana as Ms. Merriman could make such unsupported statements without being challenged," said Graham.

"Is there anything else Ms. Merriman has spoken about that troubled you?" asked Kosten

"Yes," said Graham. "She closed the class one day by saying, and I am paraphrasing, that social workers have a duty to challenge the system. She said we must be like termites that burrow deep into the foundations of our established institutions and destroy them, and then out of that chaos, a new and better system can be created."

"No further questions, Your Honor," said Kosten.

Steve Foulke stood up and walked toward Cheryl Graham with something in his hand. He took the handbook from her and turned to a particular page of pictures. They were disturbing photographs of young girls and the FGM that they had experienced.

"I have in my hand two pictures of Keisha and Kara Campbell taken during the autopsy of both girls' genitals. He held them up for Ms. Graham to see.

Graham had difficulty looking at them.

"Ms. Graham," said Foulke, "are these pictures consistent with the pictures shown in Ms. Merriman's handout of West African girls subjected to FGM?"

Without hesitation, Graham said, "Yes, they are quite consistent with the examples shown in the booklet that Ms. Merriman gave us."

"Can you turn to the front cover of this booklet and tell me the name of the author?" asked Foulke

"Shirley Merriman, MSW."

"Thank you, Ms. Graham, no further questions, Your Honor," said Foulke.

As the witness stepped down, Foulke turned and caught the eyes of Merriman glaring at him.

Kosten stood up and said, "We have additional evidence to present this afternoon that will prove Keisha and Kara were not on that plane. That, in fact, they were murdered by being drowned in that warehouse water tank filled with sea water. We will show that sea water in their lungs did not come from the waters off the coast of Miami but came from farther north on the Florida seacoast. We have someone that witnessed the events in the warehouse and will testify by closed-circuit camera from another state that Keisha and Kara were sexually assaulted by another Black man. In addition, we have an international witness available by closed circuit television that will corroborate that neither Keisha, Kara nor any of the 23 girls recovered were on the Oasis 747. In addition, we believe that Mark Campbell's life is in danger if he remains in custody, and we request that he be released on his own recognizance pending a determination by the Osceola County Sheriff that the evidence presented here today is corroborated."

Steve Foulke stood up "Your Honor, we agree with Defense Counsel, and we have no objection to the immediate release of Mr. Campbell on his own recognizance."

"No!" shouted Merriam, who had come forward to approach the bench. "No, this man is guilty of molesting these little girls. NO!" Merriman said. "I intend to bring the full force of my office to bear on this matter." Merriman glared at the judge as if to say, "Don't you dare cross me on this."

The judge stared back at her. He looked down for a moment. Then he said, "I will consider the Request for Release over the noon recess, "Bailiff, please take special precautions for Mr. Campbell's protection. We will reconvene at 2:00 p.m.," he slammed down his gavel, stood up and walked out.

Merriman looked at Foulke. "Whose side are you on?" she practically spat out the words.

Kosten stood beside the both of them as Foulke replied "The side of justice. What side are you on, Ms. Merriman? Are you tone deaf? Do you not comprehend the magnitude of what was testified to here today by Ms. Grainger and Ms. Campbell?"

"I will have you removed from this case," Merriam said as she turned and stormed out the same door the judge had used to exit the courtroom.

Judge Hardy had sat in the front row during the entire court proceedings. He remained seated as all the sharp exchanges took place around him. His face displayed no reaction.

As Deputy Jenkins led Campbell out of the courtroom, once again Cynthia caught her father's eyes. She snapped to attention and saluted him.

Foulke shouted out to Jenkins, "Wait! I am coming with you." Jenkins waited until Foulke caught up with them. Foulke turned back to the courtroom and saw Cynthia mouth the words

"Thank you, Steve." She turned and walked toward the back of the courtroom.

It was just the three of them: Campbell, Foulke and Jenkins as they walked slowly along the hallway and entered the elevator. Jenkins and Foulke were both shaking. They were clearly nervous. Campbell was not. As the door closed Campbell looked straight at Foulke and said, "The shark is in a feeding frenzy today."

Foulke nodded slightly and said nothing. He knew what Campbell meant.

They got off the elevator and passed a couple of the new holding rooms.

Jenkins' cell phone rang. He answered, "Jenkins here."

It was a female voice. "Take Campbell out now!" she said and hung up. Jenkins put the phone back on his belt clip.

"You know, Steve," said Jenkins, "it is not necessary for you to be back here. We've got it under control."

"I'm staying with Campbell," said Foulke.

They walked a little farther and Jenkins stopped. He unshackled the ankles of Campbell and then his wrist. He stared squarely into the eyes of Campbell. Jenkins raised his eyebrows slightly and Campbell took notice. Jenkins unlocked the door to the holding area. The three men stepped in to find about a dozen other inmates there, including the six skinheads.

"Foulke turned to the deputy and exclaimed, "What the fuck are you doing Jenkins? This room should be empty."

"Sorry, Steve, change of plans. Please forgive me," said the deputy, as he stepped back and fell on the floor as if he had been hit but he hadn't. The camera mounted above did show a portion of Jenkins' body on the floor but did not show what Jenkins just did. The security personnel watching the monitors took a moment to assess the situation and the alarms sounded.

There were two men in the back of the holding area. One hoisted himself up on the shoulders of the other and ripped the camera from the wall.

Four of the men came toward Campbell and Foulke backing them into a corner. The two from the back ran forward and joined in. Three of the men each pulled out a shiv. One thrust his blade toward Foulke in a slashing motion that surely would have sliced open Foulke's stomach. Campbell swiftly kicked the arm of the man, deflecting the blade from reaching Foulke. The man turned his attention to Campbell and thrust the shiv at his abdomen. Steve was scared shitless. He knew he was going to die along with Campbell. Foulke lunged at the man as hard as he could, and the man fell without cutting Campbell. The shiv fell to the floor. Foulke rolled over against the wall as fast as he could. He was able to scoot the shiv with him.

The other two men with shivs came at Campbell and were about to reach him when suddenly, the six skinheads entered the fray. The two men with shivs were quickly disarmed and hand-to-hand combat ensued. Foulke managed to get back to his feet.

What Steve Foulke had thought was twelve against two and a cowardly deputy lying on the floor, suddenly turned into six defending Campbell and six trying to kill him. Foulke was able to kick the shivs across the room toward the door. Playing out a few feet in front of him was a display of martial arts that Foulke had only seen in an action movie. At the center of the action was Mark Campbell striking his opponents with extremely efficient and brutal counterattacks.

It seemed like an eternity, but in just a few moments, all six assailants were on the floor incapacitated by the blocks, kicks, punches, and open-handed strikes, as well as varying forms of takedowns administered by Campbell and the six skinheads. Deputy Jenkins suddenly appeared with a half dozen handcuffs and began cuffing the attackers to a bar on the far corner of the room, as the skinheads dragged them over one by one.

When it was safe, the six skinheads approached Mark Campbell, lined up, smartly saluted him in unison and said "Sgt. Campbell, Sir, U.S. Marine Corps Reserve Special Operations, at your service, Sir."

Sgt. Mark Campbell stood at attention and returned the salute.

Jenkins voice broke the brief moment of silence and said "and one old, very-tired former Marine at your service, Sir:" and then Jenkins saluted.

One of the Marines spoke again, "Sgt. Campbell, Sir, Ambassador Krewe and Lt. Col. West send their regards, Sir."

Campbell pursed his lips for just a moment and nodded slightly in acknowledgment at what the Marine had just said.

"Thank you, gentlemen," said Campbell as he saluted all of them once again.

There was banging at the door, as a number of deputies were trying to get in and fumbling with keys. Jenkins opened the door. "Hold up," he said. "These six stay here in this holding area and not one of you is to breathe a word about what happened until I say so. These two and these six are free to go."

One of the six Marines said, "No, we are staying until our mission is complete and Sgt. Campbell is free to go home."

The eight of them and Jenkins walked down the hall to another room and waited where they could talk.

"Jenkins," said Foulke, "why didn't you tell me what the hell was going on?"

"There was no time Steve," said Jenkins. "After that stunt you pulled in court, she wanted Campbell dead now and his court case over. She cannot stand losing."

"Hold on," said Jenkins, as he pulled his phone from his belt and called someone. When she answered, she said, "Jenkins?"

"Campbell is dead," said Jenkins, "killed by some of the inmates."

"Good work," she said.

"Are you sure they won't talk? asked Jenkins.

"They have the same incentive to keep quiet as you do," she said coldy.

"Can we pick up the kids now?" asked Jenkins.

"Yes," said Merriman.

Jenkins hung up.

"She had your grandkids?" said Foulke.

"Yeah, they've been in foster care."

"Why didn't you tell me about the Marines?" demanded Foulke.

"It was on a need-to-know basis," said Jenkins, "And you didn't need to know until you showed up at the last minute to walk with us. It was just too late then. I was confident the Special Ops would protect you."

"Okay. It's all good," said Foulke, "I thought for sure I was a goner. Campbell saved my life."

"Now, we need to call the emergency vehicles, like this is the real thing, or Merriman will get suspicious," said Jenkins. "We are instituting lock-down procedures. No one goes in or out. No information goes in or out until the lockdown is lifted. You need to leave Steve, now."

"Bill, I need you in court at 2:00 p.m. Be there," said Foulke.

Foulke left immediately and found a private place to call Cynthia.

"Cynthia, it's Steve. My God, you were magnificent," said Steve.

"You mean on the stand or in bed?" asked Cynthia.

Steve had not expected that comment and was momentarily flustered. "Both, I guess," said Foulke, "but I was only thinking about your testimony."

"You called to tell me that?" said Cynthia.

"No listen to me," said Foulke, "Listen and do not react. Your father is fine. He is not hurt. He is safe. Merriman tried to have him killed. He is fine, Cynthia. You are going to hear that he is dead. He is not. We don't want Merriman to know her plan was foiled. If you hear it, you must react in a credible way to the news. Got it?"

"Got it," said Cynthia.

"There will be court at 2:00 p.m. make sure you are there. It may be continued to tomorrow morning," said Foulke.

"Okay."

"One more thing," said Foulke. "Your father saved my life. While he was being attacked by six men, he deflected a knife intended to disembowel me. Your father is incredible."

"You just now figuring that out?" said Cynthia.

"Yeah, but I don't have you figured out yet," said Foulke.

"Bye, Steve," said Cynthia as she hung up.

Steve walked through the courthouse and people were running around. He looked out the windows and emergency vehicles were everywhere with their red lights flashing.

He grabbed his coat and walked several blocks to a restaurant. It wasn't that cold for the first week in March. He wanted the opportunity to get a good look at the protesters. The streets were filled with anti-Campbell signs and racist chants. When he reached the restaurant, he sat down and had a quiet meal, as chaos was taking place outside in the streets. He knew it was even worse inside the courthouse.

As he was eating, he was checking news headlines on his phone. He watched clips of cable news outlets panel discussion of the "Hail Mary" pass from the Campbell defense team. They viewed as scandalous the outrageous allegations made by Campbell's daughter and Annie Grainger. They pointed out that the mother of this same Annie Grainger, Alice Brooks, had once proclaimed the Oasis was somehow behind some sinister plot. The panel took great satisfaction in attacking the legal ethics of John Kosten defending Mark Campbell, while also representing Annie Grainger in a civil case against Oasis. They scoffed at the testimony of a Christian social worker as not relevant to the facts of Mark Campbell's molestation. A professional social worker on the panel extolled the virtues of Shirley Merriman's well-respected reputation of advocating for children. An Oasis spokesperson on the panel explained, once again, how devastated the Oasis Corporation was at the loss of life in the accident and promised to do everything humanly possible to help the families.

Reports were beginning to come out of Osceola County, Florida suggesting the Sheriff's Department was conducting a massive investigation at a remote warehouse location. News helicopter views of the warehouse area clearly showed the site could have been used for a landing strip. Official vehicles were everywhere around the warehouse. The authorities were not speaking to the press yet and there was little the reporters could do but speculate on the connection to the events in Anderson, Indiana.

Foulke looked out the windows of the restaurant. More reporters and news vehicles were showing up in the streets of Anderson. Unconfirmed reports were circulating that Mark Campbell was dead. Other reports said he was in the hospital in critical condition. A few news media outlets simply reported that something had happened regarding Mark Campbell, but without confirmation, they could not report any of the rumors. They reported the holding area was on lockdown and there would be no information available until the lockdown was lifted.

Half a world away in Dushanbe, Tajikistan, the JAL 747 had taken off for its fifteen-hour flight. Callie could hardly drum up any enthusiasm. She was worried about her dad. She had to have faith and know that he would be okay and come back to her. She had been the leader of this group, and she had a role that she had to fulfill.

Once in the air and at altitude, Callie got up and shouted at the top of her voice, "Next stop U-S-A." Once again, the plane erupted in cheers. "We Rock," shouted Callie and the girls shouted "We Rock."

Then Callie started a song by one of Indiana's native sons, John Cougar Melloncamp. All of the girls knew the song. Soon the 747 was filled with 275 girls singing "R.O.C.K in the U.S.A."

Chapter 24

As 2:00 p.m. approached, Steve Foulke walked down the street to the Madison County Courthouse. He was surrounded by reporters shoving microphones in his face and shouting questions. He said little until finally, he was ready to step into a guarded entrance at the courthouse. He turned and waited a moment for the reporters to position their mics and the photographers to frame their shot.

"I have heard the same rumors and reports that all of you have," said Foulke. "The holding area is in lockdown, no one is going in or out. No information is available until the lockdown is lifted. I am awaiting an official briefing on what happened. I have court in just a few minutes, and I am confident all of the details will be known at that time."

He made his way to the courtroom and entered through a back entrance instead of from the main hallway.

Cynthia and Mrs. Campbell were sitting together just behind John Kosten. They both looked very somber. The courtroom was packed. Judge Hardy sat in the first row behind Foulke's seat at the prosecutor's table.

Shirley Merriman entered from the back and walked down the aisle looking very smug. She sat down in the front row next to Judge Hardy. Mrs. Campbell was directly across the aisle from Merriman. The woman glared at Merriman as their eyes locked upon one another. Merriman broke the duel of eye contact and shifted her eyes to Cynthia, who was staring directly at her. A slight trace of a smile came to Merriman's lips.

"All rise," and everyone stood up as the judge entered and sat down and called the Court to order.

Kosten stood-up.

"Your Honor, the defendant is unable to be here at this time. The prisoner holding area is on lockdown, and no one can leave that area until the lockdown is lifted," said Kosten. "Mr. Foulke and I have agreed that, in the interest of justice, we can continue this portion with the defendant in absentia."

The judge looked at Foulke and said, "This is fairly irregular. I am not sure we should proceed without the defendant being present."

"Your Honor," said Kosten, "in the interest of justice, I beg the Court's indulgence and would like to have the critical testimony of the next two witnesses offered into the record. This was Mr. Campbell's expressed desire."

"I have no objection, Your Honor," said Foulke.

The courtroom was buzzing with people whispering to each other. Everyone had heard that Campbell was dead. It had even been reported on a couple of the TV stations as breaking news.

The judge fumbled a bit and looked around the courtroom and caught Merriman's eyes. She sat in the front row smugly savoring her victory and the lost cause that was unfolding before her eyes. She moved her head slightly to the left, then to the right indicating her disapproval in a manner that only the judge could have seen. The judge was in a bind. It was a high-profile case and the request was not unreasonable with both the defense and prosecution in agreement.

"Okay," the judge reluctantly said, "but I warn you I will end these proceedings abruptly if I think it becomes necessary." Merriman glared at the judge.

Kosten called his next witness. A young, high-school-age girl took the stand. After she had taken the oath, Kosten began, "Emily, how old are you?"

"Eighteen."

"Were you present last month at the high school when Ms. Merriman and a doctor performed a physical examination on a large number of Mr. Campbell's students?"

"Yes," said Emily.

"Were you one of those students?" asked Kosten.

"Yes," Emily said quietly, obviously embarrassed.

"How old were you at the time of the examination?" asked Kosten.

"Seventeen."

"Were you informed by Ms. Merriman that you or your parents had the right to refuse the examination that day?" asked Kosten.

"No, she said we had no choice," said Emily.

"At any time during the examination," asked Kosten, "were you touched by Ms. Merriman in your…excuse me, Emily, I am sorry. Were you touched by Ms. Merriman on your vagina."

"Yes," she said quietly and looked down.

"Did you observe other girls that same day being touched in the same way by Ms. Merriman?" asked Kosten.

"Yes, I couldn't see for sure, but I know they were," said Emily.

"No further questions, Your Honor," said Kosten.

"No questions Your Honor," said Foulke.

The witness stepped down and slowly made her way to the back of the courtroom.

"I would now call my next witness, Ms. Shirley Merriman."

"I object, Your Honor," said Merriman, "I am not subjecting myself to Mr. Kosten's courtroom antics. I refuse."

Foulke stood up immediately. "Ms. Merriman is in no position to object. She has been called as a witness and must take the stand."

The judge looked around the room. He looked at Merriman and he knew he needed to end this. He was in an impossible position, "Very well," he said, "but the patience of this Court is at an end. The Defendant is not present, and there will be no more witnesses after this without the Defendant present."

Shirley Merriman approached the stand defiantly and took the oath and sat down in the witness chair.

"Ms. Merriman," said Kosten, "did you just hear the sworn testimony of Emily who was one of the girls you examined last month at the high school?"

"Yes," said Merriman smugly and with disdain.

"Did she accurately describe her examination," asked Kosten.

"Yes." said Merriman.

"It is your testimony that you touched her vagina and those of the other girls you examined that day, taking great care to change gloves after every examination?"

"Proper medical procedures require that, and I always insist on following proper protocol," said Merriman.

"Are you a doctor?" asked Kosten.

"No," said Merriman.

"The doctor who was present for the examinations was under the belief that you are a registered nurse," said Kosten. "Is that correct? Are you a Licensed Registered Nurse in the State of Indiana?"

Merriman suddenly froze and didn't answer.

"My office has conducted an exhaustive search of Indiana Professional Licensing and the licensing of every state in the nation," said Kosten, "I have found no record that you are a registered nurse or that you have any medical credentials that would permit you to perform such examinations or even assist in such examinations. Is that true?"

Merriman suddenly exploded "I do not have to sit here and listen to this. I am the Director of Child Protective Services, and I have been performing these examinations for years. She stood up and looked at the judge. "Do something," she said. "This is a farce."

Steve Foulke immediately stood up and approached the witness.

"Ms. Merriman," said Foulke, "we obtained a search warrant to examine the files in your office. We found this BSN diploma with your name on it buried in your files." He held it up for Merriman to see. "Funny thing, though, my office checked with this school and they have no record of you attending."

Deputy Jenkins had moved closer to the witness stand when Merriman stood up. John Kosten stepped out of the way.

"Deputy Jenkins," said Foulke, "place Ms. Merriman under arrest for the sexual assault of Emily and the suspicion of sexual assault of numerous other victims."

Merriman stormed off the stand "You are out of your mind!" she exclaimed.

She strutted across the courtroom toward the aisle. In her path stood Mrs. Campbell, who had stood up and blocked her from entering the aisle.

Merriman and Mrs. Campbell stood face to face for only a moment. Merriman took another step forward. Mrs. Campbell raised her right hand to within inches of Merriman's face. The powerful, lobster-like pinchers of her Krukenberg hand opened and were poised to clamp upon Merriman's neck. Merriman froze in her tracks. She had felt the power of Mrs. Campbell's grip once before.

Jenkins had quickly come up behind Merriman, pulled her arms behind her and handcuffed her. "Ms. Shirley Merriman, you are under arrest," said Jenkins.

Foulke pointed to the side door and said, "The lockdown has been lifted." The whole courtroom could not help but look, including Merriman.

The side door of the courtroom opened and in walked Mark Campbell in his orange jail jumpsuit. His arms and ankles were not shackled. The courtroom erupted. People were shouting. Flash photography was going off. Cynthia and Mrs. Campbell ran to Mark and embraced him. Sgt. Mark Campbell stood tall in the courtroom with one arm around his wife and one arm around his daughter.

The judge was pounding his gavel. "Order in the Court, Order in the Court."

Finally, a semblance of order came to the courtroom and quiet was restored. Two more deputies approached the bench as Merriman stood handcuffed in the aisle dumfounded and speechless. She looked at Jenkins. He smiled a big grin. It was beginning to sink in to her.

Foulke continued, "Ms. Shirley Merriman, you are also being charged with the attempted murder of Sgt. Mark Campbell."

Again, the courtroom erupted in chaos but it was short-lived. Foulke raised his arms to the crowd and gestured for the crowd to calm down and they quickly did.

"Judge," began Foulke, "you are under arrest for conspiracy to commit murder." The two deputies quickly approached the bench, handcuffed the judge and marched him out of the courtroom.

Judge Hardy quickly approached and stepped up to take his seat at the bench. "Order in the Court, Order in the Court," said Judge Hardy, as he rapped the gavel. Everyone became quiet and listened to the judge's words.

"I am assuming jurisdiction over this Court. Everyone be seated and be quiet! Deputy Jenkins, place Ms. Merriman in the front row behind Mr. Foulke. I want her to hear the rest of the testimony in this case first hand. You can handcuff her in front. Next witness."

"I call the Madison County Coroner, Larry Crawford," said Kosten.

The Coroner came forward and took the stand.

"Mr. Crawford," said Kosten, "you have been gathering evidence in the death of Keisha and Kara Campbell. Is that correct?"

"Yes," said Crawford.

"Have you completed your report on the cause of death?" asked Kosten.

"No, but I can share some pertinent information that has just been confirmed in the last twenty-four hours," said Crawford.

"Please summarize some of your findings," said Kosten.

"Keisha and Kara Campbell were drowned in seawater from the Atlantic Ocean. The seawater analysis shows that the water taken from their lungs contained certain characteristics that are not found in the seawater off the coast of Miami and did contain characteristics of seawater found off the coast of Cocoa Beach one-hundred-eighty miles farther north."

The courtroom erupted again as it had that morning.

Judge Hardy rapped his gavel once and everyone became quiet.

"Please continue," said Kosten.

"I have been in contact with the coroner's office in Dade County and Osceola County, Florida. Many samples have been taken from a warehouse located southeast of Orlando. Seawater was recovered from the lungs of Keisha and Kara, as well as several other girls believed to be on the Oasis plane. The seawater found in a water tank inside that warehouse is consistent with seawater found in the lungs of the girls tested so far. Blood stains were found on the floor of the warehouse that is a DNA match to Keisha and Kara. Two pairs of underwear were found on the warehouse floor that have a DNA match to Keisha and Kara."

The courtroom silence was occasionally punctuated by gasps from the room but remained quiet for the most part.

The Coroner continued, "Semen samples previously taken from Keisha and Kara have now been matched to at least two male Africans recovered off the coast of Miami near the Oasis wreckage. These two male Africans had previously been identified as having fallen overboard from the ship, Lobito. This ship was involved in recovery operations of the Oasis plane wreckage. Mr. Campbell's DNA was not a match to any DNA taken from Keisha and Kara."

"I thought that Mr. Campbell's DNA had been matched to the semen samples on the day of his arrest," said Kosten.

"That was a rush to judgment. There was indeed a preliminary match to an African-American male. An unwarranted assumption was made that no other African-American males had access to the children except their father. Further tests determined the semen was not from an African-American. It was from two African males who have been identified as citizens of Guinea-Bissau."

"Have you drawn any final conclusions?" asked Kosten.

"My report is not finalized, but I can tell this Court that there is no evidence to support the charge that Keisha and Kara were sexually molested by their father that day. There is irrefutable evidence that supports they were raped by at least two African men who have been positively identified. Keisha and Kara were murdered in the warehouse and their bodies dumped into the Atlantic off the coast of Miami."

"Have you given any thought as to why Keisha and Kara were selected by these men to be raped?" asked Kosten.

"Yes, I have two thoughts on that, but it is speculation," said the Coroner.

Foulke sat silently and did not object.

"This speculation is based upon facts you have ascertained in listening to the testimony in this case. Is that correct?" asked Kosten.

"Yes," said the Coroner, "The two men have been identified as citizens of the nation of Guinea-Bissau. They spoke the same language as Keisha and Kara. This may have caused the men to take a special interest in the girls. The men could reasonably assume that the girls had been subjected to the custom of female genital circumcision. All of the other girls in the warehouse that day would have been considered unclean because they had not endured that procedure. Keisha and Kara were considered clean and suitable for sexual penetration."

Kosten paused for a long time and allowed that point to sink in to all that were listening. Finally, he asked, "Is there anything else?"

"Yes," said the Coroner, "The Osceola County Sheriff Department has found the remains of a man buried in a shallow grave near the warehouse. He has been identified as the bus driver who had been employed to drive the red-and-white bus to the Orlando airport from the Hilton where the girls had been staying."

"Your Honor," said Kosten, "I have a few questions of Mr. Crawford that do not directly bear on the cause of death for Keisha and Kara but are related to the events surrounding their molestation and death."

Steve Foulke quickly stood up and said, "I have no objection, Your Honor."

Judge Hardy said, "Proceed, Mr. Kosten."

"Mr. Crawford," said Kosten, "are you familiar with Ms. Grainger's testimony regarding the placement of the Oasis logo on the tail wing of the 747?"

"Yes. We have been in communication with the NTSB. They have a copy of Ms. Grainger's video in their possession. They also have the actual vertical tail wing of the 747 recovered off the coast of Florida. They have been able to scale the dimension of the logo placement from the video and compare the placement on the actual tail wing that was recovered. On Ms. Grainger's video, the logo was determined to be six inches from the edge of the vertical tail wing. On the recovered wing, it was measured to be just over nineteen and five-eighths inches. Or, to put it another way, it measured one-half foot on the video and one-half meter on the wing recovered from the Atlantic. A simple mistake in metric conversion was made in the placement of the decal on one of the wings."

"What conclusion has the NTSB drawn from this discrepancy?" asked Kosten

"The NTSB will not make their findings public until their investigation is complete. For the purposes of my report, I can confirm that Keisha and Kara were not on the plane that took off from Orlando with the other girls. I can also conclude that the wreckage recovered off the coast of Miami was not wreckage from the plane that took off from Orlando. Seventeen of the 300 girls were recovered off the coast of Florida the first day of the search. The bodies of six more girls were recovered within the next few days. This leaves 277 girls unaccounted for, some large number of which were on the 747 that took off from Orlando and no wreckage from that plane has been discovered."

Is there anything else you can tell us about the wreckage?" asked Kosten.

"Not without speculation on my part," said the Coroner.

"Now Mr. Crawford, are you familiar with the collection of DNA material from the African nation of Namibia that has a bearing on the missing girls?" asked Kosten.

"Yes, I am," said the Coroner.

"Can you explain?" asked Kosten.

"The Oasis Corporation collected DNA samples from every finalist in their selection process of the girls. As a result of a court order, those DNA samples were made available for analysis. In the nation of Namibia, near the Angolan border, two 55-gallon drums of sand and dirt containing human waste and other material was analyzed for DNA. A number of viable DNA samples were recovered and matched to the DNA samples collected by Oasis. There were ninety-three positive DNA matches." said the Coroner.

"Can you draw any conclusion from this information?" asked the Kosten.

"Yes," said the Coroner, "At least ninety-three of the 300 girls who were in Orlando together, were also at the Angola-Namibia border together."

"Thank you, Mr. Crawford. Just one last thing," said Kosten as he handed the coroner a photo. "Can you identify this photograph?"

"Yes," said the Coroner. "The NTSB shared it with me. This is a picture of the cargo ship Quelimane. It left the Mozambique port city of Beira a few days after the DNA samples were collected in Namibia. It is a highly detailed picture of the cargo ship taken by satellite imagery. It shows several white containers on the top of many stacked containers. The white containers are arranged in a pattern to create sort of a courtyard in the center of the ship. If you look closely you can see dozens and dozens of blonde females aboard this ship."

"No further questions, Your Honor," said Kosten.

"No questions Your Honor," said Foulke.

A large television screen was rolled to the front of the court.

John Kosten clicked a remote and a picture of a young, Hawaiian girl appeared on the screen.

"I call my next witness, Lani Kealoha."

"Lani," said John Kosten, "can you hear me/"

"Yes, Mr. Kosten, I can hear you."

"Lani, were you one of the girls selected by Oasis to perform in the Super Bowl and did you leave the Hilton Hotel on the way to the Orlando Airport that day with the rest of the girls," asked Kosten.

"Yes," replied Lani.

"In your own words can you tell the Court what happened?" asked Kosten.

She began her story. It was transmitted by satellite from Hawaii to the courtroom. Her testimony was being uplinked unencrypted for any news organization to pick up. They had been tipped off and all the major cable news organizations had interrupted their programs with the breaking news.

Lani began by telling how she boarded a red-and-white bus with Keisha and Kara. "There were 24 of us on the bus," she said, "We drove mostly east and came to some kind of warehouse. An orange truck that was carrying everyone's luggage was also there."

She described what happened. She broke down when she got to the part about the girls being drowned in the water tank. All the girls struggled when they were thrown into the tank. "I just held my breath when I was forced under the water," she said. "They took all of us out of the water and strapped us into seats. I played dead. They put us on a plane. They put life vests on us. Then they threw our seats from the back of the plane. I had a plan. I unfastened my seat belt. I threw my safety vest off on the way down. I dived the way my dad taught me to my whole life. I knew I would hit too hard if I still had the vest on. I hit the ocean hard and it stung. I hit the water with tremendous force. It was dark when I surfaced. I could see some of the other girls floating in their seats. I knew they were all dead but I checked anyway." She began to cry. "I am sorry but I had to take the life jackets off three of the girls to survive. I made sure they were still strapped securely in the floating seats for the search and recovery teams to find."

She continued, "At one point, I came across a Black man floating in the water. I know he was dead but I didn't check. I was afraid to get too close to him."

"I had three life jackets and I found two seat cushions floating," she said. "I used some of the metal debris as a knife to cut the fish I was able to catch. There were some search planes but I could not get their attention. When it rained, I was able to drink a little fresh water. After a while, I could see lights at night to the northeast. I just kept trying to go that direction. I was afraid the current was going to take me right past it. I never made it to the lights. I came across a small, flat island. I just stayed there on the land. Sooner or later, I thought a ship would come along. I was able to catch fish and there was a grape tree that I ate for fruit, I could stay under it for the shade. I would drink the water off the leaves when it rained. I weaved a bowl out of twigs and leaves so I could catch some water when it rained. One day this yacht passed by. I caught their attention. They picked me up and took me to Port Royal. Then they took me to Freeport and my parents came."

"Lani," said Kosten, "I know this is difficult. What can you tell us about Keisha and Kara?"

"Keisha and her little sister Kara were drowned in the water tank in the warehouse the same way as the other girls. We were the last three to be thrown into the tank. There were these four Black men that didn't speak English. Keisha could talk to them in their language. It sounded a lot like Portagee. At first, we thought that was a good thing, but it wasn't. They took Keisha and Kara into another room and raped them, even little Kara. The men were laughing the whole time. The girls were screaming for their mom and dad. I knew they were going to kill all of us."

She paused. The courtroom remained totally silent.

"Mahalo, Lani," said Kosten. "I have no further questions."

Foulke stood up, "I have no questions, Your Honor. I would like to drop all charges against Mark Campbell," Again the courtroom erupted in a clamor.

Foulke continued, "That's what I would like to do. But Sgt. Mark Campbell has specifically requested that I not do that. He wants the Court record to show his name totally cleared. This whole proceeding from day one has been a travesty of justice that I unwittingly played a role in. Sgt. Mark Campbell wants the record to show he was found not guilty."

Then Judge Hardy turned to Kosten and Campbell.

"Mr. Kosten," said Judge Hardy, "may I address your client directly."

"Yes, Your Honor," replied Kosten.

"Mr. Campbell," asked Judge Hardy, "has the prosecuting attorney clearly stated your desire to hear the verdict of this Court."

Campbell stood up and looked straight at the judge.

"Yes, Sir, Your Honor," said Campbell.

"NOT GUILTY," said the judge.

Chapter 25

Jasmine had lost track of time. She didn't know if she had been in the Zindon Prison cell for only one night or two. She thought one but she just didn't know. She had fallen asleep, maybe for eight or ten hours, or maybe it was eight or ten minutes. They had brought her a disgusting soup that she could not eat. Her toilet was a pot on the floor. There was no paper, there was no running water. Again, she prayed to Allah and felt nothing.

It was dark and she could see the night sky through an opening in the wall of her cell. She positioned herself around the cell so she could see the stars. Then she saw Al Jabbar. The constellation Orion was bright in the night sky. "Dan Grainger," she thought "Can the guardian hunter of your daughter guide you to me?" It had been Jasmine's mission to save the lives of the women of Bukhara and she failed. But she knew she had at least helped save the lives of 275 American girls from a life of sexual domination and horror. She would have to be satisfied with that for her life's work. She made peace with herself and decided that was enough. She fell back asleep.

Once she awoke and she could sense a still and quiet voice gently speaking to her, trying to comfort her. She believed it was her grandmother counseling her and keeping her safe. That voice offered her the only comfort she had.

The doors opened. Elite Guards came in and shackled her arms and feet and marched her over to the Ark. She could hardly open her eyes in the bright morning sun. She was dirty and her clothes were dirty. She could only shuffle her feet when she walked, due to the chains on her ankles. She was taken into a nice, clean room. Alim appeared at the door. He came over to her and ripped off her clothing. The clothes dangled from the shackles on her wrists. She stood before him completely naked. He stepped closer with the most wicked smile on his face. He touched her and ran his hands across her shoulders and down along her sides and then toward her breasts. She mustered all the strength she had and brought her shackled arms up and struck Alim under his arms, forcing them away from her. The chain hit him under the chin. He stepped back from her.

"You bitch," he said. "Defiant to the end just like your infidel grandmother."

"Unshackle her," he said. The Elite Guards removed the shackles from her wrists and ankles. She stood there in front of him. Her eyes locked on him as he grinned with amusement.

Alim grabbed her long dark hair and threw her against the wall. "Clean yourself," he said, "and prepare to meet your fate."

Alim was elated. Finally, he would be ridding himself of Abdullah and his two cousins. He failed to listen to news stories coming out of an obscure city in Indiana that would soon unravel the mysteries surrounding the crash of Oasis One.

He failed to consider that the American girls had actually escaped Bukhara and would not be found by the Elite Guard.

Alim left the room, leaving Jasmine lying on the floor against the wall. She managed to get up. There was a shower and soap and a fully-functioning, modern bath. She tried not to think of what was about to happen. After her bath, there was only one piece of clothing for her to put on. It was a simple white gown. She put it on over her head and slipped on the pair of sandals.

Her captors entered the room and tied a black sash around her waist that bound her arms to her body. She was escorted to Registan Square outside the Ark. She could see the pit that had been prepared for her. There were three Islamic clerics standing nearby. Nasrullah was with them. Then she saw Alim appear, pushing her father in the wheelchair. Her father appeared distraught when he saw Jasmine. "Is this why you have brought me here?" he said, his voice stronger than she had heard it in years.

She looked around. There were two other women in white bound as she was. There were two large blue sacks on the ground near them. The yellow and black front-loader was nearby with a bucket full of very large stones. The engine was running. For a moment, she wished that she would get the front-loader. She knew that would not be the case. Her eyes kept returning to the hole that had been dug in the ground. She knew it was for her. A small crowd had gathered about fifteen feet away. There was a pile of stones near them. Merchants continued to sell their wares, taking little notice. The usual chess and backgammon players could be seen playing their games and sipping tea, women separated from the men.

Jasmine's face was fully exposed to the crowd. Nasrullah began reading a proclamation. "This young woman is the daughter of the Emir of Bukhara. She had a duty to live her life as an example to all the women of Bukhara. She must pay the price for her sin in the full public view of the people she has betrayed."

"Abdullah tried to rise from his chair. He nearly did so but could not quite summon the strength. He fell back into the chair. "No," he said, "I will not permit it."

"It is beyond your authority to commute her sentence. These three clerics have examined photographs that show her in adulteress behavior with an American Christian," said Nasrullah.

One man playing chess boldly stood up and said, "I am that American Christian and she is my wife." It was Dan. He walked directly up to face Nasrullah. Jasmine could not believe her eyes. Dan was walking into certain death.

Nasrullah was startled. Alim looked at the American in disbelief. Abdullah said, "Listen to him. You must listen to him."

Dan turned to one of the clerics and handed him a piece of paper. It was an officially stamped marriage license in the State of Hawaii, showing Lahaina, County of Maui as the place of their marriage.

Dan continued, "We were married in Maui last month and stayed there for our honeymoon. Nasrullah and Alim have been the bearers of false testimony. I am told that to give testimony on a matter wherein one has no knowledge, or to purposely testify with the opposite of what is known to be the truth, is a great sin in Islam." Dan's eyes locked onto Alim's.

The three clerics each examined the paper.

"It does not matter," said Nasrullah, "It is forbidden for a Muslim woman to marry a non-Muslim. The penalty is death by stoning." Alim's mind was racing. "This American was supposed to be dead," thought Alim. His trusted advisor Al-Qadir had assured him that the American died in Sydney. Alim began to wonder if Al-Qadir's treacherous lie explained his absence.

Abdullah had somehow found the strength to stand. He looked at Nasrullah and then Alim and then to the three clerics. "In Bukhara," said Abdullah, "only the family has the legal right to pronounce the sentence of death on the woman who has married a non-Muslim. This is to preserve the family honor and the honor of Islam. I am the father and I will not permit it."

The clerics stunned, conferred for several minutes and then one said "The Emir speaks the truth. This woman is married to a non-Muslim. Only the father or brothers can pronounce the sentence of death. Free her."

Nasrullah angrily disagreed, "This is an outrage, the Emir cannot bring dishonor on the entire nation of Bukhara. I will not permit it." He motioned to the Elite Guards to take her. Suddenly, the sound of machinery drowned out Nasrullah. It was Ricky Gibraltar operating the large front-loader. He dropped over one-thousand pounds of stone in front of Jasmine and her father's wheelchair, as Dan shielded them away from the falling stones. Ricky then lowered the bucket. Several Elite Guards were crushed under the stone. At the same time, eleven women playing chess and backgammon in beautifully colored Islamic dresses removed their automatic weapons from under the long tablecloths where they were seated. The T-Girls opened fire on the armed Elite Guards. Nasrullah, Alim and the clerics managed to take cover behind the stones.

Dan whisked Jasmine into the front-loader bucket, grabbed her father and pulled him in too. The front-loader sped away from the Ark toward the park, with its bucket lifted in the air to protect Jasmine, Dan and the Emir. The few Elite Guards remaining began firing at the front-loader. Several of the T-Girls hopped on the forklift and returned fire. The remaining T-Girls backed up alongside the forklift and continued their barrage of gunfire toward the Elite Guard. As more Elite Guards began to appear, they were immediately mowed down by the T-Girls. The merchants and the people near the Ark scattered for safety. It was complete chaos.

Nasrullah, Alim and the clerics scampered into the Ark for cover. Alim headed straight for the secret passages of the Ark confident that his Elite Guard would quickly neutralize the attackers.

Ricky stopped the front-loader in the park near the entrance to the tunnel. He lowered the bucket. Dan and Jasmine helped her father into an awaiting, old, beat-up Mercedes driven by Kaliq. The Mercedes sped off through the park carrying Dan, Jasmine and the Emir to safety within the city. The city was filled with dozens of old, beat-up Mercedes.

Ricky turned the front-loader around and pointed it toward the Ark. He put in into gear, jumped off and let it take off on its own through Registan Square toward the Ark.

Ricky and the T-Girls slipped into the secret tunnel. They stopped and changed clothes into the full combat gear they had pre-positioned in the tunnel. Then it was off to the studio. They entered into the underground film studio with their weapons blazing. They had determined that all the male actors appearing in the porno movies were actually members of the Elite Guard or the three-thousand-man regular military of Bukhara. The T-Girls ushered the women back into the cells, as they systematically took out all the men that would not immediately surrender. The captured men were packed into the cells meant for the women. It was a large studio and most of the men were nude and unarmed. Many men raised their hands and ran into the cells voluntarily, hoping to save themselves from the automatic gunfire all around them.

The T-Girls began their escape plan by making their way into the main hall of the Ark. It was necessary to take out all the hostiles they could to prepare for the next operation. Elite Guards of the Ark showed up in force to stop them. Small arms fire was exchanged as the T-Girl Special Forces worked their way to the roof. The Elite Guard may have served as great studs in the films, but they were not an effective fighting force.

The Ark was a massive fortress, designed to defend against external invaders from the outside, not internal invaders. Room by room, the T-Girls took out the remaining members of the Elite Guard that had not fled from the firefight. Once on the roof, they had command of the Registan Square below. The Ark itself was largely free of any Bukharan hostiles.

From the roof, Ricky surveyed the situation. A hundred or so Elite Guard had formed in front of the Ark. In the distance, she could see the Bukhara Army of several thousand approaching in their military vehicles.

Ricky looked at her watch "Where the fuck are they?" she screamed. Then she heard the unmistakable sound of Russian Mil Mi-8 military helicopters. She looked to the east and there were twelve approaching helicopters. Ricky grinned.

Ricky and her special forces continued to return fire to the Elite Guard on the ground around the Ark. The regular Bukhara army was getting closer to the Ark. It was just a matter of time before the Elite Guard would enter the Ark, over-run the roof and take them. The Elite Guard had to be stopped from entering the Ark.

As the Mil Mi-8 Tajik attack helicopters approached the Ark, the helicopters opened fire. The Elite Guard fell to the ground. Two of the helicopters provided cover for a third, as it hovered over the roof of the Ark and dropped a ladder. Ricky's Special Forces scurried up the ladder while being covered by the others on the roof and the other two helicopters. Ricky was the last one up the ladder and into the safety of the helicopter as it lifted high into the air above the Ark.

A familiar face greeted Ricky. It was Prince Adil of Bukhara. Jasmine's brother was dressed in a full, military-combat uniform. Adil stretched out his hand and said, "Welcome aboard the First Brigade of the Rapid Reaction Force of the National Guard of Tajikistan."

The helicopter gained altitude and backed away from the city safe from any fire. The other eleven attack helicopters continued to engage the Elite Guard and the Army that had now reached the Ark. After a few minutes, resistance on the ground was futile.

Two Bukhara military helicopters attempted to take off from the airport and were immediately shot down by the Tajiks.

What was left of the Elite Guard threw down their weapons and held up their hands in surrender. The Army near the Ark did the same.

The portion of the Army that had not yet reached the Ark turned and retreated to the west. They fled on the main roads to the northwest and southwest leaving the city. The attack helicopters stayed in pursuit. The fleeing convoys on the ground on both roads drove right into the fortified positions of the armed forces of the Republic of Uzbekistan. The Uzbeks had assembled at the Bukhara-Uzbekistan border, lying in wait for the retreating Bukhari ground forces. All of the ill-trained Bukhari forces surrendered.

Adil had carried personal letters to the President of Tajikistan and the President of Uzbekistan from Emir Abdullah requesting the intervention. Abdullah was highly respected by both presidents. Both nations gladly offered the requested assistance to the Emir.

In less than two hours, the battle for Bukhara was over. When all the Bukhara ground forces had surrendered, Tajik paratroopers were deployed from the helicopters and took complete control of the Ark.

The helicopter carrying Adil and Ricky's Special Forces set down right in front of the Ark main entrance. Adil ran into the Ark searching for Alim. It took a while but he found him hiding in the Zindon prison. Adil was in the secret passage and Alim had no idea he had been discovered and was being watched. Alim approached the edge of the very Bug Pit that Adil had been imprisoned in for so many years. Alim would often come and taunt him.

"Your sister's treachery continues!" shouted Alim into the pit as he raised the pit cover. She escaped from me today, but tomorrow I will triumph." Adil suddenly realized that Alim had been hiding in the deepest recesses of the Ark and Zindon Prison. Alim clearly did not know the battle was lost.

Alim had a spear, and in the dimly lit Bug Pit, he never realized the man he was speaking to twenty feet below was the wrong man. "I have allowed you to live too long. I will make sure you do not survive to foil any of my plans," said Alim. Al-Qadir tried to cry out to Alim, but the sounds he made without his tongue were unintelligible. Alim took aim and threw the spear into the abdomen of the man below. The man screamed in pain.

"It is too late, my cousin," said Adil, as he came up behind Alim. Alim turned, his eyes adjusted and he recognized him. "Adil! You are Adil. It cannot be!"

Alim stepped back. Adil stepped forward and said, "As you judge, so shall you be judged, and the measure you give will be the measure you get." Adil pushed Alim into the pit. It was a favorite scripture of Adil's Christian wife, Farah.

After the fall, Alim struggled to his feet. The stench was unbearable. The insects had crunched under his body when he fell. The vermin were crawling all over him. Adil spoke to him. "The first louse is an unbearable shock; the one-thousandth is of no consequence at all."

Alim shouted, "You cannot leave me here. I will die."

"No Cousin, you will wish you were dead, but you will not die," replied Adil, as he closed the pit cover. Adil headed along the tunnel to return to the Ark.

Alim was left in the pit but he was not alone. The man he had speared lay dying beside him. He suddenly recognized his missing advisor, Al-Qadir Ravshan. "Your treachery has allowed this to happen!" shouted Alim, as he twisted the spear in Al-Qadir's gut. The screams of Al-Qadir's agony pierced the silence of the tunnels until he was no more.

Adil walked over to the Ark in the bright sunlight. The area was totally secured by the Tajik Special Forces. People had come out to the Ark when the commotion had stopped and began going about their business. The merchants were again selling their wares. A group of Tajik National Guardsmen came out of the Ark with Nasrullah in handcuffs. The three Islamic clerics had reassembled in the very spot they had stood before.

A nice, new, black Mercedes pulled up. Kaliq was driving. Jasmine got out. She again was dressed as royalty. She helped her father into his wheelchair. Kaliq pushed the Emir over to Nasrullah. Jasmine and Dan followed.

Abdullah stood up and said, "I charge that this man, the Foreign Minister of Bukhara, has attempted to overthrow the rightful Emir of Bukhara. He has a duty to live his life as an example to all men of Bukhara. He must pay the price for his treachery in the full public view of the people he has betrayed."

Abdullah paused to let the words sink in to Nasrullah.

"I sentence him to death by stoning," declared Abdullah.

"I protest," said Nasrullah. He turned to the clerics. "He cannot do this."

One of the clerics answered, "The Emir of Bukhara has lawfully sentenced you to death by stoning. The three of us have personal knowledge having witnessed your treachery. Bind the prisoner."

Jasmine offered the black sash that just a few hours ago had bound her arms. The sash was tied around Nasrullah binding his arms to his waist.

He was placed into the hole that had been prepared for Jasmine and was covered up to his waist. There was a crowd that had gathered fifteen feet away near the pile of stones. Nasrullah displayed no emotion.

A man in the crowd hurled the first stone and it crashed against Nasrullah's left shoulder causing his body to lurch backward. Nasrullah regained his composure and made himself as erect as he could. A second stone was handed to a woman in a burka. She immediately threw the stone with great force, striking Nasrullah in the forehead. His head lurched violently backward. Another woman in the crowd threw up her hands in approval and cheered. The crowd cheered and the stones rained down on Nasrullah.

Chapter 26

The girls on the JAL 747 knew only that they were going back to America. Even Callie didn't know where they were landing. Her dad had not told her. After the plane took off, the girls removed their contact lenses.

Callie soon realized that free Wi-Fi was available on the plane. She spent a lot of time surfing the Internet on her phone for stories about them. Most stories were just about the crash and a few days after. She learned for the first time that 23 of the girls had died in the crash. Except Callie knew there was no such crash. She read about Lani being rescued in the Bahamas.

She finally fell asleep. She was awakened by an e-mail alert from her dad. She checked her e-mail. The message said that he was safe and Princess Jasmine was safe. Her dad explained about Jasmine's sentence to be stoned. Her brother, Adil, came to the rescue with a coordinated attack by the National Guard of Tajikistan, and the Uzbek Army surrounded the country. Jasmine and her dad were safe.

She began searching reports on the Bukhara invasion. It quickly became clear that another big news story was out of Anderson, Indiana. She read all about it, including Annie's name and all about her testimony. She even saw the clip of her mom and sister getting on the elevator and Annie saying "Stay tuned, you ain't seen nuthin' yet."

Seeing her sister, seeing her mom, it was all too much for her and she began to cry. Other girls noticed and were concerned and began crowding around Callie to see what was wrong. She decided she could not tell them. They knew nothing of the 23 girls that had been drowned. They knew nothing about the whole world presuming they were dead until just a few hours ago. If they knew her phone could surf the web, she would be bombarded with requests. Her dad had a plan that was working He was orchestrating everything from behind the scenes. If he had wanted her to know all of this, he would have told her. She had been placed in a position of leadership and needed to keep order.

Callie wiped the tears from her eyes and gave some of the girls a hug and said "I was just thinking about my mom and dad and my sister. I am so happy to be going home."

The girls were fed several times during the fifteen-hour flight. Many were able to sleep and many giggled and milled around in the aisles. Well into the flight, the girls were given a red T-shirt, white shorts and sandals. They were instructed to put in their brown contact lenses.

After what had seemed like an eternity, one of the girls somewhere in the plane cried out, "I see land and city lights." Other girls tried to get to a window to look out. Callie looked out the window and could not believe her eyes. It was dark but she could see the silhouette of mountains rising out of the ocean. She caught a glimpse of the bright lights of the U.S. Arizona Memorial reflecting off the waters of Pearl Harbor.

The stars and stripes of the American flag blowing gently in the trade winds were clearly illuminated by the flood lights of the memorial. In the distance, she recognized another site she had seen a dozen times in her short life - the Waikiki shoreline of hotels reaching toward the sky and the outline of Diamond Head.

"It's Hawaii!" shouted out Callie, "It's Hawaii. That's Honolulu! It's America!"

Another girl shouted "God Bless the U.S.A.," and with that the entire plane was filled with song *"I'm proud to be an American, where at least I know I'm free."* As the song finished with the words "God Bless the U.S.A.," the plane touched down at Honolulu International Airport, the speakers immediately began blaring out "Aloha 'Oe," as they taxied to the terminal.

The girls were excited and were told to calm down. They were led into U.S. passport control. Several female U.S. Marines were there and helped escort them. Each girl now had her own passport and the older girls helped the younger ones.

Annie and Alice had arrived in Honolulu about two hours earlier and were waiting anxiously for Callie to appear. While on the flight Annie read a text message that had been sent much earlier. It said:

"OASIS TWO has cleared Bukhara airspace, Dan and 275 girls are safely on board."

"Oasis Two?" thought Annie. "That was a nice touch." She understood completely. Her dad and Callie were safe.

Lani and Kahekili Kealoha met Annie and Alice when they arrived. After they collected their luggage, they were escorted to await Callie's arrival. Lani introduced herself to Annie and explained how her dad had met with them in the Bahamas. Lani and her family had returned to Hawaii that morning.

Kahekili had made arrangements to care for all the girls on the JAL747 once they arrived Hawaii.

There were about fifty female volunteers from Kahekili's church waiting with them.

After an eternity, the girls started pouring into the area where Annie was waiting. They were all brunettes but Annie recognized them.

"There they are!" she exclaimed. "That's them."

Alice started jumping up and down.

Then Callie appeared. Annie screamed "Callie, Callie."

Callie saw them "Mom, Annie!" she screamed and she ran toward them. "Mom, Annie!"

The three came together and the tears began to flow from all of them. Alice sobbed loudly and the three hugged each other for the longest time. The other girls looked on longingly, most with tears in their eyes, wishing that they had someone to meet them.

"Where's dad?" asked Annie, suddenly panicked by his absence.

"He is okay. He had to go back to Bukhara to save Princess Jasmine. He sent me an e-mail they're safe. Annie, I know about your Anderson testimony and the other girls that didn't make it. None of the other girls know anything about that. We can't let them find out yet."

Kahekili shouted out, "Girls, Girls," as he pointed to the group of female volunteers. "These are your guides. They will call you by name. Come forward when your name is called and stay with them at all times."

The girls did as they were asked. The guides called off the names of the girls, and their passports were collected and checked. Each girl had a beautiful flower lei placed around her neck and was greeted with "Aloha."

Kahekili often met large tour groups at the airport. There was nothing unusual about this exercise for him. Group by group, they were escorted to buses waiting outside. The names were checked again after boarding.

The caravan of buses left Honolulu International Airport and began the one-hour drive to Kahuku on the North Shore. Annie and Callie sat next to each other with Alice was across the aisle from Callie. They laughed and talked and giggled and cried.

It was dark and most of the girls fell asleep on the bus. In about an hour, they pulled into the Turtle Bay Resort on Oahu's North Shore. There were another ninety guides from Kahekili's church to meet them as they got off the bus. The girls were escorted, two girls per guide to their rooms. Annie, Alice and Callie shared a room. They were all told to wash the dye out of their hair and remove their contacts. The guides helped the little girls in each room and sat with them in their room as they fell asleep.

Another group of phone-bank volunteers from the church began calling parents and informing them all across the United States, with 7:00 a.m. phone calls in the east and 4:00 a.m. phone calls in the west, that their daughters were safe.

The parents were not told where the girls were, just that they were all sleeping and in the United States. Mobile phone numbers were collected from the parents and a text group was created to keep the parents informed.

Early in the morning, John Kosten received a contrite phone call from the Oasis corporate office. They requested a meeting to determine an equitable settlement offer for all his clients and any other clients he might acquire.

The national media had erupted in a frenzy of speculation. The day before, they had even questioned whether Annie's video was legitimate. The media appeared in large numbers at the warehouse area in Florida and peppered law enforcement with questions that no one had answers for.

The evening cable shows the night before interviewed one uninformed guest after another that pontificated on what had really happened. Then word came in to local news outlets all over the country from parents. Local morning news shows had interview after interview with apprehensive but thankful parents who had received early-morning phone calls. Nothing was known by anyone, except the girls were alive and well and countless hours of airtime was filled with speculation.

Aviation experts and "mishap" experts explained endlessly how there was no way the smaller plane carrying the drowned girls could be mistaken for a 747. Other experts explained how it actually could have happened. They debated the "glitch" in the Miami radar around 8:23 p.m. that night. Some said it was because the control tower was switched to backup power because of a failure in the primary power. Others said the "anomalies" were not that unusual but would have to be studied to gain a true understanding.

Other experts raised the specter of white slavery and sex trafficking. Muslim groups were out in force on all the networks proclaiming Islamophobia for any such suggestion. Anti-government groups wanted to know where the U.S. government was in all of this and how they could not have known. Senators, congressmen and congresswomen on the networks all across the nation filled airtime with promises of congressional investigations into Oasis.

National Social Worker's Association spokespersons were heard everywhere, defending the policies of Child Protective Services and the need to protect the nation's children from abuse. Representatives of Christian social workers and churches made the case that many social workers were extremely liberal and shared the same agenda as Shirley Merriman.

The national news media swarmed like locusts on the one place in America that had provided the only accurate information the day before…Anderson, Indiana.

A press release had been sent out that there would be an important announcement at 1:00 p.m. from the park across the street from the courthouse. Early in the morning, ENG trucks and satellite trucks were everywhere in downtown Anderson. Many were parked in the lot on the south side of the park. Verizon, AT&T, Sprint and every other wireless company scrambled to set up emergency cell sites to handle the increased bandwidth of calls, texts and video.

A stage was set up along Ninth Street on the south side of the Madison County Government Center. A photographer's stand was set up along the north side of Citizen's Plaza Park facing the stage. Large video screens had been set up for the public. Many of the downtown streets were closed. Indiana State Police and local law enforcement coped with the traffic and the influx of reporters and the general public. The day was unseasonably warm at 66 degrees and sunny.

Gone were the protestors with racist signs and chants. American Flags and U.S. Marine Corps flags were everywhere. The crowd was diverse and all in support of Sgt. Mark Campbell and anxious to hear the latest word. John Kosten had organized the event and asked churches all across Central Indiana to show up in force. Steve Foulke got all the local government approvals. Dan's friend, Mike, coordinated the technical satellite feeds that were to be shown during the event.

At 1:00 p.m., John Kosten took to the podium as television stations all across the world interrupted programming to join the announcement. "I am John Kosten. I have the privilege of serving our Lord and Savior Jesus Christ, as he guided me in the task of defending Sgt. Mark Campbell of the U.S. Marines. I can tell you that partly, as a result of Mark's dedication to duty, along with the efforts of dozens of other individuals around the world, hundreds of young girls have been safely returned to the United States of America. Let us pray."

John led a brief prayer followed by the "Star-Spangled Banner."

"I would like to introduce Mr. Steve Foulke, Prosecutor for Madison County Indiana and a defender of equal justice for all," proclaimed Kosten.

Steve Foulke stepped to the microphone. "I want to say, first, that I am disappointed in my city and my county for the demonstrations against Sgt. Mark Campbell. I am ashamed of the racist protests that took place on these very streets as recently as yesterday. I am ashamed of myself for unwittingly participating in bringing the false charges against Sgt. Mark Campbell. Due to his courageous choice to remain in jail, risking his own life, Mark Campbell has been instrumental in building a case against corruption in Madison County. I also would like to thank Deputy Bill Jenkins for the role he played in protecting Mr. Campbell, while his own grandchildren had been unjustly taken from their mother to be used as innocent pawns by the Director of Child Protective Services in Madison County."

Bill Jenkins was on the stage behind Foulke. He was accompanied by his grandchildren and daughter. Today, they are all reunited as a family. Jenkins raised his arm and waved in appreciation for the applause.

Foulke continued, "I have never in my life met a finer man than Sgt. Mark Campbell. His selfless devotion to duty in the past saved his fellow Marines and a U.S. Ambassador. That same selfless devotion to duty saved my life yesterday and has brought down corrupt Madison County officials. John Kosten had evidence weeks ago that would have exonerated him. Mark Campbell insisted upon remaining in jail at great personal risk to his life until he knew the abducted girls were free from their captors. Ladies and Gentlemen, Sgt. Mark Campbell."

The band struck up the Marine Corps Hymn as Sgt. Mark Campbell in full Marine Corps dress blues came to center stage. He was flanked by his wife, his step-daughter, Kima, his son, Jimmy, and his daughter, Cynthia. The crowd cheered. When the hymn came to a close, Sgt. Mark Campbell stepped to the microphone to address the crowd.

Standing in the front row were the six "skinheads," clad in U.S. Marines dress blues. Mark looked directly at them, saluted, and said "Semper Fi." He looked out at the huge crowd that had assembled.

"Thank you all so much for this show of support," said Mark. "I want to thank my attorney, John Kosten, for the blessings of his wise counsel. This man was truly an answer to prayer. Thank you, John." Mark turned and acknowledged John.

Campbell continued, "Too often in this country, prosecutors blindly pursue a conviction at all costs. They ignore and withhold exculpatory evidence. Prosecutor Steve Foulke was motivated in this case to pursue justice rather than a conviction. In doing so, he risked his own life trying to find the truth. Thank you, Steve Foulke."

Campbell turned toward his family and smiled before continuing "Thank you to my family, my wife, and daughter Kima. A special thanks to my son, Jimmy, and my daughter, Cynthia. They not only believed in my innocence, but they struck out on their own to prove it. I am truly blessed. Together, we all mourn for Keisha and Kara. I have devoted my entire life to the defense of liberty and to fight injustice wherever I find it. In this pursuit, I am no different than any other Soldier, Sailor, Airman, Coast Guardsman or Marine. Thank you and God Bless America."

Sgt. Mark Campbell turned and shook the hand of John Kosten. Steve Foulke stepped forward intending to shake Mark's hand, but Campbell did not seem to realize he was there. Campbell shook the hand of Deputy Jenkins and greeted his grandchildren and daughter. Then Sgt. Mark Campbell raised his arm to the crowd as he and his family left the stage.

Steve stepped to the microphone and said, "I want to call your attention to the monitors and I want to introduce you to one brave young lady who escaped from her captors and provided invaluable information to track down the location of the other girls. Live from Jerusalem, Ilsa Johansson. Ilsa, can you hear me?"

The television screen illuminated with the video of a young blonde girl. She said, "Yes, Mr. Foulke."

"Please tell us what happened after you boarded the Oasis flight in Orlando," said Foulke.

Ilsa recounted all the events from boarding the plane, landing in Angola, being placed on the C-130s, being held in the Quonset huts, and then her trip down the river where she made the decision to fall overboard.

Ilsa ended that part of the story by saying that "I knew if they found out I was Jewish they would kill me."

She then explained she was found in pretty bad shape in the jungle by someone who contacted her family. She did not go into details about who saved her or cared for her. She just explained that she went to her family in Israel, to maintain secrecy until the other girls were rescued. She said she would be returning home with her parents soon. She never mentioned Dan.

"Thank you Ilsa," said Foulke, as he motioned for John Kosten to step to the microphone.

John Kosten spoke, "For those of you who followed the testimony yesterday, you are already familiar with Annie Grainger. I have Annie now on the big screen. Annie, can you hear me?"

"Yes, Mr. Kosten," said Annie, as a medium close-up of her filled the screen.

"Annie, can you tell us where you are and who you are with?" asked Kosten.

"It is 8:45 in the morning and I am in Hawaii with my sister Callie. She was among the 276 girls who were on the Oasis 747. Except for Ilsa, who is safe in Israel, all 275 of the remaining girls are here in Hawaii and they are all safe." The camera switched to wide shot that panned the hundreds of girls standing on the beach in the early morning sun. Here is my sister, Callie."

"Hello, Mr. Kosten," said Callie.

"It is such a blessing to hear your voice, Callie," said Kosten, "and to see all the girls with you. How much can you tell us about what happened to you?"

Callie was never nervous in front of a microphone. She had known John Kosten since she was little. Her dad admired him and often said he was the finest attorney he had ever known. Callie knew what needed to be said and she knew what should not be said. She knew all about video and television news from her dad. She needed no coaching.

"I will tell you the highlights of what I can," said Callie, "There are so many people to thank that I know about, and there are so many people to thank that I don't know about. There are many people that can never be publicly thanked, as they risked their lives to save us. You know who you are,

Thank you. I want to thank my dad, who taught me and my sister to never give up, and we didn't. Thank you, Daddy."

Callie gave a brief account of being transferred through Africa inside shipping containers, then across the Indian Ocean in the containers, and then being flown to an Islamic country that she did not name. She came right out and said they had been abducted to become slaves in a harem. She explained what their life was like. She also took great care to assure those listening, especially the parents, that they were not physically harmed. They were captives but were treated well and fed well. She said, "The future held something horrible for all of us, but that future never came."

Callie then said, "I want all of you to see us yesterday during our escape. Some of you may have already seen this and had no idea."

The video switched to the girls dressed in Polynesian outfits and performing in the parade. The video played for a few minutes and came back to Callie as she continued.

"That was us, as brown-eyed brunettes in the city of Bukhara during the International Women's Day Parade. We were saved by the princess of Bukhara. You cannot make this stuff up. Her name is Princess Yasi Min Hassan, but she is known by her friends as Princess Jasmine. Sorry Disney."

"After our escape," continued Callie, "Princess Jasmine was arrested and sentenced to death by stoning. That was this morning, March 9th, in Bukhara. Miraculously, she was saved by persons that I can never identify and by her brother, Prince Adil and the National Guard of Tajikistan, supported by the Army of Uzbekistan. I'm telling you people; you can't make this stuff up."

Callie continued, "I can thank Princess Yasi Min of Bukhara, Mr. Toguchi and the Japanese Dance Troup, Japan Airlines, the President of Tajikistan, the President of

Uzbekistan. I want to thank Kahekili Kealoha and his LDS church here in Hawaii for sharing the spirit of Aloha with us. I have covered the highlights and you will learn more details later. I want to ask everyone hearing me to think of us girls. We have lost five weeks of our life. We want to go home to our families and our schools. We don't want the press camped out at our homes and following us to school and disrupting our lives further. We don't want you to ask our friends and family and us how we feel. We feel blessed! That's how we feel. We want to go back to our lives and be given the opportunity to catch up on our school work. Please, everyone, think about that."

Callie turned to the girls around her on the beach. The camera switched to a wide shot and Callie said

"Okay, so now, all the girls are going to pass by the microphone and give their names so their families can see them. Parents you have already been contacted and will be contacted again about arrangements for you to come here or your daughter brought to you. Thank you, Jesus and God Bless America."

One by one the girls passed by the microphone and gave their names. It was well over an hour for that process to complete. The older girls helped the younger ones just as they had through the whole ordeal.

Chapter 27

Steve Foulke had done interview after interview for media outlets across Indiana and the world. He received a phone call from the state party chairman. The chairman asked Steve to meet with him and a few selected Indiana House and Senate leaders for an 8:00 a.m. breakfast the next morning in Anderson.

Steve agreed. He could not help but think his political career may be taking a turn for the better. He was tired and yet, for the first time in a long time, he felt he had actually done some good.

When Steve arrived home his cell phone rang.

"Hi, it's me," said the female voice.

"Hey, Cynthia," said Foulke.

Cynthia replied, "I wanted to thank you for all that you did for my dad and the great things you said today."

"Cynthia, it was my honor," said Steve. Your father is a remarkable man. It was a privilege to actually serve justice for once in this crazy legal system. You don't need to thank me; I need to thank you."

"That's not necessary Steve. Is it possible for me to drop something off to you now?" asked Cynthia.

"Yes, sure." said Steve surprised at her request. He was suddenly hopeful that something might happen between them.

'I'll be there in fifteen," said Cynthia.

In a few minutes the doorbell rang and Steve opened the door. There was Cynthia dressed as elegantly as she had been earlier in the day. She stepped into the room and faced him as he shut the door.

"Steve, you are an idiot who cannot control himself," she said, as she poked her index finger with her sharp fingernail into his chest. "You said a lot of fantastic stuff today. You could be governor or senator or whatever you want one day. Except, you won't be."

"What do you mean?" he asked.

"You are going to get caught," said Cynthia, "And after today with your picture plastered all over the country you can't go anywhere and pick up some girl without being recognized. They like to brag. You will be blackmailed. You will get caught, and soon. Your whole world will come crashing down around you."

"I know," said Steve. "I know."

"Do you really, Steve? I don't think so." said Cynthia. "These girls you see on the side, do you think they really want to be with you? Have you ever stopped to think about them? I mean really think about them. Sure, they're using you and you're using them, but they don't really want you slobbering all over them and breathing heavy and doing your business. They are doing what they have to do to survive in this society. They have kids to feed, rent to pay, gas to buy, tuition to pay, or maybe it's the only way they can get money for the nice clothes they want. For a while, it's actually fun just to control men. They may have been the unpopular girl in school and now they are suddenly very popular. They may have had one loser boyfriend after another, but now at least they actually have something for doing the same thing they did with the losers. Every time they are with someone like you, they give up a tiny piece of themselves, until finally nothing is left."

"What about you?" asked Steve. "Do you include yourself in that description?

"Oh no, I'm the exception. No one gets even a small piece of me. No one."

Cynthia continued, "My dad just did his part to help save Annie's sister and all those girls kidnapped to become sex slaves. In that part of the world, men control a woman's sexuality. Here, we women control men with our sexuality. Wives do it with their husbands, girlfriends do it with their boyfriends. Some girls learn they can control any man with their bodies to get what they want. Sometimes, it is the only way they can get money. Steve, you are an integral part of this country's sex slavery. True, the girls think they chose to do it but did they really?"

Steve just sighed. He knew she was right about the other girls but he just couldn't stop. He did not want to stop. Steve was still trying to think of something to say but couldn't. Cynthia could see he was lost in thought.

"Here take a look at this while you're trying to think," said Cynthia, as she tossed him a smartphone. "Play the video."

He touched the screen. It began to play. The lighting was poor but it didn't take long for Steve to realize it was a man and woman getting it on in the front seat of a moving vehicle. Once in a while, the oncoming headlights of an approaching car lit up the people. It was Steve. It was Cynthia, although you never could see her face clearly. You could easily identify Steve. It was their wild ride to Cincinnati on I-74.

"It's the original. There are no copies, Steve," said Cynthia. "You can keep the phone. It's a throw-away."

"What's your point? Why did you tape it?" asked Steve.

"I didn't know you," said Cynthia. "You were the guy that was trying to put my dad away. I would have stopped you whatever it took. It would have killed my dad to actually know what I am capable of," she paused. "Then again, I don't think anyone could tell it was me. But you can be seen clearly."

Steve just listened trying to comprehend all that she was saying. He was at a loss for words.

"I never wanted to use it, or the video," continued Cynthia. "It was just insurance."

"You make a compelling case, it's almost like you're making a closing argument," said Steve. "You should have been an attorney."

"Oh, didn't I ever mention it, Steve?" said Cynthia with a big smile, "School is the University of Georgia. I have taken pre-law and I graduate with a B.A. in business in three months. So far, I have a 3.87 GPA. Just passed the LSAT last month with a 171, and have been accepted to Georgetown Law in DC this fall. Although Harvard and Yale are possibilities, it's too damn cold up there. Just three more years, and then I can do what this girl wants to do instead of what this girl's gotta do."

Steve just stood there dumbfounded.

"Another thing, Steve, the night we met, that was no accident," said Cynthia.

"What do you mean?" asked Steve somewhat cautiously.

"I knew exactly who you were before I ever left Atlanta. You just made it easier for me when you pulled into the strip club."

She opened the front door "It's been good, Steve, really it has. But now I am going home to be with the only man a girl can ever really trust, my daddy." She slipped out the door and was gone.

Steve was numb. He spent the rest of the evening trying to make sense of it all. He wondered if anything he thought he knew about Cynthia was even real?

He did not sleep well. Morning came quickly. Steve Foulke had been asked to attend an 8:00 a.m. breakfast meeting at the Cracker Barrel in Anderson. Several Party leaders were seated at the table. Present was the Indiana state party chairman, the Madison County party chairman and the party leadership of the Indiana House and Senate.

The national news events of Steve's role in the Campbell case had made him a cause célèbre. Steve's future was the main topic of discussion. Governor or senator were being tossed around as real possibilities. Stories were surfacing all over Madison County and elsewhere about Shirley Merriman's abuse of power. The morning local TV news outlets were reporting the impending resignation of two Madison County judges. Steve's corruption probe was gaining tremendous momentum.

Steve sat there enjoying the attention and continued talking with whoever remained. One by one, the power brokers left to return to Indianapolis. The Indiana General Assembly was still in session this month. This left only Steve and the Madison County party chairman at the table. Steve spotted a familiar face across the room.

A couple of men dressed in black suits had stood up and were leaving a table in the far corner of the room. They were very somber. Their departure revealed the figure of Mark Campbell sitting in the corner.

Steve felt so convicted. He had searched his soul wondering how he had let all of the events surrounding Mark Campbell's arrest spin out of control. He wondered why he simply took Merriman's word, rather than thoroughly investigating the matter before bringing charges. At least things had turned out properly, and he had gotten his act together in time.

The chairman picked up the bill and headed to the cashier. Steve got up and walked over to Mark just as he was standing up. He had just placed his dark overcoat over his arm. Sgt. Mark Campbell was impeccably dressed in perfectly creased black slacks, a white shirt, with a gray and black patterned sweater. His black shoes were perfectly polished.

"Sgt. Campbell," said Foulke, "what a privilege to see you here today."

"Mr. Prosecutor," said Mark, somewhat coldly.

"I never thought I would have any opportunity to speak to you privately and certainly not so soon," said Foulke. "I want to apologize for all that you and your family have been through. I particularly regret that I allowed charges to be brought against you without first conducting a thorough investigation. I am so sorry."

"If that's what it takes to ease your conscience, fine, apology accepted," said Campbell. "Now if you will excuse me, I am in the midst of making funeral arrangements for my daughters."

Foulke was taken aback by Campbell's tone.

"I'm not sure I understand, Sergeant," said Foulke. "Sometimes justice takes time to prevail. We had to work at it awfully hard in this case, but we got to the right place in the end. I am so sorry for the impact it had on you."

"Mr. Foulke," said Campbell, "I am not the least bit concerned about the minimal hardship I endured while you figured out how to do your job. You were never going to get a conviction. I knew that the moment I was arrested at the airport. I knew immediately it was Merriman's handiwork. You were just an unwitting pawn in her power play."

Steve was stunned.

Campbell continued, "The things that Kima had to endure at the hands of Madison County officials are unforgivable. She is the one that you should apologize to, not me. I was just doing my duty?

"Your duty?" quizzed Foulke.

Campbell continued "My wife visited me my first night in jail. We decided right then that we would give Merriman enough rope to let her hang herself. You have been the prosecutor for several years. I voted for you in your first term. For your entire time in office, she has conducted a reign of terror on many innocent, Black families, as well as poor, white families. We decided it was our duty to stop her. Where were you then? Where was justice then?" said Campbell.

"I…I didn't know," said Foulke, bewildered by Campbell's words.

"This was all on your watch," said Campbell. "It was your jurisdiction. It was your county. You should have known. You should have investigated. You should have done something before your ass was on the line. I did your job for you, Mr. Foulke."

"What do you mean?" asked Foulke.

"The first thing I did when I brought my family to America was take the girls for medical evaluation and treatment. They were victims of FGM and their exact physical condition was thoroughly documented at that time," said Campbell. "Those pictures and expert testimony about their condition were always available to me at any time of my choosing."

"Did John Kosten know this?" asked Foulke.

"No," said Campbell. "I never told him. He would have insisted upon using it immediately to free me. We needed to bait Merriman. When the Dade County report identified DNA from an African-American male was present on my daughters, I knew right then that something very sinister had happened. I thought it best to remain silent until I could figure it out. I didn't have to wait long. The Lord immediately brought me John Kosten and his client, Annie Grainger. That was all I needed. Through the attorney the Lord sent me, I learned how high the stakes were for the missing girls. John told me during our first meeting. I immediately knew what my duty was."

"I'm sorry I didn't understand my duty until more information came out," said Foulke.

"When did you decide what your duty was, Mr. Foulke?" asked Campbell.

Steve thought for a moment. He seriously searched his soul and his memory before he answered. "I think it was when I first cross-examined your daughter. It was her testimony and her impassioned defense of you. I will never forget the way she stood at attention and saluted you as you left the courtroom that day."

"Do you always lie to yourself?" asked Campbell "Do you believe your own lies?"

Foulke was totally mystified now. "I...uh...I...I don't know what you mean?" He stammered out the words."

"No, Steve, that was the day you were trying to figure out how to save your ass and keep anyone from finding out you were sleeping with my daughter," said Campbell coldly.

Steve put his hand on the table for support. He slowly slumped to the chair and sat down. Sgt. Mark Campbell seemed to tower over him now. Steve felt insignificant in his presence.

"I love my daughter unconditionally. Cynthia is the spitting image of her mother. She has a lot of her mother in her and I think that makes me love her even more. Her mother would have given you no quarter, Cynthia's mother would have destroyed you."

"My daughter must have seen something within you worth salvaging. Cynthia simply neutralized you. I know who my daughter is, and, I know her potential. I know with certainty the woman she will become," said Campbell. A note of intense pride was clearly in his voice now.

"Does she have any idea you know?" asked Foulke.

"No, and she never will. I am proud of her. My job is to love her, protect her and get her through life until she learns who the Lord made her to be," said Campbell.

"I see," said Foulke. "You've taught her well, Sir. She is a daughter to be very very proud of…" his voice trailed off.

"As for you," said Campbell, "you are insignificant. You're just a footnote. You are never going to amount to anything if you remain on the path you are on. You have no core values. You exhibit occasional flashes of brilliance that are quickly eclipsed by your own personal desires and ambitions."

Campbell's word cut like a knife as Foulke just sat there listening.

Campbell continued, "In every situation, you must learn to do the right thing. It's never hard to identify. But, you Mr. Foulke, you weigh every decision against your career ambitions. Just do the right thing and your career will take care of itself. You have been charged with the sacred duty of protecting the citizens of Madison County. A real man is required to exercise that obligation with honor. A real man pursues justice with total disregard of his own personal interests."

Campbell let the words sink in as Foulke just sat there unable to look up at the man.

"Go make something of yourself, Boy," said Campbell.

Sgt. Mark Campbell walked from the restaurant area. He smiled and shook hands with several of the patrons who had recognized him.

Foulke scurried toward the men's room as fast as he could. He saw Campbell in the gift area and hoped he would not be seen. He slipped into the stall and closed the door. He had somehow held his emotions until now. He had a painful lump in his throat from the verbal dressing down he had just received. He sat down and sobbed quietly as tears rolled down his cheek. He knew Campbell was right. He did not honestly know if his motives were to save an innocent man or to hide his relationship with Cynthia and protect his political future. He didn't know. "Why couldn't it be both?" he thought. He knew that Cynthia was right about him. He was screwed up.

There were many things Steve Foulke could have decided at this moment of truth. There were many things he could have resolved to do from this day forward. There were so many things running through his mind. But he could only think of one thing he wanted to do.

He pulled out a burner cell phone and stepped through the contact list. It was before noon and most of the girls would still be asleep. He picked out a name and called. A familiar female voice answered. "Hey, Baby." she said.

"Are you available? asked Steve. "I can come over now?"

Chapter 28

Nasrullah had been stoned to death. He endured the same fate that he had inflicted on so many women. Alim was imprisoned in the same Bug Pit where he had held Adil for so many years. The reign of terror of Nasrullah and Alim Hassan had ended forever.

After the execution, Adil went to Alim's quarters in the Ark. He and Kaliq searched through Alim's computer and personal effects. They found a safe in his room. Kaliq did not know anyone in Bukhara who could open the safe. Adil contacted Ricky and he was brought to the Ark with a couple of the T-Girls. Ricky was dressed in a stunning gown, with long, flowing, light-brown hair dangling to her shoulders. Adil just looked at Ricky and said nothing. In less than fifteen minutes, Ricky had cracked the safe. It was a gold mine of sensitive information on the entire studio operation. In just a few minutes several things were obvious. There were dates and times of the visits of numerous world leaders. There was apparently video of their activities with the girls they had come to see. There were financial records showing bank accounts with billions of dollars in Switzerland and other western nations. Then, there were the special, very-sensitive files.

Adil checked first on his sister and found a developed roll of film with the damning pictures. He looked at the first one and it was just a picture of Jasmine on a tropical city street.

"Kaliq," said Adil, "I need to speak privately with this person." Kaliq stepped out of the room.

"Ricky," Adil began, "you have seen the pictures of your friend with my sister?"

Ricky nodded. "You look at these," said Adil. "I do not want to have to block the images from my mind."

Ricky looked at them and made sure all the pictures were accounted for on the single roll of negatives and no pictures were missing. There were only 33 pictures and all were black and white. The roll of film had not been completely shot. Some of the pictures were very pleasant showing Dan and Jasmine together in Hawaii. A few of the pictures were damning enough for any husband to divorce his wife. Many of the pictures showed Dan and Jasmine cuddling on the Ka'anapoli beach in the sun lounges. There were no explicit pictures of Dan and Jasmine having sex in either room. The last picture was taken from above with Dan and Jasmine embracing in the Oriental Garden of the Honolulu airport. In this Muslim country, just the pictures of them cuddling on the beach would get both Dan and Jasmine executed.

"You know," said Ricky, "you should let me give some of the nice ones to your sister. I will tell her the others have been destroyed. I think it would give her some peace of mind."

"And I would never have to address the subject with her?" said Adil

"That too," replied Ricky.

Ricky burned the negatives and the rest of the pictures.

Adil then came across a file on his grandmother. It, too, was damning but not in the way Adil had always been told. She was actually charged with being an infidel and stoned to death. There were pictures of her in Hong Kong standing next to an American, but they were not of adultery. There was another picture of Adil's grandmother that was even more damning. The accompanying documents explained what she had been involved in.

Adil did not want to share this with Jasmine yet. It was too delicate.

"Do you know this man?" asked Adil.

Ricky took the picture, studied it for a minute and said, "No, but I see him on TV all the time in New Orleans. Dan would know who he is."

"Thank you," said Adil. He summoned Kaliq and told him to take Ricky and his two friends to Jasmine. Kaliq knocked on Jasmine's door. When she answered, she saw Ricky standing there in her beautiful gown."

"Honey, we gotta talk girl to girl," said Ricky in a sweet but insistent feminine voice.

Jasmine let Ricky in while Kaliq and the others stayed outside.

"Here, darling," Ricky said. "You may want these as souvenirs. The others that Alim and Nasrullah possessed have been destroyed, along with the negatives."

Jasmine looked at them. Some of the pictures showed Dan and her strolling along the shops of Lahaina. They were holding hands and she was wearing the beautiful, Pikake lei around her neck. She shook her head wistfully and said, "This was such a nice day; seems like such a long time ago."

"You have many nice days ahead, girl." said Ricky "You have many great days ahead and a great life in store for you.

All great lives need great sex. Now, let's talk about that clitoris of yours."

Jasmine's eyes widened. She was stunned but before she could speak Ricky continued. "Your grandmother took you to Paris. She knew exactly what she was doing. You still have it. It was not removed. It was surgically sewn over and camouflaged."

Jasmine remained stunned and speechless.

"Now, you get that pretty little derriere of yours back to 'Paree' and get that operation reversed. It is actually a very minor outpatient operation and voila', you'll be just as good as new."

"How could you possibly know this?" Jasmine finally sputtered out the words through her embarrassment.

"Let's put it this way. Honey," said Ricky. "You got your chime rung in Maui for the first time in your life. You can't ring a doorbell if the button is not right there at the entrance to the door." Ricky hopped up and went out the door and said, "Ta Ta."

Jasmine just sat there in disbelief and let what Ricky said sink in.

Chapter 29

The next morning Dan was asked to come to the Ark to meet Emir Abdullah. Adil met with Dan first. He showed him the pictures of his grandmother in Hong Kong. The resemblance to Jasmine was striking. Do you know this man?" asked Adil

"Yes, I do," replied Dan, "He is Dr. Lester Sumrall. He is from Indiana. He was a great man of God. He went to be with the Lord many years ago. The New Life Temple in the picture was founded by him many years ago."

"It turns out that my grandmother was stoned for being an infidel," said Adil.

Adil showed him another picture of his grandmother. "Do you recognize this?" asked Adil.

"Holy shit!" exclaimed Dan and he sighed deeply. Of all the things in the world, this was the last thing he expected to see. "Yes, I not only recognize it, I know where it was taken. I have been there."

"Do you comprehend what this could do to Jasmine?"

"I do," said Dan.

"That's why I am going to leave it to you tell her," Said Adil.

"Me? Why me? I am leaving for home soon," protested Dan.

"No, Dan, you have one last mission for the new Bukhara. My father will explain," said Adil.

Adil led Dan to the Emir's quarters. Jasmine was there. She was surprised when Dan walked in.

"Mr. Grainger," said Abdullah "I owe you a great debt. The people of Bukhara owe you a great debt. You have saved my family from death, and I must thank you personally." The Emir extended his right hand and Dan cautiously extended his. They shook hands.

"I have one more request of you, and I think you are the only one that can make this happen," said Abdullah.

"What is it, Your Royal Highness?" replied Dan.

"I have a grandson. You have special relationships that I need no knowledge of that can arrange passage to where he is. I want you to accompany Jasmine and Adil to where Adonijah is located and arrange a meeting with Farah, his mother. It is my hope that Adonijah and his mother will come to Bukhara so he can be raised as the heir to the Emirate.

Dan did not betray his doubts that he could succeed. He did think it possible that Benjamin Johansohn would entertain such a mission.

"I will be honored. Consider it done," Dan said.

"My personal jet will be at your disposal, when the arrangements are finalized. I can arrange everything until you reach the King Hussein Bridge," said Abdullah.

"Thank you," said Dan.

"I want you to be assured that all of the women held captive and debased in the studio will be freed and given assistance in finding their families. All of the websites owned and operated by Alim and Nasrullah will be taken down and materials in our possession will be destroyed," said Abdullah.

"Now, Mr. Grainger," continued Abdullah, "you are welcome to accompany Jasmine, Adil and myself to the Ark balcony where I will address the people and introduce them to Adil, and their heir to the Emirate. I will speak, Jasmine will speak and Adil will speak."

The Emir could plainly read the reluctance on Dan's face.

Abdullah spoke again. "I understand completely that, even though all of us would like to thank you in front of the whole world, you may not want such attention."

"With your permission, Your Royal Highness, I will observe this momentous occasion from a discreet distance," said Dan.

"I expected that," said Abdullah, as he smiled.

Dan followed the group to the balcony of the Ark overlooking the grounds below. Jasmine was able to whisper to Dan, "Do you have any concept of how amazing it is for my father to speak to you with such gratitude while knowing what we have done?"

"I do," said Dan, "feeling very convicted."

"Ricky visited me last night," said Jasmine.

"Why on earth did she do that?" quizzed Dan.

"It was girl talk. Seems Ricky is recommending minor surgery in Paris," Jasmine said with a twinkle in her eye.

"I see. It will soon be springtime in Paris," said Dan.

"I will be scheduling the visit soon," said Jasmine. "I have much to do there. I must recruit professors for the university I am planning."

"How about Paris in the summer?" she said, "after I have had some time to…uh…recover and plan?"

"The recovery will not take that long. I much prefer Prague," said Dan. "Spring is magnificent there. The Prague Spring International Music Festival begins the middle of May."

"Prague in May. Sounds delightful," said Jasmine, "and there are many professors there to interview for the university. Will you join me?"

"Jasmine, I wouldn't miss it for anything in the world," said Dan, as he smiled wistfully.

Thousands had gathered below to hear the Emir of Bukhara. Television cameras were broadcasting the event. The whole world was watching. Abdullah stood up from his chair and the people cheered. The people had never seen their leader so vibrant. He introduced his son, Prince Adil, and the people cheered. He introduced his daughter, Princess Yasi Min, and the people cheered.

He briefly recounted what had occurred. He praised Allah. He thanked the Presidents of Tajikistan and Uzbekistan. He thanked what he called a long list of individuals whose identity must remain secret. He apologized to the world for what Bukhara had done, explaining that more details would be forthcoming. He announced that Alim had been imprisoned in Zindon Prison and Nasrullah had been executed by stoning. The crowd cheered so loudly at this news that it was deafening. He then turned to Adil, who stepped forward to say that he was pleased to have been saved from the prison that Nasrullah had held him in. Alim said there would be changes in the fundamental way people were allowed to live in and exercise their freedom in Bukhara.

Abdullah then introduced Jasmine by saying that she would be in charge of a university to open in six months devoted to the education of women from any nation that wished to attend.

Jasmine came to the front and began to speak. "We just celebrated International Women's Day in Bukhara. I am here to tell you that from this day forward, every day in Bukhara will be the day of the woman. No more will women be stoned," she said. "No more will women be required to cover their faces or remain under the veil. No more will our young girls be purified in the heinous practice of female circumcision. Khifad stops today! Any family, any mother, any grandmother, any cleric who continues this practice in Bukhara will be dealt with severely." There were muted cheers but there were cheers.

Jasmine continued, "Bukhara began its noble existence as an oasis in the desert. It was a place for travelers to rest and quench their thirst. It was the cultural heart of Central Asia. Great monasteries and places of learning were established here in Noble Bukhara, the Pillar of Islam, *Bukhoro-i-sharif.* Today, I announce that a great university will be opened here in just six months. It will be an oasis for learning. A new generation of Islamic women will be welcomed from all over the world to attend and quench their thirst for knowledge. The arts, the sciences, philosophy, engineering and mathematics will be taught here. Scholarships will be awarded to attract the best and the brightest. We will raise a new generation of Islamic women to return as leaders to their own nations to show an enlightened path to the future."

The broadcast was carried live all over the world. Commentators spoke of little else on the cable channels, except the rescue of the girls and the role Princess Jasmine played in the rescue. The subject of an Islamic woman's university was analyzed every way possible, both positively and negatively. The world knew nothing of Dan, and that is precisely the way he wanted it. The networks and the cable news channels hastily put together special reports on the history of Bukhara and on Princess Jasmine. The request for visas by journalists to visit Bukhara reached record levels.

When Dan returned to his hotel room, he made contact with Benjamin Johansohn. Benjamin already knew the request was coming. It had been approved by the Prime Minister of Israel. They could come tomorrow if they wished. Dan informed Jasmine by e-mail. She replied that he would be picked up at his hotel at 5:00 a.m.

Then Dan e-mailed a good friend of his in Indiana, Lester L. Sumrall, the grandson of Dr. Sumrall. He attached the picture he had taken with his phone of Jasmine's grandmother and Dr. Sumrall in Hong Kong. Dan didn't know the date, but he knew Dr. Sumrall had often visited Hong Kong.

He knew approximately when Jasmine's grandmother was stoned. He asked for the archives of Dr. Sumrall's mission trips to be searched for any more information they could find about the woman. They would be able to estimate Dr. Sumrall's age and select his mission trips to Hong Kong within a reasonable time range.

Dan surfed the web for a while. He looked at all the events that had occurred in the U.S. after the girls had returned. He watched with pride the short speech of his daughter, Callie, as she addressed the world about their ordeal. Callie was now safe with her mother and her sister. He teared up and closed his eyes as he prayed, "Thank you, Lord. Thank you," he said.

He decided to click on one of the Indiana ministry websites. It was a very pleasant surprise when he saw a particular ad for Israel Tours. The timing was perfect as God's timing always is.

Just before going to bed, an e-mail response came from his friend in South Bend. The reply was amazing. They had found a short-archived video of Jasmine's grandmother with Dr. Sumrall. He downloaded and saved it on his computer, his phone and on a separate jump drive. Its contents were unbelievable.

His wake-up call came quick at 4:30 a.m. and he was in the lobby waiting at 5:00 a.m. when the Mercedes appeared. Kaliq was driving and Jasmine and Adil were in the car. By 6:00 a.m. they were in the air, bound for Amman, Jordan. He had an opportunity to become very acquainted with Adil. This was Adil's and Jasmine's first opportunity to speak at length since his recovery. Jasmine asked Adil all about Farah. They talked non-stop.

Farah lived in Safed, north of Nazareth and Lake Tiberias. Dan knew the area well, having visited the Sea of Galilee, as he called it, many times. Adil explained that Farah was a Christian Arab and that she spoke Arabic. His son, Adonijah, was six.

Jasmine replied, "It will please Father that he can speak to his grandson in Arabic."

Often, Dan and Jasmine's eyes would lock but nothing personal was ever spoken between them. Kaliq came along but remained silent and sat away from the three.

It was about three-and-one-half-hours when they landed at Amman. A Mercedes was waiting for them as they headed for the Jordan River crossing. A Jordanian military officer sat in the front passenger seat. It was about an hour before they reached the King Hussein Bridge. Adil had a Bukhari passport now. The Jordanian officer collected their passports and spoke to the officials at the Jordanian border-crossing terminal.

He returned and the Mercedes drove them across the Allenby Bridge to the Israeli border terminal. Two Israeli Defense Force officers were standing by as the Mercedes stopped. The two IDF officers escorted Jasmine, Adil and Dan to a passport control desk where their passports were examined but not stamped. In a few minutes, they were in another Mercedes driven by IDF soldiers. They traveled through the West Bank north toward Tiberias.

They had been driving for well over an hour when they came to the south end of the Sea of Galilee. Dan spoke. "Adil," he said, "I could certainly use a rest stop. Yardenit is a great place for that and is up ahead just off the main road."

Dan caught Adil's eyes when he said this. Adil did not know Dan's reasoning for the request but accepted it."

Adil asked the IDF soldier if they could stop at Yardenit to freshen up. In a few minutes, the driver pulled into the Yardenit Baptismal Site on the Jordan River. The beautiful green trees were like an oasis compared to the desolate rocky desert they had been passing through on the West Bank.

Jasmine exited the Mercedes, "This is clearly a Christian site. Why did you want to stop here?" she asked.

"I love the place. I was baptized here many years ago by Lester L. Sumrall, the eldest grandson of Dr. Lester Sumrall," said Dan.

"I see," said Jasmine with some hesitation as she looked at Adil. "Brother, are you okay with this?" she asked.

Adil replied "My wife is a Christian and my son is a Christian. Listen to the people singing. It must be a blessed place of the prophet Jesus."

The four used the facilities. Adil and Kaliq looked around the area with great interest. Adil suddenly realized why Dan wanted to stop here but said nothing. When Jasmine came out of the restroom, Dan directed her along the walkway to the Jordan River, its banks lined by beautiful, lush trees. They climbed up some steps and looked down on the baptismal site. There were hundreds of Christians lined up, many in white robes. In the water, several pastors were baptizing the people one at a time. Jasmine watched as each person was prayed over and then leaned backward into the Jordan River. When they were lifted back up to their feet, all the people sang. Jasmine had never heard so many "Hallelujahs" in her life. A voice inside her stirred and she could feel the power of the blessing these faithful were receiving. A photographer was capturing the event for each of the participants.

They went back to the gift shop and joined Adil and Kaliq. There was a place that displayed all the individual photographs taken of the faithful at the moment of baptism. Jasmine stopped for several minutes to look at the faces in the pictures. The still waters of the Jordan River, lined with trees, and the stone walls along the walkways provided the perfect backdrop for such a momentous occasion in the life of a believer in Christ.

As they re-entered the parking area, Jasmine noticed for the first time that several of the tour buses had a banner on the side that said "Israel Tours" and had a picture of a pastor. She looked closer and the name under the man's photograph was Dr. Lester Sumrall.

The four returned to the Mercedes.

"Dan Grainger," she said, "you have a reason for everything you do. What was your reason for showing me this place?"

"I just wanted you to see where I was baptized," he replied.

Jasmine did not believe him. But she let the matter go. The Mercedes continued along the Sea of Galilee to Tiberias. Dan suggested they stop at an Arab-Israeli restaurant for lunch. It had Mediterranean and Middle-Eastern cuisine. Dan had eaten here before and loved the hummus and pita bread.

After lunch, they continued along the northwest side of the sea. They turned up a winding, paved road, passing several tour buses along the way. Finally, they arrived at the Church of the

Beatitudes. The IDF officers and Kaliq remained at the car. Dan led the way for Adil and Jasmine through the gate leading to the church.

They entered the grounds. It was a beautiful Italian Catholic Church of Byzantine design. The walls were constructed of marble, and there was gold mosaic in the dome. The floor plan was octagonal, representing the eight blessings from Jesus' Sermon on the Mount. There was a columned walkway around the church. Just to the left of the north entrance stood a woman and a small boy of perhaps six years old. Adil's face lit up. "Farah!" he shouted out. "Adil!" she shouted in reply. The little boy ran to Adil shouting a word that sounded like "Abba." Adil scooped the boy up in his arms and said "Adonijah." Adil continued toward the woman. Perhaps Farah specified this blessed place for their meeting, so that she could throw her arms around Adil. She could not have done that in her village; not in any place frequented by Muslims. It would have been inappropriate. But here, outside the church, surrounded by Christian pilgrims, little notice was given to the emotional event. Jasmine approached slowly.

In Arabic, Adil introduced his wife and son to his sister. The boy wrapped his arms around Jasmine as she leaned down and kissed him on the forehead. The two women looked at each other face to face for a moment and both smiled. Jasmine said, "It is our father's greatest hope that you, Farah, and Adonijah will come with us to Bukhara to live with us at the Ark."

Farah replied in Arabic "It has been all that I have dreamed of for all these years. I would be honored."

Jasmine embraced her warmly and then stepped away so that Farah and Adil could speak privately.

Jasmine and Dan stood some distance away. In a few minutes, Adil came over and said, "We are taking Farah and Adonijah back to her village to say goodbye to her family and to pick up her things. You can come if you wish, or we can come for you in a couple of hours or perhaps less."

Dan caught Jasmine's eyes before speaking and then he said "We will stay. I will not be going back to Amman with you. I am staying in Tiberias for a few days and then flying home to Indiana."

Adil, Farah and Adonijah headed for the gate.

As they watched them leave, they heard a voice from behind them, "Mr. Grainger!" the voice said. He recognized it instantly as the voice of a certain young girl. He and Jasmine both turned.

"Ilsa," said Dan as she ran into his arms. Jasmine watched the tenderness in Dan's manner as he held her, and the care he took in speaking with her. Benjamin Johansohn approached a moment later. He was dressed in the uniform of an IDF officer. After a few seconds, Ilsa introduced her uncle and Dan introduced Jasmine. The four spoke for several minutes.

This was difficult for Jasmine, as she hid her disdain, and said, "Mr. Johansohn, I suspect I have you to thank for locating my brother, and my father's new-found health, among so many other things that I know nothing of, including I imagine, arranging this visit. Thank you."

"And thank you, Princess Yasi Min for the hope you have brought to your country and the critical role you played in saving so many. The world owes you a debt of gratitude. You are an international celebrity now, and in the coming days, you will be in great demand by the press and paparazzi."

"Not in Bukhara. I can control them there," said Jasmine.

"Yes," said Johansohn, "but you certainly must travel to Europe, Asia and America to find the teachers and professors for your university."

"If my celebrity status can help me recruit the best of the best for my faculty," said Jasmine, "I can live with that."

The four spoke for a few more minutes. Ilsa and Dan gave each other one more hug, and then Johansohn and his niece walked out the gate of the churchyard.

Dan took Jasmine's hand and walked her around the church to the far south end of a fenced-in area. It was beautiful. The church sat on high ground overlooking the entire Sea of Galilee. Jasmine and Dan sat down next to each other under the shade provided by the trees.

"One of my favorite blessings from this church is tailor-made for you today, Jasmine," said Dan. *"Blessed are those who hunger and thirst for righteousness, for they shall be filled."*

Dan pulled out his cell phone and said, "I must show you this." He handed her a jump drive and said, "I want you to keep this, so you can look at it again when you get home. He started a video on his phone and held it for Jasmine to see and hear.

The first words Jasmine heard were, "and all the people said," followed by a chorus of "Amen." The camera took a shot of thousands in the crowd listening to the man. Many of them were Asian. The camera came back to the man and Jasmine recognized him immediately from the tour bus banners as Dr. Lester Sumrall. The camera widened out to reveal a woman holding a baby.

"Where are you from?" asked Dr. Sumrall.

"Tajikistan," said the woman.

"What is your name?" he asked.

"Yasi Min," the woman replied.

Suddenly, tears began to form in Jasmine's eyes "It is my grandmother!" she exclaimed, "This is not possible!"

"You were a Muslim?" Came the words from Dr. Sumrall.

"Yes, I was born a Muslim and raised a Muslim, but I have been saved by the blood of Jesus Christ," said Yasi Min.

"You are a Christian?" said Dr. Sumrall.

"Yes," she replied

"You have risked your life to become a Christian. I understand you are returning to your family after you leave Hong Kong. You are in great danger from your family and the clerics of Islam," he said.

"Yes," she said defiantly.

"Why are you here today?" asked Dr. Sumrall of the woman.

"You are a great man of the Christ," she said. "I want you to bless my grandchildren that they might remain safe."

The camera widened out to reveal a little girl standing next to them.

Dr. Sumrall placed his right hand on the girl's head and asked, "What is her name?"

"It is Yasi Min."

"Named after her grandmother," he said.

"And the baby? His name?"

"Adil," replied Yasi Min.

Dr. Sumrall handed his microphone to another pastor who came up to receive it and hold it as Dr. Sumrall prayed over the children. Dr. Sumrall placed his left hand on the baby and kept his right hand on the little girl's head

"Father, Bless these children, Adil and Yasi Min, and keep them safe. Hear them when they cry out in despair. Comfort them when they are all alone and can hear nothing but the still quiet voice of your presence. Become a secret treasure deep within their spirit to guide them one day to you, Lord." Then Dr. Sumrall began speaking in tongues and his voice grew loud and powerful."

Suddenly, his words returned again to English, "Bless these children in the name of Jesus Christ." The crowd roared.

Dr. Sumrall placed his hands on the forehead of the grandmother and said, "Bless you, Sister, in the name of

Jesus." Then he shouted, "and all the people said," and the crowd shouted "Amen!"

The video clip ended.

Dan handed her a photograph and said, "Adil found this in a safe in the Ark. It was a picture of Jasmine's grandmother standing tall in the Jordan River, wearing a white robe with water dripping from her hair. She had a huge smile on her face after being baptized at Yardenit.

"I can't believe this is true," said Jasmine. "All of these years, all I wanted to do, all I wanted to be, was true to my grandmother's faith."

"You can be, Jasmine. It's very simple," declared Dan.

"I have failed her," said Jasmine.

"No," replied Dan forcefully. "It is never too late to make Jesus the Lord of your life. Will you pray with me?"

"Yes," she replied meekly.

"Repeat after me, Jessie. Lord Jesus," said Dan.

"Lord Jesus," began Jasmine. These words were so foreign to her and they contradicted everything she had believed she was for her entire life, yet she softly repeated all that Dan told her to say.

"Forgive me my sins," she repeated. "Come into my heart. I make you my Lord and Savior."

She didn't know what she was feeling as the words slowly sank in. She remained silent.

Dan broke the silence "By praying that simple prayer, Jessie, you were born again, just as your grandmother was born again so many years ago."

Jasmine just stared, not at Dan; she just stared upward as if she was listening to something deep within her soul. It was a still and quiet voice gently speaking to her. She had heard it before when she was troubled and needed guidance. She had always wanted to believe it was her grandmother counseling her and keeping her safe. In the most difficult times of her life, she had often heard that voice and had never known until this moment what it was, or who it was. The Holy Spirit had awakened within her.

Tears began to form in her eyes and her face suddenly exploded in an unbridled expression of joy. "Praise the Lord," she said, "I'm a Christian!"